PRAETORIAN

***

THE NEMESIS BLADE

D1519399

by S. J. A. Turney

1st Edition

For Simon Elliott, who loves the Severans and Rome's frontiers. And for Sara, who, like the wives of all Roman historians, put up with him like a saint...

BY THE SAME AUTHOR:

LEGION XXII (Egyptian-Roman Military Adventure)

Capsarius
Bellatrix

AGRICOLA (Romano-British military adventure)

Invader
Warrior (2025)

THE DAMNED EMPERORS (Roman Biographical Novels)

Caligula
Commodus
Domitian
Caracalla

OTHER ROMAN STANDALONE NOVELS

Para Bellum
Terra Incognita (2024)

THE LEGION (Children's Books)

Crocodile Legion
Pirate Legion

THE VALENS NOVELLAS

I - Vengeance
II - The Hunt

THE TEMPLAR NOVELS (12TH-13TH Century Medieval)

I - Daughter of War
II - Templar: The Last Emir
III - Templar: City of God
IV - Templar: The Winter Knight
V - Templar: The Crescent and the Cross
VI - Templar: The Last Crusade

THE OTTOMAN CYCLE (15TH Century Mediterranean Adventure)

The Thief's Tale
The Priest's Tale
The Assassin's Tale
The Pasha's Tale

WOLVES OF ODIN (11TH Century Viking Sagas)

I - Blood Feud
II - Wolves of Odin: Bear of Byzantium
III - Wolves of Odin: Iron and Gold
IV - Wolves of Odin: Wolves Around the Throne
V - Wolves of Odin: Loki Unbound (2024)

COLLABORATIONS AND CONTRIBUTIONS

Hauntings
A Year of Ravens
A Song of War

TALES OF THE EMPIRE (Roman-Themed Fantasy)

Interregnum
Ironroot
Dark Empress
Insurgency
Invasion
Jade Empire

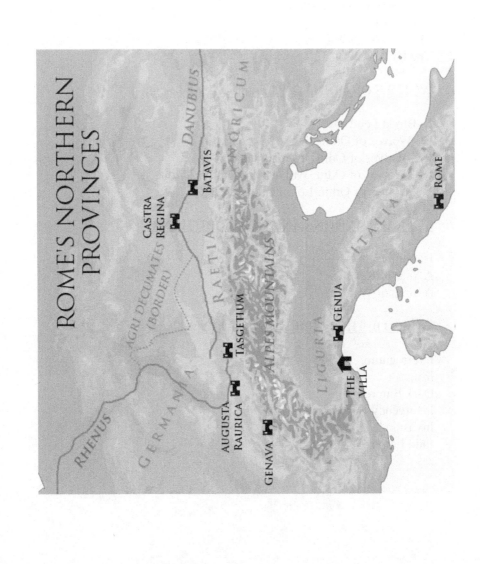

ROME'S NORTHERN PROVINCES

RHENUS

DANUBIUS

AGRI DECUMATES (BORDER)

CASTRA REGINA

BATAVIS

GERMANIA

RAETIA

NORICUM

AUGUSTA RAURICA

TASGETIUM

GENAVA

ALPES MOUNTAINS

LIGURIA

GENUA

THE VILLA

ITALIA

ROME

ROME'S RAETIAN
BORDER C. AD 198

THE
CAMP

CASTRA
NUMERA

TANNIUM

ICINIACUM

CASTRA
REGINA

ABUSINA

SORVIODUNUM

DANUBIUS

BATAVIS

AUGUSTA
VINDELICORUM

'Get him.'

The Roman ducked the overhanging branch, rain battering the leaves, and dropped down the riverbank, desperate eyes glancing left and right. There was no way out. And there were too many of them. Only the river held any possibility of salvation, now.

He looked down into the churning white waters, and then up and across to the far bank.

This river, like all rivers, had a god or goddess. Somehow, though, he felt less than inclined to pray for her aid, and more to hope she overlooked him. He could hear the roar of powerful falls off to his left, and less so to his right. At least the noise might hide him long enough. And it would be hard in this light to see someone battered and churned by the waters.

He shrugged swiftly from the chain shirt, keeping only his belt pouch and the sword at his side, took a deep breath, and threw himself into the black and white waters, freezing river closing over him and bringing a shock for which he was unprepared. All he had to do was get to the other side, and maybe he could slip away.

It took enormous effort to pull himself up to the surface, and he was aware that the powerful current was pulling him towards those falls every moment. His head broke the surface, and he looked around, blinking. He was out in the flow now, and being carried downstream at breakneck pace.

'There he is,' called a voice.

The goddess of the river had not ignored him after all…

1

PART ONE

ROMANI

Nemesis, winged tilter of scales and lives,

Immortal Judge! I sing Your song,

Almighty Triumph on proud-spread wings,

Lieutenant of fairness, Requiter of wrongs.

Despise the lordly with all Your art

And lay them low in the Netherdark.

- From "Hymn to Nemesis" by Mesomedes of Crete,
translated by A.Z. Foreman

CHAPTER ONE

Rome, Spring AD 198

Rufinus turned at the sound of a clatter and stopped, drumming fingers on crossed arms while he waited for the clerk to gather up the wooden-cased wax tablets he'd been carrying in a precarious pile. Once the soldier gave him a sheepish nod, he turned back and strode on again, teeth gritted at the sound of the young lad following, struggling to hold his burden.

And *what* a burden. A month's worth of sick lists, duty rosters, equipment requisitions, troop transfers and every other minutia of military command. A veritable banquet of tedium. Grudgingly, deep down, he had to admit that it was the poor young clerks like the lad following him who did most of the actual work. He just had to give them a once-over to make sure they looked correct, then sign and seal them for the records office.

That was all the army was these days: paperwork.

He sighed, kicked at a pebble, and then cursed quietly as his knee twisted slightly. He seemed to be becoming prey to small nagging pains that had no source these days, too.

When had he got old, he wondered? All his important birthdays had passed without really being marked. At eighteen he'd been halfway across the empire, furious at his father, running away to join the legions. At twenty-five, he'd been rather busy saving Commodus from his sister. At thirty, he'd been comatose following a fall from a cliff in Dacia. At forty... well, last year, he'd been working hard to prepare for this year. Now here he was at forty-one: practically ancient. And he felt it. Not just because of the aches, which he suspected might be willing to leave him alone if only he exercised a little more, but also because what had always been an exciting career (for good or ill) was just rather dull now.

That was probably the rank, though. Tribunes of the Guard probably all felt like this. When in garrison, anyway. He paused, listening to the sound of tablets being rescued once again, without even turning this time, and sighed once more. Of course, *some* tribunes were living the exciting life. *All* the tribunes of the Praetorian Guard right now, in fact, except one Gnaeus Marcius Rustius Rufinus. Because all the other tribunes were in Parthia with the emperor, conquering and looting. Every cohort of the Guard was out there fighting for Rome.

Except one. Because even though the emperor and his court were away, the Guard still had to maintain a presence in Rome. The palaces still needed guarding, even in their master's absence. Imperial business in the capital did not stop because the emperor wasn't there. Indeed, in some ways it actually increased, especially in the matter of paperwork.

The cohort that remained in Rome, of course, had been formed of all the sick-listers, the malingerers, the disaffected and plain disobedient, the lazy, the stupid, and those men with whom there was nothing really wrong, but you wouldn't trust them to slice bread without cocking it up. In short, the worst cohort imaginable. All so that the real soldiers, the men with a hint of go about them, could be with their emperor, fighting in the east. This lot it didn't really matter about as long as they looked the part and were seen in the right places.

Fully half his day's paperwork was always regarding illness and hospital reports or rule infractions and punishment duties. And he knew that Severus had left him here not as a punishment but as an honour, but that didn't make it any better. Severus knew him to be strong and dependable, and whichever tribune was left in charge of Rome during the campaign would very much need that to run this cohort. In truth, there wasn't much actual running involved. The centurions, because the centurionate were invariably dependable, did the actual keeping of control. Rufinus just had to back them all up and do the paperwork.

Clatter.

He stopped again. Now, he was in sight of his house as he waited for the sheepish signal to move on. The tribunes of the Guard each had a house of excellent size and quality in the heart of the Praetorian fortress, and though he still owned both the town house and the villa at Tarraco, Rufinus had felt that he needed to live full time in the fortress while he was the sole senior officer present. Senova had not argued, especially since the tribunes' houses were well kept and well appointed, and the tribunes' wives usually lived with them, which meant her presence was perfectly acceptable.

Rounding the corner of the principia, Rufinus looked across the street to where two men strode side by side in conversation. They were, to Rufinus, the very epitome of the officers that had been left behind. The bulk of the cohort that remained had done so because they were the scum that floated to the surface of the brew, and the officers, apart from Rufinus, had also been left for good reasons. Not that they weren't solid men, good at their jobs, but there was still always a reason. Take the centurion there, Cornelius Scapula. He was an excellent officer, very knowledgeable and experienced, and well he should be. No one knew how old he was, and it wasn't even in his records, but estimations ranged from sixty to one hundred and sixty, and he was most certainly the oldest serving member of the Guard. And his optio, who strolled along beside him, Felix, was another fascinating case. Though he was an excellent optio, and young enough to be virile, he was from some backwater African town, and his accent was so thick that you really had to listen hard to understand him, and even then, there was a good chance you wouldn't.

He smiled at the sight of the two men, then turned another corner into the street where the row of tribunes' houses stood. He stopped suddenly, and behind him there was a surprised noise and yet another wooden clatter. Ahead, a soldier in his duty uniform, armed and booted for service, sat on the kerb, snoring like a bull, an empty wine jug lying on its side between his feet.

Rufinus clenched his teeth and walked on, leaving the clerk to pick up his fallen tablets, striding over to the drunken soldier. He was going to have to do something. There were hundreds of misfits serving in the fortress, but he was fairly sure he knew this one, and had seen him in his office a couple of times over the past month. Rufinus bent closer to the man and cupped a hand to his mouth.

'Ad signum!' he bellowed. 'Fall in!'

The soldier shot to his feet, blinking awake, fell over as his wobbly legs failed to hold him up, then struggled to his feet again, this time swaying slightly as he saluted Rufinus with wide eyes.

'Sir.'

'Laelius, isn't it? Perhaps a little unfit for duty?'

'Sir, I was…'

Rufinus folded his arms. 'Let's not compound the fault by lying, Laelius. Even if I were faintly convinced you weren't blind drunk on duty, this is the third time in a month, so really, I have to do something about it.'

'Sir, I…'

'I just haven't decided what yet. And I need to get these tablets back home,' he added, gesturing to the clerk behind him.

Laelius collapsed in a heap, groaning. Rufinus exhaled noisily, rolled his eyes, and turned. The centurion and his optio had followed the shouting and were now close by. He gestured to them, and they marched over,

'Felix, do me a favour and lift this creature up and drag him back to my house, where I have to decide on a fitting punishment. I'm considering having him drowned in wine.'

8

'Snar ill doo mons,' the optio appeared to say with a grin, then stooped and lifted the drunken soldier with ease. Rufinus looked across at Cornelius Scapula. 'Actually, I need to speak to you about some irregularities in requisition requests, centurion, so perhaps you'd join us, too?'

The officer bowed his head, and Rufinus led the way towards his house, with his motley parade in tow: a clumsy clerk, a drunken soldier, an unintelligible optio and the oldest man in the world. He gave a snorted chuckle as he approached his house. Really, they must be a peculiar sight.

At his approach, the front door of his house swung open. He'd argued that they didn't need a servant doorman, who cost him far too much money to do essentially the work of a hinge, but Senova had been adamant. As an ex-slave herself, she would not have slaves in the house, which meant that all the people that did the work were actually being paid weekly, with the result that he was haemorrhaging money all the time. And they didn't need a guard for the door anyway, in the middle of the fortress, probably the safest place in the empire right now. Still, the door was opened, and he walked in past the ex-gladiator, who bowed his head in respect. Despite an impressive level of professionalism, the man couldn't help but frown in surprise at the carnival his master had in tow. Ahead, down the corridor, past the shrine of the household gods, a figure appeared in the open entrance to the atrium. Rufinus smiled at the sight.

Sheba, the dog he'd brought back with him from Syria, was no spring chicken herself, yet she remained elegant and lithe as she stepped into the open, tail twitching as she waited for him. She had quickly become Senova's dog, the pair of them inseparable, but she always showed her affection when Rufinus appeared, even if in small ways.

Then, just to confirm that he was definitely home, the *other* dog appeared. Orthus was a different matter entirely. The offspring of Acheron and Sheba, Orthus had managed to retain her colouring and his build. The creature appeared suddenly, at a run, lolloping past his mother and bounding down the corridor at Rufinus like an over-friendly cavalry charge. He hit his master like a runaway cart and sent Rufinus staggering half a dozen paces backward. In truth he was a lot smaller than Acheron had been, but that was still larger than most dogs, and all of it seemed to be muscle. Certainly, very little of it seemed to be brain, Rufinus noted wryly as the creature paused to start licking private parts of himself. He was, in effect, a large bundle of shaggy, white muscle. Not very bright, but extremely enthusiastic, and very loyal. *Orthus* was Rufinus's dog, and at three years old, he still seemed to be in the puppy stage, despite his size.

Scruffing the dog behind the ears, Rufinus smiled, a smile that slipped a little at the sound of wood clattering on marble behind him. He took a steadying breath and gestured off ahead and to the right. 'My office is in the usual place. Do me a favour, all four of you, and wait there for me.'

As they all trooped past in their peculiar splendour, heading for his office, Rufinus instead went the other way, where he found Senova in her usual haunt, a well-lit room with a colonnaded window overlooking the peristyle garden. She was stitching something. He didn't know what. The arts of sewing and his wife's interest in it were still a complete mystery to him.

'Another tedious day of office work,' he muttered. 'Only brought an hour's worth home tonight, though.'

Her head tilted up, and she gave him a smile. He felt his knees tremble. That smile still had the same effect on him as it had fifteen years ago, when it had first seen his defences crumble at the sight of her.

'Your dog has been a nightmare waiting for you to come home. You need to train him.'

'I *have* trained him.'

'Not to maim people, Gnaeus, to do as he's told under normal circumstances.'

10

'It's not all combat training,' Rufinus bridled. 'I taught him 'latrine' so he'd go where I pointed, and 'scram' so he'd run and hide when you're on the warpath!'

'Well done,' she said with an edge of sarcasm.

Rufinus shrugged. 'I like him as he is.'

'Wild and untamed. Like me?'

This time her smile *really* set his knees going. His eyes darted about. 'Look, I've got a little business to attend to, but the paperwork can wait. Give me quarter of an hour and meet me in the bath.'

She chuckled. 'You have other work too. There's a courier waiting in the triclinium. He's brought you a message and wouldn't deliver it to me. Had to be you, and he's waited for you to confirm receipt.'

Rufinus nodded. 'Sounds quick,' he grinned. 'Same time, still in the bath.' Leaving her to it, he departed the room and trotted lightly across the atrium once more, Orthus rising from where he'd been drinking out of the fountain and following him. He walked past his office with its weird collection of denizens and straight over to the triclinium. A wide, comfortable, and light space, the room's only occupant was a tired looking man in dusty, travel-worn clothes.

'Can I help you?'

'You are the master of the house, Domine?'

Rufinus nodded, and the man reached into his capsa, the leather satchel at his side, and pulled free a tablet wrapped tight and bound with cord that was sealed with wax. It was proffered to Rufinus, who took it. The man then held up his confirmation panel, with a corresponding soft wax stamp, and Rufinus dutifully folded his finger and held forth his signet ring, pressing it into the wax to confirm receipt. The man bowed his head and hurried away, one of the house's staff leading him away towards the door once more. Rufinus was alone as he turned the package over and looked at it. It had come some distance, judging by the slight wear and the road dust. Then he saw the seal properly for the first time and he stopped turning it, blinking.

'What is it?' Senova asked from the doorway behind him where she had just appeared.

'It's from Publius.'

'Your brother?'

He nodded.

'Where is he at the moment?'

'Up on the Raetian frontier somewhere, commanding an auxiliary cohort, making a name for himself. I think he's always been jealous that I got to serve in the wars and in exotic and dangerous places, and even when he managed to get himself assigned to the military, it turned out to be in boring camps. A little like my current position,' he added wistfully. 'He angled for a border role for a while, hoping to secure somewhere like the north of Britannia. Again, I think he was a bit disappointed with Raetia. Since we pulverised the Marcomanni, the Danubius-Rhenus border has been pretty quiet.'

'So, he's filling his time sending you letters?'

Rufinus nodded. 'Probably. He'll be complaining about his men. Last time he wrote was before Saturnalia, and nine tenths of the letter was little more than a list of names and complaints.'

'I remember.'

Rufinus cracked the wax seal and pulled the tie aside, opening the tablet. That was unusual for a start. When Publius bothered writing, it was usually on parchment, or vellum, rolled up and stuffed in a tube. Frontier posts often wrote on wooden sheets, because wax tablets, while useful for temporary lists, had an unfortunate tendency to get accidentally melted or scraped clear. The writing on this one was messy and hard to decipher at first sight. Rufinus carried it across to the window and laid it on the sill, leaning forward.

GNAEVS

I CANNOT SAY TOO MVCH HERE
SO THIS NOTE WILL BE BRIEF
IT IS MY BELIEF THAT ALL POST IN
THE LIMES REGION IS BEING
MONITORED
SVSPECT MY LIFE IS IN DANGER AND
POSSIBLY THE IMPERIAL BORDER TOO
HAVE LEFT MY POST AND AM GOING
SOUTH
MEET AT THE VILLA HE COVLD NOT
SELL

PVBLIVS

Rufinus frowned, then re-read it as though it might contain something different a second time round.

'What is it?' Senova asked, clearly sensing something wrong.

'Something's happened. Publius thinks he's in danger.'

He crossed to a desk and pulled out some of the ledgers in it, looking for the border itineraries that the Guard had drawn up after the last war, and pulling out a couple of the rare maps that were kept. As he started to sift through them for the right ones, Senova reached across and pulled the tablet away, perusing it.

'He sounds worried. Desperate, even.'

'Yes.'

'He's coming south. Where's this villa?'

Rufinus waved a hand vaguely north without looking up. 'Ligurian coast. Belonged to an aunt of ours. When she died, Father tried to sell it, like he did with everything, but she'd run it down. The vineyards were all ruined, the place falling apart, and the gardens overgrown. When she died, she was down to two slaves, and *they* were pretty overgrown and falling apart too. He couldn't sell it. No one wanted it. It's still nominally our property, so it's somewhere safe he can go hide and wait for me. Looks like he needs his big brother to pull his backside out of the fire again.'

'You can't go, Gnaeus. He'll have to come to Rome.'

Rufinus frowned. 'What?'

'You are in command of the Praetorian Guard in Rome until the emperor and his prefects return. You can't abandon your duty to go off and help your brother.'

Rufinus shook his head. 'This place pretty much runs itself. No one needs much controlling, and the centurions can handle the day-to-day business. All I am really is a glorified administrator at the moment. They can pile up the work and I'll sign and seal it when I get back.' He glanced up at her. 'Or maybe you could do it?'

He pulled one of the maps of Italia out and slid his finger back and forth across it.

'Six days, I reckon. If I get to Ostia this afternoon and secure passage on something fast – a trireme of the fleet, maybe – I can be up the coast and past Genua in four or five. Then along the coast on a horse for the last day, since the villa's inland a little and not close to any good harbour. That means I can get to him, sort this out, and get back all in maybe as little as twelve days. They'll barely have opened the next roster lists by then. I'll have a word with the seniors. By happy chance, I have the most senior centurion left in my office this very moment. And when I say senior, I *really mean* senior.'

As Senova still made uncertain and disapproving noises, he hooked out other maps and itineraries. His questing fingers fell on the tablet again, and found something jagged. He looked at it.

'There's still the remains of a cursus seal here.'

'A what?'

'Seal of the cursus publicus. Marks it as being sent from an imperial station and carried by the courier service.' He dug around for another ledger, then opened it and started thumbing through pages of seal copies, listing the waystations of the cursus. He found what he was looking for on the sixth page.

'Tasgetium. The mansio there. That's where this letter was sent from.'

He started tracing his way across a map of the Alpine region, and took some time, eventually stabbing his finger at a particular point. 'Further north than I expected.' He put one of the small black stones he used for holding down scroll corners on the place he had found, then slid his finger down to the Ligurian coast and placed another. 'That's where he sent the letter from, and where he's going.' He started shuffling through another stack of letters, finding odd ones, and scanning them before discarding them. The fourth one captured his interest, and he let go of it with an exclamation.

'Aha.'

'What?'

'I knew he'd told me his unit and station in one letter. He commands the Ninth Batavorum at Batavis on the Danubius.' He picked up a third black stone and scanned the northern border for some time before nodding and placing the stone. 'There's his command at Batavis, where he started, before he went to Tasgetium. Alright, then, he left his fort, and took the southwest road that comes to the western Alpine passes, which would give him good access to northwest Italia and the Ligurian coast. Makes sense. Nothing in the empire moves as fast as the courier service. I reckon it would take one man on a horse maybe twelve to fourteen days to get from Tasgetium to the villa, even if the passes are clear. But the cursus publicus could get a message from there right the way to Rome in less time. The way I see it, if he's been moving steadily, I might get to the villa about the same time, or at least not long after.'

'Are you sure about leaving your post, Gnaeus? I mean without asking the prefect or the emperor's permission.'

'By the time my request found them out in Parthia I'd be back in Rome. Look, I've commanded here for four months already, and the most exciting thing that happened was that blocked latrine and the incident colourfully remembered as the 'shit wave'. Nothing's going to happen, and you're in the safest place in the world right now.'

'Gnaeus, I shall be coming with you.'

'No, you won't.'

She fixed him with a hard look, but he shook his head, adamant. 'No. You read the note, and you recognised the fear. Whatever this is, it's dangerous, and I'm not walking you into that. You get to stay here where it's safe. I'll assign men to look after the house.'

'Who will you take?'

'No one.'

'Gnaeus, you just told me it was dangerous. Use your head.'

'I am. Publius said he thinks the post is being monitored. That means he doesn't trust anyone. And I know it's a long way from here to Raetia, but I don't want to do anything that brings trouble down on him or us.'

'So, you don't trust the people here now?'

'What?'

'Well Publius doesn't trust his own people at the border, so that leads you to not trust the people here, yet you're happy to leave me here where it's safe rather than take me into danger?'

Rufinus sighed and rubbed his neck. 'I *do* trust the people here. I'm just being cautious. I'll take Orthus.'

'You certainly will. I'm not having him moping around here for days on end while you're away.'

'Alright. Come with me.' With that, he left the room and went across to the office, where the four soldiers were waiting for him.

'Alright, you lot. Things have changed. I have to go away for a short while on a personal matter. I can't say more right now, but I shall be away a number of days, though I anticipate being back within the month. In my absence, there will be paperwork.' He gestured to the pale-looking clerk with his stack of records. 'My wife is an excellent administrator. I mean top-notch. I give her full authority to check the figures on anything. And you, Guardsman…?'

'Varro, sir.'

'You, Guardsman Varro, can have my spare signet during my absence. When Senova checks things, you can seal them and send them on. Thus, no paperwork will go untouched.' He turned to the centurion and the optio. 'Scapula, as senior centurion of the cohort, the job of Princeps Castrorum is yours. You are now senior commander until I return. Try not to cock it up,' he added, though in the privacy of his head, he noted the man's age and added *or die in the position.*

'That leaves *you*, Laelius,' he said, turning to the drunken Guardsman who was leaning against the wall but trying to look as though he was standing free. He straightened, or at least made a solid attempt to do so.

'Sir.'

'I've tried docking your pay for your infractions, but gambling is one of them, and somehow you always seem to recoup the losses and afford more wine. I've tried having you put on punishment duties, from kitchen patrol to latrine unclogging, and none of that seems to phase you. Indeed, I believe you were one of the heroes of the 'shit wave.' Thus far I've stopped short of beatings or floggings, not because I don't think you deserve it, which you plainly do, but because when you're sober, you're actually good at your job, and with what I've been left with in Rome, there's precious little of that about, so I don't want to waste it. So, you see, I'm troubled about the appropriate punishment for you, but I think I have the solution.'

'Sir?'

'Pack your campaign kit, Laelius. You're coming with me.'

The man blinked. He saw Senova in the doorway behind with a wry smile, and turned back to Varro, Felix, and Scapula. 'The three of you are probably the most able characters in this whole fortress right now. I know we're safe here, but with me gone, I want you to add my wife and household's safety to the list of highest priorities. If so much as a window gets broken, the culprit gets punished. If a man dare stick out a tongue at Senova, I want a nail hammering through it. This place is to run smoothly and safely in my absence, or there will be consequences on my return. Got that?'

The three men addressed saluted. 'Sir,' they all answered in unison.

In the corner, Laelius frowned. 'Campaign gear?'

'Right. I have things to get ready. You two take Laelius back to his barracks, throw a few buckets of water at him, feed him a bowl of dry porridge to soak up some of that wine, and then make sure he packs everything he'll need for time on the road and the water.'

As the two officers grabbed the drunken man and heaved him away, Rufinus turned to the last soldier. 'Varro, go about your business and leave these reports here. Senova will send for you when she needs you.'

The clerk saluted and scurried away, leaving just the pair of them in the room.

'You're sure you don't want me with you? I can be useful. Remember Dacia?'

He winced. Of course he did. Without her to nurse him back after that fall, he'd have died out in the wilds on the edge of the empire. But that didn't mean he wanted to put her in danger again. He shook his head. 'I trust the men here to go on doing what they do, but I would be happier with someone with a little extra brain dealing with my paperwork. You happy with that?'

She smiled. 'You know I'm actually better at such things than you.'

18

'Quite. Trust Varro. He's young, and clumsy, but he's straight as a die, and good at what he does. I'll send you messages whenever I can, at the very least once I get to Liguria. And if there's anywhere I can confirm I'll be, you can send messages back, too.'

'I don't like it when you go away without me.'

'I know.'

He walked over and threw his arms around her. 'If it were anyone else – *anyone* – I would stay,' he added, speaking into her hair as he hugged her tight.

'He is your brother. If you did not help him, you would not be the man I married. Be safe. Brigantia watch over you.'

'I'm sure she does. Certainly, *something* makes me itch from time to time.'

He grinned as he let her go and she turned and walked away, Sheba running over to join her. As she disappeared from sight, a lolloping mop of shaggy white hair appeared in the doorway. 'Yes, Orthus, we're going on a trip. Hopefully you don't get seasick.'

He smiled at the animal. Maybe Orthus was no Acheron, but in an odd way, Acheron had been no Orthus either.

'Come on. Let's get ready. Liguria awaits.'

CHAPTER TWO

Liguria

Rufinus reined in and shielded his eyes from the dying sun ahead. Beside him, Orthus stopped running and padded around looking excited, which was more than could be said for Laelius, who, if one had to say anything about him, it would probably be that he was no more a natural horseman than he was a sailor.

'My arse feels like I handed a plank of wood to a bath house masseur and bent over for a planking. Whoever invented saddles must not have had an arse, or they'd have made them differently.'

Rufinus rolled his eyes at the latest complaint. He had been determined that he would rehabilitate Laelius. He himself had been in the grip of the wine monster at a dark time in his life, and he knew how enticing it was, how hard to break. He would bring Laelius back to a lighter life, make him an effective soldier all the time, or that had been his plan. Then they had set sail from Ostia Portus. It turned out that Laelius had been on a ship precisely three times in his life. The first one had been diverted in a storm, and they had spent three weeks living off forage on the forbidding north African coast. The second time, the ship had sunk, and he had clung to a rock until he was found in the morning, and the third time he had spent the whole trip fighting off the advances of the trierarch, who had taken a fancy to him. In all, his opinion of sea travel was not the best. Though their journey had been peaceful and uneventful, Laelius had found fault with the smallest of things, had been the voice of doom and gloom, and had truly ruined every hour they had travelled. By the time they'd landed at Genua Rufinus had nearly bought the man a jar of wine just to make him less irritating.

Then they'd bought horses at one of the city's stables, gathered all they needed for the journey, and set off west along the coast. By the time they were a mile from Genua, it became clear that snails were going to move faster than them. Laelius not only had absolutely no skill or affinity with horses, but he also disliked them intensely, something that seemed to be reciprocated. It had been the slowest and most soul-destroying journey, and Rufinus was just immensely pleased that it was almost over.

'Does your arse not hurt, sir?'

Rufinus bit into his lip. 'No,' he growled, in an effort to end what passed for conversation in their travels.

He knew the route, though it had been many years since he'd last taken it, and he knew it was a day-long journey. He'd planned to get there in time to make an evening meal and settle down for the night. In the end, by sunset they had made it almost halfway, and Rufinus was regretting bringing the man along. Perhaps he should just have had him beaten after all. But now, the second day out of Genua, they were closing on the estate as the sun slid its last few feet into nothingness.

The villa was smaller than he remembered, but then that was no great surprise. He'd been here twice in his life, that he remembered: once as a boy when visiting the aunt, and once when she died and his father wanted to assess it for potential sale to fund his ever-desired return to court. From this distance, it looked as though part of the roof had fallen in. Really, it probably needed demolishing now and selling off as a bare plot. Maybe one of the neighbouring estates would buy it at a knock down price to extend their own vineyards and orchards.

His brother had apparently beaten him here, for as the light dwindled, he could see golden twinkling among the walls, where a light shone from windows.

'Come on.'

He walked his horse on, heading for the gateposts of the drive, the gates themselves long since fallen away and rotted. The first time he'd visited, there had been an avenue of neat cypresses, interspersed with colourful shrubs, down both sides of a white gravel drive with a clean drain. Now it looked more like woodland alongside a country farm track. With Laelius hissing with discomfort at every clop of hooves, and Orthus bouncing along excitedly beside him, Rufinus made his slow way up the long drive towards the dilapidated house on the hill crest.

The door stood open, and now that the sun had set fully, and the light had dropped to a deep indigo, the golden dancing of a fire was reflected around the walls and pillars just visible inside. He reached the front of the villa and slipped from the saddle, tying his horse to a post as Laelius dropped to the ground with a curse and rubbed his nethers soothingly, then followed him and the dog to the house, walking bow-legged and grumbling.

'Publius?' he called, tremulously, into the half-light.

He stepped into the vestibule, long since stripped of anything valuable. The marble tiles were cracked and the wall painting peeling and faded, the pictured gods having seen better days, the small shrine to the household gods little more than a marble block, the gods themselves long gone.

The atrium was little better, the pool in the centre full of leaves and detritus, no water flowing. The bronze faun with its twin horn that had spouted water in better days seemed to have become a nest of some sort. He turned and followed the light.

He wasn't sure what it was that alerted him to the fact that something was not right. Perhaps it was the silence... no response to his call? Whatever it was, something set his senses tingling, and as he stepped towards that room with the fire, he pulled his sword free of its scabbard. He waved a hand at Laelius, warning him, and then stepped into the room carefully, slowly, alert and ready.

The attack came in an instant.

As he stepped through the door, a man came from the left, sword out, swinging. Rufinus charged past, throwing his own sword in the way to parry as he backed into the room, towards the fire. Laelius followed him in, but was still pulling his sword out and only just avoided death as he ducked.

Rufinus took the situation in at a glance. Three men. Two to the left of the door as he looked back, one to the right, all hidden from the approach and ready for an ambush. They were warriors, dressed in chain shirts and dun-coloured tunics, scabbards belted at their sides. All of them were bare-headed, but had shaggy hair and beards. They looked quite un-Roman. Indeed, at a glance, they resembled the Marcomanni who he'd fought across the Danubius all those years ago before joining the Guard.

The one on the right, the one who'd attacked him as he entered, he reckoned was the leader. The other two men were both bigger, but wore less gold and bronze. They were all using long swords.

Laelius staggered past them, only just, still struggling to get his sword free.

Take the leader down first, but keep him alive in order to find out what this is about. Then move on to the two big men.

Plan laid, Rufinus pointed to Laelius and then to the big fellows. 'Keep them busy.' He then stepped towards the smaller, better-dressed one, who rolled his shoulders and swung his sword in wide sweeps, ready. Orthus, in the doorway, recognised the danger to his master, and was advancing on the leader as though stalking prey. Rufinus whistled to get the animal's attention. He could handle the man himself, but Laelius was facing two opponents. As Orthus looked round at him, Rufinus pointed at one of the bigger warriors.

'Balls!'

The dog moved in an instant, turning, bounding across the room and launching himself at one of the big warriors. His jaws opened wide as he leapt, and snapped shut beneath the hem of the man's tunic, just below the chain shirt. The big warrior

24

screamed as he turned, but the large dog remained attached to his manhood by the teeth, turning with him, but slower, and with a horrible tearing sound. His sword fell as he started to make weird wailing noises.

Rufinus left them to it, and advanced on the leader, who looked considerably less confidant now.

'This was a mistake. But if you tell me what you're doing here, you might yet walk away.'

The man issued a low growl and then said something short and sharp in a guttural language. Rufinus continued to advance, for he'd not expected the man to back down. As he came close enough to engage, the warrior swung once more, a competent enough blow, but rather predictable and not fast enough. Rufinus dropped his own sword in the way to deflect it, and spun as he did so, bringing his blade round, using the momentum of its contact with the opponent's weapon to add to his own swing as the sword came round and smashed into the man's left arm, just above the elbow. He heard the arm break in an instant, and the man yelped loudly, but was not out of it just yet. He stepped back, panting, glanced down at the damaged limb, then lifted the sword in his other arm, gritting his teeth.

The next blow was better – a lunge, which was unusual with such a weapon, and could have been surprising enough to land on Rufinus – had he not been watching the man's eyes and his feet, the former betraying his action before he carried it out, the latter bracing in such a way as to confirm what that action would be. Rufinus spun again, twisting away from the blow, this time in the other direction, and when his blade swung this time, it hit the sword arm. The man's second arm broke.

Rufinus had to give it to the man, he was no coward, and fought through the pain. Impressively, the warrior lifted his sword a little, even with a slight break or fracture in the arm, hissing at the agony, but readying for another swing regardless.

'Don't be a fool. Arms heal, and you could still walk away.'

The man took a step forward and managed, through sheer strength of will, to pull his sword out ready for another swing. He looked determined, even though he knew he was bested, which was impressive. Rufinus raised his own sword easily, point levelled at the man. 'You've lost. Now talk to me and this might still end well.'

The man took another step forward, bracing himself for something, and so Rufinus lifted the blade, the tip hovering in front of the man's throat.

'Don't be...'

He was not prepared for what happened next, though. Instead of taking that last desperate swing, the man leapt forward onto the point of his sword, the metal shearing into his throat, burying itself deep and bringing forth a spray of crimson. As the Roman pulled away his sword, too slow to prevent the man dying now, he was perturbed by the look of grim satisfaction in the man's expression. He stepped back, and the leader fell in a heap, dropping his sword, blood jetting out to form a lake around him. As he rapidly paled, Rufinus looked around. He'd have liked to have interrogated the leader for obvious reasons, but one of the others would have to do.

He was disappointed at what he saw. Orthus was facing his own victim. He had let go after a while, but the big warrior had cast away his sword and sat, legs wide, against the wall, face white with horror. His trousers and the floor beneath him were soaked with blood. The dog had caught an artery with his attack, and the man had already almost bled out, even as he faded in agony and shock. The other warrior wasn't going to be any more help, either, for he lay in a heap with a smashed face, like something hanging on a butcher's hook in the market. Laelius was leaning on the wall nearby with his back to Rufinus, shaking slightly. None of their attackers was going to reveal anything.

Damn it.

As he cursed silently, Laelius turned, and Rufinus's eyes widened. As his front came into view, Rufinus saw the huge belly wound the Guardsman had suffered, coils and glistening things held in only by desperate, blood-coated fingers. That big warrior had given as good as he got, and there was little doubt that Laelius was going to follow him into the afterlife.

'I'm killed,' the man said, voice hollow, lost.

Rufinus would have liked to have comforted him, to have told him that everything would be alright, but that was so clearly not the case, and they both knew it. He was done for, but because of the manner of the wound, it would take quite some time for him to die, and it would be agony every step of the way.

'What do I do?' mewed Laelius.

Rufinus walked over to the wall, leaning his sword against it, then walked back. He reached up, a hand on each of the Guardsman's cheeks, giving him a comforting smile, leaned in as if for a hug, and at the last moment, jerked his hands left, ripping Laelius's head in a half circle. He heard the crunches and tears as the spine broke, along with other critical parts. He'd had to prepare himself for that. It sounded like an easy thing to do, but the first time he'd ever done it, it had surprised him just how much effort it took to break a neck. Luckily, he was stronger than most men, and knew what he was doing. Laelius fell, exhaling his last, hands coming away to allow his innards to slither free. A broken neck was not the neatest death, but it was quick and could be delivered with the minimum pain to the victim. Certainly quicker and less painful than a slow death from a belly wound.

By the time he'd finished and turned to look at the rest of the room, it was all over. He and Orthus were the only two survivors, the man with the ravaged groin now white and still, in a pool of his own lifeblood.

'Damn it, but I wanted to question one of them,' he sighed. 'Maybe their possessions will answer a few questions, I suppose. But I'd best first make sure they were alone.'

Taking advantage of the last glow of sunset, in the purple light before the real dark set in, he set about searching the building. There was no sign of habitation in any of the other rooms, and he even checked the outbuildings briefly. Behind the house, he found three horses corralled, confirming that the three attackers had been alone. He noted that the horses appeared to be well rested, and the grass well-grazed, suggesting they had been here for several days. Returning to the room, the first thing he did was to check over Laelius. He removed the man's rings and purse and any accoutrements that were personal or valuable, and then went back out front and put them in the man's bag. Later, he would have those effects sent to whatever relatives were listed on his service record back at the Castra Praetoria. The body was a different matter. He rummaged and found a coin, then slipped it under the man's tongue. Cremating Laelius would be troublesome to say the least, so inhumation was the only viable option, but he didn't really want to spend half a day digging a grave either. Another search revealed what he'd hoped for: a sunken stone water tank that would hold rainwater for the summer. At the moment it was dry, apart from some sludge at the bottom. There was little he could do about that, so he carried Laelius out to the tank and lowered him into it. He then found an old, broken shovel in one of the outhouses and spent half an hour filling in the makeshift grave. As an afterthought, once he was finished, he tipped a few cups' worth of wine from the jar among Laelius's belongings onto the grave, and then went back inside.

The fire was starting to die down, but the three men had been here for a few days, and a stock of dry wood had been piled up in an adjacent room, so he brought a few armfuls through and fed the flames until the room was warm and bright once again. With the golden flickering light to aid him, he went to the bodies. First, he checked the two bigger men, but they had little on them that was any more informative than what he could see at a glance. Content that there was nothing to learn from them, he carried them, one after the other, across the atrium and dumped them in a different room.

The leader had a few personal items about him, and a purse of coins, but nothing that truly identified him. What they told

Rufinus in basic terms, though, was that the man was German. Whether from some tribe beyond the border, or from one of those that was nominally Romanised from this side of the great rivers, he couldn't say. But it did limit the man's rough area of origin.

After he'd dumped the body with the others, he went through their packs, which confirmed their Germanic origin again and again. Moreover, it made it clear that they had been camped here for days, and were equipped and supplied for a few days longer yet. In one bag he found a wine jar, unopened, and marked with its origin, a winery in a place called Phoebiana. He cursed himself for not having brought any of the maps or itineraries with him. He probably should have done. Sitting in the dust, he traced a rough map of rivers and main roads from memory, then marked the three locations he already knew about: Batavis, Tasgetium and this villa. He ran through the maps in his memory over and over, for Phoebiana was a familiar name, and he'd seen it on them. He was fairly confident when he finally placed it in context with the others, and nodded to himself. It was somewhere between that same border zone and here, confirming that these three Germans had come from the Raetian border region. That meant there was absolutely no accident in this meeting, not that he'd thought for a moment that there was.

They were German, had come from the German border to this villa and then set up camp. That meant they were waiting for someone, and in Rufinus's opinion that list could be narrowed to two names, one more likely than the other. Either they had got ahead of Publius and meant him harm, and had been lying in wait for him here...

Or they were expecting Rufinus. That was less likely, but a lot more worrying. If they knew Rufinus was coming, then they had learned as much either from reading Publius's correspondence, or from the man himself. Once again, he cursed the fact that none of the attackers had survived to be interrogated.

Satisfied that he had been through everything that was there to be found, he set about making ready for the night. He found the well he'd played around as a child, and managed to bring up a couple of buckets of water. He then used those and the Germans' cloaks and spare clothes to sluice down the blood pools and wash them into a corner and then mop them dry and cast the clothes into the fire. It was not that he was averse to blood, of course, for he'd both seen and spilled plenty of it in his time, but the odour tended to flood one's nose and become cloying, and, once the room had been cleaned, it was considerably more pleasant to stay in.

Just in case, before he set up his bedroll for the night, close to the fire, he removed from his pack a spool of thread and a few small, delicate glass bottles he'd collected for this very purpose, and went round the entrances to the villa, setting up low, barely-visible tripwires that, when activated, would pull a bottle off a surface and smash it on the floor. His early warning system in place, he returned to the fire and settled into his blankets. Orthus wandered over and collapsed in a heap, sort of next-to, and sort of on top of him, a comforting if heavy pile of fleecy dog. He leaned back in his blankets, one arm cradled behind his head on the makeshift pillow of folded cloak, the other scruffing his dog's neck, eliciting sighs of canine pleasure.

'Never used to be able to do this with Acheron,' he noted. 'I was never entirely sure he wouldn't go for me. After all, he hadn't always been my dog. Not like you,' he added as he stroked.

His mind wandered back to the main subject. The three Germans had plainly come down from the Raetian border, where Publius thought there was something happening that put him in direct danger, and possibly even the region, too, and that the post was being monitored. That last suggested something that involved either the Roman authorities or some important person therein.

He'd done some studying of the few records he had at his fingertips before leaving, including military unit disposition listings. The most senior military man in the zone in question would be the legatus commanding the Third Italica Legion at Castra Regina, who was also, worryingly, the governor of Raetia. He, therefore, had to be potential trouble. His procurator, of course, would also be able to influence the post and courier service, not to mention a number of senior administrators. He wasn't so sure about the commanders of auxiliary units, but presumably they would have influence only over their own unit and fort. This sounding like an internal Roman issue made it likely that the three men who'd attacked them had been from an allied tribe within the Roman border rather than Germanic barbaroi from beyond it. The chances of them being unconnected with whatever had Publius so nervous were minute. So, whatever had Rufinus's brother on the run from his unit, heading south, had perhaps initiated the unidentified villain sending some trusted locals to hunt him down. And whether they had come here to wait for Publius or to wait for Rufinus, that they had come here and stayed at all made it highly likely that Publius had not yet come this far. For a horrible moment, he wondered if they had killed him here and then waited for Rufinus, but he was confident that he'd searched the place well enough that if Publius or any of his gear was here, he'd have found some sign. No, he relaxed back down once more, Publius had not reached the villa.

That meant he was somewhere between Tasgetium, the last place he had definitely visited, and here, a destination he had yet to reach. He'd been travelling for some time, but still it might not be a surprise that he'd not moved fast. Publius had grown up, after all. He was in his thirties now, not the child Rufinus remembered being impetuous and rash. He was clever, and experienced enough now to be careful. He would be moving as slowly as safety required, keeping out of sight, making sure not to leave too obvious a trail for his pursuers. That, Rufinus decided, was probably why they'd come here. They had totally failed to catch up with him and find him, so they had come to where they knew from his letters he was going, and waited for him.

Comforted by that logic, he relaxed back to try and sleep, also secure in the knowledge that his shattering glass tripwires would wake him more surely than any lazy picket.

In those last moments before sleep, when his mind whirled through a number of things, he found himself pondering on Laelius. The lad was probably no worse a soldier than Rufinus had been back in the days of Cleander, when he'd been addicted to one narcotic or another in an attempt to forget the horrors of torture and the unsightly marks it had left upon him. Rufinus felt a little guilty in dragging him from the safety of the camp to his death here, but then the man was a soldier, after all. And he'd done all he could, really, giving the Guardsman a coin for the ferryman, an impromptu burial that would at least keep the body safe and stop scavengers picking it over, and gathering his effects for his relatives. When he got back, he would erase all the negatives from the man's record. His family didn't need that black mark, and they could be proud when a note was added that he had died in battle against Germans, saving the life of a tribune. He wondered momentarily whether an award would be fitting, but decided against it. That might be going too far. But he would write a letter to the man's family. That was all he could ever do, and if they wanted his body, he could at least tell them where to find it.

His mind drifted on. Tomorrow. He had only planned on coming this far and speaking to Publius. The timings he'd given Senova would have seen him on the road on the way home already. Instead, he had a new mission, and one which would only take him further away. His duty really should now drag him back to Rome, and Severus would give him such a dressing down if he went any further. This much, he was content he could get away with, but an extended absence was different. Of course, the emperor would not be back in Rome for many, many months yet. The next town he passed through, Rufinus would have to visit the imperial waystation and send a letter to Senova explaining why he had to go further, and perhaps giving her a target destination that she could send messages to where he could pick them up.

Tasgetium.

That was the name that kept cropping up like a bad sestertius.

The last place he knew for sure Publius had been was Tasgetium, up in the Alps of southern Raetia. He was either still there, or somewhere in between, but unless he happened to find a hint of the man, Rufinus was going to have to go to Tasgetium and start there. Waiting here seemed like a simple option, but there was no guarantee that Publius was still coming, and had not been waylaid, and the next people who did come here might be a score of dangerous Germans. Only at Tasgetium could he realistically hope to find some sort of sign of Publius's passing through, and from there he could work back. At least then he'd be heading south again, back towards Rome.

That decision made, with the comforting thought about his direction, he let himself drift into sleep.

The night was interrupted only once. He leapt from his blankets at the crash, half expecting to find a hundred Germans tripping his wires, but instead found a guilty-looking Orthus peeing against a wall, where he'd knocked over the sword that Rufinus had forgotten to pick back up.

The next morning, his first task was to clean his sword, which was now not only coated with gore, but also soaked in dog pee. He washed it thoroughly with water from the well, and dried it, but no matter what he did, he was convinced he could still smell piss on the leather wrapping of the hilt. He gathered everything together, and then went through the rest of the kit. He took a number of perishables and valuables from the Germans, including what coin they had. He'd not planned on a longer journey, and might be better financing it privately rather than relying on his rank and connections, especially if there was someone in the Roman provincial or military hierarchy where he was headed who could not be trusted. He rounded up all five horses, and loaded three of them as pack animals, carrying all their combined gear, including the arms and armour of the Germans, if for no other reason than he could sell it to help pay for his journey. Finally, mid-morning, he was ready to leave, with a spare riding horse, so that he could change mounts every couple of hours and therefore move fast without tiring the animals. The spare horses were all roped together and tethered to his saddle horns, and it began as an easy ride.

It was not until he reached the end of the drive that he realised he had not decided on the precise path of his journey onwards. There were three ways across the Alpes. He could either ride far to the east, to Verona, and then north from there, but that would never be the route that Publius would follow. The most direct route from here to Publius's home fort of Batavis would be north and east, through Mediolanum and the central Alpine passes. But the fact that Publius had travelled southwest from Batavis, through Tasgetium, suggested he was aiming for the western Alpine pass, down through Genava. That, then, had to be the route Rufinus should take. He would travel north and west, climbing the lower slopes, all the time keeping his senses alert, looking and listening for even the slightest hint that Publius had passed by.

With five horses, a small hoard of booty, an enthusiastic dog, and a sword that smelled of urine, Gnaeus Marcius Rustius Rufinus, tribune and acting commander of the Praetorian Guard in Rome, set off from the known, in the form of a ruined Ligurian villa, for the unknown: the high, snowy passes of the Alpes.

CHAPTER THREE

Raetia

Rufinus was tired. It had been a while since he'd spent this long in the saddle, and the terrain had not been easy. He had cause more than once to wistfully recall Laelius's complaints about horses and saddles, though at least the main roads that led up to the western pass were well-maintained and easy. He had never been to Raetia before, his experience with the Danubian frontier entirely further east, past the mountains, in the plains and low hills of Pannonia. He was impressed with this land, even through the tiredness and difficulties.

The hills of the Ligurian coast had given way to the wide flat plains of Northern Italia, but it did not take long to cross them, and soon he had begun to climb. It took a day, then, in the hills and lower mountains, to reach the city of Augusta Praetoria Salassorum, the gateway to the Alpine pass. From that time on, traffic on the roads had thinned, for on the whole only merchants and the military were to be found in the high passes. He'd climbed still, following the great valley until he reached the plateau and the ancient Helvetian city of Genava, nestled by the lake.

Following the road ever northwest, he rounded the lake, and passed another impressive body of water a day further on, approaching the hills and valleys on the far side of the great plateau, and with a few questions directed to the locals, knew he was closing on Tasgetium now. On the entire journey, he had been careful and circumspect, yet observant and thorough. He had used imperial stations and managed to check the registers for his brother's name, finding nothing. He had enquired of local hostelries, merchants, livery stables and so on, and all to no avail. If Publius had come this way, he'd done it virtually invisibly, little more than a ghost.

Tasgetium was to say the least underwhelming. A small, fortified site sat on a low hill overlooking the river at the northern end of a lake, guarding a bridge, and the town, such as it was, had grown up around it, little more than two score timber structures clustered around the walls for protection. The mansio, imperial courier station and layover point, sat just outside the walls, displaying the insignia of the cursus publicus above the door, one of the guards from the fortlet standing beside it, looking bored.

As he moved into the street that led up to the mansio and the fortlet gate, he passed several houses occupied seemingly by grubby children and a mangy hound that barked incessantly at Orthus as they entered, then a small general store and a tavern by the name of the Brawling Gaul. He'd passed through a number of towns and villages since leaving the great pass and entering Raetia, and though it had been a new world in terms of physical geography, the culture and people had felt little different to those he had left behind in the plains and hills of Liguria and Northern Italia. Here was a different matter entirely. The place felt raw and dangerous, a frontier zone, even though he was still some way south of the actual border. The main thing that contributed, he decided, looking around him as he moved, was the people. They no longer looked properly Roman. Hair was longer, shaggier, braided sometimes, beards or moustaches were in plentiful evidence, occasionally on the women, he thought, rather unkindly. They were dressed more like Germans or northern Gauls, and on the odd occasions he heard them speak, they either used a local tongue or spoke Latin with a strong Germanic twang.

Somewhere amid the fertile plateau lands of Raetia, he had seemingly moved into a different world.

And it felt unfriendly, too. Eyes followed him as he rode, and they were not filled with warmth. Conversation either stopped or lowered nearby, and the atmosphere grew frosty. Even Orthus, usually excitable at even the smallest things, seemed subdued and tense. That atmosphere was particularly evident around the tavern, where men were sitting outside at tables, drinking local brews, and watching him with hooded eyes. It occurred to him, a not entirely comforting thought, that the men he was seeing here bore more than a passing resemblance to the three men he had stumbled across at the villa.

It was something of a relief when he reached the mansio. He visited the stables first, and saw to the horses. Over the days of travel from Liguria, he had somewhat streamlined and shed goods. He'd sold a lot of the acquired equipment and three of the horses, netting himself a tidy sum to cover a good half month of journeying, and so now he had just his own mount and a spare horse, kit for himself, with a couple of left over souvenirs of the fight in Liguria, and Laelius's personal effects, of course. Divested of the bulk of his gear, he moved into the mansio itself and approached the desk. The man behind it felt rather out of place here, for he and the soldier outside were the only people he'd seen thus far in Tasgetium who looked Roman. This man had a short, curly beard, neatly trimmed, and a rather severe hairstyle, resembling the Trajanic trends. He wore the uniform tunic of the cursus publicus, and his identity amulet on a thong around his neck, theoretically a symbol of absolute trust, although Publius's vague hints had thrown a shadow over that for Rufinus.

'Can I help you, officer?'

Rufinus was impressed. His armour and weapons were with his kit, in storage in the stables, and any badge of rank he had was either packed or hidden from view, including his Praetorian insignia, covered by his cloak. He was clearly military, for he wore nailed boots and a plated military belt, but even his tunic was a civilian one, for he'd eschewed Praetorian white in favour of something a little more subtle. Still, the man worked for the cursus and would see all forms of military in his work. That he might recognise a man as an officer, probably by his bearing, should be no surprise.

'Hello. I may need a room for the night. I have my papers with me.'

'Of course, sir. *May* need?'

'I am also seeking information. I believe the man I am looking for visited here, though he may not have stayed overnight. As such, he may not be marked in your register. But he sent this from here.'

He reached down to his belt and withdrew the letter, turning it so that the official could see the remnants of the cursus-stamped seal.

'Most definitely one of ours. And yes, I remember the fellow. It is not often I apply a seal to a wax tablet, for they are rare in use in this region.'

'You remember him? Tell me what you remember.'

The man leaned on the desk and rubbed his chin. 'He arrived some time in the early afternoon, I think, around a month ago, and he was in something of a state of urgency. He carried with him military identification, that of a prefect of a unit up on the lines, though I cannot remember which one. He arrived on a horse that he'd almost ridden to death, such was his hurry. The horse is still in our stables, as it took days for it to recover. The animal had come from our sister station at Guntia, some hundred miles or so northeast for here, and I would not be surprised to learn he had tried to push the horse all the way.'

Rufinus nodded, leaning in, attentive. He'd known his brother was worried and potentially in danger, but the scale of that danger was brought home by the details of his clearly desperate journey. A hundred miles in one ride, nearly killing the horse?

'Tell me more.'

'Well, he had me send that document, of course. Actually, he asked me a number of rather personal questions first. I felt as though I was being investigated by the service, my oath called into question, but he seemed happy with the results, enough to trust me with sealing and sending his letter at least. To be honest, with the speed he'd arrived, I was not convinced the letter via the service would go any faster than him.'

'So, he didn't stay the night, I guess?'

'No. He took a fresh horse and set off southwest, heading for Augusta Raurica. I admonished him on his treatment of the animals and warned him to take more care with our mount.'

'It is a fast road? The one to Augusta Raurica?'

The man nodded carefully, though doubt creased his features. 'Yes, although I personally do not believe he used that road.'

'Oh?'

The man straightened and rubbed his arms. 'The state the horse from Guntia arrived in suggested that he had not been using the metalled roads, but rather riding across country, in the wild, through the mud and even rivers. The animal was filthy, sodden and exhausted. If he had not used the roads to get from Guntia to here, I see no reason why he would change when he moved on. I doubt he stayed on the Raurica road for long after he left town.'

Rufinus nodded again. Once more it made perfect sense. If Publius was afraid of being followed, and believed he would be in danger, one of the first ways he could employ caution would be to travel off the beaten track, remaining as hidden and incognito as possible. He'd even been careful to make sure of this man's loyalty before trusting him with a letter.

'The western pass.'

The official frowned. 'Sir?'

'That's where he was going. He came from the frontier, from the fort at Batavis, via Guntia to this place. If he was going onwards to Augusta Raurica, and I know his destination was Liguria, that pretty much confirms that he was using the western pass by Genava.' He leaned forward. 'If he was not following the road, but was headed for Raurica, where do you think he would go?'

The man sucked on his teeth, frowning, then placed his palms down on the counter. 'The main road follows roughly the same line as the Rhenus River, parallel and a distance to the south. It varies, of course, for the road is straight, while the river bends and moves, but if a man were to go from here to Raurica without using the road, the most direct path with a guiding feature to follow would be the river.'

Another nod from Rufinus. Perfect. If it had been him, *he* would have followed the river, and it seemed highly likely, therefore, that Publius had done the same.

'How far is Augusta Raurica from here?'

The man shrugged. 'Officially, on the road system, sixty-eight miles. Nearer sixty as the bird flies. Following the river, it will be considerably further, perhaps even edging towards a hundred.'

A hundred miles. More or less what Publius had done to reach this place, and it was therefore not unrealistic that he had done the same moving on, heading for the next station. Rufinus had not visited Raurica on his way north, for it was an extra dogleg on the journey. His brother had probably chosen it based on the combination of taking the less expected route, and there being another mansio he could use there.

'One last thing. My wife may have sent a letter to this station. It would be addressed to Gnaeus Marcius Rustius Rufinus, Tribune.'

The man nodded, crossed to the postal shelves and searched with the expected efficiency, then returned. 'I'm afraid we have nothing for that name.'

Rufinus nodded, sagging slightly. He'd hoped to have word from Senova, but then it had not been long since he contacted her, and it was a long shot that a letter might have got here yet. 'Thank you. You have been more than helpful,' he said, placing several coins on the counter in gratitude. 'Three more quick things: am I the first to ask after him, and did you house anyone in a similar state in the following days? And I would appreciate it if this conversation slipped your memory when I leave. It is a rather important matter,' he added, and this time, he pulled aside his cloak to show the Praetorian scorpion brooch on his tunic.

The man frowned. 'I am not accustomed to secrecy and clandestine affairs. There are *other* imperial services for that.'

'Believe me, I know. But sinister forces may be at work in Raetia, and I am simply trying to buy myself sufficient time to investigate. You have the word of a Praetorian tribune.'

'No offence, Tribune, but the Praetorians' reputation has come rather close to sinister at times too. Still, while I will not withhold information in the line of duty, I give you my word that I will not volunteer it readily, and I will be sure to whom I am speaking first. As for your other queries, I had no one following in a similar state in the next few days, and you are the first to ask this of me. I pray you are the last, and my truthful nature not be put to the test.'

Rufinus nodded. The man was the stalwart type that typified the cursus publicus, who maintained its reputation for honesty and efficiency.

'Thank you again. You may well have been of great service to your empire today.'

He tipped the man again, just to be sure, and then walked back out towards the stables. There was still several hours of daylight left today, and he was aware that time was passing rapidly, while his brother's fate may hang in the balance, and the Guard remained in Rome without a senior commander in his absence. It might have been sensible to stay at the mansio for the night, but he felt the need to press on, to find more. To find anything.

Publius had left his post at Batavis, apparently alone, fearful for his life, and believing that someone might be reading his correspondence, possibly with good reason. He had then raced to this place called Guntia, and changed horses there. After that, he had ridden across country, away from where he would be expected, and had ridden so hard and fast that he'd almost killed the horse, arriving at Tasgetium, where he sent the letter to

Rufinus, after making sure he trusted the official, then changed horses again and seemingly followed the Rhenus southwest towards the Alpine pass to Italia. Rufinus had known he reached Tasgetium. Now he knew where his brother had gone thereafter. The next step would be to confirm that he arrived at Augusta Raurica. He toyed with following the great river in his brother's footsteps, but decided that he had less reason to hide, and so he would use the main road and head to the next place, and there check for signs of Publius's passage. The next step would have to be the mansio at Raurica, a place where this frontier world met the civilised.

That was his goal.

He retrieved the two horses from the stables, impressed that they had been fed, watered and groomed in just the short time he had been inside with his enquiries. When he retrieved his packs from the holding area, he checked them through to be sure they had not been tampered with, each of them fastened with a single thread across the tie which would betray their being opened in his absence. The threads were all intact. Whatever fears Publius had over the regional authorities, it seemed that this mansio at least was above reproach.

Satisfied that he had achieved everything he could at Tasgetium, he mounted up and rode back out of the mansio. For all the satisfaction of what he had achieved here, though, he was also haunted by a thought. Publius had left Tasgetium and not arrived in Liguria. He was therefore somewhere between the two, and the more Rufinus discovered, the less likely it was looking that Publius was safe and sound. A lot would ride on what he discovered at the Augusta Raurica mansio.

He rode back down that street, and on the way out of town, he was once more sharply aware of the less than friendly looks he was receiving from those men outside the tavern. He toyed with throwing them a friendly smile to see what happened, but he wasn't feeling particularly friendly right now, and so in the end he did not, simply ignoring them and riding away, though he could feel their gazes boring into his back as he left.

He departed the town by the main road, noting the distance marked on the milestone with a smile, given that the official had been spot on from memory. He rode steadily, so as not to exhaust his horses, but he did not dawdle, and changed mounts after an hour to allow the first to rest a little. Still, he had covered not more than half the distance by the time night fell properly, which brought home to him just how hard his brother must have ridden.

He found a farm near the road and rapped on the door, then asked a boon of the farmer in the form of a place to stay in one of his barns for the night. The farmer turned out to be more than helpful and instead gave him a bed in the bunk house used by the farm workers, while his horses recovered in the corral outside. In the morning, he paid the man handsomely for his kindness, and then moved on.

It was near noon when he approached the city of Augusta Raurica. Unlike Tasgetium, this place was a thriving metropolis, a true Roman city, and he could see the high arcades of theatres and amphitheatres, the roofs of temples and other grand buildings rising above the houses. The great Rhenus River was here crossed by a long and impressive bridge, small fortlets sitting at either end, though more suburban sprawl had begun to grow on the far side. The mansio was not hard to find. A quick question to a local, who seemed considerably more Roman than at Tasgetium, and he was directed to a large complex not far from the south end of the bridge, where a road marched off into the heart of Raurica,

The mansio was a much larger affair than the last one, and held several buildings all within a walled complex. Rufinus followed the same procedure, leading his horses into the stables. This time, his gear was placed in a locked container to which he was given a key. He moved into the main hall, and found a desk manned by three people, all busy dealing with guests. He waited his turn and was rewarded with a small, rotund man in the uniform of the cursus publicus.

'Can I help you, sir?'

Rufinus nodded. 'I am trying to trace someone who came through here a little over a month ago. He would be riding a horse from the mansio at Tasgetium, and would be looking fretful and nervous. His horse would probably not be in the best state, and would have been ridden hard, across country. I doubt he would have stayed the night, although it is not impossible, and he may have dispatched a letter from here, although I doubt it.'

The small man gave him a look that suggested he had much more important things to do than answer rather random questions.

'Name?'

Rufinus frowned. 'If he gave a name, it would probably be Publius Marcius Rustius, although I don't know whether he would, and there is always the possibility that he used an assumed name.'

The man tutted. 'An assumed name would be no good. If he wanted to change horses or use our facilities, his name would have to match the documentation he carried.'

Rufinus nodded and let the man work. He went through a number of ledgers, and sent for the head groom. When the man arrived, he pointed him over to Rufinus, who repeated the details of his brother's horse and ride. The groom shook his head. 'Definitely not. If anyone had brought a beast in here in such shape I would know about it, and I would blow my top at him. I will not have riders mistreating their mounts, especially ones we have a vested interest in. I can tell you straight away that no one in such a state has been here in at least half a year, since I took over as head groom.'

The small man leaned across and took over. 'And there is no record of the man's name in any of our ledgers. There is, in fact, no evidence that the man ever set foot here. There is another mansio a few miles away, on the far side of the river. Perhaps it was there he went?'

Rufinus thanked the men and then went and retrieved his animals and gear. With a sinking feeling, he followed directions to this second mansio, on a different road, heading north beyond the river. There he made similar enquiries, but with identical results. There seemed no record of Publius utilising a mansio at Augusta Raurica.

He spent a short while there, as his horses were prepared, deep in thought. All the evidence pointed towards Publius having left Tasgetium, but never reaching this place. Whatever happened to him therefore happened along the hundred mile stretch of the Rhenus between the two places. He dismissed the notion that Publius had instead visited a private stable in the city. If he had been using the cursus all the way from Batavis to Tasgetium, it seemed highly unlikely he would change his modus operandi thereafter.

It was, in fact, looking increasingly like the three Germans he had met in Liguria had caught up with Publius somewhere along this stretch of the Rhenus and had done away with him, but not before learning that he had sent a letter to his brother, arranging to meet at the villa. They had therefore dumped the body and raced to Liguria to meet Rufinus and tie up a loose end.

Damn it.

His spirits sank even lower. It was becoming increasingly hard to see any other possibility: Publius had to have met his end between Tasgetium and Raurica.

He would make sure, though.

While his animals were being prepared, he headed back inside and strode across to the counter.

'Where can I hire a guide?'

The man on duty shrugged. 'We're a waystation, not an outpost. Perhaps you could ask at the fort?'

Before Rufinus could answer, a voice behind him, with a faint Germanic accent, said 'What do you need a guide for?'

Rufinus turned. A man in travel-worn leathers was sitting by a fire, picking his teeth with a long splinter. A bow was propped against the wall nearby. His hair was braided in the German style.

'I want to search the Rhenus from here to Tasgetium for a sign of my brother, who, I fear, went missing somewhere along that stretch. There has been rain, and tracks will be hard to find after so long.'

The man stopped picking his teeth again, and wagged the long splinter at him. 'I'm a hunter by trade, but I know the land. I'll take you along the Rhenus and help you look, for three aurei a day, doubling the fee either when we reach Tasgetium, or when we find what you're looking for on the way.'

Rufinus gave the man a fierce smile. 'Done, my friend. When can you be ready?'

'I can start now, but there's only five hours of daylight left, and it'll still cost you a full day.'

'Agreed. I will see you in the street outside in a few moments.'

With that, he returned to the stables and retrieved his horses and gear, saddled up and led them out front to find the hunter already astride a horse, a bow tied behind his saddle. He himself had now strapped his sword to his side. Thus far he had only been travelling main roads and visiting imperial stations. This was going to be something different, a time in the wilds in a place he did not know. He nodded to the man, who returned the gesture, and then led the way, trotting along the road alongside the great Rhenus. They moved out into the countryside, leaving behind the last few houses, and as they did so, Rufinus paused, frowning.

'What is it?' the hunter asked.

'Those men,' Rufinus replied, pointing back along the street. 'I think I've seen them before.'

The hunter frowned and shrugged. Rufinus peered. In the gateway of a stables near the edge of the town, four men stood, watching. They were attired and coiffured in a Germanic manner, and, although that was hardly unexpected here, so close to the German border, he was willing to wager that they were the very same men who had sat outside a tavern in Tasgetium and watched him leave, yesterday. He could not be absolutely sure, for he'd not committed faces to memory, but he would certainly put money on it. And the way they were watching him and the hunter only added to the suspicion.

As the pair rode on, leaving those men behind, Rufinus felt a chill run through him. The men's presence raised several unpleasant thoughts. Firstly, it no longer seemed that this whole thing was the work of three Germans in the employ of some nebulous villain. Now, it looked as though there were more men involved, and that the forces arrayed against Publius were more of a network than just a dangerous few. And the other thought was that if those three Germans had known of Rufinus and gone to the effort of riding as far as Liguria just to remove him, then he was in considerably more danger here. Why had they not made a move, though? The answer was simple. At both Tasgetium and Augusta Raurica they were in the wide open in front of plenty of witnesses, including Roman authorities. And on the main road between the two, the highway had been busy with merchants and travellers, yet more witnesses. But now they had picked up his trail at Tasgetium and they were on him. And he had just made the decision to ride into the wilderness with only a hunter as a companion. Indeed, it even occurred to him that it was faintly possible the hunter was in league with them, and was leading Rufinus off into the wilds and a death that awaited.

He eyed the hunter carefully. The man *seemed* honest enough. Rufinus would have to seriously keep his wits about him along the stretch of river between here and Tasgetium.

He spent the next few hours nervous, following the hunter, always watching the man, yet at the same time letting his gaze frequently strafe the countryside for any sign of pursuit. He saw none, though that did not mean it was not happening. The hunter moved slowly and methodically, checking for foliage broken by human passage, potential hoofprints in areas under cover where the rain a couple of days ago had not disturbed the ground, examining anywhere where the riverbank was accessible. As the sun began to slip into the hills behind them, the man reined in.

'Since we left, I have noted evidence of the passage of endless wildlife, one or more other hunters about their work, and fishermen coming from local villages to use the river, but there has been no noticeable sign of a horseman. I am content that your quarry did not reach this point in his journey from Tasgetium. However, the light is now fading, and it is pointless to continue our search until dawn, for there is a very good chance that we would miss any clue that awaited us. I think it would be sensible to make camp for the night. Would you like to trap a rabbit or bring down a bird for an evening meal, or search for dry firewood, while I do it?'

Rufinus glanced back over his shoulder. 'I know it is not ideal, but I rather fear pursuit. I think we would be sensible not to light a fire. We will stay in the dark in our blankets, one of us always on watch, and eat only cold food and hard tack.'

'If you are happy to pay a discomfort charge as well.'

Rufinus nodded, and the two men set up camp as best they could, locating a nicely secure and obscure dell surrounded by trees and bushes. They tethered the horses in the shelter of trees and then set out their blankets. Rufinus would take the first watch, and so the two men ate a rather bland and boring cold repast, washed down with water, and then settled in, the hunter wrapped in his blankets, Rufinus finding a nice position where he had a good view of the countryside inland from the river.

As the last of the gloomy evening light disappeared, his suspicions were given new grounds.

A mile or so away, probably close to the main road, a campfire flickered into life in the darkness.

The game was still on.

CHAPTER FOUR

By the Rhenus River, somewhere between Augusta Raurica and Tasgetium

Rufinus rode slowly, warily. The hunter continued to examine their close surroundings, taking note of every leaf, tree and sod of earth in his attempts to find any sign of Publius's passing, but Rufinus had other matters in mind. He lacked the hunter's skill and would undoubtedly miss things, so he left the man to his work, while he himself kept his eyes on the middle distance.

The camp Rufinus had seen last night had to be the Germans. No one else would have planned their journey so as to end their night in the open land between towns, in a time and place where banditry was rife enough to occasion the fortlets they kept spotting in small towns and open countryside. Rufinus had watched that flickering campfire for the first half of the night, making sure he did not spot human shadows against the golden glow coming their way. He'd swapped watch shifts with the hunter, then, who had taken his place. The man claimed not to have dozed off, and perhaps he did not, but it was clear that the Germans had decamped some time before dawn, for as the sun came up, a thin and dying column of smoke showed that the fire over there had been extinguished manually while darkness still reigned. The Germans had been on the move before dawn, and if they'd known for certain where Rufinus was, they could probably have found and overcome them quickly.

That meant, as far as Rufinus was concerned, that the men were out there somewhere, four of them, and almost certainly

49

looking for the Roman. Hence, his wary watchfulness as they travelled.

His surprise, then, when they found the Germans rather suddenly, late in the morning, was palpable. He'd been watching the horizon and the middle distance, and instead, as they rounded a bend in a small copse of trees, they found two of the men on horses ahead of them, blocking the path.

The morning had dawned grey with a little drizzle in the air, and something of a chill, and the leaden cloud lent a strangely morbid atmosphere to the scene. The two Germans had their swords sheathed still, and from the way they looked at one another briefly as they met, Rufinus was willing to bet they were as surprised to stumble on the Romans as the other way around. Rufinus and his guide pulled their horses up and sat facing the two men, Orthus hovering close by, watching, a low rumble growing in his throat.

'A fine day,' Rufinus said in a flat tone.

The two men frowned, and one put a hand on his sword hilt, the other still on the reins. When he spoke, it was with that thick Germanic accent with which Rufinus was starting to become rather familiar.

'Praetorians have no place here.'

'I am not here as a Praetorian,' Rufinus countered, carefully.

'Take heed of this warning,' the man growled. 'There are matters that do not concern you. For the good of your health and the Pax Romana, take your shit and piss off back south. Go home and forget you ever came here.' The man's gaze slipped down to Orthus, then back up, seemingly discounting the dog.

Rufinus could not stop one eyebrow rising. The demand seemed odd, given that their compatriots had ridden all the way to Liguria to face him. He looked at the two men, at their body language, and decided he knew what was going on.

'We will ride on, at least as far as Tasgetium. After that: who knows? I offer you a counter suggestion. Get out of our way and you won't be picking boot leather and hobnails out of your arse for a week.'

The two men shared a look again, and Rufinus smiled. He had been right, he decided. He sat tall, confident, for now he had to be the commanding presence. The Germans' hands danced near the hilts of their swords, but the weapons remained sheathed as they bowed their heads and turned, riding back out of the copse, and then off to the side. The quiet growl that had been emanating from Orthus finally stopped once the Germans were out of sight.

The hunter let out an explosive breath. 'I felt sure they would attack us.'

Rufinus nodded. 'They would have. That's their goal. They will kill me at their first opportunity, but they'd split up to look for us. Two on two was a little uncertain for them. They couldn't guarantee a win. Now they go to find their friends. We'll see them again soon.'

The hunter shivered. 'Maybe we should stop the search for now and ride to Tasgetium? Ask for help from the fort?'

Rufinus shook his head. 'You may find broken leaves and bird tracks, but you missed something important with our friends back there.'

'Oh?'

'They may be dressed like natives, and have their braided hair, but they wore plated military belts and heavy boots. And best of all, they had their swords sheathed on the right.'

'So?'

'So, they are soldiers. Auxilia from one of the German infantry regiments. Only Roman soldiers are trained to draw their swords from the right, to make shield walls work effectively. No use running to the nearest auxiliary fort and asking for help against four of their own. My brother thought there was something going on with the Roman authorities in the region. Given that it seems to stretch into the military, I think he was right. At this particular moment, there are four people in Raetia I trust: me, you, my brother, and the commander of the mansio at Tasgetium. Everyone else could be an enemy.'

'I don't think you're paying me enough for this,' the hunter muttered.

'I'll treble it.'

The man had been about to give up and ride away – Rufinus knew it from his face – but greed suddenly got the better of him.

'Alright. What now?'

'We keep going, as we were, but be prepared for trouble.'

They continued on their way, the hunter continuing his search, Rufinus more alert than ever. They managed less than a mile. As the hunter examined horse tracks in the mud near the river, Rufinus held up a hand to stop him, then put a finger to his lips. Ahead, he could hear voices. He strained. German, speaking in their own tongue, and at least three different tones. The pair had found their friends. That meant there would be no dissembling or ultimatum this time. He was content that the moment they saw Rufinus, the attack would begin. He turned to the hunter and mimed the drawing of a bow. The hunter nodded, loosened his sword in its scabbard, and then quietly and carefully removed his bow, drew an arrow, lifted them, nocked, and prepared for trouble.

Rufinus slowly slid his sword free and reached back for the other blade he had kept from the fight at the villa, another Germanic long sword, suitable for cavalry use. The two men moved close together, to the centre of the clearing they were in, eyes locked on the path ahead, listening to the approaching voices.

'What do we do?' mouthed the hunter, trying to stay quiet.

Rufinus mimed seeing them appear and loosing an arrow. He was in no mood for delay. He was not going to let these men get in the first blow. The hunter nodded, though he did not look happy. Rightly so, really. Rufinus had dragged him into something big, he suspected, and the man was now being asked to shoot a

Roman auxiliary. Such a move could be disastrous, and see the aggressor crucified for his actions.

A moment later, horsemen appeared in the gap, and it took only a heartbeat to confirm that they were the same men. The same as they'd met a mile back, the same as he'd seen in Raurica, even the same as he'd seen in Tasgetium. The hunter had clearly listened and accepted his task, for he let his arrow go in an instant. The shaft flew straight and true and thudded into the chest of the lead rider, aimed well, for they knew from the earlier encounter that these men were not wearing armour. The rider gave a cry and slumped in the saddle, his horse skittering off to one side. The attack girded the other Germans, and they broke into a gallop, racing into the clearing.

Rufinus braced himself, swords out, content that with a man down, two against three was favourable enough. Then his plan crumbled. The next three men burst into the clearing, but there were more behind them. In total, *seven* men were now riding at them. It made sense, he thought with a curse. If they were auxilia, then with the dying one they made an eight-man tent party.

'Fuck,' the hunter barked, echoing Rufinus's sentiments fairly succinctly.

Rufinus felt a moment of panic. These were insurmountable odds. Three, he could have considered. Seven was too many. But there was no time to run. He gritted his teeth, remembering the Germanic peoples, the Marcomanni, they had fought in the war. They were brave, but they were prideful, individual. Add to that the need for brotherhood among the Roman auxilia, and it left one possibility. He had to cause enough damage, quickly, to make them back off, and afford him time to get away. A sharp bark drew his attention for a moment, and he realised that Orthus could be in even more trouble here. This was an unwinnable fight, and his dog could be of little use against cavalry. He made the hard decision. In their time at home, he had taught Orthus only those three commands. 'Balls' was useful, and 'latrine' was another good one, but 'scram' was perhaps the best of all.

Whenever Orthus had done something naughty as a pup, and Senova was angry with him, Rufinus had trained the animal to flee into hiding.

'Scram,' he snarled. He risked a momentary glance to see Orthus loping away towards the trees, though not looking entirely happy about it.

He returned his attention to the enemy riders, who had sized up their prey already, for of the seven, two raced towards the hunter, while the other five all rode at Rufinus. He ignored his companion. The man would have to look after himself, for Rufinus had enough trouble on his own. He braced himself. All his life, whenever he had faced danger, he had retreated to that skill he'd learned in boxing. Size up your opponents, prioritise, and plan. Then execute. The problem was that with five of them, that was rather a tall order. All he managed to do as they raced towards him was to pick the two most dangerous looking ones. Those two were coming at him ahead of the others, hungry for blood, one to each side. Rufinus knew he was strong and had a good reach. They were prime requisites for a successful boxer. And though he'd been fitter in his youth, he had kept in fair shape, better than most officers his age.

He'd once seen a dimachaerus – a two-sword gladiator – in the arena at Tarraco. The gladiator had managed to get his opponent up against the wall, and had his swords crossed in front of the man's throat. He'd waited for the call of permission and had then scissored with the two blades and removed the man's head.

This was a sort of expansion on that move. He crossed his arms, his swords coming up and back, behind him. He watched the men riding at him, and carefully judged the timing. It needed to be precise, or he would just open himself up to extra trouble. Fortunately, he was no novice to war, and had been fighting villains and enemies of the empire since these Germans had been sucking their mother's tit.

His timing was good. As the two men took the lead and came to either side, Rufinus used his knees to nudge his horse in the neck. It bent its head in response, just as the twin swords swung out across the animal in mimicry of the dimachaerus and his scissor-kill.

Both blades found a home, one biting into an arm, deep enough to touch bone, before ripping back out into the air, the other grating against ribs. Neither was a guaranteed kill, but both were sure to take a man out of the fight. That narrowed the odds considerably.

He'd no time to plan beyond that first twin blow, though, and the remaining three coming at him had free rein. There was little he could do. The man to his left swung his sword, but too late. These men may be on horses, but they were trained auxiliary infantry, as he'd noted by their shorter swords worn on the right. Thus, the man was not used to mounted combat and misjudged his swing. Rufinus threw his arm in the way. The limb bore no armour, and he didn't have time to bring the sword up, but he was wearing two bracelets that Senova had given him, a tunic, and a leather glove for riding. He caught the swinging sword with a painful thud, and knew that it would blossom into a truly impressive bruise, but the man had been too close to deliver a cut.

To the other side, he managed to get his sword in the way just fast enough to knock the man's blade away. Unfortunately, he had only two arms, for three opponents.

The last man was clearly the thinker of the bunch. While his friends launched into their attacks, he timed his own strike and placed it carefully. In the wake of his friends, he ducked low, avoiding any possibility of Rufinus swinging at him, and the dagger in his off-hand thudded into the throat of Rufinus's horse. He let go, leaving the dagger embedded, and danced his own mount out of the way.

Rufinus's horse screamed and bucked.

He was faced with a horrible selection of options. He could try and hold the animal steady, bring it back down. It would die from the blow, but with the dagger still in place, he might get another few heartbeats of action out of it, although it might buck again. Or he could try and pull it away, but if it fell, he could end up trapped under it, and that was not a pleasant thought: being cut to pieces by Germans while he nursed a crushed leg. The only other viable option was to flee. That in itself was no simple task, when wedged into a four-horn saddle. He put his boot against one of the enemy horses nearby and straightened his leg, pushing hard. The momentum threw him free of the saddle and he fell.

He hit the ground hard, dazing himself for precious moments, and as he shook his head to clear it, he realised he was amid the dancing hooves of several horses, including his own mortally wounded one. Coming out of the temporary fug, he found himself in dire straits, desperately rolling this way and that, to avoid being crushed or trampled. He saw a moment of freedom and scrabbled for it, darting under another horse and out into the open. As he emerged from the press, he rose to his feet, tottering. He still had hold of both swords, but he was unhorsed, and still faced a number of men. He turned and discovered to his dismay that the hunter had died and had only managed to wound one of his own attackers. Rufinus was alone, and faced seven men, at least four of whom were intact. The odds were not good.

He closed his eyes for a moment and tried to picture the situation in its entirety. What remained was chaos. A lot of it involved panicked or pained horses, and the men riding them were not trained cavalry. They would have at least half their attention on the animals, trying to keep their own mounts under control. No one was currently looking at Rufinus, for they'd lost track of him under the horses. Only one man was looking roughly his way, and that was one of those who'd attacked the hunter.

Resolved on a path, he ran and dived into a roll, disappearing under that last man's horse. As he passed beneath it, he stabbed upwards with both swords into the horse's unprotected underbelly. The result was unpleasant: a sluice of blood, a coil of intestines, and a bucking horse. The rider cried out in panic, but he was already lolling badly in the saddle, poor horseman that he was. The result was what Rufinus needed. All eyes in the chaotic clearing turned to the leaping mare and its panicked rider, and no one looked down at the man who had rolled beneath it, then kept going, under the horse of the next German. He found himself at the fallen horse of the hunter, the man lying glassy-eyed, staring up at the damp grey sky. Another corpse left in Rufinus's wake.

He scrambled across the body of the horse and dropped down behind it, pulling himself close in to the animal. He'd had but moments to get out of sight before someone looked past the chaos and spotted him. He lay there, still, hidden by the bulk of the horse, swords by his side, and listened.

The urgent conversation that ensued around the clearing was in some Germanic tongue, and Rufinus silently cursed that he could understand not a word of it. But its tone was worried and angry, which suggested they were still in chaos and had not seen him go into hiding. For a few heartbeats he was safe. The moment the riders started bringing things under control, he was screwed, for they would inevitably find him, and he knew now, as his arm started to become numb, that he was unlikely to survive a second encounter with them. He had to get away. He was never going to win this fight, and all that mattered now was walking – or limping – away from it. He took a deep breath and looked around. He spotted a white blur amid the undergrowth at the edge of the clearing, and realised that Orthus was watching from cover. That was where Rufinus now needed to be. *He* needed to 'scram' too. He glanced to his right.

The body of the fallen hunter lay nearby, cleaved and bloody. Oddly, neither his sword nor his bow was in ready evidence, but the small arm-purse of coins Rufinus had already paid him lay in the wet dirt. It was a purse of Germanic design, after a Roman model, decorative and bronze. He smiled, grimly. The hunter might do him one last service. He reached out and slowly, carefully, slid the coin purse towards him. Once it was in his fingers, he gripped it, pulled his arm back, and hurled it with all his might across the clearing.

The gods were with him. The purse hit a tree trunk at the other side of the open space, with a dull thud and clink, and disappeared into the undergrowth. As if their spell of inactivity had been broken by the sudden noise, the men in the clearing began to shout and turn their horses, all eyes seeking out the unexpected sound.

The moment their gazes moved away, Rufinus was up and running. He tried not to pant, and ran on the balls of his feet, trying to keep his steps light despite the speed, making as little sound as he possibly could. He did not look back, for that would just waste time. That the Germans continued to shout to each other, and no one bellowed a sudden warning over the top of them, told him that he'd been unnoticed in his flight, and he ducked into the undergrowth beneath the low tree branches with a sense of hope. Five paces from the open ground, he joined Orthus and stopped sharply, standing at a crouch, completely still, forcing his breathing into tiny, quiet breaths as he listened.

Still no urgent cry. He'd worried that as he pushed into the undergrowth, the noise would attract their attention, but it seemed that the group moving their horses to investigate the sound of the purse had covered his flight. Still, he remained quiet and motionless, listening. They were still moving about the other side of the clearing, arguing. Holding his breath, he gestured to Orthus to follow and moved another five paces until he found an old fallen trunk, mossy and rotten, and slipped behind it, lying in the damp, listening. The riders were frustrated, arguing more and more, and he could hear them spreading out, now, moving around the clearing. He tried to think back, to remember whether where he ran had been grass or mud, for the latter would give his location away fairly quickly, but he simply could not remember, from the chaotic few moments. Time went on, as he lay in his hiding place, listening, but it was becoming clear that he had left no obvious trace, for the sound of anger and frustration was clear even in the unintelligible tongue of the Germans.

He chewed his lip. From here, in his hiding place, though he was seemingly safe, he also had no idea what was happening. Regulating his breathing again, he looked about carefully, eventually spotting a place where low greenery would provide another good hiding place closer to the clearing. Watching his footing, he rose and began to slowly and lightly pick his way back, pausing whenever the sound in the clearing dropped for a moment, then hurrying when there was a flurry of noise. Orthus followed, surprisingly quietly and deftly for such a large hound. After what seemed like hours of creeping, Rufinus rose from a crouch behind a bush, and could see a small part of the clearing, though only low, around the legs of the Germans and their horses. He could see the hunter and his dead animal, and a number of other men and horses around the clearing, from the knees down. He tensed as one of the riders crouched by the hunter, for if the man happened to turn and look Rufinus's way, there was a chance he might be spotted. But the German had other plans. Rufinus watched in hollow disgust as the man produced a long knife and began hacking at the hunter's neck until the head finally came free, blood slopping out, unspeakable tendrils dangling from the mangled neck. The man rose once more, carrying the head away.

Rufinus continued to watch and listen as the men searched in a half-hearted manner, not bothering to go too deep into the woods. One of them finally found the coin purse and lifted it, bringing forth shouts and more argument. Finally one man, presumably their leader, shouted over the top of them all, and they fell silent. Orders or instructions were given, and, as Rufinus watched, four of the men gathered the horses and lifted their fallen companion, draping him over the back of one of the mounts. The other three, one of them still carrying the severed head, strode across the clearing.

Rufinus felt a moment of panic, for they seemed to be coming directly for him, and he could sense Orthus tensing, ready to attack, but as he crouched, silent and still, they passed him, only ten paces away, and disappeared into a track in the woods. He fretted again, wracked with indecision. He could really do with taking one of those horses, and all his kit was tied to one of them, too. The safest option was to slip away while they were all busy and try to leg it back to Augusta Raurica. The third option, though, was too much of a pull to ignore. He wanted to know what the three men were up to. He waited until they were safely past, and then began to move, watching his own steps carefully, and timing them so that the sound of his passage through the woodland was masked by theirs. It was not too hard, for they had no reason to creep and were making plenty of noise, even talking in low Germanic voices as they went. Moreover, their attention was all locked on the woods ahead, and they were not scanning their surroundings, so would be unlikely to see Rufinus. That they moved with such purpose suggested that they knew where they were going, which in turn suggested that these men were locals, familiar with the territory. As they moved, he could hear the river now, not far ahead.

He followed them some distance from the clearing, Orthus at his heel, and almost came a cropper when they stopped and he nearly bumbled ahead into crackling undergrowth in a sudden silence broken only by the watery rumble of the river nearby. He stood rigid, holding his breath, praying that he'd not been noticed. No sign of that arose, and he started to breathe again, slowly and carefully, as he watched through thick foliage. His view was largely obscured, but he dare not move any closer.

He could not see what was happening, and dare not move any closer. Instead, he listened. The three men murmured a little longer in their own tongue, and then began to chant in a low voice, all three saying the same rhythmic thing, presumably a prayer of some kind. Then there was a series of weird shuffling noises and dull thuds, followed by a distant splash. Another pause, another rhythmic chant, and then another strange sound, this one the groan of tortured metal and a sharp cracking noise, again metallic, followed by a clang and a thud. He waited still, silent and motionless, and then finally the three men began to talk more normally and move. Orthus had begun that low growl again, and he had to reach down and stroke the animal's head to stop it as he listened hard. The three men were heading back the way they came, and he waited, trembling, until they were past and moving out of both sight and earshot. There seemed little to be gained following them back to the clearing, and so he waited until he was truly alone and relatively safe, and then picked his way forward to where the three men had been.

He and the dog emerged into another clearing, a small one that led down to the river bank. This one was apparently looked after, maintained by locals, and the reason why swiftly became clear. This was a temple or shrine of sorts, and a grisly one. At the centre of the clearing stood a set of four pillars of heavy, dark stone, standing in an arc around a large stone bowl that was sunk into the ground. Atop each pillar was a misshapen, roughly-carved statue of a man, presumably images of their gods. Each pillar contained a series of recesses, in which sat heads. Several were old, little more than bare skulls, but some were considerably more recent, mouldering and gruesome. Their features had mostly gone, probably pecked out by birds, but enough matter remained to make them truly unpleasant to look at. In one aperture sat the head of the hunter, a new addition to the display, and Rufinus surmised that the splash he'd heard was the bony previous occupant being tossed into the river.

The bowl contained a number of broken weapons, most of them already rusty and old, though with a few more recent additions, the hunter's snapped sword now in place among them. Looking around the stones, he could see the crack where the blade had been wedged to snap it.

Offerings to the gods. A head and a broken sword.

He'd not been particularly fond of these Germans already, but now he found he truly detested them. What sort of a divine offering was mouldy human meat and a broken weapon?

A thought struck him, and it was not a nice one. Three of the heads here could be around a month old. And Publius had never made it to Augusta Raurica. There was no way he could identify the pecked and ruined heads, but it was entirely possible that one of them was Rufinus's brother. Heart in his mouth and a growing certainty filling him, he crossed to the stone bowl, crouched, and began to move the weapons around, examining them.

He knew Publius's sword the moment he found it. He'd have recognised the thing anyway, for he'd been the one who bought it for his brother, a gift when he'd first come back from service with the Seventh Legion. But even if it had not been clear, the punched legend at the top of the blade, a stamp of possession, clinched it.

P MAR RUST

Rufinus dropped to the turf, feeling suddenly hollow. He'd distanced himself from his family all those years ago, after one brother had died so cruelly in a hunting accident, and his father had begun that slide into mania and depression. He'd lost that brother, and effectively his father as well, the old man finally crossing that last river only recently. Publius had been all he had left. One brother. The only family. And he'd become closer to Publius over those recent years.

And now he was gone.

Something began to fill that hollowness.

Anger.

Yes, Publius was dead, but there was more to it than that. This brother had not died in an accident in the forest. This brother had been murdered, plain and simple. Someone was a murderer, and that someone may well be a Roman, an official, an officer, a man supposedly trustworthy.

He began to channel the anger.

Someone was at the heart of this.

Someone was to blame.

Someone had killed his brother.

And he would find out who that someone was.

He lifted the broken blade and looked it up and down, lip wrinkling in an unbidden tic. He rose to his feet and turned. He began to walk back towards the clearing, tucking the broken sword into his belt as he went. He'd lost his brother, lost his horse, lost his bags, lost his guide. He had nothing. But with nothing, the only way to go was up. Resolve was swelling in him now, hardening that anger into a cold diamond. He needed a plan. He would make it to Tasgetium, even if he had to walk there. In Tasgetium, at least, there was one man he trusted. And from there, somehow, he would make it to Batavis, his brother's command, and find out what had happened.

Someone was going to pay.

CHAPTER FIVE

Raetia, approaching the Danubian frontier

There were *some* benefits to be had from the rank and position of Praetorian tribune, Rufinus mused. He had left the clearing by the river, carefully checking the site of the fight, only moving into it when he was sure the Germans had gone. All that remained was the dead, a headless hunter surrounded by still horses. Rufinus's kit had vanished. It had then taken three days to reach Tasgetium from the clearing by foot, traipsing in light drizzle through the countryside along the river, always careful, always wary, eyes on the land around him, watching for those Germans. Arriving on the edge of the small town, he'd waited until pre-dawn, when he knew no one would be about in the taverns and streets, and hurried across to the mansio. He'd been immensely relieved to find the same man on duty, and despite having nothing on his person but weapons, a pouch of coins and his Praetorian brooch, the man had a good enough memory that he accepted Rufinus's identity and rank without the proof of documentation.

Rufinus had thus acquired from the man a horse, fresh uniform, and temporary documentation confirming his identity, written up and sealed with the cursus stamp. With that, he could make his way further without difficulty, yet still he'd left the mansio carefully, looking to avoid trouble. There were still too many of those Germans intact for him to take on himself, and in the grand scheme, they were but a *symptom* of the corruption that had caused all this, not the *source*. It was the hand that *guided* those men who Rufinus was now after.

65

Leaving the Rhenus as he departed Tasgetium, he used the main road northeast, crossing a wide and flat stretch of terrain, farmland dotted with intermittent forests, before meeting the other great border river, the Danubius. Here, as he rode, he could see signs of what had once been the frontier. Every few miles saw a suspiciously fort-shaped platform, demolished and backfilled as the border moved north, but the only settlements now in the region were small villages. Enquiring of them, he had found somewhat familiar names lurking but a day or two ahead. Guntia, where Publius had picked up the horse he had all-but ridden to death, and Phoebiana, from where the Germans at the Ligurian villa had bought their wine. The locals were all so very German, despite being well within Rome's borders these days, though the question of whether he could trust any of them was made moot by the fact that he was not sure he could trust any *Roman* in the region either.

Two days out from Tasgetium, he camped down once more in a tumbledown, disused shepherd's hut close to the river, just within sight of Guntia. He had toyed with the idea of moving into the town for the night, but there was the possibility of attracting the wrong sort of attention in such a busy place, and he was not yet sure whether he could rely upon the staff of the mansio there. Better to stay in the countryside.

Lying, wrapped in blankets in the cold shed, he wished that he dare light a fire, but decided that it would be foolish. As such, it took some time to fall into slumber, cold and uncomfortable.

The first dream woke him sharply, soon after he first slept. For some reason he had dreamed he was back in Dacia, that time when Cleander had sent him away. He had fallen with his enemy from that cliff, but this time it had been he who had been underneath, and he awoke as, in the dream, his body hit the rocks and shattered into a hundred meaty pieces. It took almost an hour after that to stop shaking and get back to sleep again.

The next dream that came was, if anything, worse.

He sat upon a rock in woodland, the sky black and oddly devoid of all stars. As he waited, a figure came to him, almost plaintively, in supplication. It carried something. He recognised with cold distaste both the figure, and its burden. Many years ago, just before he had saved the life of a Praetorian prefect in the forests of Marcomannia, he had been fighting other Germans. Here was one of the men he had killed then. He could even still see the very wounds he had inflicted that had done for the man, yet somehow he walked, and he carried a head.

The disembodied face of Publius glared at him from where it hung from a hand.

He shivered, but did not wake this time, and the dead Marcomannic warrior went away into the darkness. When the second figure, another man he had killed that winter, came forth, he too was carrying Publius's head. He stopped long enough for Rufinus to acknowledge who he was and what he carried, then he too walked off into the darkness with the head. And so it went on; an endless line of Rufinus's victims over the years, each carrying his brother's head, like an offering. He saw men he had killed across the Danubius, and in Rome, and in Dacia, and in Arabia and Syria, and now in Liguria.

But as the grisly procession went on, something in him changed. Initially he had been revolted and chastened by the presence of so many men he'd killed, but as the line caught up with current events, and the men bringing his brother's head were now the Germanic warriors he had killed in the villa, those emotions were overcome instead with the anger that had simmered in him ever since that shrine by the river, five days ago. The anger grew with each of them.

Finally, as the figure of one of the men he'd killed in that clearing with the hunter a few days ago stepped from the gloom with Publius's head, Rufinus could take it no more. He leapt up from the stone, and for some reason his sword was now in his hand, where it had not been before, and swung the blade with all his might. No plan, no skill or thought, just a powerful blow, driven by rage and hate.

His eyes snapped open.

Reality and dream blurred.

The German had been standing over him, his own sword raised, ready to fall and cleave the sleeping Roman. Even as he struck, slumber falling away in shards, Rufinus realised how deeply asleep he had been. Not only had he not heard the Germans approaching him, he had not even woken to the violent sounds of Orthus, who was hanging from the forearm of a second man, snarling around the flesh into which his teeth were buried. The man had dropped his sword as the fangs bit down, and was now howling in agony as the dog held tight. Rufinus had been exhausted enough to sleep through it all, but some preternatural sense had jolted him awake at the last moment, just in time to save his life.

The blow he had struck had been just as powerful as in the dream. There, he had leapt from a rock. Here, he had risen from his blankets. But in both worlds he had a sword in his hand, and in both worlds he had struck with all the might of anger and anguish.

The sword had hit the man in the unarmoured side, just beneath the bottom rib, and such had been the force of the swing that it had sheared through linen and flesh, slicing and mangling the organs inside until it slammed into the spine, which cracked with the strength of the blow.

The man didn't even scream, didn't have time. He died where he stood, the sword falling from his raised hands and almost impaling Rufinus by accident in the process.

Even blurred and shocked, rising from sleep, Rufinus found himself taking stock.

He recognised the man he had killed, for he had seen him close enough in that clearing. They were the same men. There had been eight, a full tent party. One had died to an arrow days ago. Three others had been wounded in that fight, enough to put them out of action for many days, one with a broken arm, one broken ribs, and the one the hunter had managed to wound had a blossom of blood on his tunic around the midriff. He doubted any of those three were still up to a fight, which left four men. One of those he had just killed, and another died just as he looked around, for Orthus let go of the man's arm and, as he hunched over, cradling his ruined limb, the dog casually tore his throat out in one horrendous action, his white hair soaked red with the sudden gush of blood. His victim toppled forward, making peculiar noises, unable to scream or speak, with a shredded hole where his throat had been.

That left two.

Rufinus pulled himself up. He had slept fully dressed, including boots, his habit when travelling like this, and so as his blanket fell fully away he was already set for battle. The man he had killed in his sleep toppled away to the side, and Rufinus spotted movement very briefly through the hut's doorway.

Two left.

He was running in a moment.

By the time he ducked through the door out into the open, Orthus was beside him again, a nightmare shape in the dark, his shaggy white form now shot through with plenty of crimson, fangs dripping gore, matching the sword in Rufinus's hand.

He could see the man now. Another of the Germans, who had perhaps been about to enter the hut to help his friends, when he saw them die and decided that *flight* might be the better part of valour. The man was running like an Olympic champion, hurtling across the grass, close to the river, trying to get away.

Rufinus felt that anger and hate rising once more. Yes, the man behind all this was his ultimate goal, but there was enough vengeance to go round, and these men were very probably the ones who had personally decapitated Publius. The German was fast, driven by panic. Rufinus was faster, driven by hate. But the fastest of all was Orthus.

Even as Rufinus ran, the dog pulled ahead, closing the distance between him and the fleeing soldier. For a moment, Rufinus considered calling him back, for he would like to be the one to gut this man himself, but there was always the possibility that the man might outrun him, so he let Orthus do his work. The German rounded the corner of a hedge, and the nightmare white blur was right behind him as he did so. As Rufinus ran on, catching up, there was a horrendous roaring sound behind the hedge, and then a scream.

He rounded the corner.

Orthus was standing calm, chewing on something, redder than ever, while the man who had been running was now staggering, limping away. With one good leg, he hop-staggered, more or less dragging the other, which was missing a large piece of calf muscle.

The man looked back, white-faced and panicked, and Rufinus gave a smile that held all the warmth of a steel trap, and about as much promise of hope. The man was hardly moving at all, now, and Rufinus settled into a steady, implacable walk. He drew the dagger from his side now in his off-hand, as he closed on the man.

The German clearly decided it was hopeless and turned, almost falling as his leg would not take the weight. He lifted his sword, wincing and panting through the agony. Rufinus closed the last few steps and launched his attack. Once again, just like his sleep-kill, there was no care or planning to this. The German tried to get his sword in the way and block, but Rufinus knocked it aside with his own weapon, then slammed his dagger into the bicep. The man let out another blood-curdling scream as he let go of the sword, and Rufinus struck again, and again, and again, knife and sword both slamming down, scything across, stabbing in, relentless and furious.

By the time Rufinus's need was sated, the man was barely recognisable. He'd have been lying, mangled on the ground but for the fact that he'd still been close to that hedge and had fallen back into it under the onslaught, the foliage holding him in position until Rufinus finally stopped and stepped back, blades running and dripping. The piece of ruined German meat toppled to the grass amid a lake of his own blood, mangled limbs and butchered face, broken body and soaked tunic all in a twisted heap.

Rufinus was panting.

'By sacred, blood-bathed Vernostonus, you are a hard one to kill.'

He turned, trembling slightly, though from effort and ebbing anger rather than fear. It came as no surprise, given the heavy Germanic twang to the voice, to find another of those men standing looking at him. He remembered this one, the leader, he believed, from the clearing. Four left, he had noted, and three were gone to meet their head-loving god. This would be the last. The man had come through a gap in the hedge a little further down, presumably drawn by all the noise.

'Stupidly, if your friends had not come to Liguria to do away with me, I might never have known what happened. And you followed me from Tasgetium, so you brought this on yourself.'

'I have killed bigger men than you,' the soldier said.

'And I have killed more men than the plague,' Rufinus retorted, remembering that seemingly endless dream-line of his victims.

The man lifted his sword and walked forward. Rufinus stood his ground, sword and dagger, still gore-coated, out to either side.

'Give me your master's name and I might let you live,' Rufinus said.

The man made no reply, simply came on with his sword at the ready.

'Or at least kill you quickly.'

Then the soldier attacked. It was a well-executed move, if a little predictable and formulaic. Like many of the northern auxiliaries, the man had eschewed the short traditional gladius for a longer spatha blade, more akin to his own native weaponry, and so he gripped the sword in a tight fist, and swung it at Rufinus's side.

At the last moment, Rufinus brought his two blades together and crossed them, making a V shape that caught the man's sword, mid-swing. As the three weapons met, Rufinus carried on pushing that V upwards, containing and driving the man's sword back, and then, suddenly, he twisted both his own blades. The motion turned the soldier's sword sharply, which caused the hexagonal bone hilt to swivel in his grip, a strange ache and discomfort rippling across his palm. Rufinus knew how it felt, for Mercator had once done it to him in a training session. He stepped back and pulled his weapons away.

The German lifted his sword again, ready to parry Rufinus's attack, but the previous meeting had numbed his palm a little, and the sword slipped and wavered, not quite held tight. Thus, it did little to stop Rufinus's own sword swatting it aside, as the dagger in his other hand came on and stabbed the man deep in the chest, close to the armpit and below the shoulder.

The man gasped and then hissed with pain, lurching back away from the fight, struggling to keep his grip on his sword. Rufinus let go of the dagger, leaving it wedged in the man's torso, where it would hurt with every movement, cutting flesh anew.

'The name?' he urged.

The man snarled. He had recovered his grip faster than Rufinus had expected, but no matter how strong he was, he was still predictable. The next swing came just the same as the last, a standard move. The man had stood at a palus in a training yard, day-in, day-out, swinging this very blow at the target, chipping pieces of wood from the stake until it was second nature. That was where a professional fighter won out. Boxers, wrestlers, gladiators, all had to learn to be inventive, to react and to launch unexpected attacks.

Rufinus's own sword knocked the man's aside easily, and in a fluid move, he flipped his own blade over so that he was gripping it back-handed, and stepped forward, slamming the pommel into the man's forehead.

The soldier swayed, making a strange croaking sound, eyes crossed, stunned by the blow. He wobbled this way and that, blood oozing out around the dagger in his chest. Rufinus took a couple of steps back. The man was bleary, his thoughts scattered, and it would be some time before he could talk.

His shock, when Orthus suddenly shot past him and leapt, was immense. He just had time to bellow 'nooooooo' at the dog, before savage canine jaws closed on the leader's neck and repeated the earlier attack, tearing out a mouthful of vital meat, including windpipe and artery. Blood sprayed wild as the stricken man spun, staggered, then dropped to his knees before toppling forward onto the grass.

Rufinus stared.

'I wanted him to talk.' He turned to Orthus, ready to bellow angrily at the dog, but the animal simply looked so proud and pleased with himself that Rufinus felt that irritation melt away. He shook his head. 'You're a menace,' he sighed as he tried to find a stretch of white hair to stroke that was not soaked with blood. 'Senova was right. I need to train you more.'

He turned and looked at the two men. Both very dead. And so were the pair back in the shepherd's hut. And one had died of an arrow back in the clearing. That left the three who'd been wounded. He frowned, deep in thought. It was possible that the leader had sent the three wounded men back to their base to seek medical attention. But what if they were not local after all? What if they were far from home, and had only found that shrine in the woods by some giveaway sign? Then they would keep their wounded with them, part of the same tent party.

He smiled, grimly.

The man outside the hut had run, but where had he been running *to*? And from where had the leader come? It was night. The man had to have been running back to his camp. And it would be from that camp the leader had come. And since he'd come in response to the sound of his friend dying, it had to be close. And if their camp was close, and they'd kept the wounded with them…

He was moving again a moment later, making for that gap in the hedge through which the leader had appeared. Reaching it, he rounded the foliage carefully, looking this way and that. The camp lay only fifty or so paces away, marked out very visibly by their fire. It sat in the lee of another hedge, and he could see figures there, two of them, sitting by the fire. Orthus started to pace past him, going into that low, stalking mode, and Rufinus gave the dog a hard look.

'No. Heel.'

'Heel' was not a command the dog knew, but he picked up enough from Rufinus's tone of voice that he straightened from that stalk into an ordinary walk, and fell into pace with his owner.

Rufinus marched towards that camp, and it took only moments for the two seated men to spot and recognise him. They scrabbled for their weapons, and one managed to pick up a shield. The other's spare arm was useless, tucked away in a sling, the evidence of their earlier clash. Indeed, as the shield man walked forward, he hissed and flinched with the pain in his ribs.

'Don't be fools like your leader,' Rufinus called. 'Tell me the name of the man who employed you for this task, and I will walk away.'

They said nothing, just came to a halt at the edge of the firelight and awaited him, weapons ready. Their eyes then drifted down from Rufinus to the creature walking by his side. Days ago in a woodland clearing, they had written off the dog as unimportant. Now, looking at the blood-soaked white hair, they seemed to be of an entirely different opinion. As if sensing their nervousness, Orthus snarled, baring his blood-rinsed fangs.

The man with the ruined arm broke. As his friend readied himself, one-arm barked something frantically at his companion, using his sword to point to the dog. Rib-man replied also in their native tongue, sounding almost as though he were ridiculing his friend. One-arm said something else, hurried, close to panic, and again his friend overrode him with a sneer. Finally, one-arm uttered one last word that sounded like a curse, and then turned, lowering his sword. He was about to flee, when the other man spun sharply and swung his blade. His sword caught his companion in the back of the neck and there was a snapping sound. One-arm fell face first to the turf, and his friend turned back to face Rufinus, expression a grim mask of determination even as he hissed at the pain in his ribs.

'Wasteful,' Rufinus noted.

The man replied, once more in his own unintelligible language, and lifted his shield. As he did so, he gasped and winced again, the pain in his ribs apparently excruciating when he used that arm.

Rufinus grinned nastily as he stepped close. The man waited for him to launch an attack, and so Rufinus obliged. He lanced out with the dagger in his off-hand, and the man naturally used his sword, which was on the same side, to parry. As he did so, Rufinus hit the shield with his sword with all his might. The man hollered with the pain this carried through to his ribs, and staggered backward. Rufinus followed up with another attack before the man could recover, and swung the sword again, this time at the sword arm. Blade met flesh and there was a nasty crack. The man's sword fell to the ground and he cursed again in his Germanic tongue.

He backed away another couple of paces, though the hedge would prevent him going much further, still clinging to the shield, now held in front of him, more or less covering him from potential attacks.

Rufinus stopped. 'You can either tell me your master's name now, or I will keep hurting you until you do. Take it from me, every man has a breaking point. You can hold against pain for only so long. I managed hours myself, even when they took the nails from my fingers and burned me with brands. But in the end,

I would have sold my own mother out to make it stop. Save yourself that and give me a name.'

Fear flashed across the man's eyes then. He was done, and he knew it. With a fractured arm and several broken ribs, he was not going to be able to fight Rufinus off. And the prospect of hours of pain would hardly appeal.

'Just a name.'

'Ingomer,' the man said. 'Alemanni.'

'What? Is that one name? Two? What does it mean? I know you can speak Latin. You're no new recruit, and the auxilia would not pay you and keep you if you couldn't. *Talk* to me.'

'Alemanniiiiiiiii', the man suddenly shouted, and his good arm appeared from behind the shield, gripping a dagger, which he lifted and thrust into his own throat.

Rufinus cursed and leapt forward, but he was too late and he knew it. Faced with a slow and painful death, and with no hope of fighting back, the man had taken his own life, just like that German back in Liguria.

Rufinus watched him expire and collapse to the turf, grimacing. He could feel Orthus by his side. 'Whoever their master is, he is powerful enough and causes enough fear in his men that they would rather kill themselves than incur his wrath. Impressive.' He wracked his brains. 'What did he say? Ingomer Alemanni, wasn't it? Ingomer certainly sounds like a German. Could Alemanni be a tribe? Like the Marcomanni?' He fretted over it. It was certainly not clear, but it was a step forward. He had a name. Now he needed to find out more. Whoever it was, he had to be linked to Publius, which made the fort at Batavis the common link, and the clear next destination, as he'd already planned.

At least those Germans were now dead. All eight were gone, which meant that, as far as he knew, there was no one else actively hunting him. He should have no need to look over his shoulder now for the rest of the journey. Even if there were other enemy groups out there, they would not know Rufinus by sight, and so he should be nicely incognito.

He returned to his shepherd hut and gathered his things, then took them to the German camp, for now he could have a fire for the rest of the night. He dumped the bodies away from the camp, where he found the packed and wrapped bodies of the other two, stomach wound and arrow kill, and made himself comfortable, then slept again, this time without dreams.

He rose with the first glimmer of sunlight, and took stock. His first chore was Orthus. The dog had been terrifying to look at last night, but now, in the morning sun, he simply looked like a bedraggled, blood-soaked sponge. Rufinus took him down to the river and managed to get the animal into the water on a low slope. Once he'd scrubbed Orthus until he was white once more, a pink stain floating downstream for a good half an hour, he returned to the camp. He went through each of the Germans' gear, that they had on their person and what they had in bags, and was disappointed, though not surprised, to find nothing useful. They had brought nothing with them that could be identifiable, and only a few personal items. Rufinus left most of it where it was, for he had neither desire nor need of loot now, though he did take one item. The leader had worn an armlet of bronze in the form of a serpent coiled four times around his bicep. It was a nice piece of work, but more importantly it was quite unusual, and was the only thing Rufinus found that might be used to identify the man. The one thing he did locate that had him heaving a sigh of relief was his own kit that they had stolen in the clearing. He had it back, including his identification and Publius's letter.

Satisfied he had all that could be of use, and with a clean dog, he saddled up, taking a spare horse from the Germans, and set off once again. Now, able to ride in the open and without worry, with a spare animal, he made good time. He passed Guntia and spotted the mansio. He contemplated dropping in, but he already had a spare animal, and he knew his brother had been through there and died afterwards, so there was nothing more to learn. Before reaching Phoebiana, where the Germans had bought their wine, he was faced with a choice. The road forked there. The left led north, following the Danubius to the legionary fortress of the governor at Castra Regina, while the right passed through the city of Augusta Vindelicorum and met the Danubius further east. He had been originally intending to follow the main road north, but after consulting a couple of merchants, he learned that the eastern road would take him more or less directly to Batavis, via the city en-route. There would be little difference in time or distance to either path, and both held a potential problem. Augusta Vindelicorum was the capital of Raetia, and would house the procurator and possibly the governor of the province, both of whom could be up to their necks in this mess. But the governor was also the commander of the Third Legion at Castra Regina, so he could be there, too.

With little to choose from, he plumped for the southern route. The northern one would bring him among numerous auxiliary forts along the border, and any one of them could be home to the men who had so recently attacked him. At least the southern route passed only through civilian sites on the way to his destination.

Thus it was that ten days after finding his brother's remains by the river, he finally set his eyes upon the place where Publius had commanded his cohort.

Batavis.

CHAPTER SIX

Batavis, on the Danubian frontier

In a way, it was so familiar. That was the thing about forts in the Roman world. They were all designed to a standard, so that a unit from far-off Syria could be posted to soggy northern Britannia and still find their way round. Actually, in practise, forts were more often varied than identical, depending upon terrain, location and garrison. But still, over so many years of war, Rufinus had been in fort after fort, and knew exactly what he could expect, even among the auxilia.

The Danubius here was wide and brown, fast and powerful, just as it had been around Vindebona and Carnuntum all those years ago when he had fought across it to suppress the dangerous Marcomanni. The fort of Batavis sat on a peninsula formed by the Danubius and one of its tributaries, jutting out northeast into the flow, the usual solid walls and towers surrounded by a double ditch, gate open, but manned by two auxiliaries.

It had plagued Rufinus for the past day's travel how to go about what he now needed to do. It was entirely possible that this place was the cause of Publius's worries and troubles, that the men here had something to do with his death. As such, walking in and announcing in a blasé manner that he was Publius's brother, and demanding what in Hades had happened, might be a short journey to suicide. On the other hand, there was only so much subterfuge that was going to get a man into an auxiliary fort with the authority to look around. In the end, he settled for authoritative and provocative.

Last night, he had rolled up a scroll and sealed it with wax by his camp fire, and had used his small eating knife to press a design into it that looked realistic enough to be the seal of an official, adding the legend PCAV. It was risky, but he had to have a reason to visit in the guise of an officer, though not as himself. He would have to trust that the men of Batavis had no more knowledge of the higher rank structure of the province than he did. To complete the guise, he had donned one of the red tunics he had kept from his travels, rather than Praetorian white, then his armour and weapons. As such, he was clearly a senior officer, but with no apparent unit identification.

He straightened in the saddle, and rode along the street of the civilian settlement towards the fort. Unfriendly eyes watched him from doors and windows as he passed, but he ignored them as he closed on the causeway across the ditches.

The two soldiers pulled a little closer together, effectively barring entry to the fort as he neared them, and, as he reined in, one held up a hand.

'Identification and business in Batavis,' he demanded in a brusque manner and in that same Germanic accent that seemed universal in the region.

'Gnaeus Cornelius Strabo, from the governor's office in Augusta Vindelicorum with dispatches for the commander.' To add weight to his words, he held out the document with his fake seal. 'From the Praefectus Castrorum,' he added, explaining the PC as well as the AV on the seal. He tried not to blink or sweat or look uncertain. He had no idea whether there was a Praefectus Castrorum at the provincial capital, or even whether there was a Castrorum to be Praefectus of, and banked on ordinary soldiers being no better informed. The two men looked at the seal, at each other, at Rufinus, and then at each other again. There was something inherently shifty about the way they were acting and looking. Nothing overt, just a distinct feeling. Their gazes slid to

Orthus for a moment, but then back without issue. Rufinus was still getting used to travelling with a dog that didn't frighten the shit out of people at first sight. He kept his expression carefully haughty and neutral, playing the visiting officer carefully.

One of the men seemed to make a decision, and nodded to the other. 'Follow me, sir,' he said. Rufinus noted with interest how the man's Latin cleared a little, the accent forced into a more Roman manner for his benefit.

As he dismounted and followed the soldier into the gate, leading his horses, he found himself pondering on the place and its occupants. The Batavi were a famous, or possibly infamous, tribe. They were renowned for certain military abilities, and had served with great effect in some of Rome's most important campaigns. They were, in fact, so dangerous and valued as soldiers, that the tribe had been immune to Roman taxes in return for high recruitment. But they had also been trouble for Rome more than once, and on one notable occasion, revolting in the wake of a year of civil war, they had almost caused the loss of Germania. And Batavis was named for them. This was the heart of their tribe. That the Eighth Batavian Cohort was based in their own lands was unusual. Rome tended to post men far from their homes to prevent exactly the sort of thing that had happened over a century ago with the Batavi. Of *course* these men still spoke with a Germanic accent. They had been born and raised in the region, and though they now served Rome, their tribe were still all around them.

He shivered, and was not entirely sure why.

The fort was tidy enough, if a little spartan. Most forts he had visited showed a little more clutter. Piles of shields awaiting mending, stacks of pila, crates waiting to be moved, that sort of thing. Batavis seemed oddly tidy, because it was almost empty of things. He wondered what the inside of the buildings were like, if they were the same.

The soldiers drew his attention, too. That they looked very similar to the unidentified Germans who had attacked him in both Liguria and Raetia was not a comforting thought, although without shield designs and standards it could often be difficult to tell auxiliary units apart, unless they had a certain amount of license with native equipment. Of course, Gauls and Germans looked much like Roman auxilia anyway, since Rome had adopted the best of their cultural armoury and clothing, and only the beards and braids really suggested a Germanic origin for these men, until they spoke, anyway.

But there was one thing that really struck him about the men.

How *few* of them he could see.

Auxiliary forts in peaceful garrison times tended to be hustle and bustle at most times of the day, and even into the night. There did not seem to be very many men around in Batavis, even on the walls, let alone in the streets between the buildings. He almost probed the matter with his guide, but decided against it. For now, he would observe, and then enquire in the commander's office. Of course, that in itself was a question that demanded an answer, since in theory it should be Publius sitting behind that desk waiting to see him. Who was he being shown to?

The bath house was not being used, he noted as they passed it. No smoke rose from the flues. Of course, if he were going to be culturally unkind, he might suggest that Batavians might not be as enamoured with the bathing process as men from the older, more southerly provinces. But that, he suspected, was not the reason. It was another symptom of the quietness of this place. A mangy hound rounded a corner and stopped dead at the sight of Orthus, growling defensively, but coming no closer. Orthus ignored the dog and stuck by his master's side.

They passed the granary last, approaching the headquarters, and there, at least was activity. As they approached, that activity stopped. Three soldiers stood on the loading platform with the granary door open, several sacks of grain on the stone floor before them, a cart half-filled. They watched him with suspicious eyes as he passed, and did not begin their work again while he was still in sight. He'd only caught a brief glance before they'd stopped, but it had looked to him awfully like they had been *loading* the cart with sacks from the granary, rather than the other way round, which was intriguing.

Then they were at the headquarters, but this time they were not challenged, the soldier on guard at the doorway simply watching, knowing that his companion had already checked Rufinus at the gate. Another soldier was called over, and took Rufinus's reins, keeping his horse for him. The two men then entered the principia, moving into the courtyard, and Rufinus once more took in everything he could. There were two statues in the square, which was not unusual. Most forts would have a statue of the emperor, and many would have one of the gods associated with the military, either Mars, Jupiter, or Minerva. Two things struck him instantly about the Batavis headquarters. One was that the god, whose base identified it as Mars, bore a distinct resemblance to a number of Germanic deities Rufinus had seen over the years, far more than it looked Roman, anyway. The other was that the imperial statue facing it across the courtyard might be supposed to be Severus, but to Rufinus it bore much more of a resemblance to Commodus. Both men had curly hair and beards, of course, and since the native artist had not been the most talented of men, it could possibly have been either. That left Rufinus with two notions. Either the unit had decided the emperors were similar enough not to bother updating the statue, or possibly they didn't care, and had not bothered with it, despite the change in regime.

This place was intriguing, in a worrying way.

The chapel of the standards, as they moved into the main range of buildings, at least seemed normal. The standards, flags and horns of the unit sat in their appropriate place, which confirmed that this fort was still considered an occupied garrison post. There was no one in the basilica, and their footsteps echoed as they crossed the stone floor. Rufinus made a last moment decision in the direction of provocation, and, unseen by the man leading him, he pulled out that serpent arm ring he had taken from the leader of the German attackers, and slipped it onto his own arm, with some difficulty, given his powerful biceps. He made sure it was visible below his tunic sleeve.

Moments later, he was shown into the commander's office.

The man behind the desk, who looked up as he entered, was a grizzled veteran of many years, with some very visible reminders of his service record carved into his flesh. His eyes were the cold blue of winter skies, his hair a straw blond and his physique every bit as powerful as Rufinus's. That alone could have told him this man was no senior officer, but a centurion, though to confirm that, a knobbly vine stick and a helmet with a transverse crest sat to one side. The crest was tall, and of black feathers. He was immediately willing to bet this man was the primus pilus, the most senior centurion of the unit.

'Yes?' the man asked, his voice tinged with only the slightest Germanic accent as his gaze passed from the soldier to Rufinus, to Orthus, and then back to Rufinus.

'A tribune from the governor's office, sir, asking to see you.'

The man frowned, looking Rufinus up and down. He flicked a glance and then a forefinger at the soldier, who left the room and closed the door behind him. Once they were alone, the man rose from his chair and thrust out a hand rather forcefully.

'Julius Segimerus, Centurion commanding Eighth Batavorum,' he announced, by way of greeting.

Rufinus held out his own arm and shook the hand, that serpent arm ring in plain sight and moving in front of the man's eyes as he shook. 'Gnaeus Cornelius Strabo.' He deliberately left out any identification of rank or unit, to see if the man probed. He did not. Nor, interestingly, did he pay more than passing attention to the arm ring. Either those German killers were not from here, or the commander did not know the man's personal gear, which was quite likely.

'What can I do for you?' the man asked. Rufinus had already put away the sealed document. Now that he was in, he didn't need it, and since it was just blank parchment it wouldn't be much use anyway. Now, he was going to brazen his way, to rely on the fact that he outranked everyone in this place, and that was clear from his uniform alone.

Rufinus went on the offensive. He had no intention of being interrogated.

'I am surprised at how quiet Batavis is. Given its importance and critical position on the border, I would have expected it to be rather busy. Instead it is quieter than an Athenian library. You have staffing issues?'

Segimerus, which Rufinus had also noted and filed away as a distinctly Germanic name, nodded. He spoke straight away, eyes unblinking and directly on Rufinus. If he was lying or dissembling, then he was extremely good at it.

'Like many border units, our effective strength is considerably lower than the strength on paper. That is not uncommon. We are a thousand-strong unit of mixed cavalry and infantry, but our last accurate strength report confirms the unit strength at seven hundred and sixty-three, pending a number of requests for funding to support a recruitment drive in the region. Of those seven hundred and sixty-three, the fort holds two hundred and ninety-one men at the moment, seven of whom are currently sick-listers. The remaining four hundred and seventy two men are variously assigned to frontier guard duties at a number of fortlets and watchtowers, a tile works, local fabricae, and on patrol duties. Frontier life involves rather a lot of external detachments, I'm afraid.'

Rufinus nodded along, though his mind was racing. It sounded so perfectly reasonable, so true. He was sure to some extent it *was* true, in fact, at least the core of it. But the man had been so quick and so knowledgeable. Centurions were the nearest thing to infallible, usually, but to be able to pluck specific figures out of the air like that...

'You are curiously able to produce such numbers,' he mused quietly.

'You have interrupted my examination of assignment duties and strength reports. The figures are somewhat fresh in my mind.'

Again, Rufinus nodded. Again, it seemed so reasonable. His eyes slipped sideways to Orthus. The dog was watching Segimerus, and Rufinus had the distinct impression that he did not like the man at all.

'Might I ask where your prefect is?' Rufinus dropped in suddenly, hoping to catch the centurion out. 'I have a dispatch for him, but it is "prefect's eyes only", I'm afraid.'

Was that a moment's irritation he caught in the man's eyes?

If it was, Segimerus rallied magnificently. 'Prefect Publius Marcius Rustius left Batavis a little over a month ago. He received a communique about which he would not speak. He told me that he needed to visit the governor at Castra Regina, and did not know how long he would be away. In the meantime, I was to take command and keep things running until his return. He took an escort of a turma of cavalry, one of the various assignments to which I referred just now with our troop lists. In truth, it has been a little too long for comfort now, and I have been starting to consider sending men to enquire after the prefect, but his manner when he left was so secretive that I was not sure whether he would welcome that.'

Rufinus was nodding again. On the face of it, that sounded so plausible. Only if you knew a little more, that said prefect's head sat in a stone shrine by the river a few days' ride from here, might you disbelieve the man. Somehow, he doubted Publius left with a cavalry escort. Or if he did, it was probably that escort who killed him. And Rufinus wasn't convinced that Publius had any intention of going near Castra Regina. If he thought someone was monitoring the post and felt he was in danger, going to the very hub where such things happened would be foolish... unless, perhaps Publius had gone to visit the governor with his worries, only to find that the governor was in on it, and had been forced to run. But if he was worried about the local military, why would he take their cavalry with him? His head spun for a moment, then he looked down to his dog for help. Orthus was quite a good judge of character, and right now he looked as though he was ready to pounce. The dog was almost trembling.

No. Julius Segimerus was plausible, calm, and a very traditional centurion, but he was also clever, sly, and a lying bastard.

Rufinus held his temper, though he could feel it starting to rage deep inside. Whatever had happened to Publius, whatever lay at the root of all of this, Julius Segimerus was in it up to his fancy crest. But right now, Rufinus had no proof of wrongdoing, and no idea what it was the man was guilty of. As such, there was really nothing he could do. And even if there was, while standing in the man's own fort, surrounded by his people, was probably not the most sensible time to do it.

'As interim commander, I should receive your dispatch,' the centurion said calmly. 'In the normal course of affairs, if a prefect is not in a position to receive orders, they should be passed to the next in command.'

Rufinus noted an almost eagerness flash into the man's eyes for just a moment. He really wanted to know what Rufinus's message was.

'Sorry, but I was given very explicit instructions. I shall have to return to the office with the document and report my inability to deliver it.'

That was another provocation. If, as Rufinus was growing certain, there was something odd going on here, the last thing Segimerus would want was the provincial authorities looking into the disappearance of his commander. The fact that the centurion did not even flinch, led Rufinus to a worrying conclusion. If the centurion wasn't worried about the provincial authorities, that was a strong suggestion that said authorities already knew what was going on and were somehow involved, a possibility that Rufinus had acknowledged from the start. Not *all* the high authorities, though, he realised, or the centurion would have known Rufinus for a fake from the outset.

'Thank you for your time,' Rufinus said to the man, then bowed his head. He gestured to Orthus and turned, walking towards the door. It was only when he reached it that he realised Orthus wasn't with him. He spun back to see that the dog had not moved, and a low rumble had begun in his throat, a sound that usually presaged violence. People might not see Orthus as a threat at first sight, as they had done with Acheron, but they never made that mistake twice. The centurion had clearly decided that the dog was more dangerous than he'd initially assumed, for his hand reached for his vine stick and he gripped it tight.

'Heel,' Rufinus barked. Again, the dog might not know the word, but he understood the tone. Slowly, and without taking his eyes off Segimerus, Orthus rose and then turned, and finally walked away to join his master. Rufinus opened the door sharply and walked out, almost braining the soldier who'd guided him here and who had clearly been listening at the door. As the man stumbled backward, swearing under his breath and rubbing his forehead, Rufinus gave a grim smile. Something was definitely going on in Batavis, and it seemed to include the garrison and its officers, but Rufinus and Orthus together had caught them out, made them a little guarded and tense. Good. Nervous people made mistakes.

He collected his horses at the principia gate once more, and began to walk them back through the fort. As they passed the granary, he noted that the cart was a little more loaded than it had been on his last passing, which confirmed that they were taking grain out, not putting it in. He wondered where the grain was going. Of course, it could be perfectly legitimate, being transferred to another border installation, or distributed among towers and fortlets.

Or it could be going somewhere else. For a moment he considered the possibility that the Eighth Batavorum were engaged in large-scale theft and corruption, stealing from military supplies and selling it to locals. Such things were far from unknown, and on a small-scale it was usually overlooked and considered to be enterprising soldiers enhancing their wage. But he pushed that notion away. It was quite possible, but he somehow doubted such theft would drive a unit to murdering their commander and hunting a man down over two provinces. Whatever this was, it was bigger than sidelining grain for sale to locals.

There were not many men here, but each one of them watched him as he passed, and their gazes were utterly devoid of warmth. He walked on past them all and out of the fort gate, where he heaved a sigh of relief once out of reach of the guards. As he mounted and then walked his horses through the dirty, slum-like streets of the civilian settlement, he mused on his next move. He was clearly not going to find anything more out from Batavis, unless he somehow managed to question someone in a slightly more private situation. One possibility lay in taking the investigation up a level. Perhaps his next step should be visiting the governor, who would either be in the capital of Augusta Vindelicorum, or in Castra Regina, commanding his legion directly. He doubted he was going to learn anything else useful without being a little more confrontational, although that brought with it a huge added level of danger.

It took only a few moments to pass through the settlement, and then he was out in the part of the peninsula where it widened, the two rivers marching off in separate directions. He stopped when he reached the junction of the main road. Milestones presented him with options. To the left, the road led southwest, inland, towards Augusta Vindelicorum, and the provincial palace with all its staff, records and potential corruption. To the right lay Castra Regina and the Third Italica, ostensibly the most loyal force in the region, but in the hands of the Governor, who may be behind all this. Both locations were extremely risky, but both offered opportunities.

He cursed and chewed his lip, indecisive.

What he would really like was a little bit more information from Batavis before taking this anywhere else. He would not get back into the fort, and the civilians outside looked no more friendly. He had the distinct feeling that *everyone* in this place was up to something. *Everyone* was involved. This was no small crime, but a big thing, possibly even involving the civilians as well, given how they looked at him. Usually, in such places, the officers were the best informed, the soldiers less so, and the civilians hardly at all. In this case, he suspected that *everyone* knew more than him.

He toyed with the idea of interrogating the villagers, but brushed that idea away. Apart from the distaste of interrogating civilians, who might simply be innocent but unfriendly, it carried with it a huge risk. If it turned out they *were* innocent, then he would be committing a crime by questioning them, or at least the way he would have to do it if they resisted.

An idea rolled into his mind, and he smiled. Those soldiers had been filling a wagon with grain, which meant they were going to take it somewhere, and that somewhere was far enough that it needed a wagon and oxen. He'd seen such details before, and they rarely rated more than three men. Three soldiers not expecting trouble, out on lazy duty with a slow wagon, would be easily overcome. And there might even only be two. Rufinus was content that even with a good ten years on these men, he could probably handle them with enough preparation and surprise. All he had to do was take them out fast, and leave at least one able to talk, and he might be able to get a little more of a handle on what was happening at Batavis. And that cart would be leaving today, else they would have left the grain inside in case of rain. He suspected the cart would come out through the village some time in the next two hours or so. And when it left, it would have to come by here, no matter where it was bound. It had to follow one or other of these two roads.

Looking around, he could see that locals on the edge of the village were still watching him. Kicking his horse, he began to walk it away to the south, down the Vindelicorum road, which curved around a large patch of undergrowth and straggly trees and out of sight. He followed that curve until he was happy no one could see him, and then found a game trail and led his horses off the road. Relying on his good sense of direction, he then slowly and carefully walked his horses back towards the junction, but now within the trees. Once he was sure he was in roughly the right area, he tethered the two animals and, with Orthus at his heel, pushed his way towards the road. It did not take long to find a comfortable enough spot with a slightly restricted view of the crossroads and its milestones. There he settled in for a wait, seated on a tree stump. Just to be sure he was sufficiently hidden, he had taken his travelling cloak from his pack on the horse and donned it, a miscellaneous brown woollen garment that blended nicely with the undergrowth.

He sat and watched, pondering.

He was in a place that was as Germanic as could be, despite being officially Roman. It was named after a Germanic tribe, housed a garrison of Germanic auxilia, raised in the surrounding region, commanded by a man with a surprisingly Germanic name. Everyone had Germanic-looking features, hair and beards, clothing styles, and Germanic accents, even the civilians. Were it not for the fort itself and the standards and weapons, Rufinus conceded that it would be very hard to tell whether they were inside the empire or outside it. He wondered just how closely the border was guarded in the region, given that the people on both sides of it had to be related. Even in the most dangerous zones, often the borders were eased to allow trade to pass through. How much more so when the border was effectively an arbitrary line drawn across a tribe's lands?

He was so lost in his pondering that he only realised someone was coming when they got close enough that he could hear hooves. He looked up sharply. It was not a cart full of grain, after all. One man on a horse had come through the civilian settlement at a brisk trot, and now that he approached the junction, he turned without delay to the northwest, taking the road that led to Castra Regina.

Rufinus paused only for a moment. He had planned on waiting for the cart, but this had to be better. The man was dressed as an auxiliary cavalry rider, right down to his arms and armour, which meant he was on business. That he seemed to be in a hurry, and had left just after Rufinus's visit was hugely suspicious, and offered a much greater opportunity than a grain cart full of bored men. This man's sudden departure from the fort simply had to be something to do with Rufinus's visit, and that meant that he had to know something useful, or was carrying something important. Even as the rider began to kick his horse and speed up, racing away along the Castra Regina road, Rufinus was already moving. He had to be careful. Here, he was still in sight of the village, and he did not want word of his continued presence to leak back to the fort. To that end, he returned to his horses, collected them, and then forced his way northwest through the undergrowth, parallel with the road until he was perhaps half a mile further away, then mounted up and pushed a way out to the road.

Scratched and bruised by branches and brambles, he kicked his horse and moved up onto the road. The civil settlement of Batavis was some distance back now, and there was no sign of the horseman ahead, but he had to be there, just having gained some distance as Rufinus found his way free. Rufinus kicked up to a gallop, racing along the good military road. After a short time, he began to encounter locals and merchants on the road, and perhaps two miles from Batavis, he finally spotted his quarry. The rider had slowed to rest his horse, which suggested he was going some distance, and that had allowed Rufinus to catch up. He took the opportunity to swap horses, which meant he could continue to move at speed. In theory, he could catch up with the man and drag him off the road, into the undergrowth, where he could interrogate him.

But he had changed his mind. Twice now, he'd had men in a position where they could be questioned, and both times those men had chosen to end their life rather than talk. That suggested that this rider would be no different. Of course, he might be carrying something incriminating. But there was another option now. It would be useful to know where the man was going, and who he intended to visit. That information might actually be more useful than anything he could wring out of the rider himself.

Rufinus slowed again. He would follow the man, and at sufficient distance so as not to be spotted.

The plot was starting to unfold.

CHAPTER SEVEN

Danubian frontier

The plot was unfolding in an unexpected direction.

The rider had clearly not considered the possibility that he would be followed, and kept his attention on the road ahead. Consequently, Rufinus found tailing the man easier than he'd expected, and given the traffic on the road, it was not hard to disappear from immediate view when the man *did* occasionally look back.

They had ridden straight past the next fort west in the defensive line without pausing, yet at the one after, the man had dipped inside, stopping for a little over half an hour before reappearing and taking to the road west once more. Rufinus had slipped a couple of coins into the hands of a lad in the nearby village and asked a few questions. The place was apparently called Sorviodurum, and was the home to a cohort by the name of the Second Raetorum. As Rufinus had ridden on to catch up with his quarry once more, with Orthus always keeping pace alongside, the significance of this rolled around his brain. For some reason the fort after Batavis had not been worth stopping at, but Sorviodurum *was*. It was, to Rufinus, rather interesting that Batavis was full of Batavians, Germans in Germany, with a German commander and a fort named for them, while Sorviodurum seemed to be garrisoned by Raetians, who must have been drawn from the local populace since they were founded. Somehow the local connections had to be significant in terms of the grand plan here, though he had yet to see how they connected.

After Sorviodurum, it had seemed almost certain that the man's next destination had been the legionary fortress of Castra Regina, which may well currently house the province's governor, and so, when they reached the city and the rider continued on past the place, upriver along the frontier, Rufinus had been forced to re-think.

He had considered from the start the likelihood that the governor was somehow involved in whatever was happening in the region, and so a rider sent to the governor with warning that Rufinus was poking around made a lot of sense. But if the rider was *not* visiting the governor, where *was* he going? *Who* was he visiting? More forts like Sorviodurum? Or was it possible that Rufinus had misconstrued, and that the rider was actually on ordinary military business and nothing to do with his visit?

No. That the man had left just after Rufinus, and had ridden at speed and with purpose, made it far more likely that it was connected to him than anything else.

Biting down on the uncertainty, and the urge to simply stop the man and beat the information out of him, Rufinus continued to follow subtly. East of Castra Regina, the landscape had been quite flat and arable, the river wide and moving in gentle, lazy bends. Continuing on to the west, those loops in the river began to become sharper and more pronounced, and hills and woodland began to rise and become more and more prevalent. Some miles upriver, they passed the next Roman installation of the border, a small signal station on a plateau above a loop in the river, though the rider did not even slow for the place, and no life or activity was obvious there.

It was as the sun began to sink behind the horizon that they appeared to reach their destination. Rufinus watched as the rider slowed. They had left an area of hills and moved once more into flat land, the river straight for a short while, and a fort stood above a slope down to the south bank of the river, torches and fires already burning to ward off the growing gloom. The rider cantered up to the fort gate, which was resolutely shut and, after a short exchange, was admitted, the great timber doors closed behind him.

A small civil settlement had grown up outside the fort's east gate, beyond the ditches, and Rufinus stopped short of the place, not sure how best to approach the matter. He could really do with knowing what was happening, who that man was speaking to, and to watch the fort's gates in case he left once more, but wasn't sure how much he dare trust even the civilians here.

The fort presumably had four gates after the standard fashion, though one would lead only down the slope and to a jetty on the river. If the rider left the fort, it could be by any of the other three gates, depending upon whether his job was done and he was returning home, or continuing on elsewhere. Utilising the gloom, Rufinus moved off the road, keeping to the edge of the woodland to the south, and continued on past the civil settlement and around the edge of the place. To his relief, he found a place in the lee of a growth of yellow gentian where he could see the fort in its entirety, including all three main access points. Better still, the bright plants, some as tall as a man, formed an excellent hiding place from which to keep watch.

He tethered the horses and set up a small camp, though making sure that everything could be collected and slung into bags for a quick departure. Resigned to consuming only hard rations because he dare not light a fire and be spotted, Rufinus settled into his blankets and watched carefully. Beside him, Orthus curled up on the spare cloak Rufinus carried in his pack for that very reason.

Nothing happened as the light dwindled its last and the purple and then black of evening bled into the sky. More lights sprung up in the fort and in the small settlement nearby, and figures occasionally bobbed along in silhouette atop the fort walls. Not as many as he'd normally expect, though, especially in a frontier fort. A similar situation to the fort at Batavis? A diminished garrison again? What was going on in Raetia?

He continued to watch for a couple of hours, and finally sat back, rubbing his eyes, which were becoming quite tired with the strain of watching in the dark. The rider had not re-emerged, and to Rufinus's mind he was not likely to now, until the morning. A lone horseman would be foolish to travel frontier roads in the dark, after all. If the rider was going to either return home or move on, it would likely be at dawn now. And Rufinus would have to sleep. He was tired now, and if he sat up all night watching the fort, he'd be useless the next day. As such, he decided that enough was enough for now, and rolled tight in his blankets.

Sleep came immediately.

The dream came almost as fast.

Publius was back in the dream, dressed in his prefect's uniform, but rather distressingly carrying his own head beneath his arm, the way a soldier might carry his helmet. Behind him were gathered a multitude of corpses, all armoured in their various manners, some Roman, some not, all prepared for war, and all dead in a variety of gruesome manners. It took only a moment to recognise them as a lifetime's worth of his own victims once again. Indeed, among the front line, he could see the bully, Scopius, still drenched and broken from that fight that had left him trapped in an aqueduct settling tank to drown.

Even in the dream, Rufinus shuddered. This was not the most encouraging of sights.

'They are yours, brother,' Publius announced.

'I know,' Rufinus replied, hoarse, hollow.

'Yours to *command*,' explained the headless prefect. 'Your new Praetorian cohort.'

Rufinus woke with a start, eyes snapping wide. He was cold but drenched with sweat, the image of Publius holding his own head still fresh enough to shimmer before his eyes. It took him only moments to realise that something was happening, that it was noise that had awoken him from the dream, and not the mix of guilt and horror he had thought responsible. Orthus was giving a low, constant growl. Alert now, Rufinus looked in the same direction as the dog, his ears adjusting to overcome the growling even as he placed his hand on Orthus and stroked him, soothing down the growls so that he could now hear the voices over the top.

He rose from his blankets and peered between the tall yellow flowers.

The civil settlement outside the fort was alive with bobbing torchlights and the shadows of moving figures, a hum of numerous voices forming a gentle drone. He watched carefully, and strained to hear. All he could make out was that the voices were speaking in their local Germanic tongue, rather than Latin, but watching them told him one thing: they were entering the fort.

Intrigued, his senses now alive and night-sweats forgotten, Rufinus lifted his cloak and pulled it about himself. The people of the village were going into the fort, which was now more brightly lit than ever, a huge, golden glow rising above it. He wondered for a moment about the feasibility of slipping in among them, but quickly brushed that aside. He would never pass for a local, even visually, let alone if one of them should ask him a question. But he wanted to know what was happening. He examined the crowd. No one was looking this way, all intent on their business. His gaze strayed to the fort's defences, and he realised that now there was no one on the walls at all. Whatever this was, it seemingly involved everyone. Even children and doddery old men walking with sticks were making their way into the fort.

Taking a breath and adjusting his sword so that it would not swing and make noise, he dipped out from the bushes, and began to move along the treeline in a series of jerky sprints, between which he would stand still. If anyone over there caught the movement out of the corner of their eye, by the time they turned to double check, Rufinus would be still, and very hard to spot. Orthus was keeping pace, but beneath the woody canopy, in the shadows, less visible despite his white colour. The tactic seemed to work, for no call of alarm went up as he left the fort and skirted around the village. He peered at the settlement as he circled it, back towards the main road that left it heading east. There were maybe twenty to twenty-five houses, as well as a small baths, what looked like it might be a shrine, and a couple of granaries or warehouses. Not a big place, considering the number of people he'd seen moving into the fort. Certainly, it had to be the settlement's entire population, and then some. He found himself wondering if people from the surrounding area had come, too. Farmers from nearby, or natives from neighbouring villages. Certainly they seemed to have emptied the settlement here.

He crept towards the houses, and reached the nearest corner, looking around it, the dog at his heel. What he saw seemed to confirm it. The place was empty, quiet and dark, every last occupant gone to the fort. He stepped out into the street and looked through the place, towards the fort at the far end, just in time to see the great gates shutting, the last visitor admitted. He frowned.

There was still no one on the walls. Rufinus was alone and unobserved.

That presented unprecedented opportunities.

Still, he waited for a time, in case guards might just appear on the fort's ramparts. None did, and he was confident they were truly empty, for he would have spotted any guard silhouetted against that great orange glow.

He moved into the village, considering whether it might be informative slipping into one or more of the houses. He decided against it. He would rather leave no evidence of his presence, and he doubted he was going to learn much from civilian locals in their natural habitat. Instead, he took in the few public structures here. Wherever Rome expanded, a man could identify the level of Romanisation that the area had achieved by its buildings. Truly barbaric frontier zones looked little different to the native lands beyond, while places that had become properly Roman boasted entertainment venues, temples to the emperor, aqueducts and so on. This place had a bath house, which was a start.

The centre of the village was an open square, probably used for markets, and at its heart stood a stump of stone, surrounded by carved blocks, scattered close. Intrigued, Rufinus crossed to it, and took it in at a glance, realising immediately what it was, for he'd seen them before in Noricum and Gaul. The blocks were intricately designed, some with the figures of gods or of representations of seasons. Six fluted stone drums had formed the main height of the column, and the four-headed stone from the top lay nearby. Of the statue that had once graced its summit, there was no sign. It was a Jupiter Column, a depiction of the supreme god, defeating chaos and instilling order, a celebration of the Pax Romana over an area. It was, in short, one of the most Roman symbols of civilisation.

It had been deliberately destroyed and the god removed.

That spoke volumes. It suggested that these locals were rejecting the law of Rome. Moreover, that it happened within sight of the fort's gate suggested that the garrison had allowed it to happen.

A lump rose in Rufinus's throat. This was bad. He didn't like what he was seeing here at all, and together with what he'd seen at Batavis, and his brother's fate, it hinted at something big. What he found as he looked around did nothing to diminish that worry. The shrine he'd seen from afar proved to be just that, as he got closer and examined it. Marks on the floor and wall suggested it had housed an altar of some sort and probably a statue of whatever god it was dedicated to, but now those had been removed, and instead stood a single, rough-hewn column. He swallowed nervously as he spotted the three distinctive recesses in the column, so similar to that shrine he'd found by the Rhenus days ago. It was for holding heads, though as yet this one had no occupants, thank the gods. A smashed Jupiter Column, and a Roman shrine replaced with a Germanic head-taking cult?

101

He shivered again.

The bath house did not improve matters. It had clearly not been used in some time. He dipped into a granary, half expecting to find it full of sacks of grain, marked with the identification of one of the local forts, part of similar activity to the emptying of the granary at Batavis. Instead, it was all-but empty, just a few remaining sacks to keep the settlement going.

He returned to the broken column. Some such monuments carried the name of their location among the carvings. It took some time in the dark to find it, but when he did, it was unmistakable. He had the name of the place now.

ABVSINA.

He stayed crouched, thinking back. He'd memorised whole sections of maps and itineraries before he left Rome, yet not for the first time he really wished he'd brought some of them with him. He was fairly sure he could remember Abusina, the next fort west along the line from the great legionary base of Castra Regina. He scrunched up his eyes, trying to remember. He'd seen it listed, and was fairly sure it housed a cohort of Tungrians from the far northern end of the Rhenus, up near the sea, though he couldn't remember its number.

Gingerly, slowly, quietly and very carefully, he crept forward through the end of the village facing the fort. There was a good open stretch between the two, separated by a double ditch that surrounded the fort, a causeway marching across them to the gate. Still no figure had appeared atop the wall, but just in case they did, Rufinus braced himself to move fast.

Then he stopped.

The noise had changed.

Instead of a general hum of voices, they had fallen into line, forming a rhythmic chanting. Whatever was happening here, it was happening now. He peered at the fort. There had to be a huge fire, or possibly several, blazing within to create that much light. He could still see no sign of men on the walls. He had to find out what was happening.

He turned, remembering the dog at his heel. He couldn't take Orthus with him, this time. Hurriedly, he grabbed a length of twine hanging from a fence beside a house and tethered the dog in place.

'Stay,' he said, showing the dog the flat of his hands, and wishing he'd taught Orthus that particular command.

Bracing himself, he broke into a run, hoping the dog wouldn't follow. There was no one outside the fort for they were all inside, the brightness over there when combined with the darkness outside would make him quite hard to spot even if someone did appear, and the growing racket from within would hide any sound. In truth, he could probably march slowly over to the fort, blowing a trumpet with a burning torch strapped to his head, and still get there unnoticed.

He broke free of the village and hurtled across the open ground onto the causeway that led towards the gate. As he crossed the ditches and closed on the defences, he had hoped to find the fort gate ajar and unattended, since everyone was clearly inside and busy, but was disappointed to find them shut tight. He stopped at the wall, panting and listening. Whatever they were chanting, it was in German, and he had no idea what they were saying, a fact he found distinctly frustrating.

He moved to the side of the gate and examined the fort walls.

He had seen many fortresses in his time. Some were built of immense stone blocks, others of brick, some very well formed with hardly any need for mortar, others much rougher. These walls were of a fairly common sort, stone blocks around the size of his forearm, forming the face of a wall with a core of mortar and rubble, extra mortar used between the facing stones. As with all forts more than a few decades old, the mortar had crumbled in places and the walls here showed signs of generations of repairs, yet were still currently in need of more.

Good.

He gripped the stones and used the gaps as finger- and toe-holes. Just off the ground, he turned and looked back towards the village. Orthus was still in place, tethered, though he did not look happy. He turned back to the task at hand. The walls were only fifteen feet high. Any enemy had to get past the ditches and defensive weapons just to reach the walls, and so they really didn't *need* to be too tall. As such, they were not too challenging a climb, and it did not take Rufinus long to reach the parapet, where he gingerly put a hand over the battlemented top and used it to pull himself up high enough to see.

He managed a glimpse for the blink of an eye, before ducking again. The fort was full of people, and his appearance above the battlements, bathed in golden light, might be all too easy to spot. In that momentary glance he saw a huge bonfire in the centre of the fort, around which were gathered hundreds of people, singing and chanting. Details, he could not make out in that short time.

Gritting his teeth, his fingers starting to ache, he carefully ducked below the wall line and edged to his left, back towards the gate and its flush-walled flanking towers. Once there, he took a deep breath and prepared himself. In one swift, fluid move, he hauled himself up, throwing himself over the battlements and landing on the wall walk, where he dropped flat to the stonework and lay there for a moment, breathing shallow, waiting for cries of alarm.

They did not come.

He waited a little more, not looking up, just listening to the incomprehensible chanting.

There was a narrow shadow where the tower met the wall, and he rose slowly and shuffled along until he was in it, where he finally stood in relative concealment and took in what he was seeing.

The fire had clearly been built over days, given its size, and extra fuel was stacked over to one side in a large heap. That meant this event was either a one-off, or at least rare, not a regular thing. The figures around the fire were in a mix of clothing, some native civilian, some auxiliary uniform, which meant the army and the locals had mixed. Given that they were all chanting the same thing, it was clear that the soldiers here spoke a Germanic tongue the locals could understand. Given that they were from the Tungrian region, at least three hundred miles away on the lower Rhenus, this was impressive. Then he shook his head. The unit might have been from there and had Germanic leanings from the beginning, but they had probably been based here and recruiting from the locals almost as long as that Raetian unit at Sorviodurum.

Of all the forts the rider had passed, he had stopped at three, and those three had contained units with a German origin or connection: Raetians, Batavians and Tungrians. Rufinus was starting to form a faint idea, though it was nebulous as yet, a little elusive. One thing he decided now, though, was that he would sooner put his trust in a criminal than in any cohort with a German connection. Maybe he could find a unit with a nice Hispanic or Greek origin to test a growing theory. They, he suspected, might be a great deal more trustworthy.

His gaze moved on, focusing on minutiae, and the next two things he spotted did little to ease his disquiet. A statue stood on a rock close to the fire, and though it was distant and hard to make out details against the dancing flames, he would be willing to wager it was Jupiter, taken from the top of the column, though changed in some way. Even from here it looked misshapen. A heap of something at the base of the rock was unidentifiable from here, though it had the distinct air of sacrifice.

The other thing was less of a surprise, if more worrying.

Auxiliary spears stood to either side of the rock, each topped with a head. Rufinus felt sure he knew where those were bound in the morning, when the fire had burned down to ash, and this grisly celebration was over.

He watched for a while, in case something important happened, as he didn't want to miss anything, but it became clear quickly that the main event was over, and had presumably involved those three heads and the heap in front of the statue, the chanting soon ending and devolving once more into the din of a party. Now, all it seemed to consist of was drunken Germans whooping and dancing around the fire.

Rufinus slipped back over the wall, lowering himself until he was hanging from his fingertips, then let go and dropped to the ground. Safe once more, he hurtled back to the village, untied Orthus and then took the quickest route he could back to his little camp site hidden behind yellow flowers, where he lay in his blankets and listened to men, who should behave like Roman auxiliaries, celebrating their beheadings.

His sleep, when it came once more, was not comfortable.

He woke at the first light of dawn, but not because of the light, or indeed through anything natural. Once more, it was growling and voices that had drawn him from slumber. This time it was different, though, for the voices were lower, more subdued, but considerably closer. He listened, trying to ascertain where they were, and decided they could not be more than fifty paces away to his left. Slowly, quietly and carefully, he rose from his blankets, soothed Orthus, and peered out through the undergrowth, staying as hidden as he could.

He could see men walking. They were soldiers, or at least wearing auxiliary tunics with belted swords. They were muttering to one another in their own language as they emerged from the trees and out into the open, where they crossed the road and headed back to the fort. He frowned, not sure whether they had been in the woods all night, or had passed him once already, before dawn, and were now returning. Whatever the case, he stayed still and quiet, watching. Some of them were wet, and he thought he could see blood-spatter here and there, which was not an encouraging sign.

He waited until those men had crossed the open space and disappeared in through the fort's southern gate, then took a steadying breath. It was still very early and the light was but a pre-dawn glow, which meant he would be hard to spot from the fort, and so he made the most of that and slipped along the treeline, ducking from bole to bole until he reached the place from which he reckoned those men had emerged. Without delay, he ducked into the woods. The men had not been careful, and had left a clear trail through the trees, so it was not hard to follow their path. He tracked it for perhaps a quarter of an hour into the woods, the light growing all the time.

Then he found a clearing.

Given the mess the many hobnailed boots had made of the turf in the clearing, it was obvious that this was where the men had come. The clearing's only points of interest were a pool some twenty feet or so across, and what looked to be fishing apparatus.

His eyes narrowed suspiciously as he emerged and walked over to the pond.

No. Not fishing. A forked wooden pole had been driven into the ground beside the water. A thin rope cable, almost certainly military, since it looked very like a tent rope, had been tied to a tree stump, then arced up over the forked stick, from which it disappeared into the water. The rope was taut. Rufinus walked over towards the stick, looking down at the pool. The water was dark and glassy in the early light. He picked up a twig from the grass and tossed it in. The water rippled around the wood, and he noted with distaste a faint pinkness to it. He'd already had a suspicion forming, but now it was building rather quickly.

Half knowing what to expect, he stood back and tugged down on the rope on the far side of the fork. It was hard, tight, and as he pressed with a good deal of effort, the rope rasped over the stick, and the water began to ripple and churn.

Then the body appeared.

He held the rope tight, as he leaned forward to look at it. The rope had bound the man's arms behind him, and Rufinus could imagine the poor bastard being slowly lowered into the water as they let the rope slacken, so that he could drown. Of course, his head was missing, but they'd probably let him drown first, *then* taken their grisly prize. Two heads last night by the camp fire, and now a third here in the clearing. And a new grisly shrine in the village with three holes awaiting occupants.

But that was not all. The body was still fresh, and had probably only died an hour ago at most, but it was neither the horrible death nor the missing head that shook him. It was the uniform the body wore. The military tunic bore the stripe of an equestrian officer. This man had been a senior man, a commander, in all likelihood the prefect in charge of the cohort at Abusina.

That was another trend to add to this matter, and one he didn't like the look of. The prefect of this Tungrian cohort, drowned in a pool and decapitated. Rufinus's brother, prefect of a Batavian cohort, also missing his head by the great Rhenus River. It reeked of revolution, removing the officers.

He looked over the body and managed to find the man's signet ring, which he slipped from the cold, dead fingers and wiped before dropping it into his purse.

There being little else he could do here, and little point in burying the body right now, he hurried back along the worn path towards the fort. At the treeline, he used as much cover as he could to shuffle back towards his little camp site, where he gathered his things and bagged them up. For a long moment he stood and looked at the quiet, calm-looking fort.

The rider may well have gone. If the man set off at dawn, which was most likely, then he'd be at least an hour away. But even if Rufinus wanted to follow, he didn't know *where* to follow. The man may have continued on along the border road, or he may have turned round and gone home. Rufinus would only find out by following one direction fast enough to catch up. But was that important right now?

He wasn't entirely sure what else he was going to find out by following the rider now, for his mind was already whirling with what he had discovered so far, and what it might mean. He had already pondered on the fact that since this seemed to involve cohorts of a local or Germanic origin, the only units he might be able to trust were non-Germanic ones. Given that, and the fact that the rider had skipped Castra Regina in his ride, Rufinus was, for the first time, inclined to put his trust in the Third Italica Legion and in its commander, the provincial governor. At this point, the best option was perhaps to bring the matter to the attention of the authorities.

Decision made, Rufinus untied his horses and then led them out onto the road, where he would be within sight of the fort. At this stage what could they do?

He turned to the east, mounted, and began to ride for Castra Regina.

CHAPTER EIGHT

Castra Regina

Rufinus found the great fortress of the Third Italica both impressive and *un*-impressive.

Impressive because it was the most powerful, unusual legionary fortress that Rufinus had ever seen. Where such fortresses were usually wide and spacious, with walls of fifteen to twenty feet in height and open spaces for the marshalling of troops and equipment, this place was built more with an eye to defence than to accommodation, its walls twice as high as normal, punctuated with huge, heavy towers of immense limestone blocks, the gates enormous and powerful. Castra Regina was no ordinary legionary headquarters, but more a defensive bastion at the core of the Raetian frontier that happened to house a legion. Very impressive. What was less impressive, as Rufinus approached the gate, was that it appeared to be suffering the same manpower problems he had seen in the other forts, for the walls were undermanned in his opinion. That was a knock to his expectations, for he had thought the legion to be a different matter entirely to those auxilia.

The men who stepped out of the open gateway on his approach, on the other hand, looked every bit the professional and veteran legionary. They wore the more recent developments in heavy infantry kit, helmets that were more enclosed and bulky than the older models, scale shirts of bronze, long spatha swords hanging at their sides. But more importantly, the way they moved

111

and the look in their eyes reminded Rufinus of the legionaries he'd served alongside in the war.

'State your name and business,' one called.

Rufinus took it as a hopeful sign that the demand was made in good Latin and without any audible trace of a Germanic accent. This time, for the first time in many days, the situation might just call for the truth.

'I am Gnaeus Marcius Rustius Rufinus, Tribune of the Praetorian Guard, and I have business with your legatus.'

The two men shared a look, and Rufinus wondered for a moment whether the commander was actually not here, and was to be found more in his gubernatorial role further south in the capital. Then the two men turned back to him.

'You have papers, Tribune?'

Rufinus nodded, grateful that he'd retrieved his kit from those Germans back on the Rhenus, and rifled through his bags until he produced his documents with the Praetorian seal. He handed them over and the legionary scanned them briefly, then bowed his head and stepped aside.

'You'll find him in his office at the headquarters, directly ahead,' the soldier told him.

Thanking the man, Rufinus led his horses through the immense, powerful gate and into Castra Regina, Orthus trotting alongside, thanking the gods that he seemed to be somewhere friendly at last, and that the governor was present. As he moved along the main street towards the towering headquarters, he made the same observations again. The place had all the usual structures and facilities of a legionary fortress, but they were tighter-packed, and more utilitarian, organised for quick muster and defence rather than ease and space. And there were fewer legionaries to be seen than he would normally expect in such a place, and fewer military slaves running their duties, too.

That worrying trend was still preying on his mind as he stopped at the headquarters gate, showed his papers once again, left his horses with a slave, and made his way inside. A clerk hurried over, glanced briefly at the dog, and then escorted him through the complex. The statues of Mars and the emperor here at least looked like who they were meant to be, the one of Severus startlingly lifelike, having been recently repainted. The chapel of the standards was impressive, too, but Rufinus noted that despite the eagle, the imperial image and the other treasures, several standards were missing. That meant either that they'd been lost in war and not yet replaced, or perhaps explained the absences another way, suggesting that parts of the legion were on detached duty elsewhere.

At the governor's office, the clerk went in and made an introduction, then returned and ushered Rufinus inside, shutting the door behind him.

The man who ruled Raetia for the emperor, who had responsibility for two hundred miles of frontier, and commanded the Third Legion, sat slumped in his chair. His features were oddly avian, his limbs long and reedy. He looked drawn and tired, bags beneath his eyes and sallow skin. He wore a high quality uniform that was in need of pressing, and he had clearly not shaved this morning. It seemed to take immense effort for him to raise his gaze to the visitor. His gaze slid to Orthus, faltered for a moment, then he shrugged and lifted a hand, waving Rufinus forward and clearing a space on the desk before him by shuffling piles of tablets and papers out of the way.

'A tribune of the Guard, I am told? You are far from home, young man, especially without an escort of men in white. Are dogs in white a Praetorian thing?' He gave a humourless chuckle, then straightened a little and his face became serious. 'I am Titus Decius Barbatus, Propraetorian Governor of Raetia and legatus of the Third Italica. I am assuming that your business here is rather important, since it dragged you so far from Rome and your men.'

Rufinus inclined his head. 'I am investigating some concerning matters in the region, governor. An unexpected report led me to believe there might be trouble among some areas of the provincial military. Might I ask… putting aside the matter of the auxilia for a moment, your legion itself seems to be in garrison as only a skeleton force. Are your men divided between two camps?'

Decius gave a snorted laugh. 'Two? That, Tribune, is something of a joke.'

'Sir?'

The man sagged a little further. 'I would have to consult my paperwork for the details, but I will tell you that three cohorts remain here in Castra Regina, their base. One more is permanently assigned to my capital at Augusta Vindelicorum. Two other cohorts of men are distributed between the more crucial sites in the border zone, as well as controlling certain logistic and manufacturing centres. That is perhaps why you see fewer men here than you expect.'

'With respect, sir, that still only racks up to six cohorts out of the ten one would expect.'

'There's almost a seventh cohort's worth in bits and pieces, including the sick. We are seriously under-strength, Tribune, just like every unit in the region. I realise that most commanders would have divided what men they had into ten cohorts, each below the usual strength, but I reorganised the Third to achieve a lower number of cohorts that could boast full strength. The barbarians out there do not know how *many* cohorts I control, especially with them scattered as they are. All they see is the *size* of the cohorts going about their work, so I maintain a fiction of a full strength legion. Jove alone knows what the tribes over the border might be tempted to do if they knew the true state of manpower in Raetia.'

Rufinus scratched his chin. The governor's explanation shared much with that of Centurion Segimerus back at Batavis. That man, he'd been sure, was lying. *This* man, he was *less* sure about. 'Why so under-strength, sir?'

The governor shrugged. 'Been this way since long before I took control two years ago. I understand manpower has never really risen above the diminished levels at the end of Marcus

Aurelius's wars with the Marcomanni. The legions were sent back to their garrisons and told to recruit as best they could to refill the ranks. Volunteers are somewhat hard to come by up here, especially given we are a poor province, and I cannot take non-citizens, obviously. Not that that matters, anyway. The auxilia have similar issues with numbers, and *they* cannot find sufficient men to take the oath either.'

He suddenly leaned forward, slamming his hands on the desk and then steepling his fingers.

'This province is a mess, Tribune. It is seriously under-profitable, contains far too much mountain for its own good, is home to a people who share more cultural links with the Germanics over the border than with the people ruling them, and sits between better provisioned provinces like Germania and Noricum. And if being given a poor and difficult province was not bad enough,' he went on, suddenly changing tack to make this more about his personal woes than the land, 'I was given the most difficult stretch of frontier west of the sands of Parthia, but just one legion and seventeen auxiliary regiments to control it. Seventeen might sound a lot, but just try dividing it between two hundred miles of frontier, and it starts to look quite thin. Just a garrison every eleven miles. And that's not allowing for the four cohorts I assign to the hinterland to keep control of the more critical areas and to hunt the bandits that seem to grow like weeds in this province. And all that is before you consider that each of those units is under-strength. The whole damn thing is a headache, Tribune, and I shall be grateful in a year's time, when I hand this gilded turd over to someone else and go back to Rome. I'll hardly have made my fortune, but at least I won't be here anymore.'

His eyes suddenly took on a faraway look. 'I had hoped for Hispania or Lusitania. Somewhere warm and peaceful, packed with silver, where good wine and oil is made.'

'It is said that the emperor Augustus favoured Raetian wines above all,' Rufinus noted.

'That was over a century ago. Palates have changed, but the wine hasn't. It tastes as though someone has already drunk it once.' He sighed. 'To be honest, almost *anywhere* would be better than this. Imagine what it would be like to command in Moesia, where the emperor has made sure that the army is of sufficient strength for its needs. Or any frontier province that has a good river to define the border, for that matter.'

'Sir, the Danubius?'

Decius looked up at him. 'Of the two hundred miles of border I control, less than half sits along the nice, safe banks of the Danubius. The other hundred miles is an arbitrary border made of clods of earth and timber stakes that marches out into the most unfriendly lands in the world. And when successive emperors, in their infinite wisdom, advanced the border north, they simply cut through native tribal lands, which then means that the peoples who been thus divided, both within the border and beyond, *both* hate you. I tell you, this place is a mess. People say that Nero was mad and bad for the empire, but at least he had the sense to confine the Raetian borders to the big rivers.'

Rufinus frowned, trying to remember the maps he had studied before leaving Rome. He seemed to remember that the Rhenus and the Danubius almost met at their sources, somewhere way back in the occupied province.

'This place is one short step from disaster at all times,' Decius grunted. 'And until Rome sends a hundred cartloads of gold up here to sweeten the pot for recruitment, we don't have sufficient strength to hold it if anything happens.'

That put a chill up Rufinus's back, particularly given the hints in his brother's letter.

'Do you really feel things are that unsafe, Governor?'

The man's eyes narrowed. 'Two years ago I came here with my wife and children. I sent them back to Rome for their own safety eight months later. Don't forget that while the Marcomanni were crossing the Danubius and causing Aurelius trouble downriver, their allies up here were busy trampling over Raetia too. But because the Marcomanni were bigger, all the effort went into restoring Pannonia and Noricum, while the sole attempt to help Raetia was to garrison the Third here. Things have never been quite right since the war, and *I* think that only the memory of what was done to the Marcomanni keeps the peace here, now.'

Rufinus frowned again. 'You make it sound dire, Governor. I wonder if you are aware of any trouble with the *auxilia* under your command; beyond diminished numbers, I mean? My brother commanded one of the units in the region, and he had concerns of his own that he shared with me,' he put in with deliberate vagueness.

Decius drummed his fingers on the table. 'What unit?'

'The Batavians at Batavis.'

'Ah yes. I thought your name sounded familiar. A competent officer, if a little fond of putting in requests.' He shrugged. 'I'm not *aware* of any specific trouble among the auxilia, I have to say. I have reassigned a few units from time to time to try and tighten border control, but no. Why?'

Rufinus folded his arms. 'Are you sure? Nothing at all has come to your attention recently?'

The governor's gaze strayed slowly across his table, noting the various documents and lists spread upon it. 'Just paperwork issues, but that's to be expected in a command such as this.'

'What issues, might I ask, sir?'

'I'm missing several months of the standard reports from a few of the units. But as I pointed out, they are at least as undermanned as the legion, if not more so. When I've occasionally sent reminders, the commanders have been apologetic, and generally blamed such matters on a lack of adequate clerks and time. And really, so little has changed for these units over the years that, short of variation in sick lists and the date at the top, it's hard to tell one month's report from the next. I've not chased them up avidly, because I find little joy in the thought of trawling through hundreds of nearly identical reports just to say I've been thorough in a job that no one really

117

cares about. Frankly, and I realise how bad this sounds, but I fully intend to fluff my way through my final year without rocking the boat, and then go home and let my successor see if he feels like putting things right.'

Rufinus tried to push the irritation that forged back down deep inside. It *did* sound bad. The man clearly was not right for the position and it could only be good for Raetia when he was replaced. But then, Rufinus had to allow a *little* sympathy for the man's plight. Rufinus might disapprove of the man's attitude, but at the same time, in honesty, he wasn't sure he'd have fared any better in the role, if what he said was true.

'You say *some* of the units failed to report, Governor. Not *all* of them?'

'No.'

'Can you tell me which ones?'

Decius threw him a look loaded with irritation, but leaned forward and started shuffling through the stacks of documents on his table. He picked up a list carefully penned on vellum and laid it beside him. Rufinus could just make out, upside down, the names of units and their garrison location, a similar document to one he had studied in his office before he left. The governor then started looking through the piles of reports on his desk and placing beads against names on the list. It took some time, for there were a lot of reports sitting waiting, but finally, the governor slid the piles back aside and turned the list round to face Rufinus.

'There you go. The persistent offenders.'

Rufinus peered down at the list.

CELEVSVM	ALA I SINGVLARIVM
SVRINA	COH I RAETORVM
SORVIODVNVM	COH II RAETORVM
ABVSINA	COH III TVNGRORVM
TANNVM	COH VI RAETORVM
BATAVIS	COH VIIII BATAVORVM

Rufinus felt alarms start to sound in his head at what he saw on the list. Five of the names perfectly matched with his working theory, and possibly the sixth too. He shivered.

'This cavalry unit, the Ala Singularium, do you have any knowledge of the unit? Of their origin?'

'I think they were something to do with the usurper Vitellius back in the bad old days. Other than that, I can't tell you much.'

Rufinus nodded to himself. Tungrians and Batavians, both Germanic tribes from the Rhenus. Three units of Raetians formed from the local peoples. And Vitellius had been the governor of Germania during the civil war over a century ago, so there was a very good chance that the cavalry ala at Celeusum was formed in Germania too. It was becoming rather hard to deny the connection he'd seen. Six auxiliary units with Germanic origins and manpower, all of whom had stopped sending reports to the governor.

'I'm aware of the locations of Batavis and Sorviodurum to the east, and of Abusina to the west. Where are the others?'

The governor waved a hand, drawing his attention to a map on the wall, and he strode over, looking at the sites marked. He found Abusina, where he'd watched that ritual, and was unsurprised to find Celeusum was the next fort along the frontier from there. Tracing a line along the border he found Tannum maybe thirty or forty miles further on, and then Surina close to the border with Germania, where the next governor would control the units.

Six units, spread along two hundred miles of Raetian border, all with Germanic links, all of whom had stopped reporting to the governor, and two of which, at least, had seen their commanders butchered. That amounted to a third of all the auxiliary manpower of the province! One thing was certain: Rufinus could hardly go back to Rome and resume his duties without finding out properly what was happening here. If he could uncover who was behind this and what the plan was, then he could pass the details to the authorities, and then go home. If Decius Barbatus did not have the resources to deal with it himself, he could always call upon the neighbouring governors. He looked back at the office's owner. The man was exhausted and filled with ennui, but for all the man's faults, Rufinus was at least convinced that the man was nothing to do with whatever was going on. He appeared to be largely useless, but at least he was likely trustworthy. Should Rufinus bring his theories to the man's attention yet?

No, he decided. As yet, he had worries and suspicions, but nothing specific, nothing to actually accuse anyone of, and no one particular to accuse yet, either. He could see the *edges* of the problem, but not the whole shape, and without more information all he had was rumour. He did not yet know what was actually going on. He needed more information. Perhaps the first thing he should want to know was who was currently in command of those six units. Of the two he had visited so far, the Ninth Batavorum were run by their very Germanic senior centurion, their prefect dead, and the commander of the Third Tungrorum at Abusina was also dead, though Rufinus had not seen who was now in charge. If this was the norm… if these six units had done away with their commanders and were now being run by men with Germanic sympathies, then that at least was something to tell the governor. And if those six men were no longer reporting to the governor, who *were* they reporting to? Who was *behind* all this? He needed to visit other forts on this list.

Decision made, he straightened.

'Governor, I need an escort.'

'I beg your pardon?'

'A bodyguard. A singulares. I am currently alone, but I fear there is something dreadful growing in Raetia, and the more I investigate, the more danger I perceive around me. I need to go to places where I may be viewed as an enemy, and to do so, I want good, armed men around me. I've seen your soldiers in Castra Regina. They are veterans. Solid. Trustworthy. Please would you arrange a detachment to serve with me during my time here?'

Decius's expression hardened. 'I have just got through explaining to you how we don't have enough men to do what we're *supposed* to do here, and you're seriously asking me to send men out with you on your travels, too?'

Rufinus felt another twitch of irritation. He let his cloak slip slightly so that his Praetorian brooch caught the light. 'Might I remind you, sir, that I hold high position in Rome, with the ear of the emperor.'

'You're a glorified bodyguard.'

Rufinus bridled. 'I am a personal friend of the emperor, and not without influence. One tent party. Eight men. That is all, and you will not find me ungrateful.'

Decius sagged again, the fight seeming to go out of him as fast as it had appeared. 'Eight men. Try not to get them killed. I need every man I can get.'

He rose from the desk, and as he crossed to the door, Rufinus was surprised at how tall and imposing the man was when he was not slouched in a chair. He had a feeling that perhaps Decius had been a strong man and a good officer in his time. He would try and find more sympathy for the man. This was not an easy position to find oneself in, after all, and recent experience with emperors had taught good men that failure at almost any level could easily be fatal.

The governor beckoned him with a finger, and left the office. Rufinus followed, and they crossed the basilica, then strode

121

through the courtyard and to the gate, where the governor waved to the duty centurion.

'Sir,' the man snapped to attention.

'Go find me Terentius Clemens.'

The centurion saluted and turned, marching away. Decius turned to Rufinus. 'Clemens is one of my best men, and he's been serving in the region all his career with the Third. He knows the border like few others. His contubernium I often assign as couriers or temporary assignments, for they are all more than competent riders and veterans with a commanding manner.' He turned a sharp look on Rufinus. 'I give you my best, because the last thing I want is to be questioned upon my return to Rome over how I managed to get a Praetorian officer killed. Do me the courtesy of trying not to get my best men killed in return?'

Rufinus nodded. 'Of course.'

They waited only a short while before the centurion reappeared with a soldier in tow. The man was in his mid-thirties, with short, sandy-coloured hair and a neatly trimmed beard. He wore a shirt of shiny bronze scale, and his uniform was neat. Half a dozen scars across his arms and a nick out of his chin spoke of a solidly martial history, too. Even at first glance, Rufinus could see why the governor valued him. He had an air of quiet competence about him. Rufinus listened as Decius gave the man his orders, Clemens simply nodding along, accepting without question. Once the exchange was complete, the governor turned back to Rufinus.

'When you are done with whatever you're doing, I would appreciate a full report. You'll be coming back here with my men anyway. If you are going to be longer than six days, I would like word sending via courier. You understand?'

Rufinus bowed his head. 'Of course, governor.'

'Then I leave you in Clemens' capable hands.' And with that, he turned and walked back across the headquarters towards his office.

The soldier thrust out a hand. 'Good to meet you…?'

'Rufinus. Tribune Gnaeus Marcius Rustius Rufinus.'

'I trust you intend to leave immediately, sir?'

'I do. My horses are over there with the slave. How long will it take to gather your men?'

'Quicker than a bird shits,' the man grinned. 'Follow me.'

The legionary waved over to the slave holding the horses and beckoned, and the lad followed them with the animals. As Clemens led them towards his barracks, Rufinus cleared his throat. 'The governor tells me you are familiar with the frontier forts and geography?'

Clemens nodded. 'I've served as a praepositus commanding small mixed units of legionaries and auxiliaries all along the Danubius and beyond, border to border, and back inland some way too.'

'And you are familiar with the forts of Celeusum, Tannum and Surina?'

'Of the three I've only spent time at Surina, but I've been to the others briefly, yes.'

'And what can you tell me of that fort's garrison, the First Raetorum?'

The man shrugged. 'Same as most other auxilia, sir. Local lads with a pompous commander sent from Rome, no offence intended. They drink a bit too much, try to shirk out of hard work, given half the chance. In other words, normal auxilia.'

Rufinus nodded. 'I want to visit those three forts at least. Perhaps not Sorviodurum, which is also on my list, since it's in the other direction. I want to get the general lie of the land in the forts, an idea of strengths, and of levels of loyalty and of sympathy for local tribes. Most importantly, I want to speak to the commanders, if there currently is one.'

Clemens' brow shot up at that, but he didn't question it.

'Do you speak the local language, sir?'

Rufinus shook his head. 'Not a word, I'm afraid. Do you have a man who does? It could prove very useful.'

Again, Clemens laughed. 'Speak it myself, sir. Served fourteen years on this frontier, so it's been something of a necessity. Two other lads in the contubernium speak it, too.'

'Good. Excellent, in fact.'

'You might find that a lot of the business at the forts you mentioned is carried out in the local tongue. If I'm not mistaken, they are all German units or local Raetian levies. These local lads tend to use their own language, because all the locals do. Only official correspondence through their commanders will usually be in Latin, because they never speak the local language. Never here long enough to need it. Do me a favour, sir.'

'Of course.'

'You outrank me, and what you say is law, but I know this area and its people. If I tell you to do something, you need to do it. You can ask me why later, when we're alone, but I ask you to defer to my local knowledge if I feel it's important.'

Rufinus bowed his head. 'Very sensible. I agree entirely.'

'Good. Hopefully this will all go smoothly, sir.' He eyed Orthus with interest. 'Your dog is good with strangers and horses, yes?'

Rufinus nodded. He thought so, at least.

Arriving at the barracks, Rufinus caught sight of a group of men loitering across the road beneath a veranda, and his skin prickled. He frowned. They looked an awful lot like the Germans he had fought back on the Rhenus, and were certainly not attired like legionaries. Before he could point them out, though, Clemens had led him in through a door, the slave waiting outside.

Seven men, all attired in uniform, if not armour, sat around the room, all looking at the door as the two men entered.

'We're off on a trip, lads,' Clemens announced. 'For the next few days we're to escort the tribune here to a few forts along the frontier. Saddle up. We're leaving straight away.'

'Before lunch?' one of them asked with a sly smile.

124

'We'll pick something up on the way. Sausage, probably. Arruntius tells me you're quite fond of a bit of local sausage,' Clemens grinned, waggling his eyebrows.

The soldier rolled his eyes as they all rose from their seats and shuffled around collecting their kit and bags. It did not take long for them to have everything ready, and as they moved to the door, Rufinus felt oddly comfortable in their presence. They reminded him of the men of his own unit when he'd served in the legions as a young man. Solid, ribald and competent. Soldiers born and bred.

Emerging into the light once more, his eyes fell straight on the small Germanic gathering across the road. They were watching him back, and their expressions were not the friendliest. He turned to Clemens, keeping his voice low.

'They're not legionaries. Who are they?'

Clemens shrugged. 'Native scouts. We use them for all business beyond the border. People think a frontier is a solid, impassable thing, but even with rivers and walls it isn't. Traders come from the north with amber and furs, and they take wine and oil and coin back with them. And there are friendly people out there with relatives on this side of the line. There's a lot more back-and-forth than people tend to realise.'

Rufinus snorted. 'When I served on the Danubius we were fighting the Marcomanni. The last thing you wanted was back-and-forth in those days.'

'The Danube makes a good, impassable frontier. In western Raetia, though, it's just a timber palisade and some watchtowers.'

'I'm not sure I trust those men,' Rufinus said, keeping his eyes on the scouts. 'Don't let any of them follow us.'

One of the legionaries in the group coughed quietly. 'You don't trust them, sir? Because they're Germans?'

'I have experience in that area,' Rufinus said. 'I found myself sword to sword with a few of them recently.'

'Not *all* Germans are animals,' the soldier grunted, his tone dark.

'No, but in this area, all the *animals* I've met were *Germans*,' Rufinus replied, rising to the bait.

Clemens turned, pointing at them both. 'Tribune, I would strongly advise keeping any opinion like that behind your teeth while you're here, for the good of everyone. And Claudius Ademus, bear in mind that the Tribune is both a visitor and a senior officer, and you might change his mind about the Germanic peoples easier by being friendly, rather than confrontational. Now wind it all in, suck it up and ready yourself. The nearest of the three forts is Celeusum, and that's about thirty miles from here, so we'll have to ride hard if we want to be there with light to spare.'

CHAPTER NINE

Celeusum

It was mid-afternoon when the cavalry fort came into view across the river, although it was hard to tell from the sky. As they had ridden west along the frontier, the clouds had gathered rapidly, rolling in from the north to fill the sky with a blanket the colour of old slate, the position of the sun only hinted at by a lighter patch in the gloom. Then the drizzle had begun – that very fine and light, yet constant precipitation that soaked deep into fabric, leaving the riders sodden and cold. Beside him, Orthus had become so waterlogged that he had almost changed shape, the wet flattening down his hair and leaving it dangling below him like a curtain. Rufinus was impressed that not once did he hear a man among them complaining about the conditions. True professionals.

He would need true professionals, he suspected.

Despite the weather, Rufinus squinted into the wet, trying to ascertain anything he could about Celeusum before they came too close, though it was difficult at such a distance. This was where the frontier departed from the line of the Danubius, the beginning of that land-bound stretch of rampart and towers about which the governor had complained. The great river flowed on slightly south of west, the scars of old abandoned forts along its bank as the border had advanced from the water to the north. Consequently, a bridge had been constructed over the river, which was here maybe a hundred paces wide, carrying the frontier road to the fort that lay perhaps a mile from the bank.

As they clopped across the damp timbers of the bridge, a little more detail became visible ahead. The walls of Celeusum were discernible as a darker grey line, the gate towers visible as a bulge at the centre. A sizeable civil settlement surrounded the fort on the south and east sides, blocking the view of the lower walls.

As he crossed the bridge, leading the riders, and trotted along the road towards the fort, Clemens pulled alongside.

'It might be best, sir, to let me take the lead until we're inside. You know how the auxilia generally feel about the legions, and that will go double for Praetorians, I think.'

Rufinus frowned. 'But you are legionaries too?'

The man smiled. 'We might be legionaries, but the Third Italica has worked with the local units often enough that they know us.'

Rufinus nodded at the sense of this. He wasn't entirely sure how he was going to handle matters in the fort. Since Batavis, he'd not had official direct contact with any other auxiliary unit, instead watching them from outside. If this unit *were* involved in whatever was going on, which seemed certain, then announcing his presence and asking questions was going to be provocative, to say the least. Still, he was going to learn nothing else from just watching, he was sure.

As they closed on the fort, they reached the edge of the civilian settlement. A bath house stood by the side of the road, and though it was not currently belching out smoke, it did at least look as though it had been used recently, which Rufinus saw as a hopeful sign. They rode between the first few buildings and quickly reached a fork in the road, where one branch ran north, alongside the fort's ditches, while the other did the same to the west. That last being the nearest gate, they turned in that direction. As they moved through the settlement, every pair of eyes that settled upon them seemed to contain malice.

'That's curious,' Clemens noted.

'What?'

'Have you noticed the locals?'

'Not very friendly,' Rufinus replied.

'And not very male. All women and children. Where are the menfolk, do you suppose?'

Rufinus frowned and looked about, noticing that fact for the first time. He jumped slightly in the saddle as a scream suddenly rang out from ahead and left, among the buildings. Orthus's ears pricked up, and Rufinus and Clemens looked at one another, and kicked their horses into speed, running along the line of houses and shops towards the sound, the dog and the rest of the riders close behind.

The cry had come from a gap between two buildings, and as they rounded the corner, Rufinus stared. Six men stood around the body of a seventh. The standing men were all garbed in the uniform of the auxilia, armed but unarmoured. Their hair was longer than military fashion usually dictated, and braided in the native style, and their beards had been grown out. They were very clearly Germans.

The body on the ground between them was not.

Most of the corpse was the same, garbed in auxiliary kit, but the head, which lay several feet from the rest, had neatly-shorn black hair and a tidily-trimmed beard, blood from the neck mixing with the rainwater that was gathering in puddles. One of the six men was wiping the blood from his long cavalry blade even as they turned to see the riders approaching.

'What is the meaning of this?' Rufinus demanded, all plans to let Clemens do the talking evaporating at the grisly and unexpected scene.

The six men focused on him, then, though he noted no particular respect, deference or fear among them, just that same disdainful anger he had seen in the eyes of so many others in this region. The one with the sword finished wiping it, held it up to examine it, then noted another spot and gave it a second clean, and only then looked back and them and spoke. What he said meant nothing to Rufinus, for it was in his native tongue. The Praetorian turned with a questioning look to Clemens.

'He says the man fell asleep on watch,' the legionary translated.
'And so he lost his head?'

There was a short incomprehensible exchange between
Clemens and the German, and then the legionary turned to
Rufinus once again.

'Apparently the man is a consistent offender. This is the fourth
time this year. He has already been punished repeatedly, and the
commander ordered his death only as a last resort.'

Rufinus's eyes narrowed. It that were the truth, then an
argument could be made that the punishment was within reason,
and the commander of the unit certainly had the authority to
order such a thing. But despite all that, suspicion continued to
lurk within Rufinus. Perhaps the man *had* fallen asleep. Perhaps
he'd done it time and again, and this was the final punishment.
But it was an impressive coincidence that the executioners were
all of native Germanic stock, while their victim displayed all the
signs of a Roman, drawn from another region. He looked at the
head. Thracian perhaps? Greek? Somewhere over in that region,
from the features. Certainly not Germanic, anyway.

'I think I might want to speak to the commander about this,'
he said, coldly.

Clemens breathed deep. 'Shall we, sir?'

Rufinus nodded, shook the gathered rain from his cloak hood,
then pulled it forward again, and the riders all turned and walked
their horses on towards the fort's southern gate. The walls of the
place were in good condition, no interval towers visible along the
length, and the gate stood open. There were men on the walls
and at the gate, and this time, Rufinus let Clemens take the lead as
they crossed the causeway over the fort's ditches.

The legionary reined in before the gate and its guards and
greeted them in their own tongue. There was another short
exchange, identification documents shown, and then Clemens
waved the others forward and walked his horse on, through the
arched gate and into the fort.

The first thing Rufinus noted here was a difference between the fort of Celeusum and those he'd seen at Batavis and Abusina. At both of those forts, they had clearly been under-strength, insufficient men on the walls, fewer among the buildings than he'd expected. Here, though, it appeared that the Ala Flavia Singularium were almost at full strength, which seemed odd, given the testimonies of both the centurion at Batavis and the governor at Castra Regina. The centurion had claimed his low numbers were largely due to his men being on detached duty at other locations. The governor had claimed that all units in his command were seriously below strength. Yet here, the fort veritably bustled with life.

There was an answer to that, suggested by simple logic.

'Some of these men are new,' Clemens noted, as if plucking the thought from Rufinus's mind.

He nodded. 'I was thinking the same thing. All the local units are under-strength, but suddenly this ala of cavalry isn't. And at the same time the civilian settlement outside the walls is missing its menfolk. That cannot be a coincidence.'

'Forced recruitment?' Clemens hazarded.

'I doubt the commander would be able to force a levy here. Besides, I'm not sure these Germans would willingly force their fellow tribesmen into service for Rome. The governor hinted that he's given his units freedom to recruit to fill their numbers. Clearly the commander here has taken him up on that and offered mass recruitment. But that leaves a question unanswered.'

'Oh?'

'The governor made it clear that Raetia is not the wealthiest of provinces, and that the imperial administration has not allocated funds to allow for extra recruitment since the war. If there has been no financial incentive to sign up for the auxilia for the past twenty years, why *now* are the locals suddenly happy to join the army?'

Clemens nodded at that, sinking into deep thought.

Rufinus looked about as they moved through the fort towards the headquarters. He was growing so used to the unpleasant looks the locals threw him that he hardly noticed them now, for they had become the norm. It was clear now that some of these men were indeed recent levies from the local settlement, wearing what uniform and armour was available, but with insufficient equipment to garb and arm them all, so some were still partly attired in their native clothes, some carrying ring-pommel swords of Germanic origin.

Rain dropped in heavy blatters from the various veranda roofs to the stone of the streets, and Rufinus shook his hood once more to remove the worst of the moisture.

Whatever men were doing stopped as the party of riders approached, and all conversations fell silent as they neared. Rufinus could not help but notice how the doors of the timber buildings they passed all closed as they came near. He was sure immediately that things were being hidden from him, which made him all the more intrigued.

By the time they reached the headquarters and dismounted, Rufinus had also noted that every single man he had seen on their way through the fort had appeared to be a native of the region, or at least of Germanic or Raetian origin. Was the man who lost his head in the village outside the last non-local? Contemplating the worrying question, Rufinus stepped around a deep puddle and shook the rain from his cloak once more.

At the headquarters doorway, he handed his reins to one of the other riders and gestured for Clemens to join him. He then approached the gate, and the man on guard straightened just a little.

'Business?' was all he said, brusquely and in a thick German accent, although it was at least refreshing to hear Latin used, however badly.

'We have come from Castra Regina on the authority of the Legatus Titus Decius Barbatus. I need to see your commander.'

He turned with a frown as he realised that Clemens was speaking simultaneously, translating that into the local Germanic tongue just a few words behind. His irritation mounted as he realised that the soldier on guard was actually listening to Clemens instead of him, and nodding along. The man jerked a thumb over his shoulder.

Rufinus, Clemens and Orthus strode through the arch and into the courtyard of the headquarters.

No statues at all here, Rufinus noted. He suspected a vague mark on the flagged ground over to one side revealed where a statue had stood until relatively recently, whether it be of a god or an emperor, but there was certainly nothing here now. The differences between this place and the other two forts he'd visited were marked, and slightly worrying. They certainly didn't alleviate his fears. On the surface it looked more like this fort was functioning normally, but attention to the details suggested otherwise. There was something just oddly... *sinister*, about the place.

Another soldier in the courtyard barked something at them in German, and Clemens replied in kind. The soldier nodded and beckoned, leading them into the basilica across the yard. As they entered, Rufinus's attention darted across to the shrine of the standards. It appeared to be full at first glance, standards, flags and other regalia in evidence, though he didn't have the opportunity to examine them closely as the two men were led away towards the commander's office. As they approached, Rufinus removed his riding cloak, shook the worst of the moisture from it, and then folded it and draped it over his arm. Orthus was leaving a trail of water behind as his thick mane drained.

A knock at the door, a brief exchange in the native tongue, and the door was left open for them, the soldier stepping away. Rufinus let Clemens lead the way, and the legionary walked into the office first, Rufinus following and closing the door. He turned and focused on the man behind the desk. He was not dressed in the tell-tale striped tunic of an officer, but just a single glance told Rufinus that the man was a decurion, the cavalry's closest thing to a centurion, and a veteran of some years.

Orthus stepped into the open space and chose that moment to shake wildly, sending droplets of rain in a shower in every direction. The decurion glared at the dog, but said nothing, and lifted his eyes to the visitors with a question.

'Where is your prefect?' Rufinus asked, bluntly.

Clemens flashed him a frown. The man had expected to take the lead.

The cavalryman frowned at Rufinus, not rising from his seat, and his expression was not one of deference. 'The prefect suffered a riding accident a month ago. Broke his back. It took him an unfortunate number of days to die,' the man announced with matching bluntness.

Another officer gone. A suspicious accident that had happened at around the same time as Rufinus's brother being removed from command at Batavis.

'And you have not had a replacement in a month?'

The decurion shrugged. 'We sent the paperwork to the governor. Of course, it may have been waylaid. There is much banditry in the region.'

'How inconvenient for you,' growled Rufinus.

'You are not the second in command,' Clemens said to the man. 'I know Flavius Catumerus, and have worked alongside him before. Where is he?'

This apparently took the man by surprise, though he recovered very quickly with just a flash of uncertainty. 'Catumerus passed away of the Gallic disease a few market weeks back.'

'Did he indeed?'

The decurion nodded, then sat, silent for a time, before asking 'so what can I do for you?'

Rufinus stepped forward. 'I am monitoring manpower levels for the governor. The ongoing crisis of recruitment in Raetia needs to be dealt with, and it seems that a number of the units in the region have not returned their figures to the governor for several months.'

'Bandits,' the decurion said dismissively. 'Tch.'

'Tch, indeed,' Rufinus replied, fighting to restrain his irritation. 'I started my rounds in the east, with the fort at Batavis, and am working west through the province, visiting any fort for which the governor has no recent strength reports. Thus far I have found those forts to be severely under-strength and lacking sufficient manpower to operate as an effective unit. That does not seem to be the case at Celeusum. I am hoping you can provide me with numbers, and explain your impressive retention of manpower.'

The decurion's eyes narrowed, betraying a touch of suspicion, and then he took a deep breath, nodded, and sat back, folding his hands behind his head.

'I have yet to do the weekly staff report, but at my last count we were at full strength of five hundred and ten, allowing for the current lack of prefect and senior decurion, though eleven of the men included in that count are on sick.'

'I think you mean five hundred and *nine*, unless you plan to stick the head back on the man we saw executed outside.'

Surprise and guarded suspicion once more flashed across the man's face, before he nodded. 'An unfortunate case, but the man was a serial offender, and I needed to make an example for the benefit of our new recruits.'

Rufinus took that in without further comment. 'It would appear that your recruitment drive took place in the civil settlements around Celeusum?'

'Of course. Where else would I go to find men?'

'And they all signed on to the auxilia willingly for the standard terms of service? You offered no bonus? Might I ask what incentive could have drawn so much fresh recruitment attention from the locals?'

The decurion shrugged again, a gesture that was starting to irritate Rufinus. 'We appealed to their sense of community. After all, the men serving at Celeusum are their fellow tribesmen on the whole, and their role here is to defend this land from any trouble. Better to live here and receive pay from Rome than live here for nothing.'

'How very neighbourly, or entrepreneurial, of them,' Rufinus said archly, fighting to control his temper and feeling his lip start to twitch. He had never heard such a blasé line of utter horse shit. The local Raetians had failed to take the oath with the auxilia for twenty years and then suddenly a decurion appeals to their community spirit and they flock to the banner? He wanted to call the man out, but was acutely aware that doing so might not be a good idea in their current position, that being around fifty to one odds.

'Might I be able to see the recruitment paperwork?'

Without blinking, the decurion graced him with an oily smile. 'I wish I could, but we bundled them all up to send to the governor's office for copying and storage...'

'And *bandits* must have got them,' Rufinus finished for the man. He turned to Clemens. 'I think I have all the information I need from here.'

'Please pass on my thanks to the governor,' the decurion said with only a slight curve of the lip, 'and my apologies for any missing paperwork.'

Rufinus glared at the man, almost astounded at his bare-faced affrontery. To his private delight, Orthus seemed to pick up on his mood and chose that moment to cock his leg and take an extended leak against the table leg. Rufinus waited patiently until he was done, the decurion glaring horribly at them, then gestured to Clemens who nodded in response, and they both turned, opened the door and walked out of the office, the dog following on. The basilica hall was empty, and so before they left, Rufinus diverted and strode over to the chapel of the standards, peering through the iron grille at the small room. Everything was there and polished up, and it took him a few moments to spot what was wrong.

The cavalry carried fewer standards than an infantry cohort. Four items stood against the back wall amid the other riches of the unit. The draco – the standard shaped like a dragon's head, with a material 'tail' that flapped along behind – was present and correct. The vexillum – the small, square flag on a spear top – usually bore a symbol or an image of a god that had meaning for the unit. This one bore a stag, which was unusual, but not worrying in particular. The main unit standard looked fine at first glance – a spear tip above a large silvered disc with the face of a bearded god, and below that the unit's stamp, on a panel bordered with tassels. Then, when one looked a little closer, it became clear that the unit's name on that panel, ALA I FL SING, had been crudely scratched out. That was a lot more worrying, but the most worrying and telling of all was the imago, the spear carrying the disc with the emperor's image. The disc was still there, but the embossed imperial image had been hammered flat to the extent it could have been anything, from an emperor to a piglet.

'Does that look to you like they're renouncing their oath?'

Clemens shivered. 'It does, though I very much hope that's not the case. Let's leave Celeusum, and not slowly.'

'Why so fast, now in particular?'

'Because while I'm not sure I believe that the prefect died in an accident, I *certainly* don't believe that story about the senior decurion,' the legionary said as he turned and marched towards the exit.

'Why?'

'You know how the Gallic disease spreads?'

Rufinus nodded. It was the colloquial term for one of the sexual diseases that was the subject of regular outbreaks among the military around the more disreputable brothels, but it was very rarely fatal unless a man didn't get the medicus to treat it.

'Flavius Catumerus didn't do that sort of thing.'

'What?'

'He was a…' Clemens lowered his tone to a whisper. 'He was a *Christian*. He didn't believe in sex outside marriage. He was waiting until he got his retirement and chose a wife. If there's one man in the *world* I know didn't die of the Gallic disease, it was him.'

Rufinus shivered. So, in *this* place not only the commander had been removed, but also his second in command who, by the sound of it was a man entirely above corruption. 'Come on.'

They crossed the open space in that fine drizzle, and dipped back out through the arch of the main entrance, where the others were waiting for them with the horses, sodden and bored.

'Saddle up,' Clemens told them. 'Time to move on, and sharpish.'

The men looked at one another in surprise. 'Sir, it'll start to get dark in an hour or two. Shouldn't we stay and use whatever barracks they can find for us overnight?'

Clemens and Rufinus shared a look, and the Praetorian turned to the speaker. 'This place is so over-manned right now there is nowhere for us to stay.' He glanced again at Clemens, who nodded. 'There's a good local place about four miles from here I've used before,' he said. 'We'll stay there. We need to leave by the east gate and head around the fort from here.'

Rufinus wasn't convinced about the wisdom of staying in any 'local' place, good or not, but he certainly didn't want to stay at Celeusum, and was willing to defer to the legionary's local knowledge in such cases. Along with the others, he hauled himself up into his saddle and turned his horse. As he did so, he glanced down the road along which they'd arrived and paused. Amid the myriad unfriendly faces there, one stood out. He pointed at the man, a rider on horseback, approaching the centre of the fort up that road.

'I'm sure he's one of the men we saw opposite your barracks in Castra Regina,' he said.

Clemens shrugged. 'I'm not overly familiar with the scouts. Could be.'

'Don't all Germans look alike?' grumbled the one called Claudius Ademus who'd pulled him up on his words about Germans back at the legionary fortress. Rufinus glanced at him, presuming that to have been a barbed sarcastic comment. He ignored the man and turned back as the nine of them began to ride away along that road towards the east gate.

They exited the fort without obstruction, and crossed the ditches using another causeway, back to the civil settlement. Rufinus felt anger and disgust fighting for supremacy as his gaze fell on the shrine ahead, on the northern fringe of the village. Once again, it was formed of three stone pillars with spaces for decapitated heads, with misshapen carvings atop, and *once again*, those apertures were occupied. Several heads were relatively recent, and any of them could have been the prefect or the senior decurion, but it was the *middle* one that drew his attention. A fresh head, still with some colour, black hair and neat beard – the soldier they had seen being executed upon their arrival at the place. The auxiliaries who'd carried out the execution were standing around in a knot by the shrine, their gruesome work done, and they were laughing and joking, presumably at the expense of their victim.

Rufinus turned away from them. He didn't want to see that head particularly at the moment. Severed heads were becoming a little too totemic of his Raetian visit for his liking, and brought back memories of Publius. As they rounded the fort's corner and set off on the military road that led slightly north of west, following the frontier, Clemens pulled alongside once more.

'I'm starting to see why you're investigating these places.'

'Something is very wrong,' Rufinus replied.

'Yes. I've been to Celeusum a few times, and I've never seen it like that. I wonder what they were doing behind all those doors they were closing to us.'

'I don't know, but the place was very busy. It had the same feel as you get in a campaign base just before the off.'

Clemens nodded. 'I know what you mean. Preparing for something big. And I don't like that the two senior officers happen to have died.'

'Then you'll love it when I tell you that I found the body of the prefect at Abusina murdered. Sacrificed in a pond. And the prefect of the cohort at Batavis, my *brother* no less, had his head taken hundreds of miles from home beside the Rhenus while he was trying to find me to tell me something. I'm starting to get an idea of what that was.'

'Shit,' Clemens whispered.

'Yes. And *neck-deep*, I fear.'

'What now?'

Rufinus shrugged. 'We stay the night in this local place of yours, and tomorrow morning we ride to the next fort on my list.'

'To Tannum, then, and I hope the place is not as dangerous and unfriendly as Celeusum has become.'

Rufinus nodded. 'I was toying with the idea of being a lot more subtle and circumspect next time, for the sake of our safety, but I think I've changed my mind. Being fairly direct is allowing us to catch them out and identify lies, and I think I'll need to do that again next time, at Tannum, if we are to stand any chance of finding out what's really going on. What can you tell me about Tannum?'

'I know it well. Better than this place by far. It's one of the most northerly forts on the frontier, and by far the closest to the actual border line.'

'Border line?'

'The actual frontier is a rampart, ditch and palisade, with watchtowers. It runs to the north of most forts all the way from Germania to the Danubius just above where we just crossed. Most of the time it's a few miles north of the forts, but at Tannum the frontier runs within a spear's throw of the fort walls.'

'And the fort and its garrison?'

'Well, they've changed fairly recently. The fort was only rebuilt in stone about twenty years ago by the Second Aquitanorum, a bunch of mad Gauls, but by the time they left three years ago, it was already falling apart. Shoddy Gaulish workmanship, I guess. We went as part of a joint force with the new Sixth Raetian to do a few repairs on the fort's main buildings. Not been back for over a year, so it might have fallen apart again by now, of course. It had a little civil settlement around it, nothing like the size of the one we've just left. As for the Sixth themselves? They're a bit nomadic from what I know. In less than a century they served in Noricum, Germania and here, and even in Raetia they've moved at least four times.'

Rufinus walked his horse on. A Raetian unit who kept getting moved around raised one major question: why? What was it about them that kept them on the move? And was it the cohort's doing that they kept moving, or was it the authorities that kept moving them?'

Something was nagging at him, and he couldn't quite put his finger on what it was. He rode quietly, letting his mind go blank, using his senses, leaving himself open to the world, trusting his intuition.

He felt it again and turned. Back in the village outside the camp, he could just see those six soldiers still standing by the shrine, little more than tiny figures now, and they were not alone. They were speaking to a man on a horse.

'We're being followed,' Rufinus said, turning to Clemens.

'What?'

'That horseman I saw in the fort, he's talking to the men at the shrine.'

'Could be perfectly innocent?'

'I don't think so. He's followed us from Castra Regina, after all.'

He turned back to look once more, and now there was no sign of the rider. For a moment, he wondered if he'd imagined it, but quickly threw that idea aside. The six soldiers were still there, and he knew what he'd seen.

'*I* can't see him,' Clemens said, looking back.

'No, he's gone.'

'Well, there's not much we can do about it now,' Clemens said. 'Let's just get to our overnight stop.'

Rufinus nodded. And then, on to Tannum…

CHAPTER TEN

Tannum

The rain was holding off now, though the sky remained leaden with portent, and the breeze was not warm. Rufinus glanced around at Clemens, who was riding alongside with the same taut, worried expression as his own. Orthus had dropped back a little, to trot alongside Oclatius, one of the legionaries, who had taken a shine to the dog and kept sneaking him pieces of dried pork.

Ahead lay the next fort on their list, although they could not see it yet. This part of the frontier ran over gently undulating ground, low grassy slopes and small areas of woodland, and it was hard to see at any distance. Occasionally, as they had closed on the place, they had seen the distant shapes of towers, which marked the line of the actual frontier, but it appeared that the fort of Tannum lay in a dip, rather than atop one of the slopes, a peculiarity of planning that was rare.

'Do you think this is the civil settlement?' Rufinus muttered, looking at the huddle of buildings ahead.

'No. Just a local village. Beyond that, in the dip, that's where the fort and its vicus lie.'

Rufinus nodded, eying the village. Formed of perhaps twenty buildings, the native settlement had clearly drawn on Roman culture and technology, from its shingled roofs to the stone footings, and even rudimentary paving to keep the locals' feet out of the worst of the muck. Near the edge of the village was a small shrine by a pool, presumably to some local god, but at least it did not feature stone pillars filled with heads for a change. A building near the centre with a wide canopy, held up by sawn posts, at the front looked as though it might be a tavern of some kind.

'Maybe we can get some advance information here, about the fort?'

'Perhaps,' Clemens said, though with more than an edge of doubt.

They rode slowly into the centre of the small village and reined in outside that building. As they approached, figures began to appear at doors and between the houses, mangy dogs and grubby children, all watching the strangers, none with a welcoming face. Rufinus beckoned to Clemens and, while the others remained on their horses, the two Romans strode over to the building and beneath the canopy. Orthus was torn for a moment, between following his master or staying near a new source of meaty treats, but finally trotted on after Rufinus. An old man sat on a bench over to one side, a stick in one hand and a wooden beaker in the other. His white hair was long and wispy, and so was his beard. He looked a little on the feeble side, but the look he threw them was as belligerent as any Rufinus had seen.

What passed for tables and chairs seemed to be logs and sawn stumps, polished only by repeated use. The door stood open, and Rufinus was about to walk over to it, when a figure emerged from the gloom within. Rufinus turned to Clemens and spoke quietly.

'Whatever they drink around here, order two of them for us.'

Clemens nodded, and addressed the local in his own tongue. Naturally, Rufinus had no idea what the man's reply was, but the tone of voice in which it was delivered was not encouraging.

'He says he doesn't serve our sort,' Clemens explained.

Rufinus rolled his eyes. 'Ask him if he has any news or gossip about Tannum,' Rufinus urged, as he fished in his purse and pulled out two gold aurei bearing the image of Commodus. He contemplated dropping one back in, but then held them out on the palm of his hand.

As he offered the coins, Clemens spoke once more to the man. Again the response did not sound overly-positive, and when the legionary seemed to press the issue, the old man in the corner joined in, snapping something angrily in their native tongue. Rufinus wondered if the owner had not yet noticed the coins in his hand. Two gold aurei was probably enough to buy his entire establishment off him, maybe even the *village*. He took a few steps towards the man and thrust out the hand with the coins in.

The German barked something at him and slapped his hand away, sending the gold coins flying out into the street. Orthus let out a low warning growl, while Rufinus stared, but Clemens quickly crossed to him and grabbed his arm.

'I think it's time we left.'

'Yes,' Rufinus agreed, emphatically, 'I think you're right.'

Rejoining the men out in the street, Rufinus wondered momentarily whether to scrabble around and find his two coins, but with distinct regret decided against it. Two aurei was a lot of money, but these people were already angry and unpleasant, and it would hardly look dignified for a Roman tribune to be on his knees in the mud, scrabbling around. Romanitas was going to have a high cost today. Besides, Orthus was still growling, and now his teeth were starting to show. If they didn't leave, it was entirely possible the dog might attack the man.

Rufinus pulled himself up into the saddle, and in moments they were off again, trotting through the village and away from that horrible place and the gathered locals with their glares of hatred.

'That was new,' Rufinus said as they left the village.

'What?'

'Open hostility. I've not found northern Raetia to be particularly friendly, but that's the first time a local has been openly belligerent. I swear he'd have tried to punch me if we hadn't left. These people are nominally *Romans*, Clemens. They've been within imperial borders since the days of Hadrian, for eighty-odd years.'

The legionary nodded slowly. 'I suppose we need to remember that they are the same people as those on the other side of the border, though. Eighty years is not enough to change that. There is a tendency among the people on this side of the border to refer to their cousins outside as the 'free peoples'.'

'But that's ridiculous. These people are free too. They're just free Romans instead of free barbarians.'

'That's because you're *thinking* like a Roman. *They* don't.' He sighed. 'But I agree, anyway, to an extent. I've served in this region for many years, and while there have always been pockets of resentment among the natives, I've never seen it on this scale, either in numbers or in viciousness. I've never been spoken to like that, certainly.'

'Something has changed in this region,' Rufinus said. 'It feels like the whole of Raetia is on the edge of revolt, and fully a third of the auxilia, who are supposed to keep the land under control, seem to be as rebellious as the locals. They *are* locals, I suppose.'

'Remember, too, that we are as close to the border now as you can get without standing *on* it. That might have something to do with the intensity of native resentment. Here, they are closer to the "free peoples" than elsewhere.'

Rufinus huffed. This place was getting to him.

'What's the plan?' Clemens asked.

'I'm not inclined to pull punches now, and I don't think subterfuge will work. We go in as who we are: representatives of Rome, and of the governor and of the legion, and we find the commander, if there is one, and make enquiries again. Depending on what we learn, we might press on to the next fort, or I might be tempted to take what we have back to Castra Regina and warn the governor.'

'Warn him of what?'

'I'm not completely sure yet, but I have a feeling Raetia is heading for a revolt like that of the Batavi all those years ago, which nearly lost us Germania.'

They rode on in silence, over a gentle hill among woodlands, and as they crested the slope, Tannum came into view. The fort was a reasonable size, surrounded by a triple ditch. It looked quite neat and reasonably busy from what he could see at this distance and angle. A civil settlement lay scattered around the southern and eastern sides. To Rufinus's surprise, a small turf-and-wood amphitheatre sat at the edge, and there appeared to be something happening there. Maybe fifty paces from the northern fort ditches, the frontier lay in full view, a rampart and fence that marched across the landscape, towers every half mile, literally cutting the German world in half. The sight of that formidable barrier brought back what Clemens had said in the village about the locals and their brethren on the other side. It did not escape Rufinus's notice that he could actually see the distant shape of a Germanic village maybe a mile beyond the rampart. The locals could actually *see* their cousins. Wooden gates were evident beside each tower, allowing movement across the border, but only when controlled by the men in those towers.

The civilian settlement, while not deserted, certainly did not appear to be busy, and as they moved among the first buildings, the locals gave them the same glowers of distrust and hatred as he had seen all along the border.

'This way,' he said, earning a surprised look from Clemens, as he turned his mount and led the riders away from the fort, along one of the other roads that led east, off towards the woodland. The others moved closer together, unsure of what was happening, and starkly aware of the general air of aggression around them.

'What are we doing?' Clemens asked.

Rufinus pointed ahead in answer. At the edge of the settlement, along this road, they could see the amphitheatre. The circular turf embankment was terraced with two tiers of wooden seats, and they could see locals atop the mound, watching what was happening, as well as a few people in the uniforms of the auxilia.

They rode towards the venue, whose central arena was surrounded by its own wooden fence. The entrance was a simple gap in the turf embankment, allowing access to the centre, which also enabled the riders to see along the opening and into the heart of the place.

Rufinus hauled on the reins just outside, along with the others, and peered at the arena.

There was a fight going on. It looked oddly normal to see what appeared to be two gladiators hammering at one another in the arena, to the cheers and boos of a crowd. He peered into the action and picked out more detail. It was not an execution, which was a relief, for that was what he'd been half expecting since he first noticed activity there. In fact, it appeared to be two roughly evenly matched warriors, one armed and dressed in the gear of a Roman auxiliary, the other garbed like a Germanic tribesman. He watched for a while, and determined that the two combatants had to be there of their own volition, for they were clearly sparring, rather than genuinely attempting to kill one another.

'What do you make of that?'

'I don't know,' Clemens replied. 'Entertainment? Training? Maybe settling an argument?'

Rufinus nodded, not entirely sure what he himself thought. 'Let's go.'

He turned his horse and led the riders back along the road, through the village, and towards the fort. The gate stood open, men in uniform and armour to each side, on duty. As they approached, the two men stepped closer together, blocking their way.

'State your identity and business,' one called as they approached.

Rufinus frowned. He'd not expected Latin. Thus far, the further into the frontier he got, the less he was hearing his own language. It was a welcome sign, and, added to the amphitheatrical combat, seemed more Roman than anything he'd encountered for some time.

Perhaps this fort was different? Perhaps it would allay some of his fears when he left here? Who was the garrison here again? The Sixth Raetian Cohort. The ones who kept moving from place to place.

Clemens was looking at him. No German translation was needed here, and Rufinus was back in command. He straightened in the saddle.

'Tribune Gnaeus Marcius Rustius Rufinus and a legionary detachment from Castra Regina on behalf of Governor Titus Decius Barbatus. I need to speak to your commander.'

The two soldiers snapped to attention and stepped back to the sides, opening the way through the gate. Rufinus inclined his head at them and then kicked his mount into motion, leading the others into the fort, Orthus back beside Oclatius, looking hopeful. The impression of normality did not end at the gate guards and the amphitheatre. The moment they passed inside, the whole place had the feel of a standard active auxiliary fort. The buildings were all intact, clean, but worn, smoke rising from a few flues here and there, soldiers about their business, some on duty, some not, some armoured, some not. If Rufinus were going to draw on one thing, it would be that there were not quite so many soldiers as there should be, but that was to be expected, given what the governor had told him about unit strengths.

One thing nagged at him, though, and he leaned towards Clemens as they rode.

'The men at the gate never asked for our identification.'

Clemens frowned. 'That's right.'

At every fort or fortress he had visited, he had been asked for his papers or identification. Here, though the soldiers had seemed perfectly normal and very professional, for some reason they had not done so.

'I wonder why. Curious.'

'Still,' Clemens noted, 'things seem more on-track here. The place seems active and normal.'

Rufinus chewed his lip as they passed a fabrica building, one end of the block open to the air, where the forges and water buckets were very much in evidence. Something occurred to him.

'*Very* active, in fact,' he said. 'I've been in hundreds of forts over the years, but the only time I've ever seen workshops that busy, crammed with men, was during the wars with the Marcomanni.'

Clemens shrugged. 'If there's been fresh recruitment, maybe they've stepped up production to arm and equip everyone.'

Rufinus nodded, saying nothing. That made sense, but it did little to ease his disquiet. They rode on past the granary, and Rufinus raised himself in his saddle to peer over the loading platform and through the open door as they passed. The place looked empty at a glance. All these soldiers and no grain? Perhaps that was what the men of Batavis had been loading their carts for?

The headquarters building sat in the usual place, at the centre of the fort, and Rufinus approached the guard there, dismounting at the last moment. 'I would like to see your commander,' he announced.

The soldier nodded and whistled. Another man appeared in the doorway from inside and bowed his head, then gestured for them to follow. Rufinus waited as Clemens also dismounted, and he and Orthus trotted forward, then they followed the soldier inside. As the man walked ahead across the compound, Rufinus leaned close to his legionary friend and spoke in a low whisper.

'Didn't ask who we were at the door.'

Clemens nodded. 'And this one didn't ask where we were going. Maybe he heard us talking before his friend whistled.'

'*Maybe*,' Rufinus hissed doubtfully. 'But does this not feel to you like we're expected?'

The legionary frowned. 'That scout?'

'I reckon so. I've not seen him or his horse anywhere, but he could easily have ridden past us that first night when we stayed in the local inn. I think he got ahead and came straight here to warn them we were on the way. That explains these little lapses in procedure, but might also explain why everything looks so suspiciously normal here.'

Clemens nodded, unable to reply, for they had crossed the courtyard now and were about to enter the basilica hall, their escort close by once more. As a last thought before they stepped inside, he looked around the open space. No statue was evident, but there was a rather tell-tale pile of fragments at one side. Just a small heap of broken marble lumps, but he could see pieces of curly hair and even curlier beard among them. It could have been a god. Or it could have been the emperor. Whatever it *had* been, it wasn't now.

In the basilica, he glanced towards the shrine of the standards as they passed, and was oddly unsurprised to see that it was empty. He tapped Clemens and pointed at it, as their guide led the way, unaware of the exchange. Clemens nodded.

The sound of another door drew their attention, and they turned their heads as they walked. A man had emerged from another office at the far end of the hall, and was walking towards the exit. Rufinus's pulse quickened as he recognised the scout he'd first seen at Castra Regina, then at the head shrine at Celeusum. He grabbed Clemens and hissed 'follow him.'

Clemens nodded and turned, hurrying back just as the German slipped out of the door.

Their guide stopped, frowning.

'Should we...?' he began.

'He will be fine. Let's see the commander.'

The man reached the office, rapped once on the door, opened it and then gestured for Rufinus to enter. As he did so, it once more occurred to him that the soldier had not needed to announce the visitor. They were definitely expected.

He entered the commander's office, with Orthus padding along beside him. The dog appeared tense, perhaps once again picking up on his master's mood. The door closed behind him, and Rufinus peered at the man behind the desk in surprise.

Given what they had encountered so far, he'd no idea who he would be shown to at Tannum, probably a centurion of one grade or another. One thing he had really not expected was to find a prefect in his striped tunic seated behind the table. The man was of medium height and build, attired neatly and in good quality uniform, with a nice sword lying sheathed on the desk to one side. He looked every bit the auxiliary prefect in his place of command. His hair was black, gradually fading to grey, his chin clean shaven, cheek bones high and eyes clear and bright, and intelligent. One eyebrow rose as Rufinus stopped in front of his desk.

'Good afternoon.'

Rufinus inclined his head. 'Prefect.'

'Tiberius Claudius Veremundus, commanding Sixth Raetorum. What can I do for you?'

Rufinus frowned, desperately trying to marshal his thoughts. He felt rather wrong-footed. Whatever he might have expected, he'd found something else, and was now not sure how to proceed. Somehow, a confrontational approach seemed inappropriate in the face of Veremundus.

'I am investigating unit strengths for the governor. Your cohort is among a small number who have consistently failed to return strength reports to Castra Regina.'

The prefect gave a tired sigh. 'Mea culpa, I'm afraid. No one to blame that on but myself. There are three major reasons, though. Firstly my only competent clerk retired four months ago, and while I'm trying to train up a replacement, my command consists of local Raetian recruits. Those who have a reasonable command of Latin still have atrocious writing. As such, ever since Simplex's leaving, I have taken care of all the paperwork myself, which is extremely time consuming, and usually has to take second place behind my other duties. Then there is the fact that we have been attempting recruitment drives as per the governor's standing instructions, but not all new recruits pass their initial training, which means that my numbers rise and fall rather drastically several times a month. Keeping track of them is becoming a job in itself. And then there is, I'm afraid, the fact that I detest paperwork, and find that I'm putting off the jobs, even without intending to.'

Rufinus listened, frowning. It was a perfectly reasonable explanation.

'I have got this month's almost ready, if you would like to see them,' Veremundus said, pulling a document from a stack and tossing it over towards Rufinus. 'It doesn't yet have on it the men assigned to frontier towers, but it would be ready by tomorrow. If you would like, you can make a copy of it to take with you?'

Rufinus shook his head. 'That won't be necessary for now, Prefect.'

He was struggling. He'd had all his suspicions torn from him, and wasn't quite sure what to say or ask. He certainly wasn't about to accuse this man, who was clearly an equestrian officer assigned from Rome, of fomenting rebellion in the province. He floundered, and found himself picturing the fort as he'd passed through it.

'Might I ask why your granary is empty, Prefect?'

The man gave an easy smile. 'Our granary has sprung a leak, or rather, *several* leaks. The roof has holes in three places, and the grain was beginning to go bad with the recent spate of rain. I took the liberty of paying off the locals in the settlement for permission to use their granary, and moved all our stock there for safety while my men effect repairs.'

Rufinus nodded. Very sensible.

'And the statue in the headquarters courtyard? There appears to have been a problem?'

The man's expression darkened. 'Yes. We had a bit of trouble there. At great expense, a few months back I commissioned a new statue of the emperor for the headquarters, as we still had Commodus on display in our fort. I unveiled it one day, and the next, four drunken soldiers took hammers to it. It turns out that Commodus was rather popular in this region. His peace settlements on his accession were generous and favoured the tribes north of the Danubius. When I took him away and replaced him with an emperor who's still an unknown quantity to them, they got drunk and angry and took matters into their own hands.'

'I trust they were punished?'

The prefect nodded. 'Although I value veteran manpower, so I did not harm them. The four men have been on latrine duty for months, and their wages are being docked to pay for a replacement statue.'

Rufinus sagged. Good. Everything seemed to be perfectly normal.

'But your unit standards? The chapel is empty.'

'They are being repaired, spruced up and cleaned. You may have seen the fabricae at work as you passed. With new recruits coming in, I wanted to have standards of top quality.'

Again, Rufinus nodded. 'One other thing that interests me is your amphitheatre. It is in use. Looks like an interesting bout. Is it your doing, or the work of the locals?'

The prefect smiled. 'We have taken to using it for initial training of recruits. I have the potential soldier adopt the appropriate kit and then face someone dressed in native manner, to get some idea of their skills and any sloppy tendencies. It is the perfect way to weed out those totally unsuitable before spending time and money attempting to train them up.'

'Very sensible, Prefect, yes.'

A moment's silence settled as he tried to think of anything else he might ask. It had all been so perfectly reasonable. There was nothing wrong at Tannum, no matter what the other forts might be doing.

In that silence, he frowned. Somewhere outside there was a sudden surge of noise, and amid it a muffled scream. Rufinus felt the hair rising on the back of his neck. He straightened. 'What was that?'

'Oh dear,' the prefect said with a sigh, leaning forward and placing his hands on the desk, 'you were not supposed to hear that.'

Rufinus frowned, realising now that something was very wrong. He sensed movement behind him. Why had he not looked around when he entered? Someone must have been in the corner behind the door. He started to turn, but something hit him very hard on the back of the head and his eyes defocused, flashing with white pain. He staggered, trying to hold together what remained of his wits, as the prefect now rose from his seat and started to move.

He turned on his assailant, an auxiliary soldier with a stout ash cudgel, opening his mouth.

'Balls,' Rufinus snapped.

Orthus moved in a heartbeat, for he had already been tensing for the pounce. His jaws closed on the soldier's groin, a mouthful of tunic, loincloth, and soft flesh, and tightened. Blood started to seep into the woollen garment from beneath as the auxiliary gave a high pitched shriek and dropped his cudgel, reaching down to try and ease the dog's jaws apart.

Rufinus was still stunned, barely able to think, let alone act, staggering and lurching. He had a sword. All he had to do was remember where it was and do something with it.

Then the prefect hit him from behind, and everything went black.

PART TWO

GERMANI

"the Germans have no taste for peace;
renown is more easily won among perils,
and a large body of retainers cannot be kept
together except by means of violence and war."

\- From the "Germania" of Tacitus

CHAPTER ELEVEN

Rufinus awoke, confused for only a moment, his head still throbbing a little. He reached up and touched the back of his skull where the blow had landed and found it extremely tender, but the hand came away clean, so there was no blood, no major injury. He pondered on that for a moment, given his own plentiful experience of head injuries in the boxing ring. It was surprisingly hard to render someone unconscious without doing real damage. Or at least, it took design and concentration. You had to be *trying* to do as much, to not truly injure the target. That meant that whoever had hit him had not been meaning to damage him, just overcome him.

Which explained why he was still alive and uninjured.

The same could not be said for the man who had first hit him unexpectedly from behind. Rufinus remembered Orthus, with his jaws locked around the man's privates, the blood beginning to flow. If the assailant still lived, he might well wish he hadn't.

Then there was the prefect.

Rufinus spent a few moments trawling his memory for details. He'd only been told the man's name once, and it took some work to recall it.

Veremundus.

A man who had seemed utterly Roman, more so than even the governor, and yet a man who had clearly proved, in the end, to be at the very heart of the matter. Rufinus frowned. He'd not come across that name before, but now that he rolled it across his tongue with time to think, and without the distraction of the prefect's presence, it had a distinctly Germanic sound to it. Why hadn't he noticed that when they first spoke? The answer to that was simple. Veremundus had managed to get Rufinus wrong-footed and on the defensive from the start. That scout had given him plenty of warning that they were coming, and the prefect had organised everything so that it looked normal. Mind you, he was clever, too, for he'd produced very logical and credible explanations for all Rufinus's questions as if plucking them from the air.

He sat in glum silence for a moment, and then began to pay a little more attention to his surroundings. He was in the dark, but there was light showing through cracks and around a door and the shutters of three windows. He was in a room, then, and one made of timbers. Looking around, he determined that it was one long room, perhaps ten feet by twenty-five, and the floor was also of timber.

He stood, wobbled for a few moments and then gradually regained full balance. He tried stretching and moving, and discovered that there was no impediment. His captors had definitely only intended to take him intact, then. He was not even bound. They had left him in his tunic and breeches, belt and boots, but nothing else. He reached up and his hand brushed a beam, supporting the roof. Not too high, then. He walked over slowly, quietly, to the door, and tried it, but was unsurprised to discover that it was shut tight. Nodding to himself in the dark, he wandered over to the window and pulled the shutter inwards.

Brilliant light flooded the room, and he swore as he went momentarily blind.

Blinking away stars and coloured spots as he turned back, he let his eyes adjust and then took everything in, now fully visible. The window had iron bars across it in both directions, forming a cross that allowed plenty of air and light, but would prevent a man from climbing through it. Not a shock, really. There were two other windows, all on the same wall, and he didn't bother with them. If one window was barred, they all would be.

The room was spartan, to say the least. A piss bucket stood in one corner, and at the far end was a bed, a rough timber and wool thing covered with basic military blankets. That was the extent of the amenities he had been granted. But then it could have been worse. That they gave him a bed at all suggested they intended to keep him alive and comparatively comfortable, for a time at least.

Where was he? It was a building entire, not part of a larger structure, and was therefore not big enough to be a barrack or stable block. It could be a disused storehouse in the fort, or possibly some structure in the civil settlement. He crossed to the window and looked out. He couldn't see anything but the blank wall of an identical building that ran across in front of him at a distance of maybe twelve feet. Such a regular pattern did suggest Roman military work, and as he listened, he could hear what sounded an awful lot like the ordinary ambient noises of fort life.

He concentrated on that for a while. Yes. He could hear the sounds of manufacturing, of military training, of menial work, and of distant, muffled conversation. Everything he could hear was in German, though.

Where were his men? Where was dependable Clemens, argumentative Ademus, generous Oclatius...

Where was *Orthus?*

That hit him, suddenly. Being without his allies was bad enough, but to separate him from his dog was unacceptable. His pulse quickened. What if they had killed Orthus? Simply done away with him? It would not be too easy to do, but a camp of soldiers could do it, and it might be a rational response when faced with an angry beast whose main form of attack was to tear the genitals off a man.

If Orthus had been hurt, there would be a reckoning.

He would find his way out of this, but they had best not have injured his dog.

He stopped, stretched, thought, took stock of the situation.

He had allies, although he couldn't get to them. His dog and eight legionaries had been with him when he was captured. If they had been allowed to live, it seemed likely they would be somewhere close by. Some eighty miles to the east of Tannum

161

was the first place he knew he could rely upon. Castra Regina, home of the Third Italica, where the governor currently resided, a man and a unit who surely had nothing to do with this. Then there was every other occupied fort on the frontier that had not appeared on his list. All six forts involved housed native or Germanic units. Therefore, logic said that the other forts, which housed units of different ethnic origins, were potential allies. He didn't know where the nearest of those forts was, but it should not be too far away. No more than ten miles at the most.

So that was what he needed: to find his friends and his dog, and then to get word to a neighbouring fort or to the legionary base at Castra Regina. Although first, of course, he had to get out of this place. And to find out what was happening.

While he mulled over those choices, he utilised the pisspot in the corner and then, decisions made, moved to the other two windows and pulled open the shutters, revealing more cross-bars and views of the back of the parallel hut. He pushed his head as close between the bars as he could, trying to get a better view. He couldn't see a lot more, but one thing was clear. A man stood near the door of this hut, and the man seemed to be wearing auxiliary uniform, from what he could see.

Ah well. Nothing ventured, nothing gained…

He walked over to the door and hammered on it three times.

'I need to speak to Prefect Veremundus.'

There was a prolonged silence, and he wondered whether he was being ignored or whether the man had somehow not heard him. Then there was a shuffling noise, and a click.

The door opened.

Rufinus frowned.

A single auxiliary, though with very Germanic features and braided hair, stood a few paces from him. The man had spear and shield in his hands, though he did not level them at Rufinus. In fact, as prison guards went, he seemed remarkably relaxed. But then why not? That the man did not seem to be afraid of him not only told Rufinus that he was confident, but suggested that the reason for that was that Rufinus was no danger to him. He had a fort full of compatriots to back him up. Rufinus nodded at the man. Taking a swing at him and running would hardly help, before he'd taken stock of his surroundings and the location of his own friends.

The man used his spear to gesture off to his left, seemingly inviting Rufinus to walk. He did so. Emerging from the hut, he took a deep breath. The air was a little chilly, but dry, and the sky had come blue. Had he not been at spearpoint, Rufinus might have smiled. He turned and walked the way the spear had indicated, and as he reached the end of the hut, realised he had misjudged at least one thing in his musings.

He was not at Tannum.

The huts to either side, and several more he could now see in ordered rows, were of rough, recent manufacture. They looked a little basic to be Roman military structures, but then were a little too neat and well-made to be native. The ground was mud and turf, and between the huts he could see a timber stockade wall, the top of a low wooden tower or fighting platform, and beyond that: trees.

Where in Hades' name was he?

He took in everything as he walked, the soldier giving him repeated directions with the spear.

It looked very much like the temporary vexillation camps the army used on campaign. Back in the days of the war, there had been numerous such camps constructed north of the Danubius to gather troops or to use as winter quarters. When only in brief use, they would be simple stockaded campsites, the army pitching their tents within, but when they were in use for a year or more, they might attract simple wooden structures such as these. Yet there was no war on.

Or was there?

He caught sight, between buildings, of the camp's occupants. They appeared, at first glance, at least, to be the men of Tannum. They were generally wearing the uniforms of auxiliary infantry, some armoured, some not. Many had their hair and beards in Germanic styles, though some did not. They seemed to be going about their fort business as normal, and briefly he could see in the distance an open space full of men performing battle drills and manoeuvres.

Then they emerged from the rows of huts into a small open area. One larger building sat ahead, with men on guard outside. Rufinus's eyes strayed to the left and he was both relieved and dismayed to see Orthus. The big white hound was in a wooden cage, although he noted with relief that it was large enough for the dog to pace around, had a bed of straw, and dishes for food and water. He was being looked after, at least.

The man with the spear spoke briefly to the two on guard at the larger hut, and then turned and walked away, leaving Rufinus with the guards. One entered the hut, and there was a brief muffled exchange before he returned and gestured for Rufinus to enter.

He did so.

This hut was apparently divided into two rooms, the first filled with benches. The two non-windowed walls were bare, but had hooks that were clearly for hanging something large. He walked on, and through the open doorway to the other room.

He blinked in surprise, for the second chamber was so very clearly a prefect's office. It looked a lot like the one at Tannum had. A desk covered in reports, cupboards around the edge, the prefect's armour and helmet on a stand in a corner, braziers, and a map on one wall.

Veremundus sat behind the desk. His expression was very neutral, presumably deliberately so. Rufinus glanced at the wall. It held a map of the 'agri decumates,' the system of frontier defences that cut across Germanic lands for four hundred miles, connecting the Rhenus and Danubius rivers. He noted with interest that this map did not appear to mark the provincial boundaries, and so the two-hundred mile Raetian section and the two hundred miles that lay in Germania Superior were presented as one. Forts, towns and way stations were marked, as well as the line of the frontier itself and its towers.

Marks north of the border, he presumed to be native fortifications and settlements, though there were not so many of them. One mark, quite large and prominent, seemed to lie just ten miles or so north of the frontier, close to Tannum, and it seemed certain that the mark identified their current location. That was worrying, for it meant they were in barbarian lands, outside the Roman borders, but at least they were not far away, still close to civilisation.

'You are a man of constant surprises,' Rufinus said, turning calmly to the prefect.

'I shall take that as a compliment. I hope you are well, not injured?'

'A headache. It'll pass. You almost had me convinced there was nothing wrong.'

Veremundus nodded. 'Unfortunate. The men you brought with you started poking around while they waited, and one of the groups they disturbed took exception to it. Matters escalated out of control too fast for any officer to stop it. Had your escort simply stayed put and waited, you could have all gone home free men.'

'For how long, before you raise rebellion in Raetia? I should have noticed other things. Veremundus, for instance. A name with Germanic origins, I presume, despite your very Italian Latin?'

The prefect gave a strangely nonchalant shrug. 'Very distantly. My family were granted citizenship by Drusus for their aid in his campaigns across the Rhenus two centuries ago. I doubt any of our blood has set foot in Germania for over a century, except perhaps in command of a cohort. I am as German as you, my Praetorian friend.' He gave an oddly wistful smile. 'Although perhaps it has given me a certain sympathy for these peoples. I do not necessarily see them as enemies, but what could be more

Roman than that? Many German tribes have served Rome well over the years.'

He leaned back and folded his arms. 'But to answer your other question, there will be no rebellion in Raetia. That is not my goal.'

Rufinus frowned. 'Evidence strongly suggests otherwise.'

Veremundus unfolded his arms again and rose from his chair. 'That is because you have seen parts of the painting, but not the big picture. You have spoken to our illustrious governor, have you not? What impression of Raetia did he paint for you?'

Rufinus was starting to dislike talking to the prefect. Even without a scout's warning, the man seemed to be able to wrong-foot Rufinus in a conversation with consummate ease.

'The governor hates being here. He considers Raetia a poor province, rather overlooked and undermanned. I suspect he sees the only solution to the issue as a massive injection of gold and manpower to the province.'

The prefect nodded. 'And he is almost correct. Almost, but not quite.'

'Oh?'

'Rome has a tendency to overreach itself,' Veremundus said, conversationally, as he came around the desk and stood in front of Rufinus. 'It has a history of doing as much. Varus moving into Germania only for Rome to find itself battered and sent running with its tail between its legs. Agricola conquering Scotland, only for it to be let go a few years later, because it was of little value when compared to the resources needed to fully Romanise it. Trajan, extending the empire way up into the Dacian mountains, out into Persia, down into Arabia, only for Hadrian, who recognised the empire's limits, to let half of that go as untenable territories. Even the great Marcus Aurelius, who I had the honour to serve in the war, as, I suspect, did you. He planned Marcomannia, a new province north of the Danubius over in Pannonia. But Commodus, for all his faults, was bright enough to see that as a fool's dream, and let it go. In fact, as I told you when we last talked, Commodus is still well-respected in this region for his sense and his generosity in settling with the tribes after the war. Had he kept up his father's martial approach, there would have been at least two more wars across the river by now. Instead, he made a peace that has bought Rome prosperity and calm in the region for twenty years and more.'

'You make a convincing argument. How does it apply here?'

Veremundus crossed to the wall. 'See this map? If you look at the lines of the forts, both those in current use, and those that have been abandoned and demolished, you can see successive advances into the tribal lands by a sequence of emperors with a poor understanding of the border. Four times, the border has been moved forward since the early days of empire, each time giving us a longer frontier to maintain, meaning rebuilding of our entire military infrastructure, the stretching of resources, and more disgruntled tribes who have been forcibly added to the empire. And what have we gained from it? Some hills, a few lakes, a lot of cows and an area of reasonable cultivatable fields. And all that land gives Rome less produce than even a small amount of African or Aegyptian or Italian soil. Those advances *cost* Rome, rather than *gaining* her anything. They were made for one simple reason: so that emperors who needed a victory could add the title Germanicus to their name.'

He drew a line along the frontier. 'Antoninus,' he said, 'about forty years ago.'

His finger then traced a shorter line, missing some of the western end of the territory. 'Hadrian. Eighty years ago.'

A third line, further back, shorter, less territory. 'The Flavians, a hundred and twenty years ago.'

A final fourth line, much further back. 'Nero. One hundred and fifty years ago. And what do you note about Nero's line in the south and east, and Hadrian's in the west?'

Rufinus studied the map. He frowned. 'Nero's system followed the Danubius to its source. Hadrian's followed the Rhenus and then this river... the Nicer?'

'Quite. Natural boundaries. Those rivers have been there long enough that most of the tribes live on either one side of them or the other, not both. Those boundaries did not divide tribes up and make half of them Roman. And with a river between you and the barbarian, you do not need all these watchtowers, gates, palisades, and closely spaced forts. It requires a lot less manpower to control. And while we currently have an artificial frontier four hundred miles long, can you imagine how far we would need a man-made frontier between the Nicer and the Danubius?'

'Not far,' Rufinus admitted, looking at the map.

'Less than ten miles,' Veremundus said, folding his arms again. 'Imagine that. A continuation of the river frontiers, with just a ten mile area of land to control between them. And what would Rome lose? Some farmland?'

'So this is your idea? To withdraw the Roman border to the two rivers and abandon northern Raetia and part of Germania?'

'And why not?'

Rufinus pictured Septimius Severus standing here, looking at the map. 'For one thing, because the emperor will never agree to it. Severus is a soldier. The idea of giving up territory will not sit well with him.'

'Nor would it with any emperor. No emperor likes to give up land. It knocked Hadrian's reputation, and Domitian's, and Commodus's. That, my Praetorian friend, is why this is happening. Sometimes a man with vision has to put things into motion himself. To do things for the good of the empire when those with the power cannot see the truth.'

'It won't work.'

Veremundus frowned. 'Yes it will. I have studied the matter in immense detail over many years before even beginning to move on my plan. Things have progressed so far, and we are close to conclusion. In fact, I do not think the process can now easily be stopped.' His expression darkened. 'Do not look at me like that, Praetorian.'

'Like what?'

'As though I were a traitor. An enemy of the empire. I am not. In fact, I may be more a true son of Rome than any of these men who seek to advance the border at any cost.'

Rufinus shook his head. 'You think it will work based on what you've achieved at Tannum. I can see that. I can see in Tannum a place where the Germanic spirit and the Roman seem to have sort of melded. You are to be commended on something I would not have thought possible before I came here. But I have seen the other forts, the other *units* you have involved. They have gone a different way entirely. And looking at how they smashed the imperial statue at Tannum, even your own fort may not have escaped. They are changing.'

'Oh?'

'Roman-haters, head-hunters. They are butchering their officers, and I take personal offence at that, since one of them was my brother.'

'Ah. That is unfortunate. And yes, I know that things have gone a little beyond my initial intent in places. That is the fault of my partner.'

Rufinus felt a pit opening up beneath them. 'Partner?'

'This cannot be a Roman plan alone, you understand? The tribes here have to play a part in it. There needs to be an irresistible force facing the authorities so that they understand the impossibility of maintaining the current system.'

'What have you done, Veremundus? And who have you done it with?'

'I enlisted the aid of a number of Germanic tribes and their kings. We are working together, Roman and German, to put in place a plan that will reunite their divided tribes, while giving Rome a stronger, more sensible border to maintain.'

'You are strengthening the Germans. Can you not see a danger in that?'

Veremundus shook his head. 'Not when they are our allies. Which they are, because the plan benefits us all.'

169

'And in the meantime they go around Raetia butchering any officer who is not one of their own?'

'That is Ingomer's doing.'

'Ingomer? One of these kings?'

The prefect nodded. 'I left Ingomer working on things while I visited parts of the neighbouring province to advance the plan there. In Germania, we only have to pull back a very short way to maintain the Nicer border. I was gone almost a month, but in my absence, Ingomer took it upon himself to remove from the region anyone he thought might stand against us. I have spoken to him about this behaviour, and I do not think it will happen again.'

'This Ingomer is powerful, isn't he?'

'The kings sort of elected him to speak for them.'

'A king of kings. I've heard that title before. One such rules Parthia, and look how much trouble *they* have been for Rome over the centuries.'

'You are missing the point,' Veremundus said with an edge of exasperation. 'Some small sacrifices have to be made for the greater good. There is danger, and there are upheavals. Men will be injured and killed, and it is entirely possible my name will be spat at for generations. But it matters not. In the long run it will save many thousands of lives, a huge amount of money and resources for Rome, and may well foster beneficial relations with the German tribes for all time. Sometimes the cost is worth paying.'

Rufinus sighed. 'You are an idealist. You are not making the tribes more pro-Roman. If anything, you are making them more *anti*-Roman.'

'Really? Come with me.'

Suddenly, the prefect was marching from the room, through the outer chamber and into the sunlight. Rufinus hurried after him.

'See this camp?' Veremundus asked, gesturing around them. 'An advance camp for thrusts against the Hermunduri during the

170

last war, as they were allies of the Marcomanni. It lay empty and overgrown for decades until we reoccupied it. But this is a camp of Romano-Germans, my friend. Buildings of quality, made to Roman design by German hands. And they are organised into cohorts, as we do.'

He was walking now, and in moments they emerged between two of the huts to see the large open area where soldiers were practicing manoeuvres.

'And look here. Romans training Germans. We are making them a little more like us. They will be brothers to Rome in time.'

Rufinus shook his head. He'd thought Veremundus was clever for a while. Then he thought he was a mistaken idealist, but every step deeper into this plan was cementing Rufinus's new opinion, that the man was a complete fool.

'You are not Romanising the tribes, Prefect. What you are doing is teaching them how to beat Romans. You are organising and arming a force, and training it how to achieve victory over us. Can you not see the danger in this?'

'It is but a step in the process.'

'It is a step into an *abyss*. I've seen the others you are relying on. Those men at Batavis, at Abusina and Celeusum. They will never see Rome as anything other than an enemy. You will start something that you believe will result in a stronger border, but I see it differently. You will give the German tribes free rein in a land already poorly-equipped to fight them. You have to stop this madness while you can.'

Veremundus's expression hardened. 'I had hoped you would be able to see the value of this. To see the vision. You are as blind as the rest of them.'

Rufinus straightened. The man was clearly not going to see sense. 'What have you done with my men,' he asked.

'They are detained in one of the huts, much the same as you. Unlike Ingomer, I am not seeking to kill Romans unnecessarily. Indeed, I am trying to *save* lives. You and your men will remain my guests until the command is given and the plan goes ahead.

Then, there will be no stopping it, and you will be released to go your own way.'

'You are a bloody fool, Veremundus.'

'I had planned on releasing you, giving you liberty within the camp to be part of the great plan. If you cannot see it, then I'm afraid you will have to go back to your hut and stay there for a while.'

Rufinus had not noticed, but unseen and unheard, two soldiers had come up behind them, shields ready and swords out. The prefect nodded to them. 'Show our guest back to his quarters.'

'At least let me have my dog.'

The prefect winced. 'Having seen what the animal is capable of, I am not inclined to do so at this time. I am no hater of dogs, though, and I would not see him harmed. He will be fed and looked after until this is over and then you will be reunited.'

Rufinus glared at the prefect, but the two auxiliaries gestured with their swords, and he turned his back on the man and walked away. As he moved through the huge campaign base, he shook his head in disbelief. The man had started his explanation so well. The moving of the border *did* make sense. They should probably never have advanced beyond that river line of Nero's. But it had been done. The tribes had been divided and conquered, and attempting to *un*-conquer them, and to recombine them, was only going to have catastrophic results.

Training Germans how the Roman army worked was never a good idea. Hadn't they learned that lesson two centuries ago, when Arminius of the Cherusci had been trained with the Roman army, only to use his knowledge and skills to lead three legions into oblivion and lose any hope of a Romanised Germania?

Fool.

He had combined a third of Raetia's auxilia with their German relatives from across the frontier, and trained them together as an army. Rufinus had seen the other cohorts, and at the moment, Veremundus's army was clearly spread out along the border. The moment that lot were organised properly and gathered, though, they would overcome the remaining under-strength garrisons of Raetia without a great deal of difficulty, and Rome's northern border would be open for raiding.

Gah!

He realised he was no longer walking calmly, but stomping angrily.

He certainly had no intention of sitting quietly in his wooden cell for a month and watching Veremundus destroy Roman control of the border. His earlier plan held. He had to get word to the governor and the Third Legion, for only they could drag in the forces of Noricum and Germania and flood the region with extra troops. To do that, he would need to be back over the border and among allies. That meant one of the auxiliary frontier forts manned by a non-Germanic or -Raetian unit, who had no reason to be part of this. And to get there meant getting out of this camp. He might be able to run back that ten mile journey alone, but he would stand a lot more chance with Clemens and the others. And more than that, Clemens knew the region. He would know what fort to run to and where it was. So before they left this camp, he had to get his friends out too. And his dog.

Before he could do any of that, though, he needed to get *himself* out.

A call attracted his attention, and he looked across to see several familiar faces at another barred hut window, peering out at him and calling over. Clemens was among them. He nodded to them and walked on. Good. At least now, he knew where everyone was being kept. That was a start. Next, he needed to find a way out of his own hut, though the best way to do that would be to have the freedom that Veremundus had offered him. He cursed himself silently for not nodding and smiling and accepting that freedom. He had messed up there. As they neared his own hut, he looked ahead and could see the camp's timber palisade and towers. He turned to his escort.

'When you have dropped me back, please deliver my compliments and apologies to the prefect. I was startled by his plan. If he has the opportunity I would appreciate the chance to learn more.'

The two soldiers shared a look, then one nodded.

Moments later they were at the hut, and Rufinus walked in calmly and waited for them to shut the door behind him, then strolled over to the bed and sat down.

There was one more thing. He'd already known he had to escape and get word to the governor to put an end to this insane idea, but now he knew one other thing. This German king, Ingomer, was the man ultimately responsible for Publius's death.

Somehow, somewhere through all of this, Ingomer had to die.

CHAPTER TWELVE

'I hope you are not expecting me to welcome you with open arms,' Prefect Veremundus said, his tone frosty.

'I still think your plan is irrational and dangerous,' Rufinus replied, stepping out of his hut and ignoring the glare of the door guard, 'but I am willing to admit that the *basis* of it is sound, and perhaps the goal is even a good thing.'

The prefect seemed to consider this for a moment, and then huffed. 'I am not convinced of your good intentions, but let us proceed as though I were.'

Rufinus nodded as they moved between the huts. 'Your *theory* is sound, I admit. The defensive line drawn by the Nicer and the Danubius *is* a sensible one. It is more defensible, follows natural geographical boundaries, and creates a land border zone that would require much less work and manpower.'

'Thus far, this is only what I already explained to you.'

Another nod. 'But that's where it ends, for me. If we want to withdraw to such a line, the only sensible way to do it is to seek imperial approval and do it as a recognised military and political decision.'

'You said yourself that Severus would never accept it, and I know this. No emperor willingly gives up territory, for it damages their reputation.'

'It is all about timing,' Rufinus replied. 'As we speak, the emperor is busy conquering Parthia, an age-old thorn in Rome's side. Like Trajan, a hundred years ago, he will form a province of Arabia. And I know for certain he also has his eye on reconquering those parts of Dacia we abandoned, as well as completing control of the island of Britannia. You are simply moving too early. Allow Severus a notable conquest, where we

175

gain a land of either political or commercial import, and he could probably be persuaded to let go of a few hundred miles of mountainous German farmland. He could do so without losing face if it is overshadowed by a great conquest.'

Veremundus's eyes narrowed. 'You *sound* as though you are speaking sense, so why can I not shake the feeling that you are playing me?'

'Because you are involved in conspiracy and treason against the state,' Rufinus replied flatly. 'When you are engaged in such things, fear and even paranoia become the norm. The way your plans are progressing, you will open up Rome's borders and invite disaster.'

'You think I am a fool?' Veremundus said, though it was clearly not a question. 'My timing is *precise*. I need my strategy to move on before Titus Decius Barbatus is recalled to Rome, and some new, hungry politician takes his place, and that will happen within the year. My timing relies upon Barbatus.'

'Oh? How so?'

'You have met the man. He would rather be anywhere else in the empire than here. He has little interest in, or control of, the border. When the German tribes suddenly appear in strength, Decius Barbatus will panic, for that is the best he can manage. He will not know what to do, and so he will turn to his officers. Fully a third of the army of Raetia is now in my camp. Together we will put forward a plan to withdraw to the line of the Danubius, which is considerably easier fortified. He will agree, of that I am certain. We can be persuasive enough to guarantee it. Rome can thus fall back to the new defensive line in the face of increased threat, without losing whole units. Then we have our sensible border. And pulling back to the Nicer line in Germania Superior will be inevitable once this happens in Raetia. In the blink of an eye the border will have been relocated. In fact I imagine we will already be fortifying the new line before news of the change even reaches Rome. There may be the odd man lost in the process, but think how many we will save in the long run. And once we give up that land and re-form at the river, we will never retake it. The border becomes permanent.'

'The governor will, of course, spend the rest of his life in disgrace for losing the land,' Rufinus noted.

'Better one man retire in shame to a rich estate than thousands of soldiers die to maintain an unmaintainable border.'

Rufinus winced. Veremundus had a disconcerting talent for making the insane sound sensible, and when he put it that way, it was enticing. He shook his head.

'There is still too much that can go wrong. The governor could unexpectedly prove to have a backbone and take offence at a German threat. Or the other officers could overshadow you and persuade him to make a stand. Or the Germans could do what they always do: lull you into a false sense of security, then spring a trap and massacre legions. I urge you again, wait until Severus has his grand victory, and then do this slowly, carefully, politically, and openly. In the end you might even be lauded for it.'

As the prefect listened to this, considering it, Rufinus came to a halt, at the end of the hut lines.

Their conversation had been nothing new, to him at least. To Veremundus, it was, but Rufinus had been working through everything he knew and had guessed about the prefect's plan while he sat alone in his hut, waiting to be sent for. It had been written out in his mind, ready to recite like a speech, requiring very little effort to change depending upon conversational swings. That had allowed him time to take in other things as they walked, despite appearing to concentrate on the conversation.

The time it took to go from the door of his hut to that of the one in which his eight legionary friends were being kept, he logged, although when he did it for real, he would have to take a much more circumspect route.

Then there was the cage in which Orthus paced angrily. That should be an easy task, for the door was held shut with just a single peg.

The location of at least one storehouse and armoury he noted. He'd glanced through the windows of half a dozen huts and spotted the gleam of weapons and armour inside. Always good to know where to grab a sword. And the general form and makeup of the huts used as barracks, too.

He would need more than one such trip outside, though, and he would need to be inventive to get to parts of the camp that he had no real business visiting. There were so many things he needed to see and know before even planning any escape attempt. Hiding places. Troop barrack locations. Guard positions. Warning systems. Blind spots. So much to discover. Fortunately, he had a feeling that Veremundus loved to talk over his plans. Probably he'd not had much opportunity to do so with his Germanic allies.

Rufinus frowned to himself. He thought back over all the things he had heard the Germans say. He plucked a pair of the more common words he'd heard, and strung them together, speaking to the prefect, raising the pitch at the end to make it a question. He had absolutely no idea what the words were, but had to fight down a smile when Veremundus frowned in response.

'You will have to re-phrase that in Latin,' he said coldly.

'I asked how many,' Rufinus lied glibly, pointing out to the hundreds of men training on the open ground in front of them.

Veremundus coughed. 'You probe for information.'

Yes. But not for what you think. Rufinus shrugged. 'You have six auxiliary units, which means probably somewhere between six and eight thousand men, and you face twice as many who will remain loyal to the governor. Add the Third Italica to that, and your six to eight thousand face at least twenty thousand men. If anything in your plan goes wrong, you will be hopelessly outnumbered. I know you have Germans on your side, but can you count upon twelve thousand of them, and are they strong enough to face legionaries? Be careful, Prefect. I am thinking here of saving lives, not of my own skin.'

178

'Our numbers will swamp theirs,' Veremundus replied confidently.

Rufinus felt a cold stone sitting in his belly at that. In two heartbeats, the prefect had revealed two different facts, and both were horrifying. Firstly, that he had no command of the German tongue, which meant that he had been negotiating with German kings without a command of their language, everything he thought he knew coming from interpreters. And secondly, he was relying for success upon a force of Germans at least twice the size as that of the Romans he could call up.

Rufinus had little experience with the Germanic peoples, except as enemies in the Marcomannic Wars, but he could only picture the glee their leaders had enjoyed at this revelation. A Roman officer had offered to pull his military back from the border, had told them that the governor was ineffective and could be persuaded to panic and run away, had offered to place the larger operational share of this in their hands, and the man had not even spoken their language as he did all of that.

'And what of your six Germanic and Raetian units?'

Veremundus's brow creased. 'What do you mean?'

'You have built all of this on six auxiliary units of native blood. What do you intend for them in the end? What do you think they will do?'

'I do not understand what you're driving at, Rufinus. They are auxilia. They may be German, but they are doing this for their peoples. They will pull back and form a new border to allow their tribes to occupy the lands traditionally theirs.'

'You believe they will hold to their Roman oath and help maintain a new border?'

The man frowned, saying nothing.

'You do not think for even a moment,' Rufinus said, 'that they will now have more in common with the tribes than with Rome, thanks to your work? That the moment Rome takes a step back, these men will renounce their oath and fall in with their countrymen, launching attacks against Rome?'

'You try to persuade me using spurious logic,' Veremundus rumbled. 'I am not so easily dissuaded.'

'Look,' Rufinus said, gesturing to the open space. 'What can you see?'

'Manoeuvres. Training.'

'That's what *you* see. Do you know what *I* see?' Rufinus replied.

'What?'

'I see eighty soldiers – *auxiliaries* – forming the testudo, a formation traditionally used by the legions. I see you have even had these men supplied with shields the correct shape for legionaries. I used to form a testudo, you know? I may now be a Praetorian tribune, but back in the mists of time I was a legionary serving with the Tenth Gemina. I formed that shape on a hundred exercise grounds and at least a dozen times on active duty. Shields used to make walls and a roof around and over the men. The principle is solid, the idea good, but it's a different thing in practice. Legionary shields are rectangular, but they have a curve to them. That means that when they are used as a roof, they create a series of half-moon shaped holes at the top of the front line. I will tell you from personal experience that this is fine as long as the enemy are infantry or those inside the testudo keep their heads down and present their helmet to fill that half-moon gap. But even on the best days, a testudo needs to know they are still going in the right direction, and that means that at least occasionally the men inside need to look up. If the enemy are armed with bows or slings, and are good with them, then this happens.'

He'd been half watching, and waiting for this.

The Germanic attackers were launching arrows at the advancing testudo, and it was only a matter of time. Suddenly, an arrow disappeared into the small gap, there was a scream, a man died, and the whole formation fell apart, each man scattering, running for cover.

180

'I mean, they would notice the weak point themselves eventually, and put a good archer on it. But it needs the legionary to be looking up at the time, face in the gap, and a damn good archer. And that I happened to be able to draw attention to that at just such a time tells me one thing. Can you guess what it is?'

Veremundus frowned and shook his head.

'It tells me,' Rufinus said in a low growl, 'that your men are instructing the German tribes in exactly how to beat our men. In all the little loopholes they need to overcome us. If you look into the background, you can see Germanic cavalry using light Roman-style javelins from horseback to destroy a defensive contra-equitas formation before they reach it. You are training Rome's enemies to beat her, Veremundus. I understand your position. I understand *why* you're doing all this. But you're making a mistake.'

The prefect faltered. 'I… I prepare them to be as impressive as they can.'

Rufinus bridled. 'Then why teach them how to take out legionaries? The only legion in Raetia is that at Castra Regina, and I thought your plan was that the army would withdraw at your suggestion before there was ever an actual fight?'

Another bumbled response.

'Your trainers went to such lengths as to replicate legionary shields just to show them how to kill legionaries,' Rufinus nudged.

'I think this walk of ours is over,' Veremundus said coldly.

Two days passed before the next visit was sanctioned. In the meantime, despite their differences, Rufinus had made no overt move against the Veremundus's plan, and had not tried to escape, and the prefect had, in return, allowed him to use the public latrines under guard, meaning he could finally dispose of the stinky pisspot from his room.

He emerged from his hut and nodded to Veremundus. 'I have new questions.'

The prefect smiled. 'I have no doubt. I thought that today, however, we would have more of a personal discussion. Let us stroll into a quieter part of the camp.' Rufinus inclined his head. Two soldiers followed closely, to make sure the prisoner did not try a move on their commander, though Rufinus had no such intention. Putting down the lunatic Veremundus sounded on the surface like such a good idea for the good of the empire, but he had already put something in motion, and without him, that would continue, just in the hands of other men, probably German kings or Germanic centurions. It might be better to leave a hopelessly misguided Roman in charge than let command fall to a native.

It almost made Rufinus smile as they strolled the other way for a change, and soon came to the defences, walking along their interior. It was, as the prefect had noted, an old Roman campaign camp. The ramparts were perhaps four feet high, having sunk a few feet over the years. The stockade atop it was rough, though still solid, as were the towers. They had been formed of upright corner beams with crossed struts, in a very Roman style. Rufinus smiled. He'd climbed such structures in the old days of the war. It had been excellent training for his boxing, allowing him to build body strength, from core all the way out to fingertips.

As they walked, he took note of where any blind spot might lie, of where huts provided cover, and of the locations of each tower, and how many men stood atop them. There were no clear points of departure, but there were definitely places where the defences were stronger, and places where they were weaker. He could work with that, as long as he could remember where they were.

As they walked and talked, he tried to picture the place from above. He'd always done that for a fight, imagining it as a boxing ring, but now he extended that based on the shape and size of a legion's staging camp beyond the frontiers. As such, he was pleased to discover he could picture the whole thing, and every position within it. That would be something he'd have to think of alone in his hut, though, when he didn't need to be attentive.

'I know you don't want to think about this,' he said, 'but you have spent months appealing to the German and Raetian blood in your favoured units, and what that has done is made them less Roman. It's sent them back to their roots. I've seen Dacian units who still actually use their falx, their native weapon, in combat. I've seen Thracian auxilia who use the curved sica knives of their homeland. I've seen Roman cavalry lancers and archers from Sarmatia and Parthia, who use their native weapons and standards. The auxilia are not citizen soldiers. In some cases, they're just the throw of a pomegranate from being barbarians themselves. You've taken units based in their homeland and made them feel more and more native. Think what they will achieve.'

'I think you overstate...'

'No I don't. That's bollocks, Veremundus. You think you know everything, but you don't, because you're an equestrian officer assigned by Rome to the army for a few years. *I* know this army from the ground up, not the top down, having come from the bottom rung. You have trained the ordinary men of your units to favour being German over being Roman.'

'I think...'

'No you don't. When all this is done, unless it happens to fall out precisely as you hope, and I give that a one in a hundred chance of that, those units you have trained are going to abandon their oath and simply fall in with their cousins and march on Roman territory as easy pickings.'

'You vex me, Tribune Rufinus.'

Rufinus gave the man a smile, which took a lot of work. 'That is because I speak sense, and no matter how much we differ, you and I both want what is best for Rome.'

Veremundus sighed and straightened, folding his hands behind his back. 'I would be lying if I said the questions you have raised recently have not given me food for thought, and this matter is as much one of those as any. I feel I want to ponder on this in my

183

office. I am aware that you are a nobleman of Rome and that I am keeping you confined in a prison. If you give me your word that you will not try to escape, I will henceforth allow you freedom of the compound at arranged times, under escort of course.'

Rufinus bowed his head. 'I presume the same is not granted to Orthus?'

'Your dog?' Veremundus snorted. 'I would love to. But he has already maimed two of his keepers just through the cage. Let's leave him where he is, eh?'

'And my men? They are legionaries. Roman citizens.'

'I will think on that. Bear with me.'

Rufinus bowed again. 'Then I give you my word that during these strolls I will not attempt to escape.'

The prefect gave a troubled smile, inclined his head, and walked off. In the silence of his head, Rufinus clarified that it was *only* during these strolls. With free rein over his wandering, Rufinus was careful. While Veremundus went back to his office, Rufinus made sure to cover what he could of the perimeter and of the rows of huts, all looking as innocent as he could manage.

He woke from a troubled sleep at the hammering of a fist on the hut door. He sat upright and shouted his readiness. The door opened, and the usual bland soldier stood outside. The man said something that sounded as though it may have been Latin but spoken in such a thick German accent that he couldn't tell. He stepped out towards the man, who used his spear to point the way as usual. He nodded and followed the direction, and in a matter of fifty heartbeats was escorted to the sizeable hut that made do as a headquarters. He looked to the soldier, who stopped at the bottom of the three steps that led up into the hut, and the man gestured for him to go on.

He walked up and opened the door, entering that outer room of the hut. Those hooks on the wall had been made use of now, and held a huge map inscribed on the back of a pelt, showing the entire Raetian, Noric and upper German border, with its forts, installations, roads and towers. Sitting facing it was Prefect Veremundus. The officer looked to his side and gestured to a seat, and Rufinus wandered over and dropped heavily into it.

'Prefect?'

'I do not like the picture you repeatedly paint of my plan.'

'I'm not about to apologise,' Rufinus said.

'I know. You make me question decisions I made over the past two years, upon which I have built my plans. I do not like the doubts you raise in me.'

Rufinus shrugged. 'We are there, yes?' he asked, pointing at the marker on the map.

'Yes. Some ten miles into their lands.'

'And this is Tannum?' He pressed, drawing his finger down and pointing to the nearest fort, just south of the frontier on the map.

'Yes.'

'What is this?' he asked, pointing to the next fort east from there.

'A small fort, a fortlet, by the name of Castra Numera. Garrisoned by men from Iciniacum – riders of a unit from Bracaraugusta.'

Rufinus nodded to himself. A unit of Hispanic horsemen, who almost certainly had no connection to this, and who were only a small distance further away than Tannum, maybe eleven or twelve miles. He smiled quietly to himself at that, then realised Veremundus was narrowing eyes at him, so quickly changed the subject, pointing to somewhere a lot further south. 'One of your Raetian units was based at Vindonissa. Do you control the routes south?'

Veremundus's expression suggested that he knew Rufinus was deliberately changing tack, but he went with it, regardless.

'I'm presuming you lifted that piece of information from some official documentation. The Sixth Raetorum spent a few months there making bricks for the locals to use. That's all.'

Rufinus sighed. 'If you truly mean me no harm and intend to release me in the end, I don't suppose you would be willing to let me write to my wife? The last time I sent her a message was from Liguria, telling her I was heading north. She will be worried sick. I suspect there's a small pile of letters from her waiting for me at the mansio in Tasgetium.'

Veremundus considered this for a moment, then nodded. 'I will, of course, want to read the message before I send it. You will mention nothing of any of this, nor your current or recent locations. Assure her that you are well, and no more, excepting simple platitudes. Do that, and I will send it on for you via the cursus publicus. I may even, if you are a model prisoner, consider sending to Tasgetium for any post awaiting you there. This, as well as your future liberty, rests, of course, on your good behaviour.'

Rufinus inclined his head in acquiescence. He had no intention whatsoever of being a model prisoner. The moment the opportunity presented itself, he would be gone. But it was complicated, as he had to get eight other men and a dog free at the same time.

'Come,' the prefect said, rising and striding into his office. It occurred to Rufinus that in here he and the prefect were alone. There was a very good chance that if he made a move, he could subdue, or even kill, Veremundus quickly, possibly without even drawing the attention of the guards outside. It was quite brave of the man to allow him such latitude, really. But he knew he wouldn't do it, and probably so did the prefect. Given the scale of this plot, and how he had already devolved part of the control to trusted auxiliary officers and German kings, killing him would not only be unlikely to stop the plot, it would remove the one man who might still have a small level of control over it, and instead open it up to the whims of much more dangerous men. He put aside the notion and followed the man into the office.

As Rufinus joined him, Veremundus cleared an area at a secondary desk to one side of the room and shuffled the chair over to it, providing a sheet of vellum and writing materials. Rufinus strolled across and was about to sit down when his gaze fell upon an object he had not expected to see, but one that filled him with relief. A broken sword sat atop a cabinet. A simple thing, but one that meant a great deal to Rufinus.

The prefect noted him pause, spotted the object of his attention. 'Yes, an interesting piece of luggage. When I had your gear searched, and I apologise, but it was a necessity, that rather stood out. The rest of your equipment and possessions are stored in hut fourteen with those of your men, but I was intrigued by that. "P MAR RUST," the blade says, and if I remember correctly, you are Gnaeus Marcius Rustius Rufinus. A leap in logic suggests that this belonged to your brother, the one who commanded at Batavis before his unfortunate demise.'

Rufinus nodded, saying nothing.

'Broken?'

'The work of your German head-takers.'

Veremundus winced. 'Again, my apologies and my condolences. Such things should never have happened and were not a part of the plan. I intended to hold any officer who resisted in a similar manner to yourself.'

Rufinus simply grunted and took a seat, dipping the pen in the ink and starting to write. He was careful and circumspect. He told Senova he was following up investigating his brother's death, and that he was a guest of the governor at Castra Regina. He still had work to do but was in good health and as good a spirit as could be hoped in the circumstances, and that he would be home as soon as he could. If that was not imminent, then he would write again. The message was short, and he had another piece of investigating to do now, outside in the camp, and he wanted to get to it. He'd not realised the huts were numbered, and if they were, then those numbers must be visible somewhere. Hut fourteen, he now knew, held his gear and that of his men. That would be paramount to their survival when they escaped, and so now he had an extra goal.

Two extra goals, in fact. He had no intention of leaving this camp without the broken sword of his brother, and that would mean getting into the prefect's office, somehow.

A commotion outside made him stop, just as he was finishing up the letter. He turned to the door, as did Veremundus. Argument was clearly audible outside in the Germanic tongue, and then heavy, booted footsteps coming closer, clomping on the timbers of the hut floor, and more than one pair. Rufinus tensed.

The figure that appeared in the door was new, and impressive. A native, clearly, the man had long grey hair that was pulled up into a top-knot, excepting a single braid that swung free, weighted with an amber bead. His beard was long and wild, and became almost indistinguishable from the folded and tied paws of the bear pelt he was wearing in the manner of a cloak. His biceps were decorated with arm rings of gold, tattoos beneath them, and his tunic of blue was belted with a girdle of gold and precious stones. At his side hung a good sword with a jewelled pommel. But the thing that Rufinus noticed instantly was his face, and in particular his eyes. The man, obviously a chieftain or king, was not a young man, by any means, yet Rufinus immediately recognised how dangerous the man still was. The scars on his lined face spoke of a lifetime of war, and his bright, gleaming eyes were clever and cruel. He remembered reading somewhere about Germanic leaders – the leaders of many of the northern peoples, in fact. They often became king not because of parentage, but by sheer force, and only retained power by staying the strongest and most feared warrior in the tribe. Rufinus could see straight away why this man ruled his people.

'I was not expecting you so soon, Ingomer,' the prefect said, his tone cold.

Rufinus had already almost assumed this to be that very man: Ingomer, the German who had become the spokesman for all the Germanic kings involved in this madness. The king of kings, after a fashion. The man who had the most power in this matter after

Veremundus, or possible even *before* him. In fact, possibly the man with the most power in the whole of Raetia right now.

And the man responsible for the death of Publius, along with several other Roman officers.

Behind the king, other Germanic warriors were lurking in the outer room.

'Have you finished teaching the men,' Ingomer said bluntly, his Germanic accented Latin thick and deep, hard to follow without intense concentration. Rufinus was rather surprised that he spoke Latin at all and did not simply use an interpreter.

'This batch are almost fully trained, yes,' Veremundus replied. 'I want them to study cavalry moves for a few days, and then you can take them. How many more warbands have you waiting?'

'Two, but this waiting angers me. Train them together.'

'Unless they are small warbands, there is not room here, and I will have insufficient manpower to adequately instruct them. I set the system up myself and planned it all out. You know that. Things will proceed as ordered. Two more warbands at ten days apiece, plus travelling time. That means that by the end of the month we will be ready to start moving.' He turned to Rufinus. 'And once the tribes are on the move, I will take my officers and visit Castra Regina, the plan will be in effect, and you can be released.'

'Who is this?' Ingomer suddenly snapped, pointing at Rufinus, who had stopped writing, listening carefully, his hand closing on the pen he was using and slipping it into his belt.

'A prisoner.'

'Another Roman officer. He should be killed like the rest.'

Veremundus pulled himself up haughtily. 'The others should not have been killed either. Their deaths put the whole plan in danger.'

'Gah. I care not.'

'Then look at it this way,' the prefect snarled. 'We have a month to go. The suspicious deaths of officers, should such details reach the governor, will alert him to danger. All those men we wish to frighten into pulling back will instead be mobilised for trouble and your own job becomes that much harder. That is why this man lives. Because I do not wish to kill my countrymen when it can be avoided, but also for simple expediency. Each notable death you incur makes it more likely the governor will hear, understand, and prepare to resist.'

'Train the men faster,' Ingomer snapped, and turned on his heel, marching from the room.

Veremundus was trembling slightly, and Rufinus seriously considered grabbing that broken blade and racing after the German, sinking it into his back, though he would never have got there in time. The other warriors out there would stop him.

But the time was coming. Along with all the other steps to his escape, he added one paramount item: kill Ingomer.

CHAPTER THIRTEEN

Four days had passed since the meeting in the headquarters upon the return of Ingomer. The current group of native trainees had departed the camp that morning, and another warband was expected imminently. Rufinus had managed one more tour of the camp the next morning before the German king had argued Veremundus into putting a stop to such things, citing the alternative, since Ingomer was all in favour of simply killing Rufinus and the other captives.

Rufinus was ready. Actually, not *quite* ready. He'd rather have had more time to plan, but with the reduced population of the camp right now, there would not be a better time, and every day spent here with Ingomer in residence was risking an offhand beheading. At least he had managed to identify hut fourteen in his last visit, and so now he knew what he had to do.

He had started work the moment he returned from the hut that day. All he had was the pen he had stolen from the prefect's office, a simple bronze stilus with a point at the end, stained black from years of ink. He'd looked at every way out of the hut, but the door was constantly watched, and the grilles on the windows too solid to move. The only feasible way was through the timbers. He'd found the weakest board, handily on the back wall, and had started to use the pen to pry the nails out, slowly, one by one. It had been slow, painstaking work with such an inefficient tool, and he'd limited the work to times when the ambient noise of the camp would help cover any sounds, in case the guard out front should hear anything. Then, today, he'd thrown caution to the wind. He'd managed to remove six of the ten nails over three days at such a rate, unheard, but now that the camp was half empty, he needed to go, and so today he'd worked out the last four without waiting for such cover. Still, he'd clearly not been heard, and had felt a small elation as he lifted the board carefully aside and was rewarded with a space just large enough to shuffle through on his back.

The sun had gone down perhaps an hour ago. That meant that all major activity in the camp had stopped, but the tribesmen and auxiliaries both would now be preparing food and drinking beer and wine to recover from their day's efforts.

Rufinus lowered himself to the floor and poked his head out through the hole, looking left and right. The space between here and the next hut was empty and dark, the only sound the distant hum of conversation and camp life. Carefully and slowly, he pulled himself out through the hole and into the dust. At least it had not rained for some time, and the ground was dry. Rising slowly, he looked about again to be sure there was still no movement, and then paced quietly along the length of the hut and ducked briefly around the end to view the next alley.

Empty and quiet.

His next stop was hut fourteen, and so he turned and dashed to the next hut corner, pausing and peeping around it. Two more repeats of the process, and he found himself at the end of the row that contained hut fourteen, wherein he would find their gear. He peered briefly around the corner, and ducked back, cursing silently. A German warrior and his woman were... *busy*, against the door of hut fourteen. There was plainly no way he was gaining access to that, for a while at least.

He amended the plan in his head. He had intended to take his pack from the hut and then go and break out the men of the Third Italica. Then, while they took their own things from hut fourteen, he would dip into the headquarters and collect the broken sword, free Orthus, and then they would meet up at a point he had identified as the weakest in the monitored defences. Now, he would have to break out the men first, and *then* look at hut fourteen once those two Germans' exercise was over.

192

He backtracked two huts and changed route, moving down a different alley. Briefly, he caught a glimpse of the front of the hut the others were being kept in, and could see the auxiliary on guard there, then dipped back into a dark, unoccupied space. One of the huts he was moving alongside, which he knew to be barracks, was apparently unoccupied, for the windows were open and the interior dark and silent. Reasoning that at this time, if there was anyone in there, there would be lamp light or snoring, he reached the door and gently edged it open. It seemed not only unoccupied, but unused. Probably the accommodation given to the natives when they visited to train, who had now gone once more. With the relief of confirmation, he ducked into the empty hut. The men controlling this camp may be Germans and looking to commit treason, but they were still trained auxiliaries, and so they had organised all the huts the way soldiers always did, including stacking spare kit on the shelves at the end.

Smiling to himself, Rufinus grabbed a stack of auxiliary uniforms and picked up the three swords that lay on a shelf, all he could reasonably carry. As an afterthought, he juggled his armfuls and hooked out a multi-tool that sat to one side. That would be faster to work with than his stilus.

With his burden in hand, he checked the coast was clear and then nipped back out of the hut, along to the end, and then round the corner. The alley he wanted was dark and empty. He grinned. Dropping to the ground, he examined the hut's boards and found that they were just as he remembered. These huts had been built by the natives to a Roman design, and so they lacked a little of the uniformity of Roman construction. *His* hut had been boarded from the inside, the nail heads internal, while *this* one had been hammered together from the outside. Convenient. He would have to thank Fortuna with an offering the next time he found one of her temples.

He put his pile of gear over to one side, swords on top of the uniforms, and gripped the multi-tool. This was without a doubt the most dangerous moment of his plan so far. He unfolded the device so that the single pick-blade protruded at the end and used it to dig into the wood of the lowest plank, around one of the nails that held it in place. Gritting his teeth, he dug and levered at the nail head until he managed to pull it far enough to stand proud of the surface. Taking a deep breath, he unfolded the twin-pronged fork at the other end of the tool and jammed it around the nail behind the head, using it as a lever to pull the nail free. It took some work, and at one point he slipped and panicked. The noise of metal sliding along metal sounded deafening to him in the silence, and he waited, tense, expecting the soldier on guard at the other side of the hut to appear at any moment.

He did not, and so Rufinus went back to work. A few moments more and he had the nail free. Carefully, he repeated the whole process on the nail above. He then tested the plank to see if it would move. It did not, and so he silently grumbled as he set to work on the next two nails along. After what felt like hours, he had four nails free, and then reached to the end of the plank and pulled once more.

It bent out slightly and as he leaned down to look through it, he found himself face to face with Clemens.

'Shit,' whispered the legionary, 'I thought it was rats.'

'I'm going to take out the rest of the nails, then move the plank. Then you all need to slide out one at a time, and as quietly as possible. We don't want to alert the guard.'

'And then?'

'Shhh,' Rufinus hissed as quietly as possible. On the far side of the hut, he could hear talking. Hardly daring to breathe, he listened. Two voices in German, murmuring. Then a laugh. Footsteps fading with distance. A cough. The guard was alone again.

No more whispering. Too dangerous. He motioned to Clemens to back away, and then let the board fall back gently into place. Quickly, he moved along and started work on the next nails. As quietly as he could, he levered out those two, and moved on. He noted with a wry smile that the shoddy work of the

194

natives showed in that they'd skimped and missed out two of the ten nails on this plank. At the far end, he levered out the first nail, and then had to hold the plank in place as he worked on the last one. It came free with a creak and Rufinus stopped dead for a moment, holding both his breath and the loose plank, waiting for discovery.

Nothing happened. He counted to thirty to be sure, folded away the tool and tucked it into his boot, and then lifted away the plank and propped it against the hut, a little further along. He then scooped up the uniforms and swords and nipped to the corner, looking around it. No one. With a fierce smile, he ducked across the alley to another corner, checked around it, and then turned to look back. One of the legionaries was carefully shuffling under the gap. It took what felt far too long to Rufinus, but finally he pulled himself free, looked this way and that, then nipped across to the wall of the hut opposite and lurked there, looking nervous, while the next man began to escape.

Rufinus fretted. It was taking too long. They were being too slow, but he couldn't hurry them, dare not speak in case he attracted attention. Instead he stood, trembling. For a moment, he considered running over and freeing Orthus, but decided against it. His dog was a wonderful animal but sometimes not all that bright. He might just decide to make a noisy fuss of Rufinus, and so he needed to save that move for the end, when they were ready to make a run for it.

A third man was coming out now, two already standing together next to the hut opposite. Gods, but it would take forever for the whole lot to escape at this rate. Rufinus almost jumped as the soldier on guard at their hut suddenly appeared around the corner in the main alleyway. Rufinus ducked back out of sight and, seeing him do that, the two men opposite pressed themselves against the hut wall, eyes wide. The man halfway out lay still.

Then there came the sound of a long, arcing stream of urine from the alley, and Rufinus heaved a silent sigh of relief. He'd honestly thought they'd been discovered, but in fact it was just that man relieving himself in private without bothering to visit the latrines.

Rufinus made a frantic gesture to the legionaries, and the man on the ground began to shuffle free, making the most of the urinating soldier's noise to cover the sound. Freeing himself, he ducked across to join his friends as a fourth man began to emerge. He slowed once more as the guard finished peeing, and returned to his post by the door at the other side, and then began to move again. In moments he was free and moving. Four men had escaped.

Rufinus breathed slowly. It was working. Not as fast as he'd hoped, but it was working. Now, Clemens appeared in the gap and began to shuffle to freedom. Rufinus turned and looked the other way, preparing for the next step. Hopefully those two German lovers had had their fill now, and the door to hut fourteen was clear. It was possible the door there was locked, but he doubted it. Most huts seemed to be left unlocked and many did not seem to have locks or bolts at all. He was wondering how he could use the multi-tool to open a lock, should it be required, when everything went wrong.

A shout in German from the front of the hut sounded urgent, alarmed. It was echoed by other shouts further away, and Rufinus looked across at the legionaries. Clemens acted instantly, sliding back under the boards into the hut, out of sight. The four free men threw panicked looks at Rufinus, as running footsteps sounded among the huts. Rufinus swore.

Another of the legionaries dropped and slipped back under the wall into the hut, leaving three men out.

Those three were too late to return to their hut. At that moment, two Germans appeared at the far end, spears out, and shouted angry words. The three men turned to flee towards Rufinus, but two of the auxiliaries appeared from this end, trapping the escaped legionaries.

Rufinus caught their panicked glances, and had but a heartbeat to make a decision. He couldn't help them. He would have to hope they were sensible and did not try to fight their way out. But *he* could not be caught, for if he was, then Prefect Veremundus would be very unlikely to allow Rufinus such continued freedoms. He would be back to being locked up and peeing in a bucket.

He ran. It was only four loping steps to get out of sight of the growing presence of men. More of Ingomer's native Germans and the Germanic auxiliaries of Veremundus were closing on the hut and the revealed escape attempt. Rufinus ducked around another hut and stopped dead, leaning back in the shadow, pressing himself against the wall as two men with spears in hand ran past the end of the alley.

He had to get back to his own hut and to safety, pretend he had not been part of any of this. Otherwise there would be no way to move on and have a second attempt. He waited until those men were safely away and then got to the end of the hut and looked out. He ducked back again as another three men ran past, and waited, heart pounding, in the shadow. Another look and the coast was clear. He ran to the next hut and dipped into the shadows.

What, he wondered, had alarmed the guards back there? They had not been discovered until after the shouting, so what had caused the shouts? Had the guards *heard* them? He fumed as he ran to the corner.

The next move was perilous. He had to cross one of the wider thoroughfares. That had been fine before, when the camp's occupants were going about their ordinary business, but now they were alert to trouble and rushing this way and that, it seemed very likely the street would be busy. He glanced out. Miraculously, it was empty, although it was in full view of one of the towers on the camp's defences. He was fairly sure the man in the tower was looking away, along the wall and at one of his mates, and knew that if he didn't go now, the street might fill with angry Germans at any moment, and then he would be cut off from his hut.

197

He ran. Straight out into the open, in view of that tower, and, knowing he had a wide space to cross in the shortest time possible before he was safe again, he ran fast and hard. Unfortunately, he was struggling to keep hold of his burden, and as he ran, halfway across the street, the swords slipped from the top of the pile in his arms.

He faltered for a moment only. He didn't have time to stop, and tried to grab them as they fell while still running, the net result being that he ended up dropping half the uniforms as well. In moments he was into the shadows and relative safety of the alley opposite and swore, panting. He was holding two pairs of auxiliary trousers and one tunic, everything else he had taken now lying in a heap in the middle of the street.

He looked wistfully at the strewn clothing and weapons, but the man in the tower was now looking this way, and the sound of approaching men confirmed there was just no hope of getting them back. He turned and ran on.

At the next corner, he almost ran into a German, and threw himself back into the shadows and down to the ground as the man ran past, sword out, and glanced briefly at where Rufinus had been a moment earlier.

He picked himself up once more and ran on.

There, at last, was the back of his hut with the missing board at the bottom. He'd made it. A quick glance left and right, and he dashed across to that alleyway. He would try all this again. It might be harder to get the other lads out next time, now that the board had been discovered, but he would think of something. He dropped to the dusty ground and began to shuffle back through the gap.

He knew he was in trouble that very moment. His first view of his hut revealed two pairs of boots. There were *men* in his hut, although right now from the position of the feet, they had their back to him. He wrestled with the sudden decision. The game was up. He either had to climb through and surrender, in which case he would lose all the liberties he had gained, or he had to duck back out and make a go of it. That would mean trying to free Orthus and make it over the defences out into the woods without the legionaries, and it would be highly unlikely that he would get his hands on the broken sword.

The decision was made *for* him a moment later. Something grabbed his ankles and pulled hard, and he was unceremoniously yanked back out of that gap, into the darkness of the alleyway. As his feet were released, he rolled onto his back and looked up. Four Germans stood over him, all locals in their native gear rather than auxiliaries. The one who'd had his ankles was the only one without a sword bared.

It was definitely over now.

One of the men snapped something in his own language, and when Rufinus did not answer, kicked him hard in the side. Rufinus grunted at the blow, the air driven from his lungs. The man motioned for him to get up, and he did so, slowly, grunting again at that pain in his ribs. The moment he was standing, the four men were on him, two with their weapons ready, a third sheathing his sword so that the others could grab him by the upper arms and manhandle him round the hut to the front, where the door stood open.

An auxiliary was having an argument with one of the natives outside the hut, and as Rufinus was bundled into view and then towards the door, the soldier barked something angry and urgent, and then turned and ran off, full of purpose. Rufinus flinched. That, he did not see as a good sign.

There were two oil lamps now guttering in his hut, one at each end, sufficient to light the whole room, and certainly sufficient to light the two men already in there. Rufinus's spirits sank at the sight of King Ingomer and one of his men standing in the centre of the hut. The German king turned at Rufinus's entrance, and his lip wrinkled with distaste. He let out a stream of angry sounding words in his own language, which Rufinus ignored, since he had no idea what they meant anyway. He seemed to be expecting a reply from Rufinus, who knew he should play this carefully, with respect and meekness, hoping to get through with the minimum of trouble, but it was impossible. He found that just the sight of this man inflamed him. This man who had seen to the offhand butchery of Roman officers, including the beheading of Rufinus's own brother. He simply could not treat the man with anything less than spite.

Ingomer barked out another demand.

Rufinus gave him the coldest smile he could muster and spoke, lip wrinkled.

'I do not speak your language, you murderous, slimy sack of dog vomit.'

To punctuate his sentence, he hawked and spat at the king's feet.

Ingomer's eyes flashed with fury and he suddenly lashed out with the back of his hand, a heavy slap that caught Rufinus on the cheek and sent him staggering. He was about to launch back with a punch of his own, when the other warrior stepped in the way, sword up. The four who'd escorted him in were on him again, then, the two with free hands restraining his arms.

The king said something, this time to his men. Something smashed into the back of Rufinus's legs, behind the knees, and he dropped with a stifled cry. He was on his knees now, clearly as Ingomer had intended, but the men had not let go of his arms. Rufinus struggled, but despite his strength, he was on his knees, with painful legs and face, and ribs that were still tender from the kick. His struggling was rapidly overcome. Those men who had hold of him changed their grip then, sliding down to hold him by the wrists instead. He struggled again, but their grip only tightened, and then they twisted his arms so that it wrenched the muscles all the way up and almost broke his elbows. He hissed in pain again, and was now held in an excruciating position.

Ingomer looked past him at the other men behind, and Rufinus had a rather dark premonition about what was to come. As if to confirm it, he heard a whetstone being run along the edge of a blade.

200

Well, shit. This was not how he'd imagined his own ending. He wondered if it had been like this for his brother. Rufinus had not seen one of their stone head-shrines in the camp, but it seemed likely there was one somewhere, and he'd be the latest to occupy it.

'What is the meaning of this?' snapped an angry voice in perfect Latin.

Rufinus had never been so grateful to hear his own language, and he could never have imagined being relieved to hear Prefect Veremundus, but by all the gods, he was.

He looked up. He was still being held, and could not crane his neck enough to see what was happening behind him, but he could see Ingomer, and the king was angry, not just at Rufinus, but also at the prefect. The king spoke again, this time in thickly-accented Latin and to Veremundus.

'You should have killed him straight away. Him and all of his men. And his dog. They should have been beheaded and disposed of before they ever left your lands. To bring them here was foolish, to let them live even more so. And now they try to escape, just to show you once again how foolish you are being. Kill them. Or let me kill them.'

'No. I was already furious over your butchery of my countrymen when I could not do anything about it, but I will not let you kill my people in front of me, in my own camp.'

'*Your* camp in *my* lands,' growled Ingomer in a dangerous tone.

'Still, this is *my* strategy and *my* camp. We do this *my* way.'

'I grow *tired* of your way.'

'Tired or not, I command here and you will not stand against me. Release the man this instant.'

Rufinus hissed in relief as his arms were let go, and he managed to pull them back in, folding them and massaging the painful muscles. He tried·to rise but his knees hurt, and he fell back to the floor for a few moments before making the attempt again, this time a lot slower and more carefully. He managed to get to his feet on that second attempt, wobbling slightly. The four men who'd caught him had shuffled over to stand with their king, and now six natives faced just three Romans: Rufinus, Veremundus and the guard who'd fetched him. It did not escape Rufinus's notice that if the German king suddenly decided to kill him anyway, there was actually little the prefect could do to stop it. But Ingomer did not move. Instead, he levelled an angry finger at Veremundus.

'If you will not kill this man because he is an officer, then make sure you keep him locked up better from now. on'

With that, he stomped past them and out of the hut, his men at his back.

Rufinus breathed in slowly, eyes watering, still rubbing painful joints and muscles.

'I am extremely disappointed with you,' the prefect said finally, once the Germans were gone. 'I have given you all the latitude you could wish for, every possible freedom short of sending you on your way. And you repay that by attempting to escape anyway, and to free other prisoners in the process.'

'What did you expect?' Rufinus sighed.

'A little respect and gratitude would be nice. And now I will have to assign men I cannot afford to spare to keep an extra watch on you and your men. You will have to say farewell to our brief walks and discussions, though I now recognise that you were only using them to lull me into a false sense of security while you planned your flight.'

There was a long pause, and Rufinus finally interrupted the uncomfortable silence.

'Thank you.'

'What for?'

'For stopping them killing me.'

Veremundus sagged slightly. 'Listen, Tribune. I do not want to be your enemy, though you are making that increasingly difficult. But as well as trying to put my plan into place within very tight timings, I have to constantly fight to keep my allies in their place. You making a fool out of me and proving failures in my security only damages that, and gives the Germans ammunition against me. You are hereby confined to this hut for the duration. I heartily recommend that you do nothing else to anger the king, for he will acquiesce to my demands only so long.'

He rubbed his chin. 'I am presuming you have some sort of tool you had used to pry out the nails. Hand it over.'

Rufinus nodded, removed the stilus he had stolen from the prefect's office, and passed it over. Veremundus took it and turned it over a few times, looking at it. 'Clever. I should have noticed you taking it, really, though Ingomer distracted me. There will be no such options in future,' he announced, tucking away the pen.

With that, the prefect turned and walked away with his man.

Rufinus staggered over to the bed and sank to a seated position with a sigh. He sat there as the door was closed and locked, and as that plank was put back in place and nailed on from the outside. As extra boards were hammered over the window, and the room sank into darkness, Rufinus sat and listened. He had failed. His captors had removed from him all chances of repeating the process.

He reached down to his belt and pulled free the multi-tool.

Almost all chances.

Now to start planning anew.

CHAPTER FOURTEEN

The dream was different, yet horribly familiar. In a strange and eerie dream version of the woodland camp, a hundred headless Romans sparred with and trained a thousand furious Germans, some of those still carrying the Romans's severed heads.

He recognised a few of the Romans, and two of the nearest were his brother and Prefect Veremundus, both identifiable by their clothing and gear, even without a recognisable head.

The swords rang and clanged, whined and grated.

And suddenly there was a loud bang instead.

The door of the hut slammed open, wrenching Rufinus from the dream, which, given the subject, was a mixed blessing to say the least. He blinked awake in the bed at the far end of the room and took in the situation in a heartbeat.

It was around dawn, for the level of light revealed in the open doorway was low and at a shallow angle. That light revealed three shapes, and even the outline alone told him that they were natives in furs and arm rings, rather than the men of the auxilia, which boded ill.

He rose from the bed slowly, for his ribs, knees, arms and cheek all still ached from the night's beatings, although they were already gradually numbing. The options ran through his head as they always did when faced with potential violence, although in this case rather pointlessly. Really, they boiled down to two choices: resist or capitulate. A beating awaited him at the very least, he was certain of it, but it might be just that and nothing worse. Beatings he had taken more than once and walked away from. If he attempted to resist them, they would simply add another beating here, first, in the hut, before taking him wherever they planned. There was no real chance of overpowering them, either. Rufinus had no idea how many native warriors Ingomer had brought with him to the camp, but he was a king, so there would be a reasonable number of them.

Accepting whatever fate lay ahead sat poorly with Rufinus, but in the end it was clearly the only viable option.

One of the Germans barked something and gestured at the exit. Rufinus nodded and walked steadily across the hut and out of the door, into the early morning sunshine. The sky looked prepared for a balmy day, a deep blue, though it did little to lift Rufinus's spirits. Three more German warriors waited for him outside the hut, and all of them had their swords in their hands. Clearly Ingomer had no intention of underestimating the Roman. Rufinus knew that he was still in formidable shape, and the marks and scars that defined him would have alerted the king to Rufinus's martial strengths.

A warrior stepped out ahead of the rest and began to walk, and Rufinus looked to the other Germans, one of whom motioned with a sword for him to follow. He did so, at an easy pace, alert, head turning, eyes playing across the camp as he walked. He could see no one else around, and so he listened carefully. In the distance, he could hear the sound of soldiers on a morning parade, counting off by unit. The auxilia were gathered elsewhere in the camp, likely unaware of what was happening here.

That raised a whole new alarm for Rufinus. Whatever the Germans had planned for him, they had timed it so that they could do it without interference from the auxilia. A dark premonition stole over him, and he began trying to think of any way out of what he now suspected was coming.

Two more Germans joined them. Where were they all going? They were not heading towards any of the camp's gates nor training spaces, more into one largely-shunned corner of the camp. There was no headquarters or exercise ground, or anything of value at all there. In fact, all he knew of in this corner was the latrines.

Another alarm went off.

This was a move made by Ingomer, unnoticed by the auxilia, and in a place chosen for its solitude, since no one hung around the latrine area because of the ambient aroma. Indeed, he could already faintly smell the tang of ammonia as they approached.

There was no one around to help.

This was not good.

A thought struck him, and he looked up and to one side.

The ramparts around the camp were only sparsely manned here, especially at night. The residents had nothing to fear from the local tribes, after all, given that they were supporting and training them. But atop a tower nearby he could see a figure, leaning on the timber in a bored manner. Hope thrilled through him. Over the years, he had been in a hundred camps, each filled with soldiers on guard duty. That pose, the sheer tedium it represented, was a *soldier's* pose, not a native tribesman.

The man was an auxiliary.

He took a deep breath and prayed to Minerva. All the auxilia here were German or Raetian, but he did not know how far their regression into the tribal mindset had gone. Had Veremundus managed to keep them thinking like soldiers, or were they already past that? If they had gone too far native, like some of the units he had met on this frontier, they might just *help* Ingomer, rather than standing against him. Rufinus turned and cupped his hands to his mouth.

'You in the tower.'

The soldier heard, as he could tell from the way he straightened and looked around for the source of the call.

A German warrior behind Rufinus said something and cuffed him around the back of the head, He ignored the blow and continued to call to the auxiliary guard. 'Yes, you. Find the prefect.'

Another snarl from behind, and another slap. He ignored it again.

'Find Veremundus and bring him. Now!'

This time the slap was hard, nearly rattling Rufinus's brains, and then they turned away between two huts, losing sight of the tower. Rufinus prayed the soldier had heard, understood, and obeyed. If not, he was done for. He staggered on, his escort glaring at him and exchanging words occasionally in their own incomprehensible tongue.

There was an open space around the latrines, for obvious reasons. In permanent forts, local sources of running water were utilised to flush out the latrines, which kept them relatively fresh. In temporary camps, however, where they were simply a pit dug in the ground with a wooden seat atop, they tended to back up and become horrendous until they were almost full, at which point they were infilled, turfed over, and a new pit dug elsewhere.

No one wanted to spend time in the area, so there was always a space around them.

Today, that space was in use.

Rufinus felt his stomach twist as they rounded a last hut and the scene opened up before him.

Three men stood with their hands bound behind their backs. Three legionaries of the Third Italica. Rufinus felt a chill as he recognised which three men it was. The trio who had been caught outside their hut... and Rufinus, who had done the same. That was no coincidence.

Over to one side stood Ingomer, with half a dozen of his best warriors clustered around him. Another man in gold ornament and rich clothing stood a little away with his own guards, and this, Rufinus presumed, was another of the various kings Veremundus had enlisted in his scheme, presumably freshly arrived. Another score or more German warriors stood around in the open space all with weapons bared, and one, alone at the centre, was seated on the ground, rhythmically stroking a whetstone up and down the edge of his blade.

If Rufinus had been in any doubt as to their fate, that sight dispelled it.

Ingomer intended to take their heads, despite being overruled last night by the prefect.

Veremundus's grip on this place was slipping, clearly.

As Rufinus was taken over to stand with the others, Ingomer started to speak, an almost oratorical outpouring, though once more in the gruff Germanic tongue. Whatever he was saying drew hard looks and nods from the others in the open space, and the second king was also nodding along and murmuring.

Suddenly, Ingomer pointed at one of the legionaries. Oclatius, who had been so kind to the dog with his treats, blinked, and then began to stutter denials as he was pushed forward. He struggled, though his bound hands made it difficult. Two men pushed and guided him towards the warrior who had now finished sharpening the execution sword. Rufinus shivered. It was hard to behead a man, particularly in one blow, as he knew from personal experience. It required great strength and a broad swing with the blade. The sword had to be heavy enough to gain sufficient momentum, and as sharp as possible to make the cut. Even then, as often as not it took two or three blows for the head to come off.

This sword did not look quite sharp enough to Rufinus. He was icy cold now, fear rippling through him. It was said that a man could still feel it by the third blow...

Oclatius was brought before the headsman. He yelped in panic now, babbling, and tried to move, but one of the Germans gripped his arm and held him in place. The other produced a heavy cudgel and brought it round in a wide sweep behind the man, unseen and low. It struck the back of the legionary's knees in exactly the same move they had used on Rufinus in the hut last night, and with precisely the same result. Oclatius cried out and collapsed to his knees. He tried to rise, but he couldn't. The man with the sword walked round to behind the legionary's shoulder and lifted the blade.

Oclatius was crying out for them to stop. Begging. He looked up at the man who had his arm, and that man nodded to his friends and then slammed the edge of his hand into the legionary's neck. The shouts stopped instantly with the crushed throat, but that was not the reason for the blow. The victim's body responded naturally, head jerking forward. As he did so, the swordsman brought his long blade down even as the German was still pulling his hand away. Just as Rufinus had predicted, the blade slammed deep into the neck and wedged there, stuck. The German had to yank it back out with a deal of effort, Oclatius lolling for a moment, his head half hanging off, and then the second blow came and removed the head entirely.

The rest of the body folded up, pumping blood, and collapsed to the ground as one of the warriors bent and collected a head whose mouth remained open in a wide silent scream. The rest of the remains were unceremoniously dragged to one side, still in clear view.

There was a strange and grisly air of approval all round as the man with the head collected a spear from a pile, rammed the point into the skull and then lifted it, and with some effort and help from a friend, rammed the butt into the ground so that the head could be on open display.

The sight was too much for the men next to Rufinus. The legionaries were both screaming panicked pleas now, and suddenly, the man next in line made a break for it. He started to run, but without purpose, for there really was nowhere to run to. He got little more than ten paces before two warriors from the gathering around the space grabbed him and dragged him, fighting and screaming, back to the line. Sobbing, he was held in place for a moment, but as soon as they let go of him, he ran again. It was mere moments before he was caught and dragged back again.

The second king made some suggestion, and Ingomer nodded, then barked out instructions.

The man behind the Romans suddenly slammed his blade down in a low sweep and severed the tendons at the panicking Roman's ankles, damn near removing his feet in the process. The legionary screamed and collapsed to the ground. Rufinus tried to harden his heart, for he knew what was coming.

Two men grabbed the sobbing man and dragged him into the open space, where the blood of the previous victim still gleamed in pools that reflected the dawn sunlight.

The man was too busy screaming in agony to burble in panic now. He could not stand, let alone run. The Germans put him on his knees, but he simply toppled forward to lie, sobbing, in the dirt. They lifted him back to his knees, but as soon as they let go, he fell again.

The Germans grunted in irritation, but the headsman waved them away and went about his business as best he could. His sword fell low. It was far from ideal. With the body prone as it was, it was difficult to aim the blow well, and it landed more on the legionary's shoulder than neck, breaking the bones and digging a deep crimson gash in the shallow flesh. The man began to scream again as the German retrieved his blade and tried once more. This time the blow hit the back of the soldier's skull, smashing it.

Several of the Germans laughed, one of them clearly making some awful joke of it. Ingomer did *not* look amused.

The executioner hacked away a couple more times, and finally someone collected the broken head from the pile of meat and bones on the ground. The head was appended to a second spear and driven into the ground beside the first while the body was dragged away and dumped atop the previous victim's remains.

'Womanish behaviour,' the king shouted at his prisoners. 'Meet your fate like men and die well, not like this coward, who died badly.'

Rufinus steadied himself. He would like to think he would do just that, but every man had a breaking point. Was he still the same Rufinus who had held his tongue even through torture?

211

'Stop this, at once,' bellowed a voice in elegant Latin tinged with utter fury.

He thanked the gods silently, eyes rising to the sky, for the soldier in the tower had seemingly done what he asked. That was most definitely the voice of Prefect Veremundus.

Rufinus turned. The prefect was striding into the space with a centurion and two auxiliaries at his back. He stopped, facing Ingomer across the blood-soaked ground. His gaze fell upon the two heads on spears, and his lip twitched.

'Stop this appalling, barbaric display this instant,' Veremundus snapped.

'You seem to forget that you speak to a king,' Ingomer replied, his tone dangerous. All around the space, men bristled and weapons were gripped tight, all eyes going to either the king or the prefect, expectant.

'Have I not warned you about killing important Romans? About how that could come back to bite us all, if the governor learns of it, and it drives him to a militant stand? Did you not hear me when I explained that, or did your primitive mind simply not understand?'

Rufinus flinched at the look that passed across Ingomer's face at these words. The king's eyes narrowed. 'You,' he said, turning to Rufinus. '*You* are important. *He* is *not*.'

Before Rufinus could argue, two warriors had grabbed the other legionary beside him, and were dragging and pushing him out into the space.

'Stop this,' bellowed Veremundus again.

'I take your point about important Romans. Perhaps I was hasty with the prefects on the border, but *this* is not an important Roman.'

The prefect started to move forward towards the panicked soldier, face almost puce with rage, but five Germans shuffled in front of him and made it perfectly clear he was not going to be allowed past them.

'This is *my* camp,' Veremundus shouted. '*My* camp. *My rules*.'

212

'Your camp is in *my* land,' Ingomer said. Rufinus could hear a warning in the man's tone. He was at least as angry as the prefect, but his ire was contained and controlled rather than worn on his sleeve. The king gestured to the men at the centre of the space, and the soldier there was driven to his knees. Rufinus was surprised at how calm the legionary suddenly seemed to be. There was none of the panic he had seen on the previous soldier.

The man knelt there, a warrior close by as the headsman wiped his blade, ready for a fresh kill.

Suddenly, in a blur of movement, the soldier lashed out with his hand. Rufinus thought he was attacking the German for a moment, but then he saw the flash of steel and realised what was happening. With his shoulder at his captor's hip height, the legionary had reached out and snatched the dagger from the man's belt. Rather than attack him with it, though, the soldier had other ideas. Before the Germans could stop him, he'd reversed the blade in his hands and turned it to his chest even as he threw himself forward to the ground.

It was a good blow, well aimed. He hit the dirt with a thud and a grunt. The angry German at his side reached him too late, and all he could do was turn the man over. The hilt of the knife jutted out above the man's impaled heart. His face had already gone still, his eyes unblinking.

He was dead.

He had saved himself the agony and humiliation of the beheading with a clean blow to the heart.

Ingomer was not happy. He began ranting in German, waving his arms, his men answering and nodding. The executioner walked over to the prone body and in three strokes removed the dead man's head anyway, which was carried across and added to the parade of spear-pointed trophies. Rufinus had to note with a certain satisfaction that this third head had an oddly serene expression, while the previous two looked agonised and horrified.

'Take your warriors and get out of my camp,' Veremundus spat at the king, pointing angrily. 'You have no reason to be here anyway, other than this being the only place I can be sure you are not going about killing other senior Romans. The next influx of trainees should be here soon, and I will send word when they have been instructed and the final group is preparing. Until then, I suggest you return to your own people and go about your appalling practices where I cannot see them.'

'I say again,' Ingomer growled, 'that you seem to forget who it is you speak to, Prefect.'

'Yes, you are a king. I know. But here, I…'

'Here you are just another scheming Roman, trying to be more than he is. Trying to be more than a *king*.'

'This is *my* plan. *I* control the operation,' Veremundus shouted.

'You control *nothing*, Roman. You betray your own people for a dream, and even when you ask for our help to do so, you still treat us as though you are our master and we should bend our backs to your will, and thank you for it. You are a fool, Veremundus of Rome. I would have hoped, with the blood of our people in your veins, however dilute, that you were brighter and stronger than this, but no. You are a fool, and a weak one at that. But you have done what was needed now. Your plan is over.'

He turned to his warriors. 'Seize the Roman and take his sword.'

Veremundus stared, and started to bluster. The two auxiliary soldiers stepped forward to defend him, but they had been rather taken by surprise, and their weapons were still sheathed, while all the Germans had theirs bared. The two men were cut down in a heartbeat. The centurion pushed his commander back. 'Run, sir. I'll hold them.'

But he never had the chance. An arrow thrummed out of nowhere and buried itself in the man's neck, sending him backward into the dirt, choking and dying.

Veremundus was alone. He was still staring in shock, his mouth opening and closing as several Germans grabbed him, pulling his sword and dagger from his belt and pushing him towards Rufinus.

The lesser king shouted something at his senior, and Ingomer turned to him, answering in Latin. 'No. The prefect will live. His advice was not *all* stupid. His absence may be noted before we are ready to act. I had all the other prefects killed, so if we find we need one, he is the only one left. Better to keep him alive for now until we are sure. Once we cross their wall, you can have his head. You can have *all* their heads.'

Rufinus shook his own head in exasperation. He'd seen this coming. He'd tried to persuade Veremundus of the dangers, but to no avail, and now it was too late.

'Treachery,' bellowed the prefect, suddenly, hands going to cup around his mouth. 'Romans fall back to the headquarters!'

It was a feeble offering, really, and Rufinus knew it even before Ingomer laughed. 'You waste your time, Prefect. Half of your men obey me anyway, and the others are being rounded up now.'

Veremundus sagged, defeated. 'What have I done?'

Rufinus fought the irresistible slew of 'I told you so's that rose to his tongue. Instead, he straightened. 'You were disappointed in me that I had tried to escape. Now it is imperative that we do just that. Word of this has to get back across the frontier to the loyal garrisons before anything can happen.'

Veremundus was nodding. Any further conversation was impossible, though, for at that moment the Germans had grabbed them both, and were shuffling them along, away from the open ground. Rufinus caught one last glance at the three heads on spears. Next time, the escape wouldn't fail. But he suspected it was going to be a lot harder to get out with Ingomer in charge than it was with the prefect. He could hear Veremundus chuntering angrily under his breath behind him as the two men were marched back through the camp, between the huts and to Rufinus's prison, where they were both slung through the door before it was slammed and locked.

The prefect, shaking, strode across the hut and sat down on the edge of the bed.

'I honestly thought I had them in line. Why do they do this, when my plan benefited them, reuniting the tribes.'

'Because without your plan they can reunite the tribes *and* ravage Roman land for loot and fresh heads. You opened the door for them and expected them to ask politely to enter.'

'But I was in control. I *was*.'

Rufinus couldn't think of anything to say to this, that did not sound sarcastic, anyway. He walked over to the man. 'My escape plans are now *our* escape plans.'

'It will not be easy,' the prefect muttered, looking up at last.

'No,' Rufinus agreed. Now that you finally understand the very real danger, I need you to tell me everything. How many German warbands are we talking about, and where are they? What were your instructions to the six units you influenced, and do you still have any control over them? What men among those can you definitely rely upon, and what units do you know to be extremely loyal to Rome, to the extent that you would never have approached them? How was your plan to be put into motion, and what signals are used?'

Veremundus blinked. 'That's a lot.

'That's just the start. If we want to stop this, I need to know *everything*.'

'We can rely upon the men of Tannum. The Sixth Raetorum I trust implicitly. You saw them just now. Even as Ingomer turned on me they came to my aid.'

Rufinus nodded. 'And are they all like that?'

'Yes. I collected only the best at Tannum and bound them to me. All the soldiers here are either men of Tannum, or hand-picked from the other units.'

Rufinus nodded. Taking the best for this camp went some way to explaining why the auxiliary forts were so under-strength, and why only the less Roman of the men remained in garrison. Not only were they supplying men for the frontier, but also sending their best centuries here to train the Germans. 'So you are of the opinion that everyone here is trustworthy?'

Veremundus nodded.

'Then you are still dreaming,' Rufinus sighed. 'Ingomer told you that half your men follow him, and he has no reason to lie. We can no longer count on your auxiliaries, even here. They are either Ingomer's men or are being dealt with right now. If they are lucky they will be kept alive to train men, else their fate might be atop a spearpoint. We can only hope that the rest of your men back home, assuming you left a garrison at Tannum, follow you.'

The prefect let out a long, slow breath, and Rufinus sat beside him. 'I asked you about that small fort across the frontier from here. You said they were from Bracara Augusta?'

Veremundus nodded.

'Then they cannot have been part of your plan. They are Hispanic cavalry?'

'An equitata unit, mixed horse and foot.'

'Then they are our primary goal.'

The prefect frowned. 'They are?'

'They are loyal to Rome, have no reason to side with Ingomer's Germans, and best of all, they include horsemen, so they can send riders at speed to warn other units, including the governor and the legion at Castra Regina.'

The prefect just nodded, so Rufinus went on.

'We need to get out of this camp and across the border to that fort. But before that we need a way out of this hut, and to free my remaining friends from the Third Italica, my dog, and to collect our things.'

Before Veremundus could reply, there was a thump, and the door to the hut was pulled open once more. Five exhausted-looking legionaries were ushered in, and the door slammed once more. Clemens walked forward and stopped before the two officers.

'I am assuming, sir, there has been a shake-up in command.'

Rufinus rose. 'I'm glad to see you. After what Ingomer did to the other three, I was half expecting his men to just kill you all.'

'I suspect that was the plan,' Clemens replied. 'One of the warriors who came for us asked his boss if we were important. I figured that if he was asking, it could only be a good thing to be important, so I persuaded him that we were with you as envoys of the governor. I think that impressed him, in a minor way. I suspect it saved our lives.'

'Good man. I'd forgotten you speak their language. That's a good thing. That could work in our favour. We need to escape and get to the fortlet of the Hispanic cavalry across the border. They can help get word out.'

Veremundus leaned forward. 'We need to move before the tribes are ready. Ingomer may have taken control, but he's stuck with my plan to work from, as it's too late to change it. It'll take at least six or seven days for him to get word to all his warbands along the frontier. My plan was to have them appear all along the border in strength, to frighten the garrisons and the governor, but Ingomer may have other ideas. He said they would cross the border and to do that with any great ease, he will have to go through the areas held by the six units already under our sway. That means concentrating his forces, so they will have to redeploy and combine before he can move. That will all take time. If we can get out of here and get word to the governor before he is ready, the frontier can be strengthened and held.'

Rufinus nodded. 'Yes, but we cannot simply do a runner. This has to be planned carefully. I think we will only get one chance at escape.'

'What about the auxilia?' Clemens said. 'We saw them being rounded up. Maybe we can break them out and start a revolution in camp.'

Rufinus drummed his fingers on the bedside. 'Perhaps. We don't know how many we can trust right now, but it may come to that. How many tribes are we talking about involved in this?'

'There are seven kings,' Veremundus said. 'So at least seven tribes.'

'They are only talking about one tribe out there,' Clemens said, 'and it's one I've never heard of before.'

'Oh?'

'The Alemanni.'

'You know that means "all men", don't you?' Claudius Ademus noted.

'That's right,' Clemens said, frowning. 'You don't suppose?'

Rufinus rolled his eyes. 'Gods, yes. They elected a spokesman. A king of kings, like the Shahanshah of Parthia. They're not seven tribes any more. They're a confederation, like the Caledonii of Britannia that Agricola fought. Like the Gauls facing Caesar under Vercingetorix. Shit, Veremundus, you may well have put the whole empire in danger with this. You planned to strengthen the border, but in doing so, you've instead strengthened the enemy facing it. You've taken seven tribes who were quite well-disposed towards us because of Commodus and forged them into one super-tribe who sees us as an enemy, and then you went and trained them how to kill Romans.'

'What?' said Clemens, looking around suddenly.

'The good prefect here has made a nice shiny new enemy for Rome, then armed and trained them, and even given them a way through the frontier. Unless we get out of here and warn someone, the Raetian border won't just get pulled back to the Danubius. It'll get completely overrun and obliterated.'

'Alright,' Clemens said, dropping to a crouch facing them. 'What do we do next?'

CHAPTER FIFTEEN

I t transpired that what was next was work.

Hard work, too.

Ingomer, it seemed, was no fool. While he sent out messengers to his sub-kings and their various warbands to change their plan and begin moving – they saw the riders depart, and Clemens heard talk – the great king of the Alemanni decided that while they endured the enforced wait, they might as well make good use of the time.

A few of the auxilia had remained free and had thrown off their Romanness and embraced their heritage, vowing fealty to Ingomer, while the majority of their number had been rounded up and imprisoned. Those free men, though, worked with their new king to plan the effective use of their time. They were about to go to war with the border garrisons, and that meant that the better equipped they were, the more chance they had of swift success.

Prefect Veremundus had stocked this camp well and, with it being in a forest, amid plentiful trees, that meant they had all the supplies they needed to make equipment, and a captive workforce to utilise. Roman wool brought from the border garrisons was made into clothing, leather into boots and belts and horse trappings, wood into shafts for spears and arrows, and into shields, and even the iron and bronze was being forged into weapons and armour. Ingomer was clearly serious.

The captive auxilia were being kept in a palisaded compound, locked in and guarded. The auxiliaries had apparently made an attempt to break out that first night of their incarceration, but Ingomer was no fool. All the huts closest to the compound were used for his warriors' barracks, and there were sufficient guards around the palisade that no stretch was unobserved. Soldiers had poured over the wall, but the shouts from the guards had drawn all Ingomer's men from the huts. With the auxilia unarmed, and their captors using swords, the result had been an appalling loss of life before they had been rounded up and ushed back inside. They accepted their work from that moment, once they had buried fifty-two of their number, and made no further attempt to flee. Consequently, each day they received a cart full of supplies, and orders for what it was to be made into

The more important prisoners did not escape labour, either. After the daring but foiled escape attempt, the Germans were not daft enough to put Rufinus and his companions in with the captive auxilia, keeping them separate in their hut, but they were brought out daily into an open area under the watchful eyes of strong warriors, and joined the effort in arming the Alemanni.

Three days so far, they had worked. Rufinus had forgotten what such drudgery was like, for it had been twenty years since his days with the legion, since doing shifts in the fabricae. By the third day, his fingers were raw, his joints sore and his muscles aching. Even in the legions they had had breaks in the work. Not so in labouring for the Alemanni, who brought them out to work as soon as it was light enough to see, and did not return them to their hut until it was no longer so. They had one meal at dawn before beginning the labour, and one upon their return to the hut, in order to maximise their work time. Indeed, they soon learned to time their toilet habits, for they were expected to urinate and defecate in place while they worked. There was, apparently, no time to waste.

Rufinus reached down to his ribs and tested them, wincing. He'd taken another beating that first day of labour.

As men of the legions, and therefore with better knowledge of craft and skill, some of them had been put on the forges and had worked with metal. Rufinus had taken the opportunity in the middle of their shift to swipe one of the daggers they had made, and slip it into his boot. He had discovered to his dismay that at the end of the shift, those who had worked with the metal were searched very thoroughly – almost *intimately*, in fact. The dagger had been found easily, and three Germans had reprised the damage to Rufinus's ribs as he rolled around on the floor, yelping.

He'd not tried such a thing again.

After the attempted theft, Rufinus had been taken off the forges, and moved to carpentry, along with Clemens and two others. Prefect Veremundus was learning for the first time the hardships of an ordinary soldier's life, sweating over the furnaces with the rest. Rufinus had contemplated trying to filch one of the woodworking tools, but had decided against it, which proved to be the correct decision, for at the end of the second day, all tools were accounted for. Had one been missing, Rufinus would undoubtedly have suffered another beating.

Day three, and Rufinus had begun to settle into a routine, which was a thing both good and bad. It made things easier, but there was a tendency with basic routines to fall into them and switch off, which he could not afford to do. Too much was at stake.

They had reasoned it through, time and again. It would take a while for Ingomer's tribes to move into position, but if they achieved that, while the governor and his legion and frontier garrisons remained blissfully unaware, then when they came, there would be a massacre, the border would be overrun, and this new Alemanni confederation would be free to plunder inside the empire. Their only hope, therefore, was to get out and spread the word. Clemens, who knew the local tribes better than many, was of the opinion that if the Alemanni approached the border and found that Rome was alert, prepared, armed and ready to fight, they would probably disperse and retreat, for now at least. That was the only hope, then, and as always that meant escaping from their incarceration first.

This escape was going to have to be an entirely different matter to the last one.

Rufinus's previous attempt had relied upon stealth and silence, trying to get out of the camp with his friends and away into the woods before anyone knew they had even left the hut. That was no longer feasible. The Germans were not giving them anywhere near as much leeway. Guards watched their hut at all times, and guards watched the prisoner compound of the auxilia. Guards were on every perimeter tower, had sealed three gates and were patrolling the fourth. In short, they were everywhere. The chances of getting out of here without having to take down at least one of their captors were negligible.

Despite that, Rufinus had already worked out some of the plan, though he had yet to share it with the others, or to test parts of it out. The boards of the hut walls were now out. Every angle of the hut was in the view of at least one guard, they were regularly searched for tools, and a hundred more nails had been hammered into them to be sure. The door was clearly a no-go, and the same went for the windows. He had tried lifting up floorboards and digging. The idea of where they were going to hide the mud if they tried to tunnel had not needed to be addressed in the end, for it transpired that this entire camp had been formed many years ago simply by the Roman military felling an area of the forest, levelling the ground, and using the timbers for construction. Consequently, just a foot below the surface, they came across sufficient old root systems to prevent any reasonable attempt at tunnelling. It *might* be possible, but even if it was, it would take so long that the Alemanni would probably be partying in the streets of Rome before the prisoners even broke the surface outside.

That rather limited their options. They could go neither outwards, nor down. That left only one direction, though Rufinus had yet to try the beams and shingles of the hut roof.

Once they got out, they would have to take down quickly and quietly any men watching over the hut. Rufinus had settled upon Clemens's plan as the most viable. Now that they could be fairly sure that all the auxilia in that locked compound were on their side, it seemed sensible to break them out. Veremundus had expected that they would join forces with those men and overcome the Germans. Rufinus had not yet disabused him of the notion. They would still be badly outnumbered, even with the auxiliaries, and mostly unarmed. Rufinus had decided, bitterly, that they had to be selfish, for the good of Rome. They would free the auxilia, but use the ensuing chaos as a distraction, while *they* escaped separately. A major breakout was doomed from the start, but *someone* who knew what was going on had to get to Roman land and give warning. He had confided parts of his plan to Clemens, and the rest of it to no one. He would reveal the full scheme in due course, but only when it was fully formed, and he had tested out parts of it.

Rufinus swung the adze again and again, taking bulges and rough edges off the pole on which he was working, though his thoughts were far from the tool in his hands. Tonight, he would try the roof. Getting in among the rafters should not be troublesome, especially with men to help him up. His main questions were whether the roof shingles could be removed easily and quietly, and whether he would be able to climb out onto the roof unseen.

He dropped the adze back to the bench, and reached for the chisel. He shifted the pole so that the top was within easy reach, and began to use the chisel to taper the end to fit within the socket of an iron spearhead.

A curse drew his attention, and he turned to see that Clemens had nicked his thumb while working. Rufinus was about to turn back, ignoring the interruption, when he caught sight of something odd past his friend. His gaze lifted from the legionary sucking blood from his thumb, to scan out across the worksite and past the hut corner, catching momentary sight of two figures. They'd gone in the blink of an eye when he looked back, but he was sure it had been one of the legionaries he'd seen talking to a German warrior in an oddly clandestine fashion. He knew he would get told off for it, but in order to try and check what he'd seen, he took half a dozen steps to the right, so that he could look around that hut corner and hopefully confirm his suspicions.

He cursed. The two men had gone. A German barked at him and even as he hurried back to his workbench, the man smacked him across the back with a stick, centurion-style.

He'd seen two men, looking very conspiratorial, one legionary and one of the Alemanni.

He was sure of it.

He went back to work, fashioning his spear haft, but his gaze repeatedly flicked back up in that direction, and then he saw it. A man walked back around that hut and to the worksite, finding a table and picking up some rough-hewn arrow shafts.

Claudius Ademus.

And even if Rufinus had doubted himself, then logic suggested he was right. Three of the legionaries that had come with him spoke German. One of those was Clemens, who had been here with Rufinus throughout, and a second had been one of those men beheaded on the day of Veremundus's overthrowing. That left Ademus as the only man who could converse with their captors in their own tongue. It was *possible* the two men had been speaking Latin, but so few of these warriors did, that it seemed unlikely. Moreover, Ademus had form. He had been the one from the very start grumbling at Rufinus about his attitude towards the locals. Had he been working with the enemy from the start?'

His mind roved back over the previous days. He couldn't recall any particular moment that cast Ademus in a poor light. He had not been involved in the searching of the workers for metal. Or had he? Had he seen Rufinus hide the knife and warned their captors early on, so that they then found it at sunset? It was possible.

He chewed his lip. Slowly, very carefully, he began to move around his workstation, looking with each step as though he were simply trying to find a better angle for his task. It worked, he managed to move around the other side slowly without being called up on it by the guards.

He was now only three feet or so from his friend, who had wrapped his cut thumb and gone back to work.

'Clemens?' whispered Rufinus, pitching his voice just loud enough to carry the short distance, yet be lost among the work noise to their captors.

'What?' hissed the man quietly, not looking up, intent on his work for the benefit of the guards.

'What do you know about Ademus?'

'What?'

'I'm fairly sure he's in with Ingomer's men.'

'No.'

'I am. The question is whether that's a new thing, and he's just looking out for himself right now, or whether he's been with them for some time. What happened when those three men were caught leaving your hut?'

There was a prolonged silence, broken only by the sounds of furious carpentry. Finally, Clemens sighed.

'Ademus was on watch at the window. He was supposed to warn us of any approach. Of course, he had a limited view. Maybe he just didn't see them coming.'

Rufinus shook his head. 'No. I was there. I saw the escape. The shout went up from the far side. Whoever called the warning couldn't see you crawling out of the hut. Someone warned them. Someone, I might suggest, who was at the window, and could signal quite easily without being seen by the rest of you.'

Another long pause. 'He does *sympathise* with them,' Clemens said quietly. 'His grandfather was from one of the local tribes, although he was on *our* side of the border, and had gained citizenship. But then there are plenty of men in the Third, and in the auxilia, who have local blood. It's only natural. Ademus has a girl in the vicus too, a local. They plan to marry when he retires.'

'It was him. Ademus foiled our escape, Clemens. He warned the guards. That means that not only did he stop us getting away, he is directly responsible for the death of three of your men, and even had a hand in Veremundus being overthrown. The man fucked it up for all of us. And I would not be at all surprised if it was him who got me beaten for stealing a knife.'

'I still find it hard to believe.'

Rufinus shrugged. 'Then let's test the theory.' He looked surreptitiously over at Claudius Ademus, who was now using a thin metal scraper to shape the arrow shafts.

'It's got to be tonight,' he said, as if talking to Clemens, but a little louder. As he spoke, though his head was down, his eyes were still on Ademus. Nothing changed. The man continued to work. Had he not heard? Had Rufinus been too quiet? Or was he perhaps actually innocent and didn't care?

'It has to be tonight,' he said again, a little louder, and was rewarded this time. Out of the corner of his eye, he saw Ademus's own gaze flash over to him and back. The man went back to work after the momentary falter, as though he'd heard nothing. 'After we eat,' Rufinus hissed again, 'so that they think we're settling in, and leave us alone for a while.'

He could have laughed at the way Ademus slipped in his work and accidentally shaped the table instead of the arrow shaft, because his attention had flicked momentarily to Rufinus once again.

He waited for a while. Once Ademus was concentrating on his own work once more, Rufinus dropped to a low whisper again. 'Did you see that?'

'Hardly proof.'

Rufinus nodded. The legionary was right. But it *was* very suspicious.

'Watch him. Carefully.'

They returned to their work, slowly shaping the wood that could then be sent over to the 'trusted worker' area, where Germanic auxiliaries who had proven their reliability would attach the arrow- and spearheads made in the forge. Throughout the long afternoon, around and between the periodic tirades of the

Germanic overseers and the occasional smacks with the wooden rod, Rufinus kept an eye on Claudius Ademus.

The man was good. Rufinus had not seen him vanish the first time, and had only caught sight of him by pure chance, in the blink of an eye, before he disappeared. The second time was even more subtle. Rufinus slipped at one point, exhausted in his work, and a spear shaft flicked away, knocking Clemens as he worked and then falling to the ground. Clemens rushed to help him collect it, but the overseers were there in no time, drubbing both of them with the wooden canes. When they returned to their work, rubbing aches and bruises, Ademus was gone.

Rufinus craned to try and see, but dare not move out of place again. He had tested the German guards enough already, and soon they would become suspicious and might decide to do some real damage. He was handing over a finished pole when Ademus returned. The man came scurrying through the work area, with a German overseer whacking him over the shoulder with a stick. It was brilliant. A beautiful piece of subterfuge. But Rufinus had seen men beaten enough times – had been the man *being* beaten enough times – to recognise a show when it was put on for his benefit. He smiled wickedly. He was no longer under any illusion. Ademus was working with the Germans. Whether or not he had always been doing so or whether it was a recent development intrigued him, but didn't really matter. It had no relevance right now.

He waited once more until the guards were a little bored and distracted and, making sure to never let up looking busy, cleared his throat until Clemens briefly glanced his way.

'Did you catch all that?'

'You mean the fustuarium?' Clemens whispered. 'Yes.'

Rufinus nodded and went back to his work. Clemens understood. Fustuarium was the practice of beating to death as a military punishment, and its use to describe what had just happened to Ademus could only be the driest of sarcasm.

'You realise he has to go?'

Clemens winced. Claudius Ademus was not only a fellow legionary, but also one of his tent mates. They had shared accommodation, broken bread, got drunk together, fought side by side and back to back, for years. They shared trust. And they had become something more, since the governor considered these eight to be his best men. To realise he had been betrayed by one of his closest would be a hard thing to come to terms with. The legionary was motionless for as long as he dared, risking punishment, then went back to work, and gave Rufinus a single nod.

'I'll do it,' Rufinus whispered. 'No man should have to kill a tent mate.'

His memory furnished him inconveniently with an image of Scopius, the bully who had made his earliest days in guard a trial, falling back into the darkness of the aqueduct tank. He had almost certainly broken his back and then had to lie there and drown.

Rufinus shook his head, only to realise that Clemens was doing the same.

'No. This is my problem to deal with.'

Rufinus nodded his understanding. Sometimes a man had to take responsibility for his own.

They passed the rest of the day working hard, and when the sun started to descend, finally the Germans gave the order to down tools. The various pieces of equipment were returned to their tables, checked and counted by the overseers, and the last pieces of wood taken here and there, distributed appropriately. Rufinus and his friends were marched back to their hut, thrown inside, and the door locked behind them. Rufinus waited. He tried not to pay attention to Ademus, and was a little worried that Clemens was doing so, but the villain seemed not to notice, for he was distracted. Waiting for the supposed after-dinner break out, he guessed.

The cauldron of fatty meat and soaked break arrived shortly afterwards, with one wooden bowl and wooden spoon each. Food was distributed and the cauldron taken away, the door shut and locked once more. As Ademus ate, tense, Rufinus beckoned Clemens at the other end, by the bed. It didn't matter now if he looked conspiratorial. In fact, it could only help.

'I'm going to do it now.'

'No,' Rufinus hissed. Wait a couple of hours.

'What?'

'They're outside, in numbers. They think we'll try to escape after dinner. They'll be listening. Let them get bored, decide Ademus was wrong, and go away. Then do it. And when you do it, make sure you have proof.'

'How?'

'Two of the others here saw him being beaten back to his place. They may have noticed what we saw, or maybe not. But if it was real, it would have left visible bruises.'

Clemens nodded his understanding.

'Here. In case you need it.'

The legionary looked down to see the multi-tool in Rufinus's hand, which he had managed to keep hidden in the hut throughout it all. He nodded and swept it away, then turned, and the two men went back and started to eat.

The hut lingered in silence once the meal was done. Clemens, Ademus and three other legionaries, with Rufinus and Veremundus at the far end, sitting on the bed. They waited. Rufinus was darkly amused by the almost tangible frustration emanating from Ademus, who expected them to try something at any moment. Time dragged on. Nothing happened. After one hour, Ademus seemed to have given up expecting anything. After another, the ambient sounds of the guards outside suggested they had thinned somewhat. Still, Clemens waited.

Rufinus saw it coming, Ademus didn't. The senior legionary was pacing around the hut as he so often did, striving to overcome their confinement, and at the last moment, instead of turning away, he made straight for Claudius Ademus. He hit his fellow legionary, suddenly, hard. Ademus reeled, shocked, bouncing off the hut wall with a cry, but Clemens was already on him. His punch probably broke Ademus's jaw, from Rufinus's professional opinion. There was another yelp, and suddenly Clemens had the man's arm up behind his back. As he held him there, using the pressure on his arm, he used his other hand to yank Ademus's tunic down from the shoulder.

'What the fuck are you doing, Terentius?' one of the other men barked as he and his mate hurried over.

'You saw him beaten today. Where are the bruises, eh?'

It was dark in here, even though their eyes had been adjusting with the sinking of the sun, and the two men had to close to see what Clemens was talking about. 'Come on, man,' one of them said, reaching out to calm the situation. 'We're in this together. Leave him alone.'

'He sold out our last escape,' Clemens snarled. 'He warned them about Rufinus's knife, and today he told them about our plans.'

'Come, on, man, that's bollocks. We've known him for years.'

'Look at his shoulder. He got hit nine times. *Nine* times without *one* bruise? He's been one of them for a while.'

The legionary standing beside them with his hands spread wide, advocating calm, frowned.

'Ademus?'

'I don't know what the arsehole is talking about. Haven't I been here with you all the time? Is it my fault I heal well?'

It was delivered too fast. It was the first pile of bullshit that reached his tongue, and suddenly even the two men who had been trying to stop it were giving him funny looks.

'What?' Ademus snapped.

'No one heals fast enough that bruises go in three hours. Show us.'

Claudius Ademus was done. Rufinus knew it, Clemens knew it, and now Ademus himself knew it. He jerked out of Clemens's grip. 'I'm not selling *anyone* out,' he tried. 'I'm trying to find a way *in* for us. When they move they won't need us any more and we'll all be killed. I'm trying to get us in with them. Even if it's only 'til we're over the border and we run. We just need to survive.'

'You shit,' one of the legionaries snapped. Rufinus started to walk over to join them.

'Listen, Titus, we have to survive this.'

'We have to *escape*,' corrected Clemens, lip wrinkling.

'No one's getting out of here alive,' Ademus answered, 'without being part of Ingomer's army.'

'Division is what they want,' Prefect Veremundus put in suddenly. 'Falling out like this.'

Clemens turned to the prefect.

'Sir, this is not division. This is dealing with a traitor.'

Again, Rufinus saw it coming. Legionaries stood around the room. Ademus was close to the wall, Clemens in front of him, but Clemens had turned to the prefect and, right now, had his back to the villain. Rufinus, moving towards them already, saw Ademus's hand coming up, the stout piece of wood in it, presumably stolen during work and secreted about his person until now. He was about to smash Clemens in the back of the head with it.

Rufinus didn't bother running; he simply leapt.

It was too far for a proper dive, but his reaching hands found Ademus's legs and yanked even as he hit the hut floor, sending the man tumbling backward with a cry, overbalanced. Rufinus hit the floorboards first, Ademus second, but Rufinus was prepared, knew it was coming. He hit, braced, rolled, came up on top of the shocked and winded Claudius Ademus. The instinct of the fighter took over then. Ademus flailed, one hand whirling aimlessly, the other hammering out with the piece of wood rather randomly and in a defensive manner.

Rufinus's bunched knuckles hit the man on the wrist that held the piece of wood, and, with a yelp, he dropped the makeshift weapon. Rufinus hit him, then, a cross with the left hand that snapped the man's head to the side and sent his brains swimming down into his boots. As he lolled, barely aware, hands windmilling aimlessly, Rufinus's own questing fingers closed on the wooden stick the man had dropped. It came up, and then down.

Rufinus felt no pity for the man as the timber smashed into his face, pulverising his nose and bursting an eye. The second blow took out the other eye, and the third just made more mess. For the fourth and fifth, he simply let the wood fall away and beat the man with his fists. Finally, he reached down and grasped the man's throat just below the chin. He reached round with a large hand and encompassed all the critical parts of the neck, and then squeezed with all his might. There was an unpleasant and telling series of cracks and crunches, and then he leaned back, crouched, and watched the man struggle to the death, trying to breathe through a flattened throat. It was surprising how panicked the man looked, given that his wits had to have been driven from his head at least three blows ago.

He rose, slowly.

'Bet you won a lot of bouts,' Clemens said slowly, voice a little shaky.

'What?'

'You're a boxer, and a fucking good one I'd say. And, excuse me for this, but a *really* fucking good one for a man your age.'

Rufinus smiled wearily. 'No insult. I *was* a champion in my time. And *I* saw the way *you* hit him. *You've* spent time in the ring too.'

'Came third in the border tournament last year,' Clemens said modestly.

'Shit,' Rufinus breathed. 'That's been running since I was fighting. All the way from the mouth of the Rhenus to the Euxine Sea. Seven provinces and at least ten legions. I was in it myself once. Of course, I came second...'

The two men burst out laughing, and chuckled to a halt after a while, suddenly starkly aware that they were laughing over the mushed and pulverised body of a legionary, while the rest of the hut's occupants stared at them in shock and horror.

'He was a traitor,' Rufinus said simply, standing straight and flicking blood from his fists. 'He has sold us out several times. It is because of him that we failed to escape and three men died. It is because of him that I was beaten for stealing a knife. And he would have sold us again and again to his new king just to survive. I trust there are no more traitors in the hut?'

He looked around. Shocked faces was all he could see.

'Then we now have privacy. We now have the chance to do what we must without it being reported to the guards.'

CHAPTER SIXTEEN

Two more days had passed. Every day's delay increased the danger that the German warbands would be in position and ready to move on the border, but still the delays were necessary. Partly because after the excitement of that one day, when the guards had been tipped off about an escape that never happened, and when their informant had been silenced, the prisoners needed to leave sufficient time for Ingomer's men to lower their guard a little once more. And partly because when the guards came with breakfast before the next dawn and found the body of Ademus, they had given every surviving occupant a minor beating and then withheld a full day of meals. The beatings they could cope with, but if they hoped to escape the camp and make it back to imperial territory, they would find it easier to do so on a good meal than half-starved. Thus now, with a day's food and two days of recovery, they were ready.

The Germans had clearly decided the escape was off, and had once more reduced the guard on their hut to two men. Rufinus and the others had been silent for two hours, listening carefully, to confirm that number, as well as the locations of the two Germans. One was at the corner of the hut near the door, where he could see that wall and a side, while the other was at the opposite corner, covering the other two walls. It was nicely efficient in terms of visual coverage, but with the failing that while the two guards could see the whole hut, they could not actually see one another.

He looked around the hut. Everyone was tense, ready. An auxiliary prefect and four legionaries… and Rufinus.

Clemens positioned himself, stooping, and locked his hands together, fingers interlaced.

Rufinus, now barefoot, his boots by the door, gave him a nod, lifted his foot into the cradle, and launched himself upwards with a quiet grunt at the discomfort of his bruised ribs. As he pushed, so did Clemens, and in a heartbeat he had his hands round the roof beam, pulling himself up into the rafters.

He paused, his hands on the roof for balance, listening. There was no sound of sudden activity outside, so the guards clearly had not heard anything. His questing fingers moved across the wooden shingles of the roof, looking for a poorly-placed one. He smiled to himself as he found what he was looking for. Roman soldiers, when constructing fort buildings, would use two nails for each wooden shingle, one in each top corner, pinning it to the lat. Two nails made the shingle secure and stopped any movement. The work the natives had done was laughable. They had followed the Roman design in principle, but with shortcuts. In one particular area, a worker had put one nail through the corners of four tiles to hold them in position, saving nails and time. Rufinus carefully teased the top shingle and was able to revolve it around the nail, taking the others with it until he had a gap almost a foot wide in the roof. It did not take much effort then to pluck the four tiles from the beam, the nail coming away with a gentle creak.

He panicked for a moment as the nail teetered and then fell, but as he watched it go, he saw Clemens throw out an open palm and catch it silently. Again, Rufinus paused and listened. He'd made a small amount of noise, but only creaks and scrapes, and now that he was open to the air, he could hear the creaks and groans of the woods outside the ramparts, the noises of buildings in the nighttime breeze, and the sounds of men living their lives in the camp, and knew that these things had drowned out his small sounds.

He lifted the four shingles, then held tight to the beam and lowered them with his other hand until Clemens grasped them and took them away. He rose once more, then, and worked on the next row. It took time, but gradually he shifted sufficient tiles that he could fit between them. The lats were less than two feet apart, and Rufinus could feel them scraping on his front and back as he pulled himself up between them to the roof. He went into an immediate crouch, his bare feet balanced on the rough beams. He was risking splinters, but bare feet would both give him better traction on the sloping wooden roof, and, more importantly, make far less noise.

He could immediately see one of the guards, the other hidden at the far corner by the pitch of the roof. The German had not yet looked up, but it was only a matter of time. Rufinus tensed. He had to move very quickly. Bracing, knees bent, he launched himself.

It was a gamble, but it had to be done. Had he risked creeping to the edge, almost certainly the man would see him and have time to shout an alarm. Instead, Rufinus had thrown himself from halfway up the roof's slope, a drop of some twelve feet, onto the waiting guard. His aim was true, though the landing less than graceful. He hit the man hard, with a thud, and both of them slammed down to the ground. Neither shouted, as both men were winded by the collision, but Rufinus had the advantage. He had known it was coming, while the German had been taken by surprise. As such, he recovered first. While the guard rocked, head spinning, recovering his wits, Rufinus slammed one palm over the man's mouth, reached around with the other, grabbing a large handful of hair by the roots, and then twisted, hard. There were several distinct and clearly fatal cracks, and the man lurched and shook, then fell still.

Rufinus paused, yet again, crouched atop the body, listening. There were plenty of sounds to hear, but not the urgent approaching footsteps he had half feared. He had got away with it. The first stage of the plan was almost done.

He rose, then crept along the hut wall towards the opposite corner. He peeked round it. The other German warrior stood bored, picking his nose and paying precious little real attention. Rufinus hadn't counted on this. The distance between the corner and the man would make it extremely difficult to reach him without the man getting out a shout. Then an idea formed, and he danced lightly back to his victim and dragged the body into the shadows of the hut's back wall. The man had been wearing a cloak of native design against the chill of the night. Rufinus grinned. He quickly undid the man's sword belt and strapped it round his middle, then donned the cloak and pulled up the hood, before returning to the other corner.

Taking a deep breath, he walked around the corner towards the man.

The second guard stopped excavating his nose and turned, raising a hand in greeting.

His eyes only widened in realisation as Rufinus reached him, and the Roman's hand shot out from the folds of the cloak, gripping the man's throat, preventing him from crying out. The guard, choking, reached for the weapon at his side, but he stood no chance. Rufinus's left hand remained around his throat, but the right lashed out, fist balled, and smashed into his face. The German reeled, blood exploding from his nose, two teeth broken. As he gagged and gasped, Rufinus let go of his throat and he staggered back. Before he could recover, though, Rufinus was on him. He hit the man once, and then again, then a third time, and then lowered the unconscious body to the ground and dragged him out of open view to the edge of the hut wall.

He rose and crossed to the door, lifting the catch and sliding back the bolt, opening it.

Clemens was waiting just inside, and held out Rufinus's boots. Grinning, Rufinus took them and pulled them on, while the legionary crossed to the unconscious German and stole his sword. Now, two of them were armed. As the others emerged, Rufinus gestured to them.

'You know the plan,' he hissed quietly. 'Get to hut fourteen and retrieve everything. Then go to the meeting point and wait for us.'

Veremundus and the three legionaries nodded, and spun, loping off quietly into the dark.

Rufinus turned back to Clemens, who was waiting for him. 'Come on.'

He had toyed briefly with the idea of trying a stealthy escape anyway, without involving the auxilia, but had decided against it. The six of them might just get to the camp's ramparts undetected, but the guards on the towers would be alert. And if Rufinus wanted to do his other few little jobs before they left, he would need a distraction.

Like ghosts, the two men moved through the dark camp, sidling along the shadowy walls of the huts, then dashing quietly across the gaps in between, one man then the other, never both in the open, always one moving and one on watch. They passed their daytime work area, and dropped to a tiptoe, moving crouched and low, for there were Germans over there, up to something. Whatever they were doing among the tools and benches, they were busy about their task, and did not glance over at the two shadows passing by. With relief, Rufinus dipped into the shade at the back of another hut, and they resumed their journey.

Soon enough they reached the last hut in their journey and paused, looking out across the open ground. Naturally they had not seen the compound the auxilia were being kept in at night, and had no idea how it was guarded. The place was surrounded by a palisade of nine-foot stakes, a single gated entrance facing the parade ground and exercise area.

There were two guards visible from this angle, and Rufinus cursed. He knew the whole place would be watched over, for a nine-foot palisade can be climbed, but he'd not reckoned how many would be watching. Each German could see the men to either side. This was not going to be easy.

Again, he toyed with leaving them. In a way it was cruel to do what they were doing. They would free the auxilia, but there was no chance of the soldiers making it out of the camp. There

241

would simply be a repeat of their first attempt and in the morning another fifty Roman bodies would be buried in a mass grave.

Beside him, Clemens nudged him and then started miming and pointing. Rufinus watched and nodded. He was gesturing at the gate, which they could just see off to their right. Two men stood at the gate, close together, while the others were just within sight of each other. There was no hope of breaking the prisoners out undetected, but that hardly mattered. This was not about a quiet breakout, but a distraction, and so plenty of noise and activity would only work to their advantage, as long as they got the gate open. That was what Clemens was motioning. For Rufinus to open the gate while he took on the two men. The Praetorian accepted that with silent gratitude. He was starting to ache far too much, and weariness only added to that. Let the legionary do the fighting, this time.

Ducking back, they rounded two more huts and then closed on the compound once more, now closer to the gate. Rufinus looked at the two Germans there. They would have maybe twenty heartbeats to deal with them and open the gate before the other guards around the edge were on them, the alarm going up, and men pouring out of the huts. They would have to be damned fast.

Clemens gave him the nod, and they broke into a run.

They emerged from the line of huts at speed, and had crossed half the open ground to the compound before a shout went up from the German guards. The two men at the gate were then bellowing at their friends, and the others were starting to run. The pair lifted spears and held them, point first, at the approaching Romans.

Rufinus was slightly ahead, faster than Clemens despite the age difference, and as he approached the two men, he braced himself. He had to get past the pair, immediately, and he could only see one way to do it without ending up on one of those spears. As he neared them, racing as fast as he could, he suddenly threw himself forward and down, curling into a ball as he did so, hitting the turf hard, but already rolling. He hurtled between the two men, below the spears, and came up behind them, panting and wincing at new aches added to his collection. He was running even as he reached his feet.

He hit the palisade gate and bounced off it, turning once, quickly, to take it all in. Clemens had reached the two guards. He had hold of one of the spears just below the head while he parried the other with his stolen sword. To each side, more guards were coming, while one was honking some great war horn, warning the camp of trouble.

Rufinus turned back to the gate, and cursed. For some reason, he had expected it to be simply latched and bolted as their hut door had been, but it was not. What he had not been expecting was a lock. The gates were secured with a chain fed through twin iron bars, fastened with a padlock of Roman manufacture. Perhaps those two guards had the key. Perhaps not. It was irrelevant anyway. There was not enough time to find the key and open the lock without being swamped by guards.

He ripped his sword free of its scabbard, turning it with difficulty. It was longer and heavier than the swords he was used to. Lifting it in both hands as if to stab down, he rammed it between the wood of the gate and the chain, next to the iron loop. Then, when it was in place, he pulled on the hilt with all his might.

For a moment, nothing happened. He could feel his muscles crying out with the effort, and was starting to despair, for if they could not succeed here, then capture was almost guaranteed.

Then there was a bang, a ping, a groan, and the entire looped iron bar attached to the left leaf of the gate bent with a loud crack, one end coming free of the timber, the chain sliding away loose.

Rufinus staggered, numb from the immense strain of what he'd just done. Then he reached for the gate and pulled it open.

Several hundred auxiliaries stared at him in surprise.

'Well?'

Then they were running, shouting, surging towards the gate. Rufinus's head snapped this way and that. The German guards were on them now, but the auxilia were pouring out to meet them. Rufinus ducked back and ran.

Clemens had managed to take down one of his two opponents, but the other one was holding him at bay. Rufinus hit the German from behind, swinging his sword hard and smashing it into the back of the man's head. The guard screamed and reeled, falling away, and Rufinus grabbed Clemens on the way past.

'Stop playing with him and run.'

And that was precisely what they did. They crossed the open space and disappeared between the huts. Rufinus managed a backward glance briefly, to see that two of the German guards had veered off to follow them. One never made it, for the desperate flood of auxilia overran him and took him down. The other, however, was close behind as they ducked between huts.

As they hit the shadowy alley, Rufinus gestured to the right, and they dipped round the end of the hut on the right, running along the alley there, then ducking left, creating a dogleg, where they then came to a halt, gasping, at the corner of another hut. Rufinus peered around the edge, and a moment later saw the man who'd chased them hurtle past the gap, thinking he was still behind them. They stopped for a few precious moments to get their breath back.

The camp was in chaos. They could hear the sounds of furious fighting two huts over, at the compound. There was shouting all over the camp and more horns being blown. He and Clemens looked at one another, nodded, and then they were off again. They moved at speed but with care, stopping at every junction. Sometimes they saw groups of German warriors running to join the fray, and paused, or backtracked, or carefully turned away and nipped across to the next hut.

After a while, Clemens hissed at him.

'We're going the wrong way.'

'*I'm* not. You go meet up with the others. I'll be along in a few moments.'

Clemens' eyes narrowed. 'You're going for your dog, aren't you?'

'That and one other thing.'

'You'll need help. Lead on.'

Rufinus was about to argue, but he knew the look on his friend's face, and knew it for a look he himself wore often enough. The man was not about to take no for an answer.

'Alright. Come on.'

Still in that jerky fashion, running through the dark then stopping suddenly, watching and listening before moving again, they crossed the last lines of huts and reached the open stretch in front of the headquarters. Off to the side he could see the wooden cage and the great white dog pacing back and forth in it. His heart swelled with relief. He'd half expected the animal to have been simply executed by Ingomer's men, but it seemed he had not.

Two Germans were walking across the space nearby, armed and in animated conversation. Then someone ahead of them shouted, and they broke into a run, disappearing along one of those shadowed roads towards where all the action was happening.

Briefly, the space was empty.

Rufinus ran across to the cage, and as he approached, his elation took a knock. Orthus was alive, but not necessarily well. In a dozen places his white hair was matted and stained red, and as Rufinus reached the structure, he noted with fury two long staffs with sharpened points, both stained with dried blood. The Germans may not have *killed* Orthus, but they had been torturing the poor thing through the bars of his cage.

He started to mess with the catch, and then paused at noises in the headquarters nearby. Clemens waved at him to keep

245

working, then crossed to the large hut and pressed himself against the wall beside the building's entrance.

Rufinus removed the bar and pulled open the cage door, noting also with anger that the food and water bowls were both dry and empty. They had not fed or watered Orthus in the five days since the coup. The dog emerged from the cage slowly, nervously, but once he was out, and knew that the figure before him was Rufinus, the tail gave a small wag, and he hurled himself at his master. Rufinus was fighting off the affections of his dog when he glanced over at another sound and saw the headquarters door open. A warrior emerged, looking his way. He managed two steps before Clemens caught him on the back of the head with a powerful right hook. The man lurched, fell sideways, hit the open door, bounced and then collapsed in a heap. Clemens stepped over to the prone man and then brought a booted foot down hard on the German's head, finishing him off. The legionary glanced once at Rufinus to make sure he was alright, and then dipped inside.

Rufinus gently pushed Orthus off him and rose to his feet.

The damage looked worse than it was because of the dog's colouring. The Germans had been poking him with a sharpened stick, enough to draw blood but not to do any real damage. He heaved another sigh of relief.

'Come on, boy.'

He then ran over to the headquarters, pulled open the door, and followed Clemens inside.

Illuminated by a single brazier, the legionary was busy beating the life out of another warrior in the hut's outer room, and Rufinus left him to it, hurrying across and to the door to the inner room. Orthus looked a little nervous, and remained in the outer room near the door, leading Rufinus to wonder whether he had been somehow hurt in here as well.

Ducking inside, Rufinus half expected to find Ingomer there, with half a dozen of his warriors, and was surprised to discover it empty. Likely the German king shunned the place as too 'Roman' for his tastes. He was both disappointed and relieved at the same time that Ingomer was not there, though it took time for his eyes to adjust to the darkness to be sure. It would have been an excellent opportunity for revenge and to remove the bastard from the scene early on, but then it would also endanger their escape, which would hardly be productive in the long run.

As it was, he ran over to the far side of the inner room and fumbled around in the gloom until he found what he was looking for. The broken sword lay atop the cupboard exactly where he'd last seen it, and he grabbed it and tucked it into his belt. Turning, he was about to leave, but instead, as an afterthought, crossed to the stand where the prefect's armour was still in place, unwanted by the king and his men. He couldn't carry much of it, but he grabbed the folded subarmalis, the fringed leather protective tunic that sat underneath the armour, and the man's sword, and then turned and ran for the door. Clemens was standing over a body, looking impatient. His eyes fell on the stuff Rufinus was carrying.

'You came back for that?'

Rufinus shook his head and pointed to the broken blade in his belt.

'No. For *that*. Don't ask. It's personal. But I thought I'd bring the prefect's gear along, too.'

As he hurried towards the exit, where Orthus waited patiently, Clemens fell in beside him. 'You really expect him to use a sword? He's probably never even drawn one.'

They emerged into a dark space that was blessedly empty, all the general burr of noise in the camp emanating from over near the prison compound. 'I don't care whether he fights,' Rufinus said, 'and while the next auxiliary commander we find might not believe us about all this, he *might* believe an equal. Thought it best to make Veremundus at least *look* like a prefect.'

'Good thinking,' the legionary said, then 'look out!'

An Alemanni warrior had come barrelling out of the darkness, between two other huts, as surprised to see them as they were to see him. Clemens was about to run, sword coming up, when Rufinus simply shouted 'Orthus... *balls!*'

As they ran towards the man, who stood between them and their destination, the dog sudden pelted past them, still sprightly despite having taken a number of minor wounds. Clemens watched in shock as the dog latched itself onto the German, who shrieked in a piercing tone and threw away his spear and shield as his hands reached down, trying in vain to detach Orthus from his privates.

'Now I see why they kept him locked up.'

Rufinus nodded. 'He's not particularly obedient. I think he only does it because he likes to.'

They ran on, soon reaching a point where the huts ended, revealing an open space between them and the ramparts. At the last hut, the others waited for them, each with a kit bag over his shoulder, some with two. Rufinus recognised his own gear with some relief, and from the way it dragged downwards and the man carrying it was sweating, it was clearly still full, holding his armour.

'Thank the gods,' one of the men said, vehemently.

'He was wanting to go without you,' said another, gesturing at Veremundus with his thumb.

'That is *not true*,' the prefect bridled. 'I merely speculated as to how long we were expected to wait if you did not return. It was a sensible and fair question.'

Rufinus frowned at the exchange. It was odd to hear legionaries speaking down to an equestrian prefect, and Veremundus might have lost his moral and social high ground with his plan's failure, but this was the first time Rufinus had heard him taking a submissive, defensive position. Something had happened between these four men in their absence, and whatever it was had clearly put Veremundus in his place. That might not be a bad thing, of course, Rufinus noted.

'You said,' the legionary began angrily, but Rufinus held up a hand to silence him. He fell quiet, and in that nothing, Rufinus hissed 'do you hear that?'

There was a confused pause, but Clemens had spotted it. 'The noise is dying down. The breakout at the auxilia has been contained. It's over.'

Rufinus nodded, as the rest all exchanged worried looks. Their distraction had not lasted half as long as they hoped. 'We need to go *now*. As soon as they have the auxilia back in the compound, they'll come looking for us, and the defences will be thick with warriors.'

'Shit.'

They looked at the ramparts. Manpower-wise, they were at a low ebb right now. When Veremundus had been in charge, they'd been only barely manned, as defence was deemed unnecessary. Since Ingomer had taken command, they had been much stronger, with men in each tower and roving guards patrolling the palisade in between. Now, men had left their posts to help with the revolt of the auxilia, and now there was but a warrior in every other tower, but soon they would come back in force once more.

'There,' Rufinus said, gesturing.

'What?' they asked, looking in the direction of his pointing finger.

'We can't climb the walls. The stakes are ten feet high, with the tops pointed, in full view of all the towers. By the time we get over them we'll be spotted.' As he spoke, he opened his pack that was on the other man's back, and began pulling free a rope. 'But the towers have ladders, and cross-beams that can be climbed.'

'I can't climb those,' Veremundus said.

'What if you were given the choice between that, or waiting for Ingomer to come for you?'

They all pictured their likely fates if the king should recapture them. The image was not pretty.

'I might need help,' the prefect sagged.

Rufinus ignored the disdainful looks the legionaries threw the man. 'We're all in this together,' he told them. 'There are six of us and a thousand of them. Stick together.'

This seemed to end the growing feud for now, and Rufinus looked at the others. 'I'll go first. Wait till I get there, then Clemens comes across. Then another, and so on. Each time, before you run, make sure the men in the adjacent towers are looking the other way. Like now,' he added, as he began to run, still coiling the rope in his hands.

He was horribly aware of how visible he was as he crossed the open ground. All it needed was one of those men to turn and see him, and the alarm would go up. He prayed constantly as he ran, to more than one god, and realised belatedly that Orthus was at his heel and that he'd made no provision for the dog. *Orthus* couldn't climb.

Bollocks.

He reached the tower in what felt like hours, but had in truth been less than twenty heartbeats. Turning, he saw Clemens pause for a long moment, and then start to run. Leaving his competent friend to it, he looked up. Right here, he was hidden from the view of the men in the other towers by the structure itself. He crouched beside Orthus. 'Sorry, boy. This is not going to be comfortable, but it's the only way, without leaving you behind.'

He worked fast, looping the rope around the dog's chest, just behind his fore-shoulders, then tying it as tight as he could. 'Just be patient, he said.'

'What are you doing?' Clemens asked, arriving and puffing and panting.

'The lesser climbers can use the rope to move from ladder to wall, then we haul Orthus up with it.'

Clemens nodded, and the man went up several places in Rufinus's hierarchy of worthy men, for he did not even *think* of suggesting they left the dog behind.

'Stay with Clemens,' he said to the white shaggy hound, and then reached out and took hold of the ladder that led up to the tower top. Hurrying, still gripping the other end of the rope in one hand, he climbed until he was above the level of the palisade, still below the deck of the tower. He glanced back and then down. Another man was halfway across the open ground, and Clemens was keeping the dog calm below. Satisfied that everything was working as well as could be expected, he tied the rope in a loop then dropped it over his head and one arm, hooked it over a beam, and then began to monkey-climb off the ladder and onto the crossed struts that held the tower up. This part was fairly strenuous, but not difficult. He had done this a hundred times and more in days of training, and he moved from strut to strut with relative ease until he was above the palisade. He could see the fifteen-foot drop to the loam outside now. The lazy defenders had not bothered re-digging the ditch, which was visible only as a gentle dip after so many years.

He looked down to Clemens, who was no longer alone, the fourth man now running.

'Tell the others to throw the kit bags over the palisade next to the tower. We'll pick them up when we're all out.'

Clemens nodded, and a moment later Rufinus made the last move of the escape. Slipping out over the palisade, he grinned. He lifted the rope from his shoulders and then undid it before fastening it again, tighter, around the outer timber leg of the tower. He had created a rope that led all the way from the ground to the top of the palisade, using a beam by the ladder as a pulley or pivot. He then moved sideways on the timbers, making room.

'Come on.'

Below him, another man began to climb. The man used the ladder halfway, as Rufinus had, then gripped the rope and used it as a hand-guide to help him across the timbers until he was beside Rufinus, looking out at freedom.

'Get below. Start collecting the bags.'

As he spoke, men were hurling the kit bags over the palisade. Luck was with them, for each bag fell to the soft loam outside with little noise, and as yet no alarm had gone up. He looked back as the first man jumped to freedom, landing with a dampened thump and a grunt. Clemens was already coming up next, having passed the plan on to the next man.

Rufinus tensed, feeling the passing of time and the increasing probability that any moment the Alemanni would flood back towards the walls, or a man in an adjacent tower would happen to see something. Clemens reached the top, slapped him on the shoulder, and then jumped. They were almost all here. Rufinus turned back to see Prefect Veremundus lurking at the hut corner, immobile. He cursed silently, then waved to get the prefect's attention and gestured for him to run. Still, Veremundus stayed in place. Rufinus gestured again, slightly more vehemently. Finally, the man started to run.

Another legionary reached Rufinus, ducked past him with a nod, and leapt out into the darkened forest.

Rufinus looked this way and that. Veremundus was almost safe. Three men outside the rampart were now gathering up their packs, while the other was busy climbing. Rufinus held his breath, tense. A lot rode on these last few moments. The camp was almost quiet again. Then, suddenly, there was an immense noise. Horns blared, voices shouted.

Rufinus was in no doubt. They had been discovered. The Alemanni had found the empty hut and the two bodies.

The last legionary ducked past him and jumped to safety, and Veremundus was now climbing the ladder.

Far.

Too.

Slowly.

'Fucking hurry up,' Rufinus hissed down at him. The prefect looked up, nodded, and started to speed up, though not enough, in Rufinus's opinion. In what felt like ages, Veremundus was picking his way gingerly across the wooden struts. Even as the man reached Rufinus, shouts went up in the adjacent towers, and men emerged from the space between huts from which they had been running.

The prefect looked back, then down, then at Rufinus. His mouth opened.

'If you suggest leaving my dog,' Rufinus growled, 'I will push you off this beam and leave you to your fate.'

Veremundus very wisely held his silence, and jumped.

As they gathered outside, collecting the gear, and looking fearfully up at the towers, Rufinus shook the rope free of that beam used as a pivot, then began to pull on it, hauling Orthus up, one jerked pace at a time, from the ground to the wall top. At one and the same time, he was surprised how heavy the animal was, but also damned grateful it wasn't Acheron, for he doubted he could have lifted the great black hound at all.

It took far too long, but finally the dog was up with him. Men were now running across the open ground towards the tower. Rufinus took a steadying breath, and then grabbed Orthus, pulling him close. It was about the most strain the Praetorian had ever put his muscles under. He staggered, struggling with the burden, almost dropping him several times, until he reached the palisade top. It was not graceful. He managed to unknot the rope and slip it from Orthus with one hand while the dog lay across his crouched knees, and then basically threw the animal outwards with the last of his strength.

It was too much. Orthus fell out into the forest, but Rufinus lost his footing in the process and fell outwards right behind him. He hit the ground at the base of the palisade, and everything went black.

CHAPTER SEVENTEEN

Rufinus's eyes snapped open. For just a moment he was in a true daze. He couldn't work out where he was, or what was happening, whether he was in the forest in snow as the Marcomanni attacked, or at home, waking up beside Senova, or any one of a thousand other situations that flashed through his mind. He was baffled, confused, and his head hurt.

The reality of the situation hit him as thin branches smacked the top of his head. He looked up, and managed to duck again just before another branch took his eye out. He was bouncing through a woodland, in the dark.

'What in the name of...?'

He never named the god, for at that moment the legionary carrying him came to a stop, panting, lowered him to the forest floor, and waved at Clemens.

'He's awake.'

Rufinus was propped up, then his supporter let go. He swayed. Nearly toppled. Then he managed to find strength in his legs and pushed himself into action. He straightened. 'What happened?'

Clemens crossed to him, came too close for mere comfort, and stared into his eyes. 'You fell on your head. We decided you'd not broken your neck, but whether you still had your brains was a different matter. How do you feel.'

Rufinus frowned. 'A little confused. Achy. Hungry. Hang on... the Germans!'

'Yes, they're after us. Can you run? We've been taking turns carrying you, but you're not the lightest of men.'

The Praetorian tested his legs. He felt sure he could walk on them, if not run, and recent events were now flooding back in, filling his mind.

'I'll be fine.'

'Running from head-taking Germans through a forest fine, or falling over ten paces from now and muttering about your grandmother fine?'

Rufinus straightened. 'The first one. Come on.'

He staggered, and almost fell, but given Clemens's snappy comment, refused to prove him right. He jogged unsteadily, barely leaping roots and stones, among the other legionaries and the prefect.

'Give me that,' he said, gesturing to the man carrying his kit bag.

The legionary just snorted, then easily and swiftly outpaced him. Rufinus ran on.

As he ran, he listened. What he heard was less than encouraging. There was the sound of a large force of men on their trail. He could hear them, some way back, shouting to one another in their gruff German dialect. He could also hear the distinctive sound of horses out on a compacted-earth woodland road nearby.

'Does anyone know where we're running.'

'Away,' supplied a legionary helpfully.

'But I presume someone set a course south? I mean, we don't really want to run deeper into enemy lands.'

Clemens pointed upwards. 'Do you not know your night sky?'

Rufinus frowned. 'Not something I ever studied.'

'Those three stars are the belt of Orion. Follow those and we'll find the border.'

A wave of relief flowed over Rufinus that Clemens at least knew what to do. He personally had always followed his father's spurious advice on direction finding, involving what side of a tree the moss grew on.

'Stop,' he said, suddenly.

It took a moment for them all to stop running, and they shuffled back closer together.

'We're in the deep woodland. All their cavalry is on the road, and they'll be close to it. There might be a place we can hide where they'll miss us entirely.'

'Listen,' Clemens said in reply.

He did, and it took only moments for him to hear the sounds of dogs. He'd not known there were any dogs in camp, other than Orthus, but it appeared that there were, and now the Alemanni were using them to hunt the runaways.

'Shit.'

'Quite.'

'And they'll be following Orthus, even if not the rest of us.'

'Exactly.'

'We could separate,' Clemens suggested. Take the dog one way to draw them off, while others go with the prefect to warn the frontier posts.'

Rufinus shook his head. There was a certain sense to that, but they were still a distance from the border, and separating reduced their chances of survival should anyone catch up with them.

'No, we stick together. Follow me.'

He took the lead now, Orthus running along at his side. He was starting to feel a little more energetic, though he knew he was running on adrenaline, and that all this would catch up with him at some point, for the aches and pains were insistent.

He had the bare bones of a plan forming. The main thing was to hide their scent, and he had ideas about that. He was no great hunter or tracker, but he'd hunted in his childhood alongside his elder brother Lucius, and a few tricks remained with him. Staying downwind of the hunters was not something he could do anything about right now, but water should still hide the scent.

He ran on, ears pricked, listening carefully. They'd gone maybe half a mile, very tense, the sound of their pursuers never dropping away, when he thought he heard it. He stopped suddenly, the others almost running into him. 'Can you hear water?'

One of the legionaries nodded. 'A stream, I reckon.'

'Come on.'

He ran on, relief starting to blossom as they got closer and closer to the sound, until finally they burst from the trees to find a small river, more an overgrown stream. It was perhaps ten feet across, shallow, with a gravel bed, dark water glinting in the moonlight between the trees. Without delay, he ran into the flow, only out far enough for the water to reach above his ankles and a little way up his shins. Common sense told him that the further out into the river they went, the better the chance of their scent being masked, but that was countered by the fact that water any deeper than this would slow them all noticeably, and Orthus would have trouble.

He ran on, splashing, and hoping beyond hope that their pursuers could not hear them over the ambient noise of the nighttime forest and their own sounds. After all, if Rufinus could hear their dogs from here, then they must be making plenty of noise back there.

The others joined him and they ran on. The river's slow, lazy current seemed to be following more or less the same direction they had been running.

'Is there a river that crosses the frontier near the forts in this area?'

'Several,' Clemens said.

Veremundus shook his head as they ran. 'No. All the ones near Tannum are just short streams. Nothing that would go this far into the north. We are still the better part of eight miles from the frontier. This river is the Almonus, and it crosses the frontier between two towers about a quarter of a mile north of Castra Numera.'

'Isn't Castra Numera the fort I wanted to get to? The one with the Spanish unit?'

'Yes.'

'Then this river will lead us straight there.'

'With a little meandering, yes.'

Fresh resolve settled on Rufinus now. They were out of the camp, free, and they had a guideline to follow right to where they needed to be. Once they reached Castra Numera, they would find friendly faces and help. Eight miles. He tried not to ponder on the chances of him making eight miles at a run at this point. He knew he was hardy, had pushed himself beyond most men's physical limits from time to time, but he was not getting any younger, had not slept a full and comfortable night in some time, and had been beaten a few times recently. Thankfully their Germanic captors had made the beatings painful without being debilitating. They could not afford to render their prisoners unable to work, after all. But still, he was getting worryingly close to the point of exhaustion, and without a rest he would be in trouble pretty soon. And being bounced along unconscious on a legionary's back for half a mile did not count as rest.

Still, he sloshed on, the others with him. He could no longer really hear their pursuers, though he knew them to be there, for the noise of their passage drowned out anything else. He hoped once again that the enemy could not hear their run.

Orthus suddenly gave a short, sharp bark, and then settled into a growl. He slowed.

Rufinus turned.

A brown dog, lean and muscular with a sharp nose, had appeared through the woodland. For a moment, he feared the enemy were upon them, but then his ears picked up, even over the splashing, the sound of their hunters still a way back in the woods. The dog had gone on ahead, for they had released the animals to track their prey. That only one of the dogs had come across them suggested that their use of the river had worked, for if the animal had been following their scent, then surely there would be more than one dog here.

He was about to draw his sword when Orthus took the initiative. With two splashes and a leap, the white hound met the brown on the riverbank. Rufinus watched, horrifyingly fascinated. The two animals met on their hind legs, almost like wrestlers, teeth bared, forepaws raking and then clutching in a strange embrace, as the pair both tried to get their teeth somewhere they could do the most damage.

The German hound was strong, and lean, but it lacked Orthus's naked aggression, especially after being caged for days, tortured and taunted. By simple fury and determination, the white hound managed to push his opponent's head back and up, and in a heartbeat he had his jaws around the enemy's throat. He bit, and ripped, and then pulled away.

Rufinus winced at the damage. The brown dog was clearly dead, even though it was still moving. Orthus turned and trotted back into the water, and the enemy dog even tried to follow, managing three steps before its legs gave way and it collapsed onto the bank, shaking.

They ran on, Rufinus more than a little relieved at the way the dog had died. With its throat gone first, it had had no chance to howl in pain, which might have drawn their pursuers to them immediately.

'I'm not sure how much further I can run,' Veremundus gasped as he sloshed through the water.

'Til the end of your life,' one of the legionaries snapped.

Rufinus knew what they were feeling. The prefect was an officer and a nobleman, who had come from Rome straight into the job, and had never had the training or exercise of a soldier, and that was why he tired quicker than them. Superior in rank, he may be, but in any other manner, they saw themselves as better, and they were probably right. They didn't seem to have the same opinion of Rufinus, despite his rank, but then he had been there with them in all their endeavours, proving himself. Still, he knew how Veremundus felt, for he was close to the limit himself.

'He's right,' Rufinus said. 'We're getting exhausted, and the Alemanni are fresh. The moment we falter, they'll be on us.'

'So what's the alternative?'

He had no answer to that. Instead, he ran on, sloshing downstream with every step a troublesome ache. They had gone maybe another mile along the river now, so they were probably still seven from the border. The chances of getting there without collapsing first were becoming remote.

'Stop,' hissed Clemens, waving for them all to move back to the riverbank. They did so, but in the process, Rufinus hurried forward, too, to join his friend at the front.

'Look,' the legionary whispered just above the sound of the water, pointing around a tree.

Rufinus peered into the dark. The river curved to the right, and just around the corner, he could see activity. With Clemens at his side, he climbed onto the bank a little more and moved between the trees until they had reached the other side of the bend. What he saw brought forth worry and hope in equal quantities.

A track through the woods crossed the river here by means of a small timber bridge. Four auxiliary riders were by the river next to the bridge, watering their horses. Rufinus frowned. Horses and men could undoubtedly ford such a narrow, shallow flow, so why did they need a bridge, and a reasonable quality, fairly recent one by the looks of it. One simple conclusion leapt to mind. If it wasn't for horses or men, then it was probably to enable carts to cross easily. That, and the presence of the riders, suggested that this was the road that led from the camp they had just escaped from, and if that was the case, then it probably led back to Tannum, so that the prefect could ferry goods between the two locations. A slow smile creased his face, and he turned to Clemens.

'I have an idea. Go get the others.'

His friend disappeared, and moments later returned with the three legionaries and the prefect.

'Riders,' whispered Veremundus, peering at the scene. 'I know those men.'

'Of *course* you do,' Clemens grunted. 'You *brought* them here.'

Rufinus glared at the two men. Now was not the time for argument. 'I can take one. Orthus can take another. That leaves two, but we need to hit them fast and by surprise. We need them down before any man can get on a horse, or we lose. That simple. We move through the woods until we're close, and then we rush them, alright?'

A chorus of nods greeted this, and so Rufinus led the way through the trees, keeping parallel with the river in sight on their left. He moved as fast as he dared, despite the fact that this created more sound and an increased chance of falling foul of roots and undergrowth. The packs over their shoulders caught on branches and snagged repeatedly, yet still they did not delay. He was acutely aware that if they didn't hurry, the riders might mount up and go, and those horses offered a possibility they could not let escape.

The tension rose as they moved, getting closer and closer to the bridge, then he spotted the open road that led to it on their right. With a gesture to the others, they spread out so that they were moving closer and closer in a line. Each man now had his sword out and in hand, even the prefect, and the moment the riders were visible through the last few trees, they all dropped their kit bags and at a single signal, started to run.

Unencumbered, armed and desperate, the six men burst free of the trees just ten paces from the four men who stood in a knot, murmuring to one another as their horses stood in the shallow water, drinking.

It took precious moments for the riders to realise they were in danger. By the time they were moving, Rufinus and his friends were on them. Two of the men had turned to face the attackers, instinctively, hands going to their swords to draw, while the other two had run for the horses. Rufinus did not need to give the command to the dog this time, for Orthus was ahead of them all, his master close behind. Even exhausted as he was, Rufinus raced past the two drawing their swords, in the wake of the dog, splashing into the water on the heels of the two riders.

Orthus hit his man first, from behind, teeth sinking into the calf even as the man ran. He cried out in panic and pain and went

262

down instantly into the water with a splash, though that did not save him, for it merely brought all his vital parts within the dog's reach. Rufinus was no less savage with his own man. In other times he might have regretted killing a Roman soldier. In the civil war against Pescennius Niger, for instance, he'd rued the way he'd had to face his own people in a fight. But this was different. These men had taken their oath to Rome and the emperor, and had now turned their back on it. They were traitors, pure and simple.

His sword swung just as the man reached his horse. The blow was aimed low deliberately, for the man wore a chain shirt, and the sword cut into his thigh just below the jingling hem. He cried out, falling against the horse for which he was reaching, bouncing off it and dropping into the water. Before he could do much else, Rufinus delivered a second blow, this one a powerful overhand chop. He hit the man on the back of the neck as he floundered in the current, and knew the neck had snapped with the blow. The two men who'd run for the horses were down.

He turned, to see that the other two riders had their hands full, facing two men each as Veremundus stood to one side, occasionally lancing out with his sword when he saw an opening.

Leaving them to it, Rufinus reached out and grasped the reins of the horses, which had acquired a wild-eyed look at the violence in their proximity. As he held tight to the leather, he reached up, stroking them alternately, calming them. Once they were content, Rufinus turned to the other two horses, leading one pair over to the other, where he then took their reins too, calming once again.

Happy that he had all four horses and there was no danger of bolting or rearing, he turned back to the others, and led the animals towards them. He'd gone a few steps before he noticed the problem. One of the legionaries had taken a blow to the midriff during the struggle. He was an unhealthy grey colour, while his clothing from the belly down was gleaming darkly.

Rufinus had seen enough wounds in his time to know that the man was done for.

'Gods,' he murmured as he closed on them.

'I know,' the soldier gasped, wincing. 'You've got to go.'

'Nonsense,' the prefect said. 'Get this man on a horse. If there is no medicus who can help at Castra Numera, there will be one at Iciniacum.'

Rufinus shook his head. 'He won't make it back there. He'll not last a mile, Prefect.'

Veremundus frowned. 'Are you sure?'

'I know it, and so does he.'

Clemens took the injured soldier over to the trees and spoke to him quietly, and as the others stood sombre, their victims just heaps of meat in the water that left trails of pink flowing downstream, Rufinus looked his companions over. 'Alright. Five men, and four horses. Veremundus can share with me. The rest of you get one horse each, but you have to share out the kit bags, as we can't fit those on, too.'

'How will you manage behind the saddle?' the prefect asked him.

Rufinus blinked. 'I'm afraid you're mistaken. I shall be the one in the saddle, and it will be you behind.'

The prefect frowned but had the wisdom not to argue. Rufinus passed the reins of three of the horses to the legionaries, while he took the remaining one and started making adjustments. 'What are you doing?' Veremundus asked, as Rufinus loosened the haunch straps at the junction, first on one side, and then on the other.

'It's a trick the Tenth Legion's cavalry used to use in the Marcomannic Wars when they needed to carry passengers. The second man climbs up, slips his legs under the haunch straps and then bends the knees and clenches. Then the rider mounts and the passenger holds on to either the saddle horns or the rider's waist or belt.'

'That's not very dignified.'

Rufinus's lip twisted. 'Nor is being beheaded by Alemanni and displayed on a spear tip.'

'I take your point.'

With Rufinus's help, the prefect climbed up and managed to tuck his legs beneath the leather, gripping the horse tight, holding on to the saddle's rear horns with a worried look. Rufinus tightened the straps again over Veremundus's legs to help secure him, and then, with a grunt at so many aches and pains, pulled himself up into the saddle. He was hardly surprised when his sword belt suddenly bit into him as the prefect gripped the back of it tight. Bracing himself, knowing this was not going to be a comfortable ride, Rufinus grasped the reins and looked about. The two legionaries had fastened the kit bags to the other three horses, and now Clemens was walking back their way and reaching out for the reins of the other horse that were being offered to him.

As the five men were ready to move, Rufinus turned to the dying legionary over by the tree, searching his soul for any word of comfort he might offer, but was surprised to see the blood-soaked, grey-faced man standing once more, and walking towards the bridge.

'What's he doing?' he hissed to Clemens.

'He's going to draw them away from us.'

'Gods, the man can hardly move. Is he mad?'

'No. Just brave.'

That he was. Rufinus watched the man go, with immense respect.

'Alright. Follow me. This might seem a little strange, but I want to leave no trail for anyone to find.' And with that he kicked the horse into motion, the others following on. The riders now walked their horses back up the way they had come, and then milled around in circles for a short time, near the end of the bridge, churning up the earth in a confused mass of hoof prints. Then, once the hooves were dry, the riders walked them up the start of the wooden bridge before jumping the three feet into the water, a move that would leave no clear track leading back to the river.

As Rufinus urged his horse from the bridge, and the animal gave an easy small jump into the river, the prefect behind him made a small, squeaked panicky noise and gripped Rufinus so tight that his sword belt felt as though it might cut him in half. With a series of splashes, they landed in the river and began to move faster now, trotting downstream, away from the bridge and its road.

Over that sound he distantly heard a voice calling the prefect's name.

The injured legionary at work.

'I hope the poor bastard is dead by the time they get to him,' Rufinus muttered.

Clemens shook his head. 'Not likely. He *wants* them to find him.'

'What?'

'Drawing them away is only half of it. When they question him, he can tell them we took the road for Tannum. By the time they realise they've been duped we should be home and safe.'

Rufinus pulled a face. It was brave enough of a man in such agony simply to walk through the forest shouting. To do so in the expectation of being found and then tortured to death was incredible.

'What was he called?' he asked, realising he still didn't know several of these men by name.

'Aelius Celerinus.'

Rufinus nodded, committing the name to memory. When this was all over, and he could honour his own brother's demise, knowing that Publius had been the very trigger that had led to the discovery of this plot, he would also honour the name of Aelius Celerinus for having done more than could ever be expected of a man to help them get away.

They rode downstream at a steady pace, the river gradually widening and deepening as they went into a more true flow. Once a good mile further on, they paused and listened. The pursuit had fallen far enough behind that the five men could hear nothing above the rushing water and the snorting horses. A little further on, Rufinus fancied that he could hear a very distant scream as Celerinus met his end, though that seemed unlikely at such a distance, and it was probably all in his imagination.

They started to ride again, and Rufinus relaxed just a little. He could almost feel the relief and recovery of his strained physique, despite the motion of the horse and the weight of the prefect pulling at him from behind. After the beatings, then the escape from the hut, the fights in the camp, the scaling of the tower, then the desperate run through the forest and the fight with the horsemen, simply bouncing along in the saddle was such a relief, it was almost as good as sleep.

The miles passed in relative peace, and finally Veremundus, just behind Rufinus's ear, spoke.

'Less than a mile now, I think. Then we have to work out how to get across the frontier.'

Rufinus frowned. 'We announce ourselves and demand to be taken to the fort. We are Roman after all.'

There was an uncomfortable throat clearing behind him.

'What?' Rufinus said.

'This entire stretch of the border is controlled by men from Tannum.'

'*What?*'

'I told you, the unit at Castra Numera is just a small garrison from the next fort along. They don't supply the men for the towers. In theory the men of Iciniacum should cover that stretch, but part of my plan has been to control all the towers in certain areas to facilitate the crossing of the tribes and the pressure for the garrisons to withdraw.'

'Shit. So your grand plan to fuck up the empire is still coming back to bite us, even now that we've escaped. Now we have to get across a frontier potentially defended by the enemy unnoticed, or force our way in.'

'Not the latter, I think. The towers are only a third of a mile apart. They can see each other under normal conditions. Sneaking might be our only option, although I cannot picture an easy way to do it.' He fretted. 'Perhaps if they hear that the Alemanni have turned on me, they might rush to my aid, like many of the soldiers in the camp did.'

'Or perhaps they might put arrows in us, like your other auxiliaries in the camp did.'

He fumed as they rode on along the shallow edge of the river, and only a quarter of an hour later, he caught sight of the Roman border, a timber tower with flickering torchlight inside and a man atop the high walkway, leaning on the parapet. As they slowed and moved up onto the riverbank to cut down on noise and visibility of approach, Rufinus tried to take it all in. Naturally, Rome had kept the border clear and visible, and the treeline had been cut back to give the towers an open space some six hundred paces across on the outside of the frontier, handily supplying the timber for construction. He led the others to a halt just inside the treeline, then dismounted and moved to the edge, the others following suit, Veremundus with some trouble and discomfort, having to be helped down by the legionaries.

In cover and with a clear view of the open space before the frontier, Rufinus cursed quietly. He could see two towers in each direction, which meant that the men atop them could, too. And that meant that even if the men in a tower did choose to support the prefect over their Germanic relatives, those in the neighbouring towers might not.

He looked around. The river they had followed flowed across the open grassland straight to the border, where it ran through the border. The palisade itself opened for the river, now a flow thirty or forty paces across and deep at the middle, though the timber wall on each side had been carried out into the water to at least waist depth, preventing any easy passage that way.

'Where's the gate?' Rufinus muttered, looking this way and that.

'There's no gate here,' the prefect replied.

'What? You said this river led to Castra Numera.'

'It does. The fort is quarter of a mile on the other side of the border. But this low land tends to flood and become marshy, so the nearest gate was relocated to the east, on the hill.'

Rufinus sagged.

Why was nothing ever easy?

CHAPTER EIGHTEEN

Rufinus fretted, examining the defences again, aware that every moment that they delayed their crossing brought with it the possibility of the searching Alemanni catching up with them. There had to be a reasonable way through. He ran back over what they faced.

The border consisted of a stout palisade, atop a turf embankment with a rubble or timber core. In front of that lay a traditional ankle-breaker ditch, and behind it, every third of a mile, a watchtower of timber with a balcony to allow full panoramic view. The towers and ditch were positioned in the manner of a fort's walls so that any arrow or javelin sent down from the balcony could perfectly angle over the rampart top and into any attacker slowed by the ditch. Roman military engineering at its best.

Across the slightly marshy plain, the river had flooded the ditch to either side, making it twice as slow and difficult to cross as when dry.

'Tell me about the gate on the hill,' he muttered.

'It sits before the tower you can see up there. No approach from the north can be effected without being in full view of the tower, which will have the usual four men. It will be shut tight – it always is unless in use. The road winds up the hillside towards it, and passes through a long-disused native fort, its ramparts lowered by our engineers. The gate is sturdy and with twin bars of oak in place on the south side. The fore-ditch does not climb the hill, for the ground is too rocky, but the approach is harder there anyway. It is well-used as a trade road by the tribes when they visit the empire. Merchant convoys are allowed through in both directions.'

271

'If only we could masquerade as merchants,' Rufinus sighed.

The others nodded at that. Sneaking through in such a manner would have been excellent, but no merchant would be trying to cross at night, and they did not have time to wait for dawn. Half of Germania would be at the frontier looking for them by then.

'At the moment, the men in the tower will be too careful for such subterfuge anyway,' Veremundus said. 'They had strict orders from me before we left for the camp not to open the gate except to our own people. More than that, I have only part of my uniform, and none of you would pass for either auxilia or native tribesmen. I don't see how we could get through the gate, unless you are willing to test them and see whether they will side with me.'

Rufinus shook his head. 'If they do, then we're through, but if they *don't* then there's a good chance some of us will fall to arrows or javelins before we get out of range, and then they will send the alert all along the border, and *everyone* will be on the lookout for us. Right now, the men in those towers don't know we're coming, and that is our strongest advantage.'

'Alright, so what *do* we do?'

'We can't get over the palisade, and the gate is closed to us. That only leaves the river.'

Veremundus fell silent, looking at the waterway before them. He did not look happy.

Where the river reached the ditch, it flooded it before passing through a gap in the palisade. There would be no wading through the shallow margins of the river to get through, though. Since the palisade marched out a way into the flow, the only part of the river that was free-flowing to safety would be deep enough that only swimming would get them through.

'That is far from easy,' Clemens noted, drawing an emphatic nod from the prefect. Rufinus was starting to form the distinct impression Veremundus was a less-than-expert swimmer.

'Easier than climbing the palisade while people throw spears at you,' he countered.

'The river is in full view of the nearest tower,' the prefect added.

'And how will we get the horses and kit through unseen,' Clemens asked. 'It's not practical.'

Rufinus spun, facing the prefect.

'The men on border duty are your men, yes?'

'Yes. Auxilia from Tannum.'

'It's been three days since you were overthrown by Ingomer. You've queried whether they might side with you, but what if they don't know you've been overthrown yet?'

Veremundus frowned. '*Three days*,' he repeated.

'But would Ingomer feel confident in approaching the border before he was ready, even just to send word? After all, those men might have taken exception to your being removed from command. It is my theory that they do not yet know. That means that you may have a chance of crossing legitimately as yourself. You could use the gate, just not with us, because *we don't* stand that chance. They will know who we are, and will not believe you travelling alone with us, without an escort of your own men.'

'Nor *alone*, especially only half equipped.'

Rufinus smiled. 'Wear what you have. It might not be everything, but it identifies your rank, who you are, and with the sword it suggests you are still free and in charge. We'll string the horses together and you can take the front one. Lead the animals up to the gate on the hill and speak to your men. Spin them a tale if you have to, that there has been some sort of trouble and you need to get to the nearest fort, and fast. Do whatever you have to in order to get through. Then take the horses halfway to Castra Numera and wait for us.'

'And you will swim?'

'And we will swim.'

'If the guards have been warned, I will die and the horses and your bags will all be lost.'

Rufinus nodded. 'But if you *don't* try, we'll have to leave it all here anyway. There's no way we can swim through that gap with four horses without being seen or heard by the guards. On our own, though, we might make it.'

The prefect looked entirely unconvinced. He was deep in thought, lips moving silently and distrustful eyes on the water, and Rufinus knew him to be trying to find an alternative or a solid reason not to try it. In the end, he sagged in defeat. There was no better way, and at least he would not have to swim.

'Alright. This might be the end of the trail, though.'

Rufinus gave him what he hoped was an encouraging smile. 'You can do it.'

Veremundus straightened. 'It is my duty to try. All I have done, I did for the empire, even though it has failed. I am a man of honour and duty. I shall see you on the other side of the frontier, or I shall see you in Elysium.'

That, Rufinus was impressed with. Since his imprisonment, let alone their breakout, the prefect had seemed at best pessimistic and hopeless. Something of the steel of a Roman officer had seemingly crept back into him.

They spent a short while roping the horses together, and then Veremundus cleared his throat. 'I will be some time.'

Rufinus frowned. When he listened hard, he could just hear the distant noise of their pursuers. They may have taken the wrong path thanks to Aelius Celerinus, but by now they must have discovered they had been duped and resumed their search back at the bridge. 'We don't have long before they catch us. Why delay?'

The prefect gestured to the river. 'If I reach the gate bedraggled from crossing that, they will be all the more suspicious. There was a shallower stretch half a mile back, where I could cross with the horses and only get their legs wet.'

'You risk the Alemanni catching up.'

'It's a risk I'll have to take. If I want the guards to believe I've come from the camp in the woods, there would be no reason for me to be in the water.'

Rufinus nodded, tense. He didn't like it, and every moment now counted, but the man was right.

'Go.'

Veremundus nodded and started to canter back along the riverbank, the other three horses pounding along in his wake. The other four waited until he was gone, then pushed their way back through to the edge of the woods.

'This is going to be slow, and difficult,' Clemens said.

'Yes.'

'And you know there's a good chance the prefect won't get through. There are a hundred things that can go wrong.'

Rufinus nodded. 'If he fails, we lose him, the horses, and all the kit. But if he doesn't try, we lose the horses and kit anyway. And if I were to be brutally honest, I think our chances of getting through there are considerably higher without him.'

'That I would agree with. There's no way to get across the open ground close to the palisade before we swim. We'll have to go all the way in the water. Unless maybe we crawl on the bank? There is shrubbery there that flutters in the breeze, even if it's only knee high. It could disguise us.'

'I don't relish the idea of half a mile of stony riverbank on my knees,' Rufinus said, with feeling. 'Besides, the river flows south, so we're swimming with the current. That gives us extra speed. Swimming will be a lot faster.'

Unhappily, the four men returned to the riverbank and took a bracing breath before beginning. Rufinus led the way, walking out into the flow, wincing at the shock of the cold water. It was not the warmest of swims, not like the clear blue waters off the villa near Tarraco, but at least it was late spring, rolling into summer, and the icy meltwaters of winter had gone. It would be cold, but they would not freeze, and the cold would to some extent invigorate their tired and aching muscles.

He reached the point where his chin was being lapped by the flow, and finally lifted his feet from the riverbed and began to swim. Beside him, Orthus paddled easily out into the water. The dog was a good swimmer, and only his head was visible above the surface, sodden, the hair plastered back across his scalp. It seemed to take a couple of years to make it out into the centre of the river, and by the time he was starting to pull his way south, stroke by stroke, he was already questioning the wisdom of his plan. It was a long swim even for a strong and trained swimmer. He'd not asked the legionaries whether they could swim well, but no one had spoken up against the plan, which suggested they could. He looked over his shoulder to see Clemens and then the other two in a small knot behind him.

'Spread out,' he told them, 'and for fuck's sake stop doing that stroke.'

The man at the back, who had dropped into a fast front crawl, looked guilty and switched to gentle breast-stroke instead, a slower method, but with considerably less splashing about. Even Orthus had been making less noise than him. By the time they passed out beyond the treeline, they were spread out, a line of four men and a dog. Each of them kept low, their strokes slow and measured, their bodies beneath the surface and only their heads above water. They were hardly hidden, but it was the best for which they could hope, and they were as obscured as it was possible to be in this landscape, just four dark scalps bobbing along in the midst of a dark river in the dark. And Orthus's pale head could just pass for the white water here and there as it caught and rocks and eddied.

Rufinus reasoned that the towers to either side each had a staff of four men, but at the most two would be out on the walkways, the others inside, and at night, probably only one was actually on watch. Each of those men would have to watch the ground in both directions from his tower, which meant that on average only one pair of eyes would be on this area at any time. And with a wide spread of open ground bordered by the dark eaves of the forest, their eyes would most likely stray across the grass and to those shadowy boles most of the time, only occasionally passing over the river.

At least, that was what he told himself.

They were moving through the open now, slowly pulling themselves towards the Roman border one arm-stroke at a time. Rufinus could feel the fatigue returning, threatening to claim him, every pull a strain, while the cold was beginning to bite at him, to claim his flesh. He risked looking around, his pale face coming up into view for a moment, and in some ways wished he hadn't. Atop the tower to his left, the guard was looking in his direction, and, as he quickly turned away to hide his face as he swam, he could see there were actually *two* men atop the right-hand one. Neither sight was encouraging. Still, there was nothing he could do about it. They were somewhat committed now.

He swam on, praying they could all make it physically, even without worrying about the enemy.

He could see the border coming up, now, out of the corner of his eye. Without endangering them by raising his face, he could just make out the bump and recess of the water-filled ditch off to the sides, and behind it, the frontier palisade.

A shout went up suddenly, cutting through the quiet of the night, and Rufinus's heart lurched. They were discovered!

No longer worried about being seen, he lifted his head to try and work out how far they still had to go, and whether they would find any shelter from missiles on the far side. Then there was a loud laugh, and another shout from the opposite direction.

His heart battering powerfully enough to burst from his chest, Rufinus realised with surprise that they had not been seen after all. The men in the two towers were sharing a joke and laughing, looking at each other, right across the space where Rufinus and his friends swam. He dipped his head back down and slowed, not risking a full swim now, resorting to a paddle gentle enough to keep him afloat, allowing the current to do most of the work, letting him almost drift downstream in the dark, back from Barbaricum and into the waiting arms of the empire. He managed to reach Orthus and grabbed the dog with one arm, holding him afloat but restricting the animal's motion.

The ditch slid past, and, as the joking seemed to end with another raucous round of laughter that then slipped away into silence, Rufinus dared to start hoping. Then, the palisade slid past them in silence, marking their return to Roman lands, for all the good that would do, given that the border was in the hands of the German tribes now anyway. But still, as milestones in their journey went, it was an important one.

They were back.

For the fourth time in his eventful life, Rufinus had returned to Roman lands from the world beyond: Marcomannia in the wars of his youth, Dacia in his exile, Arabia when chasing spies, and now Germania. At this rate, by the time he took blessed retirement, he would have been across every border of the empire.

Still, he drifted, not daring to swim in case he drew the attention of the men in the towers.

After a while he turned his head, just slightly, to look east, and was filled with immense relief to see the nearest tower a little way back. They were past the worst danger, for the men in the towers would concentrate what attention they had on the land *outside* the frontier, not inside.

He could see a native farm up ahead on their left, and in the distance, past it, the looming shape of a small fort, torches burning on the walls. *Castra Numera* - home of Spanish horsemen, potentially the first people they could trust since waking up outside the empire. Now was the time to risk moving. With just a single hand gesture to the others to follow, he started to angle across the flow, swimming towards the east bank. It was tense, and he only felt any sense of safety as his feet finally touched the riverbed and he began to wade out of the water. He moved fast, then, in case the watchmen happened to look back his way, and ran for the shelter of the native farm, Orthus now pounding along at his heel. The place was a small affair, with a single timber farmhouse, two sheds and a barn, as well as a large, fenced area that held a herd of heavy brown cows. In heartbeats he was standing in the lee of a shed, panting and watching the three legionaries hurrying from the water to join him. Orthus began to shake, sending droplets of cold water in a cloud in seemingly every direction. Rufinus cursed and covered his face as the spray caught him.

'Shit, that was cold,' an arriving legionary said, shivering as he leaned against the timber wall, breathing on his hands to warm them.

'And tense,' Clemens added. 'When they started shouting, I almost polluted the water.'

'I *did*,' the last man added, and despite their continued predicament, Rufinus found himself musing on the fact that he had just been swimming downstream amid another man's urine. Still, it would be dilute beyond belief.

He waved them to follow, and then jogged past the cattle, causing them all to move about and low gently in worry, then disappeared behind the barn and crept along its wall. They were now at the opposite side of the farm to the river, and with a clear view of the open land between the border defences and the fortlet of Castra Numera. Rufinus looked about with some urgency. Off to the south, he could see the fort, sitting on a low rise, close to the river, its associated civilian settlement a similarly small example. Off to the northeast he could see the slopes of that ridge, the palisade marching up it, with towers at intervals, torches burning in them. And in between, he could see the road that led down from the crossing up there and passed by the fort.

The road.

The empty road.

'He didn't make it,' Clemens murmured.

Rufinus shook his head. 'Doesn't look like it. Of course, he may have been delayed.'

'Or caught by Ingomer's men. Or detained by the men at the gate. Or just killed.'

'True.' Rufinus sighed. 'Whatever the case, we cannot afford to wait and find out. We need to get word to the man in charge of that fort.'

'And ask him if he has spare dry tunics and boots,' a legionary said quietly.

'That too. Come on.'

With that, he started to jog. It mattered not about being seen now. The border guards probably wouldn't see anyway, since they would be looking the other way, but the four men were far enough from the towers now that even if they were seen, they were out of bow range, and could safely reach the fort before being caught. The four of them pelted over to the road, and then turned and ran along it towards Castra Numera.

'Halt,' shouted a figure on the ramparts as they closed on the gate of the small fort, an armoured man, scale shirt and enclosed helmet gleaming golden in the flickering torchlight.

Rufinus had never thought he would find a confrontational command bellowed at him so warming and welcoming, but it was the first time in quite a while he had met a soldier in this province who did not either speak his native language or Latin in a very thick Germanic accent.

'Praetorian tribune Gnaeus Marcius Rustius Rufinus, and these three are men of the Third Italica from Castra Regina. We do not have our papers, but it is critical that we see your commander as a matter of urgency.'

There must have been something in his tone that carried veracity for his words, as the soldier did not instantly dismiss the four bedraggled lunatics standing in front of the gate, but rather beckoned down inside the fort. Rufinus felt hope surge again, as a man in an optio's crest appeared on the gate top alongside the soldier.

'You have no identification?' the man asked.

'No.'

'You will have to leave your weapons at the gate and submit to a search. And your hound leashed, too.'

Rufinus bowed his head, and moments later the gate was opened. The men of the Third Bracaraugustanorum were gathered around the interior, at least a dozen of them, and with weapons bared. Clearly this unit was prepared for any trouble in the region. Good.

Rufinus drew his own sword as well as the broken one at his belt, slowly and carefully, proffering them hilt-first to the garrison before removing his sword belt and using it as a makeshift leash for Orthus. His swords were taken by the soldiers, as were the weapons carried by his legionary companions, and the soldiers gave them a quick check-over and pat down to be sure they were not carrying any concealed weapon. Once the optio was content that they were no great danger, he nodded to his men, who secured the gate once more, and then led the visitors through the fort. Rufinus took stock of the place as they moved between its few buildings. A large place it was not. They passed a storehouse and a small baths on the right, a single cavalry barracks on the left. As they neared the small headquarters, there was a minor granary to one side, and a workshop to the other, and he could see two infantry barracks at the far end. That was the whole fort. Perhaps two hundred men at the most, including infantry and cavalry, and no senior officer, for there was no officer's house visible.

They were led into the headquarters, and Rufinus's confidence in their security only grew at the sight of a statue of Septimius Severus on display, announcing the unit's loyalties to the current emperor. With that, he felt safe and content as they were escorted to a room next to the rather sparse chapel of the standards.

The man who sat at the small desk with a stack of writing tablets and a single stilus was wearing the same uniform as the rest of the fort's staff, though propped against the desk was a gnarled and ancient vine stick, the centurion's badge of office.

'A curious time of night for visitors,' the centurion said, brow arching as they entered.

'They insisted on seeing the commanding officer, sir. Claim to be legionaries and Praetorians.'

'Praetorians? Here?' The man frowned, though Rufinus was pleased to note he loaded the words with neither spite nor disbelief.

'Centurion, we lost our kit crossing the border unnoticed from Germanic lands, and with it all our documentation. All I can do right now is give you my word that I am Gnaeus Marcius Rustius Rufinus, Tribune of the Fifth Praetorian Cohort in Rome, and that my companions are all that remain of a contubernium of veteran legionaries assigned to me by the governor himself at Castra Regina.'

The centurion continued to frown, rising from his chair and collecting his vitis stick.

'You had perhaps better explain how you came to be outside the empire, and what your business is on the Raetian frontier?'

'Would that we had time,' Rufinus sighed. 'But time is short, and every moment counts.'

'Explain,' the centurion said.

'It's rather a complex story, but if we skip straight to the end, you'll learn that a warband of Germanic warriors, trained in methods of overcoming Roman tactics, are moving through the forest on our trail, with the worst of intentions.'

'And you thought you'd lead them to my fort. Thank you,' the man said, though he was starting to sound less convinced now. 'Why not to Tannum, where there is a *full* garrison?'

'Because the men of Tannum have gone native, Centurion. They have surrendered to the call of their Germanic blood and sided with the tribes. In fact, they also control the border towers over this entire stretch.'

'Your story is far-fetched to say the least,' the centurion said. 'I have met the commander of Tannum, and there are fewer more rigid Romans than he.'

'And if he were still in command of Tannum, I might agree, but he is either captive in the woods behind us, or sprawled dead in the open ground before the palisade wall. This is no joke, centurion, and no trick. Rogue elements among those frontier garrisons with Germanic roots have been training their free countrymen how to kill Romans. At the moment, there are just a few hundred out there, and they know that we've escaped, so they'll be at our heels. But when the signal is given, half of Germania is going to start flooding across the border, and at least six of the garrisons are in on it, granting them half a dozen free points of access to the empire. We need to get messages out immediately.'

'To who?'

'To your parent garrison at Iciniacum, to any local auxiliary fort that cannot claim Germanic or Raetian origin, and most importantly to the governor and his legion at Castra Regina. They need to be warned and ready. If they are unprepared when the Alemanni start to move, there will be massacres, and we might even lose Raetia. I understand there is a similar plot unfolding in Upper Germania, too, so messages should be sent there as well.'

The centurion gave him a curious smile.

'You're extremely convincing, I'll give you that. Early on, you almost had me. But I'm afraid your tale will not change the world here. I am not about to send out orders putting the frontier on alert and turning half the border garrisons against the other half, just so they are fighting one another while whatever nefarious plan you have put in place unfolds. I wasn't born yesterday, "*Tribune*".' He loaded the rank title with such dripping sarcasm that Rufinus felt the ground open up beneath him. They'd failed. With no proof of who they were, the centurion wouldn't believe them.

'If you won't listen, send a rider to Tannum to check my information? Or send us to your parent unit so I can speak to your prefect.'

'I don't think so. I think you will stay right here until the morning, when I will have you escorted there for questioning.'

'By morning, this place will be a smouldering ruin, and we'll be burned corpses amid it. The enemy are close behind.'

'No. I'm afraid I will not be rearranging the frontier on the word of a bedraggled and filthy vagrant claiming to be a senior officer.'

'How about on *my* word, then,' said a new voice from the doorway behind them.

Rufinus turned with surprise, and an immense flood of relief, to see Veremundus in the doorway. The man looked exhausted, but he wore his subarmalis, with his sword belted at his side, the stripe of his rank visible on the tunic.

'Prefect Veremundus?' the centurion said, looking part Rufinus.

'The man speaks the truth,' the prefect said. 'Here.'

He tossed something across the room, which the centurion caught with his free hand, then turned over in the lamplight. Rufinus recognised in an instant his Praetorian brooch. The centurion clearly recognised what it was, too, for he looked up at Rufinus then in surprise.

'If you need his papers too,' Veremundus said, 'they are in his bag on the horse outside. But I urge you to move. This is a matter of some urgency.'

'It's *true?*' the centurion said.

'It is. And worse than that, the warriors of the Alemanni were already starting to cross the open ground from the woods behind me as the border guards let me through. They will be across the frontier and at your fort gate within the hour at the latest. Our only hope now is to pull out of Castra Numera and back to Iciniacum, where there will be sufficient men to hold against them while messages are sent out.'

The centurion shook his head. 'No.'

'What?'

'I will not abandon my post. You said there were a few hundred of them?'

'For now, yes, but there will be many more coming.'

'There are a few hundred of *us*, too. We will hold this fort against your German enemies, and then, while they mourn their dead, and before any second warband can come, we will speak to my prefect at Iciniacum, and plan the next move.'

Rufinus looked around, as though he could see the fort that lay outside the headquarters' walls. 'Don't take this the wrong way, Centurion, but that does not sound like a good idea. You keep a nice, tidy and well-presented fort, but it's not exactly the most defensive place to hold against a Germanic warband.'

The man fixed him with a look. 'Frankly, I don't care whether you're a wandering vagabond, a Praetorian tribune, or Jupiter himself, you will not persuade me to abandon my command. Only my own prefect can do that. But I accept your identity on the word of Veremundus there. You therefore have the choice. You can stay here and help us prepare, or you can leave us to hold while you take your story to the prefect.'

Rufinus turned and looked at Veremundus. The prefect had a worryingly defiant expression. He sighed.

'Best show us to the armoury, then.'

CHAPTER NINETEEN

'You know this is foolish in the extreme.'

It was not a question, and the centurion nodded. 'So you keep saying. Yet you agree there are just a few hundred of them, and there are a few hundred of us. So in the eyes of the gods, we are evenly matched. But we have walls and towers and ditches where they do not. And we have Noric steel to their iron. And we have the discipline of the imperial military to the chaos of the warband. But above all that, we have one thing.'

'And that is?'

'We are Bracari!'

Rufinus rolled his eyes. He was aware of how certain Iberian tribes considered themselves superior in strength of arms from a century of brutal resistance to Rome. And they *were* fearsome, yes. But so were the Germanic tribes.

'How many men do you have again?'

'Two centuries and a turma.'

'None of them up to strength, I presume?'

The man had the decency to look momentarily embarrassed. 'Not entirely. Those who can take a place in battle number one hundred and twelve foot and twenty-six horse.'

'Twenty-three horse,' Rufinus reminded him.

The man nodded. Three riders had just left the fort by the south gate, heading east, south and west, to carry word to the forts at Opia and Iciniacum, and more distantly to the governor at Castra Regina.'

'How are you planning on deploying them?' Rufinus asked, as he shrugged into his scale shirt and began to tie the laces.

'I have the riders dismounted among the infantry, and including officers we total one hundred and thirty-five men.

287

Adding yourself and your men to it, barring the prefect, of course, we have one three nine.'

'Count the prefect. Every man is important. So that's one forty. And my dog, though he can hardly commit himself until they're inside the fort.'

Orthus sat nearby on the wall top, idly scratching an ear with one foot and then sniffing the foot suspiciously.

'Thirty-five men to each wall,' the centurion mused.

Rufinus shook his head. 'This is your first siege?'

The centurion bridled. 'Hardly.'

'Your first siege as the commander, though?'

'That much is true, yes.'

'Your horsemen are not going to be as effective on the ramparts as your infantry. They are not trained the same. Keep the riders in the interior, carrying ammunition and dealing with the wounded, and then they form the reserve.'

The centurion's eyes narrowed. 'I don't think you understand. You've not fought with the Bracari. Our riders will be better at the walls than the infantry.'

It was Rufinus's turn to frown now.

'Just watch and learn,' the centurion said, then waved to a man in a cavalry decurion's uniform, who turned and hurried over. 'Six men to each wall, yes Paccius?'

'Six to most, five to the south.'

A nod from the centurion. 'I shall deploy the infantry between them, keeping two contubernia in the compound as a reserve to plug the gaps.' He nodded to Rufinus at that, echoing his suggestion, and was about to go on when he was interrupted by a shout from the north gate.

'They're coming!'

Rufinus quickly finished arming, and then jogged over to that position alongside the centurion and his men, Orthus trotting along at heel. As he ran through a world illuminated by three dozen torches and a number of braziers, Prefect Veremundus and the four legionaries, all similarly finishing arming, converged on the gate with him. They climbed the wooden steps of the earth bank onto the stone parapet, breathing heavily. He was exhausted, and beset by aches and pains, but it did not seem the gods were willing to let him rest yet. Reaching the place above the gate, he first looked back. Men were falling into position all along the fort's walls, those in the chain shirts of the infantry, and those in cavalry scale, fastening helmet straps, hefting shields and spears... and there he suddenly realised what the centurion had meant about the cavalry. The footmen were gripping spears with a length of six or seven feet, while the cavalry had been armed with the contus, a long, lance-like spear ten or eleven feet long. The reach of that weapon from the wall could make a great deal of difference. Rufinus found himself reassessing their position. He'd thought the centurion not up to the task, inexperienced in such command, but clearly the man was more shrewd than he'd expected. It was possible after all, given the numbers and the defences, that they could resist and even beat their pursuers.

He turned back to the slope up to the border crossing, through which the Alemanni had come without question or incident. At a rough estimate he made it two hundred out there in the dark. Roughly. Not a lot more than the Romans themselves could field.

The hope that rose in him then faltered and fell away once more.

This was only the party sent out to recapture the escaped prisoners. And now that Ingomer knew they had got free of the camp, he would have no choice but to commit. His messengers would have gone out to the various other warbands along the frontier, and even as those two hundred men trawled the forest looking for Rufinus and his friends, the rest of those warriors back in the camp will have been arming up and marching out to war. There was a damn good chance they were little more than an hour behind this lot. And they might number a thousand or more. Rufinus could not even *estimate* the numbers, given the lack of freedom he'd had to explore these last few days.

A thousand? *Two* thousand? *Five* thousand? And that was without counting their friends in the border towers and the fort of Tannum. Worse still, among them were traitorous but well-trained Roman auxiliaries, experts in siege warfare and imperial tactics.

He eyed that mob streaming down the hillside in a new light. Yes, they might win this fight, but that was only the vanguard of what was to come.

He turned to the centurion. 'Listen to me. We can stand, and we can hold, but we have only limited time before the rest of their friends turn up, and then we could be facing ten-to-one odds. I know you don't want to abandon your command, but you will have to make a sensible command decision.'

The officer nodded curtly, but Rufinus wasn't sure he agreed.

He sighed. Right now they had to concentrate on their immediate problem. Another glance back gave him some little confidence, for the Third Bracaraugustanorum were clearly more than competent. They were already shuffling into position, five footmen spaced between each dismounted rider, all along the walls, the few remaining men busily moving ammunition and supplies into position from the storehouse. Of course, Rufinus said to himself, probably a little unfairly, with so few men and such a small fort it was considerably easier to prepare.

But again, the proficiency of the Hispanic auxilia and their centurion shone through. Sheafs of short, narrow-headed throwing javelins were being passed up to the walls, where the infantry were standing their swords against the stonework for swift retrieval and hefting the four-foot shafts ready for an initial volley. There was sufficient for every man to take one, and some spare, those latter being concentrated towards the gate where the officers stood.

'They will hit the north wall first and hardest,' Rufinus noted, 'and they will concentrate on it. Not only is it the closest contact point, but we are here, and they have likely already seen us. You will be a target,' he added, pointing at the centurion's crest, which tended to draw attention in combat, 'but they will be desperate to kill or capture me and Veremundus.'

'We can use that to our advantage,' the centurion said.

'Oh?'

'If you can draw their concentration, then wherever you go, their strength will follow. To that end, you and the prefect need to be ready to move. Wherever anywhere is looking weak and endangered, you two could move round the walls away from it, and draw enemy attention to a stronger point.'

Rufinus nodded his appreciation. 'An excellent idea.'

He turned back to the road at the shouts of men along the north wall. The Alemanni were almost upon them, hurtling across the open ground now, making for the fort gate, where the causeway crossed the ditch, and above which all the most important men in Castra Numera stood.

As soon as the mass of warriors neared the edge of the fort's surrounding ditch, the junior centurion among them gave an order, echoed by the two optios, and arms came up and over all along the wall, casting the light throwing javelins down at the advancing Alemanni.

Rufinus realised the mistake too late to warn anyone. Like all Roman officers across an empire and centuries of warfare, the centurion in charge of the volley had counted off the paces and readied, giving his order so that he could time the landing of the volley with the position of the enemy. Only at the last moment did Rufinus realise how much damage Veremundus had done by training the Alemanni in Roman warfare.

The warriors ran at the ditch and causeway, but at the last moment they stopped, and even managed to take a few steps back in places. It was masterfully done, in a way only a man who knew precisely what was going to happen and when could possibly have anticipated.

A few of the light javelins hit, but the majority fell short of the suddenly curtailed charge, thudding harmlessly into the grass or clattering against one another down into the ditch.

291

'Shit,' breathed the centurion nearby.

'They can't do that twice,' Rufinus urged. 'Have the rest of your javelins passed round while there's still time.'

The man nodded, shouting out the order, and light throwing weapons were passed from man to man around from the fort's eastern and western defences to those at the north who, with the centurion's command, cast them the moment the weapon fell into their grip. Now, better able to aim and to anticipate, the rest of the javelins hit home, and the throws were good, but the failure of the initial volley had made a huge difference to potential enemy casualties.

Out across the causeway, there was something happening. The Alemanni were not coming in force yet, still halted beyond the ditch, wary of the javelins arcing up and out, but a small knot were changing formation. That alone worried Rufinus. His experience of Germanic warfare against the Marcomanni suggested that they had little or no concept of formation. That these Alemanni did was yet another nod to the training they'd received under Veremundus's misguided command.

They were settling into lines eight wide, just enough men side by side to fill the causeway, but also five deep. Rufinus felt a chill as he saw men swapping out their equipment, large, oval or hexagonal shields being passed to each of those forty men in the formation. He had a horrible feeling he knew what they were doing.

His eyes darted left and right along the wall. In a siege with more preparation time, they would have gathered baskets of rocks to pelt down on the attackers, a standard, effective, and very cheap, tactic. They had not had the time, but with what was about to happen they really needed rocks as the most efficacious weapon. He fretted even as that formation began to move, trying to find anything that might act in the same manner as heavy dropped rocks.

His gaze fell upon the battlements. Like so many Roman fortifications, these were topped with heavy, shaped cap stones, mortared to the stonework below. He looked along the line. At least half a dozen of them stood above the causeway and gate, and would not need to be moved far.

'Quick. Get daggers out. Get these capstones loose.'

'Why?' The centurion frowned, as Rufinus pulled his pugio free of his belt and started to hack at the old, dry mortar holding the stones together.

'Because they're going to climb the testudo.'

The centurion frowned. 'But they're barbarians.'

'Just do it.'

The man gave the order, and along the line above the gate, those infantrymen who had already cast their light javelins pulled free their daggers and began working furiously to separate the capstones from the battlements they covered. Even as they worked, Rufinus's eyes continued to flick up at the movements outside, and everything he saw confirmed it. The Alemanni were engaged in a manoeuvre that was almost solely a legionary trick, using their large, rectangular body shields. The auxilia did create the defensive testudo from time to time, but their oval shields were less suited to full coverage, and so not unless it was particularly required. There could no longer be any doubt in the centurion's mind that these warriors had been trained by a Roman, and a Roman with not only auxiliary experience, but in the legions too. Veremundus had undoubtedly served as a tribune in the legions as well as commanding an auxiliary cohort.

They were moving across the causeway now, chanting something in a spine-chilling Germanic fashion in the dark, five rows of men, and as they moved, their shields held out forward, they formed the new shapes ready.

'Sacred Minerva,' the centurion hissed as he dug at the mortar. 'I've never seen anything like it.'

'You have. Just not on *their* side of the wall.'

As they moved into range, the Alemanni slid seamlessly into the testudo, shields held out as walls to the front and both sides, but also held overhead to form an armoured box. That was impressive enough, but Rufinus knew what was coming next, and worked harder now.

The stone was starting to lift at the corner, and, glancing left and right as he dug with his dagger, he could see similar success with the other capstones. He pushed at it, then returned to digging, eyes still on those men outside the gate, lit eerily by a combination of silver moonlight and golden torch flare.

They were out of time. He saw the testudo reach the gate and settle into position, bracing. And that might have been all there was to it: just ranks of men protecting themselves from missiles from above. But it wasn't. Even as the rear two ranks of the testudo began to rearrange and move again, the warriors back past the ditch were preparing, bracing, spitting on their hands and stretching.

'Quickly,' he shouted.

The capstone to the right must have been looser, because it was already rocking free, the men lifting it. 'Don't wait,' Rufinus panted. 'Drop it on them.'

The rear two ranks of the testudo were now clambering up on top of the roof of shields, their own boards up as a second-storey roof. They happened to be looking up as the stone was levered free, out over the drop, and let go. By a combination of preparation and blind luck, the men on the second storey angled their shields and braced, catching the heavy falling stone and managing to deflect it out into the ditch, harmlessly. Then they moved into place.

The warriors out in the darkness began to run.

The defenders were *very much* out of time.

Rufinus almost lurched out over the wall as the capstone came free, and his dagger slipped from his fingers, clattering out over the parapet and into the darkness. Forgetting about the small blade – he would replace it later – he grabbed hold of the edge of the stone and began to heave. Others were doing the same. Stones were being freed and tipped.

Down below, the rear ranks of the two-tier testudo were angling their shield roofs, higher at the front, lower at the back, creating between them a ramp that reached most of the way up the height of the wall. The other warriors were halfway across the causeway now, speeding up.

Rufinus had seen it used time and again during the wars, a way of getting over walls. A testudo that re-forms into a ramp when it reaches the defences, so that other soldiers can run up it and take the walls.

Never before had he seen barbarians doing it.

Between them, he and Clemens tipped the stone out. A wary warrior in the higher tier realised it was coming, and he and his companions managed once again to use their shields to angle and deflect the stone out and away, although a cry of pain suggested that someone had broken something in the process. But the move was not enough for them, as another capstone, being worked on by two men of the garrison, fell out only a heartbeat after Rufinus's one. While managing to deflect the first stone, the warriors were unable to move in time to stop the second, which fell through the upper roof, splintering badly-positioned shields and knocking them aside as it broke arms, ribs and legs, before smashing into the lower roof and settling there.

Even before the next stones fell, the Alemanni were beleaguered. As the upper level of the ramp splintered and separated, reeling with damage and wounds, two of the dismounted auxiliary cavalry went to work with their long contus lances, stabbing down with expert precision, each blow driving deep into flesh, adding constant injury to the reeling formation.

The enemy warriors that had run over the causeway were unaware of just how badly the formation had gone awry, and reached the rear, leaping up onto the shields of the first level, then straight up onto the floundering, disjointed shields of the upper tier, where everything fell apart.

In moments, all that remained of the attempt was a mass of warriors trying to disentangle themselves in front of the gate.

More capstones landed among them, and there were screams as heads smashed and bones broke. Many of the warriors simply took flight, pelting back out across the causeway to their friends, a few limping after them, cursing in that harsh tongue.

'They'll think twice before trying for the walls again,' the centurion said, perusing the two score corpses that littered the approach to the gate, victims of javelins, rocks and spears.

'We can't afford for them to wait all night,' Rufinus said. 'There are many hundreds more out there, not far away. If we're trapped here and they all arrive, we're truly screwed. We need to beat them fast or get away from here and regroup with the rest of your unit.'

'Too late for that,' Clemens said, pointing.

Rufinus looked out. The Alemanni, their attempt on the north gate having failed, were spreading out, moving to surround Castra Numera. They were trapped. By the time they managed to get to the south gate, that side would be covered too. 'Shit. We're surrounded, and they're staying beyond the ditch for now. They're not daft. All they have to do is wait for their mates, and they can overrun us with ease. They just need to stop us getting away.'

The centurion gave him a sly smile. 'They might think they've got the better of us, but we are Bracari.'

Rufinus had a feeling that 'we are Bracari' was a refrain that would go down in history with classic lines like Caesar's dismissive 'well the Ides of March are come,' or Vespasian's 'an emperor should die on his fee...' He suspected 'we are Bracari' could only ever precede acts of ridiculous heroism, or appalling failures. Probably the latter more often than not.

'What can we do from here?'

'We can make them wish we were anyone else,' grinned the centurion. You obviously don't know our *full* unit designation here.'

Rufinus frowned. 'What?'

'We are Cohors III Bracaraugustanorum *Saggitaria*.'

296

'Saggitaria?' Rufinus blinked, then looked round as a single noise echoed all around the walls, as every infantryman along the rampart lifted a bow and nocked an arrow, keeping them out of sight just below the battlements. He grinned. 'You sly bastard.'

'We are Bracari,' shrugged the centurion, as though that explained anything.

The man didn't need to give a command. He just lifted a hand and dropped it, and in a silence broken only by the Alemanni crowding together to form a cordon around the camp, a hundred bows were lifted clear of the walls, and a hundred arrows released in a single cloud that flowed outwards from the fort in every direction.

The effect was stunning. The Alemanni had thought they were being clever by surrounding the fort and preventing escape, and the Hispanic centurion had let them do that, not disabusing that notion, yet all the time knowing that they were unwittingly playing to his strength.

Fully half the Germanic warriors across the ditch died in one volley. Rufinus watched in astonishment as every second man surrounding the fort fell with a scream. In a very short time, they had more than halved the enemy number, and without losing a single man as yet. He almost laughed as the Alemanni fell over one another in an effort to get out of bow range, even as the men on the wall top nocked another arrow each, a few loosing, where they saw a tempting target who had not pulled back in time.

'You realise that while they're largely uncivilised, they're far from stupid,' Rufinus said quietly. 'We've outmanoeuvred them twice now, but they'll learn from every failure, and they won't repeat the same mistake. You'll run out of tricks before they run out of resolve.'

The man shrugged. 'Then at that point, we'll have to try your plan, Tribune, and run back to the rest of the unit.'

Rufinus gave a slightly crazed laugh. 'You are Bracari,' was all he could think of to say.

There was a long pause, now, as the Alemanni lurked at the very edge of the light cast by the torches, planning their next move. In that blessed breathing space, the soldiers along the wall top took the opportunity to arrange their equipment so that swords and shields were easily to hand, while the cavalry held their long spears and the infantry waited with arrows nocked.

'I can almost see into their minds,' Rufinus laughed.

'Oh?'

'They've spent months being taught Roman tactics, and the first time they've had the chance to try them out for real, they've failed. I reckon they're arguing about whether their new training has been worth a dog's spit. Watch them devolve back into their natural state any moment now.'

And they did not have long to wait. Rufinus could almost hear the frustration building to a head out there, and rather suddenly the silence and the darkness were split as a hundred Alemanni gave up any attempt to emulate Roman warfare and simply ran, screaming, swords raised, towards the fort. Rufinus almost laughed aloud, then caught the expression on the centurion's face, and actually did. It was not often in the midst of war a man could find even dark humour, but when he did, he latched on to it with the desperation of a madman.

The Alemanni ran. Some managed to funnel across the causeways that led to the gates in each wall, others simply ran down into the ditch and struggled to climb the far side. A few leapt the ditch entirely. Some even made it.

Rufinus was still laughing as, at a signal from the centurion, those men with bows along the wall let loose a second, looser, volley at the various warriors struggling to cross the defences.

The fight was going to be over very soon, and Rufinus knew it. In excess of two hundred warriors had poured down the hillside from the frontier gate. At most a third of them remained, and they had as yet to even wound one of the defenders.

The enemy reached the walls then, and the fighting broke out in a much more traditional manner. The Alemanni essentially swarmed at the defences like angry, hairy ants, using one another as a ladder, when the opportunity arose, to come ever closer to the wall top. The dismounted cavalrymen, experts with their long lances, used the weapons with their impressive reach to stab down into the furious, milling crowd of warriors. Whenever one of the Alemanni succeeded in coming close to the parapet, they became the province of the Hispanic infantrymen, who had downed their bows the moment the enemy were across the ditch, and now stabbed and slashed down with their swords in an effort to keep them from the parapet.

Rufinus watched, not committing to involvement. For one thing, these men were used to working together like this, with plans and systems in place, and Rufinus appearing in the middle of it, flailing with his sword, might do more harm than good. For another thing, he was exhausted. He was so mentally done in that he couldn't even work out how long it had been since his last sleep. And the aches and pains of beatings and repeated exertion did not improve the situation. He contented himself with watching as the auxilia made the Alemanni regret their attack. Here and there he saw a defender fall, either dead and crumpled to the wall walk, or wounded and carted off by a capsarius.

It was clear to Rufinus's expert eye that the walls were going to hold. Castra Numera was safe.

For now.

The fighting lasted maybe another hundred heartbeats before the Alemanni gave up. Totally unable to overcome the walls at any part of the fort, the survivors limped and lurched away into the darkness. There could not be more than forty of them, to Rufinus's mind, as they disappeared into the night. That grand plan of he and the prefect drawing their attention had been far from necessary. The centurion had been better prepared and more ingenious than Rufinus could have ever expected.

'*Are* you Bracari?' Rufinus said suddenly, turning to the man.

'What?'

'You have a Gallic accent, I'd say. Somewhere in the Lugdunum area? I spent some time there a few years ago.'

The centurion shrugged. 'Bracari is in the mind. Are you a *Roman*?' he asked archly.

Rufinus nodded. 'Gens Marcia, since the days of the kings and the formation of the republic.' He laughed. 'But I take your point. Rome is in the mind and the heart, and not always the blood.' He looked around at the fort. 'That was extremely impressive, and I can only commend you. I will, in fact, to your commander. But you know you won't get to do that twice.'

'I have other tricks.'

'Not enough,' Rufinus said. 'Bravery and foolhardiness are a hair's breadth apart. Make sure you stay on the right side. This was brave. To stay for the next one would be foolhardy.'

For a moment, the centurion bridled, then finally shrugged acceptance. 'You really think there'll be that many?'

'Can't say for sure, but there'll be a lot more than this bunch. And these weren't prepared for an attack. They were just hunting us through the woods. When the rest come, they'll have had time to equip and prepare. And they will probably have other auxilia with them, too.'

The man nodded. 'Then we had best move back. We need to move fast?'

'Yes,' Rufinus replied simply. He had no idea how far away Ingomer and his warband would be, but the man would be chasing them down as soon as he could, so it would not be far.

The centurion turned and waved over to the other officers. 'Have every man gather his things, and get everything we need to take loaded on horses. Not carts. We need to move fast. Anything we can't take that's of use to an enemy, burn it, including all the documents in the headquarters.'

He turned back to Rufinus as the fort burst into activity.

'I hope you're right. Prefect Quintus Papirius Maximus at Iciniacum does not like surprises. Unless he's the one doing the surprising, of course.'

Rufinus nodded absently, turning his attention back to the frontier, that line of stockade and towers that marched across the low, swampy ground and then up the slope to the ridge. Was it his imagination or could he just see a faint glow far beyond it.

He had a feeling they were going to have to move fast.

CHAPTER TWENTY

For the first time since he had left the Praetorian fortress, months ago, Rufinus was surrounded by allies. Until now the most men he could have counted on at any time had been the eight legionaries the governor assigned him. Now, he was surrounded by their remnants, but also by four hundred ridiculously self-confident Hispanics. And yet somehow still the race from Castra Numera had been every bit as tense as their breakneck race through the woodlands.

Of course, while Rufinus now had a lot more men on his side, the enemy had similarly increased, and so the difference was negligible. By the time they had been ready to leave the small fort by the river and begin the speedy withdrawal to Iciniacum and the unit's mother fortress, the enemy were well on the way. Rufinus had been one of the first to depart on a borrowed horse, his kit bag tied to the harness, but as he had looked back from outside the fort's south gate, he'd been able to see Ingomer's warband crossing into Roman territory. They were pouring through the gate atop the bluff, *encouraged* by the men in the tower, whose raison d'etre was to do precisely the opposite. They were gathering on the hillside, burning torches bobbing around among them, their numbers growing worryingly, as Rufinus and the Third Bracaraugustanorum left their victory site and began to move at a forced march southeast for the five mile journey to relative safety.

It had not been a comfortable journey. The lead elements of the enemy force had initially chased them down, but there had not been enough of them to truly threaten the retreating Romans, and so they had continued to dog their steps without quite committing. The Romans had been immensely lucky,

303

Rufinus believed, that the need for the Alemanni to funnel their force through the gate on the ridge was the only thing that had bought the Third time to flee.

Thus, they had arrived at Iciniacum in the pre-dawn light, knowing that the warband of Ingomer was but an hour behind them, and that they had only that much time to prepare, for it seemed inconceivable that the Alemanni king would allow them to slip away now.

The interview with the prefect had been less than encouraging.

'Thousands, you say?'

'Yes.'

'And they will assault this fort.'

'I cannot see other possibility.'

'And you have already sent riders out to Castra Regina and the other allied forts, the same as the one we received?'

Rufinus nodded again. 'Yes.'

'So there is nothing further we can do to warn the other units along the border or the governor and his legion. But you believe our local forts to be untrustworthy and so there is no point in sending for aid.'

'I have seen the men of several such forts working alongside the Alemanni with my own eyes.'

'So we are on our own. Against a sizeable Germanic army?'

Rufinus had nodded. 'That's about the size of it, yes.'

'A chance to prove our mettle to the governor, then.'

Rufinus blinked. He heard a short indrawn breath and turned to find the centurion who had commanded during the siege grinning. Gods, but the two men thought alike. Rufinus stood in the office of the fort then, waiting for them both to whoop like lunatics and announce that *they were Bracari*.

'I have made preparations with the time I had since your messenger arrived,' the prefect said. 'I've had all timber buildings thoroughly doused with water in case of the use of fire arrows. I have had the north, east and west gates strengthened, with carts rolled up against the timbers, and the approach bridges broken across all three ditches, leaving only the south as a potential sally route for cavalry. We do not have a lot of pitch, for recently it has been used in repairing timber roofs, but what we do have is now in pots on the walls, and braziers are being lit to further their use as a weapon. Similarly, all ammunition has been moved to stockpiles close to the wall, and every man who can walk, even the ones with the terminal shits, have been brought up to the ramparts and armoured.'

'What artillery do you have?' Rufinus asked.

'Four stone-throwing ballistae, one at each corner tower, and six smaller bolt throwing versions that have currently been sited around the walls, two to each long axis, one to each short. We also have a weapon of immense size brought here after the wars that hasn't been used since, but she needs a little work to get her fully operational. When she works, though, she can throw something the size of Cleander's ego, and the weight of Commodus's head.' He grinned. 'We call her Locusta, because she's killed more men than the Antonine Plague.'

Rufinus shuddered, and not at any of what he was hearing, but at the sheer enthusiasm in the man's tone. Enthusiastic officers were rarely a good thing. They tended to push when they shouldn't and failed to stop when they should.

'What about the civilians?' Rufinus asked.

The prefect frowned. 'What about them?'

'I saw the size of the civil settlement out there. Will you send them away or bring them inside the walls?'

'Neither. They are civilians. They have no place here, and their fate is no concern of mine. Besides, they are German. This lot will probably *welcome* them.'

Rufinus shivered again. 'I'm not convinced of that. I fear any local who has not sided with them has probably made it to their list of enemies.' He straightened. 'Alright, where do you want *us* in your defensive plan?'

'Wherever you like. Just watch and enjoy the show. Leave this to us. We are Bracari.'

There it was. That had been the moment Rufinus began to worry that they were doomed.

At least the prefect had organised his men and his fort well. He'd even, at Rufinus's insistence, assigned an engineer, an artillerist and half a dozen heavily-built men to trying to get Locusta working. Rufinus had then resigned himself to the temporary position of observer. He'd actually given serious thought to trying to get some shut-eye, but he knew the Alemanni were close, and wanted to be here to see them arrive. He'd not had long to wait. True to his own mental timings, not an hour had passed between his arrival at Iciniacum and his standing on the ramparts and watching the enemy do the same.

There were a *lot* of them. They came flooding along the road from Castra Numera, their strange horns booing, drums banging. To the west of the fort lay the remnants of an earlier timber fortress, of similar dimensions but long since reduced and backfilled, now little more than a rectangular mound of lumps and bumps. The Alemanni flooded across the old fort like seawater reclaiming buildings of sand, until they were just out of bow range, where they came to a halt. A line formed, and shields came up to face the Romans. The warriors lifted the boards to their mouths and began to moan, a low, growling sound, made eerie, echoing off the shields.

Rufinus knew that sound well, for he'd heard it while fighting the Marcomanni in the wars in Pannonia. The *barritus*, the war cry of the Germanic peoples. It was designed to get their blood up and ready them for violence and death, and simultaneously to chill their enemies to the bone. Even knowing that, and having heard it plenty before, it still worked, and Rufinus shivered.

As the Alemanni's voices rose in both volume and pitch, shields lowering to change the sound, the chant turning into a roar, and then a scream, Rufinus was impressed with how the Third simply stood around the walls and watched, impassive. The barritus ended suddenly with a single mass bark.

In the momentary silence that followed, someone over at the northern wall suddenly started ululating, loud and high pitched, and moments later every Hispanic voice in the fort was joining in, the sound piercing and nerve-jangling. Rufinus wanted nothing more than to put his hands over his ears, but also could not help but smile to see the Alemanni reacting, their confidence knocked momentarily. Their own cry was meant to instil fear, but all they could hear from the defenders was a cry of their own.

We are Bracari, Rufinus thought amid the shrill cacophony.

Finally, the noise died down, and the two units faced one another in silence across the earthworks of the earlier fort.

'See that one with the feathery helmet?' Clemens called along to the artillerist standing a dozen paces to their right. The man nodded. 'Think you could put a bolt through him?'

The artillerist thought this through for a moment, then turned to his prefect, Papirius Maximus, who gave a single nod. The range was long, and the man tested the wind, angled the small ballista he worked at, lifting it to point at a sky that was now beginning to clear for morning, night fading away. Content he had done what he could, the artillerist steadied himself, held his breath, and pulled the trigger. Even as the bolt flew up into the morning blue, the crew were already reloading and resetting the engine.

The bolt arced high, and every pair of eyes on both sides rose to its trajectory, fascinated.

It fell. Alemanni warriors tried to move out of the way, but they were jammed together in their press for the barritus. Still, the artillerist missed his target slightly, for it was an extremely difficult and long shot, yet the bolt found a new home, falling into the man *next* to the plumed chieftain, slamming down so hard that it disappeared inside his torso entirely. He fell forward to the ground, eliciting a great moan from the Alemanni. To their credit, the fort's garrison did not cheer.

The enemy pulled back another six feet, making such shots even more difficult, and then began to deploy. Rufinus made a rough headcount as they did so, and estimated somewhere just in excess of two thousand. Against maybe four hundred defenders. Not the best odds, but he'd feared it would be worse. This, they at least stood a chance of surviving.

He yawned, acutely aware that he had not slept since the night before last. Twenty years ago, as a fresh soldier serving with the Tenth, he'd not have blinked at that. Now, he could feel fatigue clawing at him. He resolved to find one of the water barrels and dip his head in to help revitalise himself, but first he watched the Alemanni. They began to spread out, surrounding Iciniacum, as they had done at Castra Numera, but at a more sensible safe distance. Towards the rear of the force, he could see a small knot of well-dressed men on horses. Though he couldn't make out details yet, they had to be the leaders, and that meant Ingomer.

'Do you notice anything?' he said to Veremundus and the legionaries.

'What?'

'No auxiliaries. Where are the auxilia?'

'They were probably all beheaded before the Alemanni left the camp,' the prefect posited. 'I'm sure Ingomer will no longer feel bound by his deal with a Roman.'

Rufinus shook his head. 'The auxiliary *prisoners* back there are probably all dead, but there were plenty who went native and joined them. And what of those men on the frontier, in the towers? Ingomer needs all the forces he can get, and men who know the ways of Rome could be useful here. So where are they?'

It was a worrying question, for which no one seemed to have an answer. Rufinus and the others watched the Alemanni's next step in dismay, despite its predictability. They moved into the civilian settlement and began to take the people from it before looting the place and burning the buildings to the ground. The locals were then brought out in full view of the Roman defenders, lined up all around the fort, and then beheaded, one at a time. Their heads were gathered together in a grisly heap, and the rest of their bodies taken away and disposed of. All morning,

Rufinus watched their horrible work, silently cursing the garrison commander for not having either sent the locals away or brought them in for safety.

It was a soul-crushing few hours of gruesome display, though he made himself watch it all, as testament to those poor folk. When it was done, he was tempted once again to go and attempt a doze, but as often as not a brief doze leaves a man groggy, and worse off than if he'd not slept at all. Instead, he found a barrel and dipped his head, blinking away cold water as he rose once more, sending spray across the nearby ground.

More waiting ensued. The Alemanni seemed to be preparing the ground well this time. They rushed into nothing, manoeuvring groups of warriors around to specific positions, based on some criteria the Romans could make neither head nor tail of. Rufinus was starting to get irked by the fact that he could actually have got a reasonable sleep in by now, though any notion of doing so was offset by the knowledge that if he tried, there was a good chance the fight would begin while he was out for the count.

Instead, he watched every movement. After a time, he nudged Clemens. 'I'm sure I've seen that lot there before.'

The legionary shrugged. 'I hate to say they all look alike, but right now I can't tell any two groups apart.'

Rufinus fell silent again, watching. He was sure they were the same men, who'd been rotated out of this position only to be brought back an hour later. A thought struck him, and he looked along the wall. He breathed in heavily. Every man was looking out at this ongoing display, intrigued, even those who were supposedly in support roles, down below the walls.

'Fuck.'

'What?'

'They're just attracting our attention so they can get a good look at us. Now they know our numbers.'

Clemens slapped his forehead. 'Shit. This Ingomer is clever.'

'That he is.'

'Shall we get the men to head back down?'

Rufinus shook his head. 'He's getting information, scouting us. We need to throw off his planning. Get everyone up here, and keep moving them round.' He turned to the prefects. 'You need to get everyone on the wall, including your few slaves, the scouts, the wounded. Get everyone armed and up here whether they can fight or not, even the men working on your artillery monster. And then start moving them in small groups the same way the enemy are. It'll make it hard for them to get a clear headcount, and work out where the strengths and weaknesses are, and there'll look to be more of us than there are.'

Prefect Papirius Maximus mulled this over for only a moment, then nodded and turned to his senior centurion. 'See to it.'

Thus began the third phase of the siege, following the enemy's deployment and destruction of the civil settlement, and then Ingomer's posturing and testing. Now the Romans were doing the same. Rufinus spent two hours watching as both sides tried to estimate numbers, while making it difficult for the enemy to do as much.

The attacks began in the early afternoon, just as the men were finishing their meals of cold rations and water, eaten in position on the walls. At first men laughed, confused. Three or four of the Alemanni would psych themselves up, bellowing and chanting, and then run at the fort over one of the gate bridges, or even trying to leap the ditch. They were fairly wily, in that they knew what ranged weapons to expect from the defenders, and so the moment an archer or javelin thrower brought their weapon into view above the parapet, those men started to weave and duck, shields up, covering the large part of their exposed flesh. Consequently while they drew arrows and javelins, only a few found a home quickly, and the Alemanni would reach the fort, touch the wall, whooping, and then race back to their kin.

It appeared to be a game, a way for them to prove bravery and daring among the Alemanni, for it went on for a number of hours in a variety of locations, and Rufinus was just wondering

310

whether they intended to keep it up in the hours of darkness when Clemens found him watching the latest such escapade.

'I've been thinking about all this,' the legionary said.

'Oh?'

'I don't think it's a game. I think they're cleverer than that.'

Rufinus concentrated now. 'Go on.'

'Each time: a new place, each time: new moves and ideas. They're testing us. They're assessing the strength at every location, and our reaction time to their attacks. And they're testing weapon ranges and reload times. All this is just more of Ingomer's information gathering. See how runners keep going to that group of leaders at the back with reports?'

Rufinus winced. Why had that not occurred to him. Damn it, but Clemens was right. 'And they're making us waste a cart load of ammunition every hour into the bargain. Ingomer really is bright. And we fell for it. Pass the word to stop trying. The men are only to loose a missile if it's a definite kill, and preferably only when they've reached the wall. I'm going to tell the prefects.' He did so. Veremundus nodded sagely. Papirius Maximus looked vaguely annoyed at the end of the game.

Over the ensuing hours, the ever-decreasing response to the small probes led the Alemanni to increasing their own attempts, throwing in more men, being more daring, trying to push the defenders into action. But the garrison knew what they were doing now, and were quiet and careful, and gradually the hours slid by. It was already heading towards sunset when the situation changed once more.

Rufinus was strolling along the wall walk when a shout went up, and men began pointing. It took him but moments to find the source of the alarm. Smoke was pouring up from the granaries. Rufinus cursed and ran over to Clemens, grabbing him and the other legionaries. Veremundus was busy in discussion with his fellow prefect, so Rufinus left him to it, while the rest of them, along with Orthus, and a small number of auxilia that were at work in the streets of the fort, ran for the burning buildings.

311

'I thought he said they'd doused the timbers with water to stop this?' Clemens huffed as they closed on the site. Rufinus looked ahead to the twin buildings. They were of stone base, up to waist height, with timber walls above and tiled roofs. The doors were wide open, and he could see the inferno within each as an orange glow, while black smoke roiled and curled up from the timbers and tiles.

'It's only so much use having a wet roof. That doesn't protect the interior.'

'What?'

'Well did you *see* a fire arrow come over the wall?'

'No.'

'Exactly. These were burned from within. Someone set fire to the grain, and grain burns like nothing else in the world. We just need to contain it and stop it spreading to other buildings. It's a good job we're not looking at a long siege, as this would make things very difficult if we were.'

'Come on. Let's get some buckets and start dousing it.'

Rufinus shook his head and pointed to the auxiliaries dashing around. 'Let *them* do it. I'm more interested in knowing who lit the damn granaries.'

Because whoever ignited the grain in those buildings could only have done it in an attempt to bring down the defenders. Whoever did it had to be allied with Ingomer.

'Who would do this?' Clemens said, as if reading his mind.

'I don't know. We brought with us only legionaries, and all the men here are Bracari. I suppose it's *possible* they've recruited a few locals who turned on the unit.' He frowned. 'No. I don't think a traitor would last long among this lot without being discovered and done in. Besides, Veremundus told me he'd only approached units that were Germanic or Raetian in origin.'

The two men turned and shared a look in an instant.

'The scouts.'

'Shit. Recruited from locals and yet kept as part of the garrison. And they're in and out of the forts all the time, ranging over the countryside. They could have been Ingomer's men for months. Years, even.'

'Where will they have gone?' Clemens mused, looking around.

Rufinus followed suit, and paused as his gaze reached the headquarters building, just ten paces from the granaries. 'Shouldn't there be a guard on that door?'

'Probably not. We *did* tell them to bring every man up to the wall earlier, remember?'

'Yes, but that was when we were trying to disguise numbers. Now things have moved on, and men have returned to duty. The orderlies are in the hospital hut, the men are back to working on getting Locusta working, and that means to me that there should be a guard on the headquarters. There's *always* a guard there. *Always.*'

He gestured to the other two legionaries with them, and all of them now drew their swords and began to walk towards the headquarters, the fort's central building, a white hound pacing alongside, teeth bared. Rufinus's sense that something was wrong only grew as they came closer. The doorway seemed innocent enough, but there were scuff marks in the gravel in front of it, and when he looked carefully it was hard to miss the faint blood spray on the building's wall. There *had* been a guard, but he had gone.

With the other three and the dog at his back, Rufinus reached the door and stepped to one side. One of the legionaries followed him, Clemens and the third man stepping to the opposite side. They paused. There was a tapestry of sound woven across the fort from a hundred different threads, and it took work to separate them out. The Alemanni outside the walls, and the soldiers atop them, the men in the fort's streets going about their many tasks in support of the defenders, the labourers working on Locusta, the roaring of the granary inferno and the hissing as water was thrown across the buildings by the bucketload.

And beneath all that, close and echoing: voices.

Germanic voices, which had no place in a Roman fort garrisoned by a unit of Hispanic origin.

It had to be the scouts.

The voices were muffled, suggesting they were several rooms away, and so Rufinus gestured to the others and dipped inside, looking sharply back and forth in case of danger. The courtyard was empty, barring the body of the auxiliary guard who'd been butchered and then dragged inside, but he could now hear the voices clearer, emanating from the basilica doorway across the open space. He passed on a plan using only hand motions, and then dashed across the courtyard to the next door, where they repeated their move, two men dropping to each side, motionless and silent, listening.

Rufinus could hear them. He had no idea what they were saying, of course. Clemens *would*. He would understand it all, but right now, Rufinus could hardly ask him. In addition to the voices, there was an intermittent sound that it took him moments to identify: wooden writing tablets hitting a stone-flagged floor. He concentrated, counting. For a while he waited, to be sure he had them all. Four separate voices. He held up four fingers. Clemens nodded his agreement. Rufinus motioned for each man to take one scout, and then started using his fingers to count down from five, oddly wondering whether the legionaries wondered why there were no nails on that hand.

He reached one.

They burst through the door, the Praetorian and his dog at the fore, and they did not stop. They were running as they entered, and all that changed then was *where* they were running. Rufinus was first in, and took in the scene in an instant. Three men were busy with the fort's records, discarding those of no interest in a large pile, and stuffing the ones they wanted into a bag. He didn't know what it was they had taken the details of, but it seemed likely to be strength reports, unit locations, passwords, military papers and suchlike, which Ingomer could use in his coming campaign, and which would otherwise burn when he took the fort. Clever bastard must have planted scouts like this in every fort on the border, just for situations such as this. But there were only three men. Even as he ran towards them, and they looked up in surprise, realising they were discovered, two more writing tablets came flying from the prefect's office.

Rufinus and Orthus angled that way, leaving the three currently going through the records to his friends. Man and dog reached the office doorway and barrelled on through. Rufinus never paused to take stock. He knew there was a man in here, and the office wasn't that big, which was why as he passed into the small room, it was a simple thing just to angle at the man by the desk with tablets in his hands. He hit the man hard, slamming him into the table and stealing his breath. The man made an 'oof' sound and bent double over the wooden surface, the tablets he'd been holding flying from his grip and scattering across the room just as Orthus's jaws closed on his ankle with a crunch. The man never stood a chance. Rufinus yanked the scout round to face him, pulling his ankle free of savage jaws, and then struck him square between the eyes with his sword pommel, which raised a loud crack, the victim collapsing in a heap. Rufinus frowned for a moment, trying to decide what to do with the man. So many times over these past months, men had died before he could question them, but now he simply couldn't think what he might want to ask. He already knew what he needed to know, and it was important in life never to leave a live enemy behind you. Without even a hint of regret, he pointed to the shaking body with one finger. He didn't even need to say a word. Orthus's jaws closed on the scout's throat and tore it out in a heartbeat.

Ignoring the sounds of savagery, Rufinus looked around to make sure he was alone, and then left the office once more, returning to the basilica. The fight there was over, but had taken its toll. Clemens and one of the legionaries were helping their friend over to a bench. He was limping, and blood had blossomed on his tunic above his hip. Whether or not it would prove to be a fatal wound was something Rufinus would only find out by peeling aside the bloody material, and there was insufficient time for that now. He nodded his approval. His fight had been more successful, but then he'd had the full element of surprise, while the men here had drawn their swords to face the Romans.

Rufinus frowned, did a quick count. Two bodies. Where was the third?

'The other?' he asked. Clemens pointed towards the small stairwell next to the chapel of the standards. The man had fled the fight and taken refuge in the strongroom, where the unit's pay was kept. It was a veritable fortress within the fort, only one entrance, lockable from both sides and barrable from the inside, underground and with a heavy vaulted roof. There seemed little chance of bringing the man out of there without him wanting to. Rufinus sucked on his lip.

'How do we get to him? Clemens mused.

'*Why* should we get to him?' Rufinus responded with a vicious smile.

'What?'

'Well, he's got nothing we want, and he can't do much harm down there. Come on.'

With the help of the other two, he lifted a bench and carried it to the stairwell, a simple straight tunnel of eleven steps that led down to that solid, unbreachable door. They threw the item of furniture down, where it slammed against the oak door, wedging it shut. Just to be certain, they threw another bench and a table down there, jamming the way solid, and holding that door shut. The man would simply starve in his safe haven. His refuge would become his tomb.

'Shit, remind me never to get on your wrong side, sir,' the second legionary, Annius, said, whistling in wonder.

'One day I'll tell you what I did to a bully called Scopius. *Then* you'll stay on my good side. Come on. Let's report this to the prefects.'

They left the headquarters, noting that the granary blaze seemed to be under control, although all the food therein had clearly been lost. As the sun began to set, they reached the walls and reported the incident to Papirius Maximus, who took it surprisingly well, claiming he would reap a replacement harvest from the locals for their part in this.

The enemy had pulled back from their various little attempts now, and had retreated to a safe distance, where they were making camp, lighting fires and preparing for the first night of the siege. Rufinus heaved a sigh of relief. 'Prefect, we have not slept in days. I feel it is important that we try to get a few hours while there is a lull. Mind if we use one of your barracks?'

The man shook his head. 'Hut nearest the south gate is transitory barracks for scouts and visitors. Use that. But be prepared for a full day when you awake, and despite what I said earlier, I fear we may need you in the coming day.'

To add weight to his words, he threw out a finger, past the camping Alemanni and towards the road that led off northwest to Castra Numera. Rufinus squinted into the darkness, and then saw it. Another column was arriving from that direction, which was bad enough news, but when he realised what the new arrivals were, his pulse picked up speed.

Auxiliaries, presumably from Tannum. They were coming in ordered groups, and were escorting wagons. Wagons that bore siege weapons.

Things were about to get nasty.

CHAPTER TWENTY-ONE

T he dream was different this time. Oddly, Publius was no longer there, and instead Rufinus was assailed by hordes of Germanic warriors all coming out of the dark and carrying the head of Veremundus. Also, he no longer seemed to be in a forest, but in some sort of labyrinthine construct of wood-shingled huts.

Rufinus woke suddenly, with a start, but for a moment could not figure out why. His gaze strayed around the small barrack room, a simple hut fitted out with just eight separate bunks, four of them occupied. Clemens was murmuring something in his sleep about a woman called Octavia, and occasionally chuckling. Annius snored gently. Orthus lay curled up on the bottom of Rufinus's bunk, his sole concession to his master's waking to open one eye, then close it again.

Tiberius Claudius Veremundus, prefect of the Sixth Raetorum, was sitting in silence on the end of his bed with his head in his hands. He was shaking gently.

Rufinus lay there for a moment, not wanting to disturb the man, nor draw attention to his own wakefulness. He had seen Veremundus move through a cycle of emotions since the moment the man had been deposed and imprisoned alongside the others. Initially there had been shock and disbelief, then withdrawn silence. He had started to fight back in his own way by giving them information as they planned their escape, and then, outside, he had begun to regain confidence, a process that built until the siege of Castra Numera, when he had seemed to gain once again that haughtiness of the Roman commander, something that had only come out stronger with their arrival here at Iciniacum.

319

This was unexpected, though. It seemed out of sequence in that process.

Rufinus lay there, thinking. It occurred to him that officers were often defined by their role, and that Veremundus was in some ways one of such men. He had a certain dignity of command to maintain and, no matter what he was personally suffering, in the presence of other senior officers he had to be the model prefect, unbeset by doubt. That had been the case in front of the commanding centurion at Castra Numera, and even more so here, with a fellow prefect. But alone, in the dark, the man was suffering something he would not reveal in public. And only a fool could not see what it was.

Guilt.

Rufinus continued to lie there, silent, not sure what to do. There was no real chance of going back to sleep, for the dream lurked there, waiting, yet he did not want to intrude on the prefect's own private moment. He lay, uncertain, but as he did, he moved about just a little, running a few checks. His limbs had stiffened with the rest, but they would loosen up as he stood and moved around. A few aches and pains still gnawed at him, but they were injuries he could overcome and deal with properly at a later date. His mind seemed alert and back in control. He was not fully rested or recovered, but what he *had* managed had certainly made a difference.

His uncertainty as to what to do in that dark room was made moot a few moments later, when a fist hammered on the barrack door, and it opened to reveal the shape of a soldier silhouetted in the torchlight. Veremundus straightened in an instant, composure recovered, a senior officer once more.

'Yes?'

'Beggin' your pardon, Prefect, but *our* prefect sent for you from the west gate. There's movement among the Germans.'

Orthus leapt from the bed, and Rufinus took the opportunity to pretend to awaken to this, as Clemens and Annius also blinked back to reality. The prefect nodded to the soldier and rose from his bunk. 'Tell Papirius Maximus that we are on our way.'

As the man disappeared, Veremundus slipped his feet into his boots and fastened them. The other three rose, stretching, rubbing and massaging muscles, and then followed suit. The two legionaries asked what the man had said, having been half awake at the time, and the prefect reiterated the soldier's words as the four of them helped one another into their armour, grunting at their aches and pains, and then armed themselves and looked about.

'Well, that was a nice rest,' Clemens sighed. 'Now back into Hades for a bit, eh?'

'What kind of an enemy chooses to fight at night?' Veremundus grumbled.

'The kind who knows that time is now of the essence,' Rufinus said. 'If Ingomer can overrun us, then his warband will have free rein on this side of the border. He needs to draw as much Roman attention now as he can, so that his other warbands can do the same at those forts where he holds control, yet he cannot afford to get bogged down. Warning has been sent to the governor, and if he delays too long, the province's forces will all be aware, prepared, and fully fielded, and the rest of the Alemanni will not cross the border so easily. He has to be loud and obvious, but fast and decisive.'

Rufinus adjusted the hang of his sword as they hurried from the hut into a world of nightmare, four men and a dog amid the chaos. Men on the walls were shouting to one another now, archers loosing where they could. Fire arrows were arcing up from the surrounding darkness and into the fort, thudding into roofs and walls more often than they missed. Some buildings simply smouldered, while others had begun to combust, the preparatory soaking the prefect had given them long since dried out. Men with buckets were at work all around the fort, fighting small fires. Things were under control for the moment.

As they ran, they ducked around the remnants of the granaries and into the open space where Locusta, the great ballista, loomed. Rufinus could not help but be impressed. He had only ever seen such large siege weapons on a couple of occasions, both during the Marcomannic Wars. The thing stood fully the height of three, maybe four men. When it needed moving it had to be taken apart and loaded on four carts, it was so immense, but when used properly, it could hurl a stone large enough to wreck a tower at a distance of up to almost a mile. How one of them had ended up here, he could not guess, but then they had to go somewhere, he supposed, and it had probably been employed in the war in this region, after all.

They paused as they passed an optio, clearly an engineer, and looked at the machine and the men working on it. 'How's it going?'

'It's *going*,' the man replied, rather vaguely.

'Oh?'

'No one here ever trained on something like this,' the optio sighed, turning to them and gesturing at the monster. 'It hasn't been loaded or used for twenty years, and parts of it are almost rotten or worn through. We're replacing what we can, and repairing other parts, and it will be ready to wind up in maybe an hour or so, but what happens then is anyone's guess.'

'What do you mean?' Veremundus asked.

'Well, these things never had the best safety reputation anyway, without twenty years of rot and a few hours of care thrown into the bargain. It might throw a boulder half a mile and kill some Germans. Or it might creak, groan, and then explode, kill its crew, and demolish half the nearby buildings.'

Clemens winced at that. Most veteran soldiers had seen a ballista malfunction at some point in their career. It was never pretty, and often resulted in multiple fatalities. A thing this size could do immense damage to either side, depending what happened.

'Just get it working,' the prefect urged. 'We may need it very soon.'

As if to provide evidence for his words, there came a sudden dull thud, and shouts of alarm. Rufinus turned to the west to see a cloud of dust rising above a stretch of wall there.

'Their artillery have begun.'

They hurried along the street towards the west gate, where the garrison's prefect waited for them, and as they ran, they watched a second stone strike a little further along the wall, another thud and crack, another cloud of dust and din of shouting. The prefect was in heated discussion with a decurion as they arrived, and the cavalry officer ran off along the walls as they came to a halt close to the garrison's commander.

'No letting up for the night, then,' Veremundus murmured.

'Looks like they've stopped messing around and testing us,' Papirius Maximus replied. 'They're gearing up for a major push. I'm guessing they intend to soften us up with artillery, then give us a barrage of missiles before coming in force, using any breach or weak spot they can create.'

'Are they concentrating on the western walls?' his fellow prefect asked.

The garrison commander shook his head. 'A large part of their force is here, and maybe two thirds of their siege weapons, but earlier on they shifted a third of those round to the south, and it is there a second artillery assault is about to begin, I believe. Those are the two areas that will take damage from flying stones. I can see why, of course. To the west they have good artillery platforms from the old fort's earthworks, and our south gate is a grand affair, designed by some lunatic former commander to look good. Even has a wooden bridge. But the gate towers there are concave, and could fall a lot easier to artillery than the other gates.'

'Concave?'

'Yes. Stupid idea. They *look* interesting, but they're hardly practical. One good shot and the Germans could bring down a whole tower.'

'So the west and the south are in danger.'

Again the prefect shook his head. 'Ingomer is no fool. He may have concentrated his artillery there, but now the lion's share of his actual manpower is gathered to the northeast. We concentrate west and south at our peril. It is always possible that he is using the siege weapons to draw our attention while he intends a full assault north or east. I have to divide my forces equally. There's no alternative.'

He straightened. 'And that is why I sent for you. I am commanding the west wall. I have sent my chief centurion, a stalwart man and veteran of the wars, off to command the east wall. If their warriors do come in force, he is more than qualified to hold there. My cavalry commander I have set to the north wall, where their long spears will help against infantry assault. That leaves the south. Prefect Veremundus, you have practise at commanding a fort, and Tribune Rufinus, I believe you have more than adequate experience in warfare. I give you the south, with its troublesome gate. Keep it safe. You will have a full century of infantry, plus a few cavalry, at your command. Make good use of them.'

Veremundus nodded professionally, Rufinus following suit, and they and the two legionaries turned and hurried south along the wall with Orthus alongside. Ahead, another stone hit, near the corner of the fort. There was an explosion of stonework, another cloud of dust, and an unearthly scream. As the four men came closer to the corner, aware that they could be hit by such a stone at any moment, they discovered the source of the scream. The southwestern corner of the fort had been home to one of the two built-in latrines. The outer wall of the latrine had been struck, and the small room had been filled with rubble and shards of flying stone. Rufinus could only pity the man who'd been answering a call of nature in there when it was hit.

They passed the corner then and were running along the south wall. Looking out over open ground, they could see more siege weapons in place now, and men were working on them, priming and loading them. A similar assault was about to begin on that wall.

As they ran, Veremundus gestured to Rufinus. 'I will have command and overall say of our tactics, but you have more experience in battle and sieges than any of us, I think. I need you to plan and to advise me on our best moves, and concentrate on the danger areas.' He turned to the other two. 'You,' he pointed at Annius, 'take control of the infantry for me, and you,' to Clemens, 'the cavalry.'

They hurried along the wall, Clemens finding a centurion, Annius a decurion. Veremundus approached the gatehouse, and Rufinus reached out to stop him.

'The tower,' the prefect said. 'Best place for observation.'

'The towers are the fort's weak point,' Rufinus reminded him. The man nodded, slowly, and found a position on the walls not too far from the gate. Leaving the man to it, Rufinus ran to the gate and examined it, entering the towers, climbing to the top and back down, bringing with him the men atop them for safety, then examining the ground and the single arch with its iron-shod timber portal. The main gate was no weaker than any other example, but whoever designed those towers with a concave face was clearly a lunatic. They seemed to have been almost designed to *catch* artillery shot. However, due to their strange shape, the interior of the towers was little more than eight feet across, and mostly consisted of curves and angles. A smile crept over him, and moments later he had the support staff down behind the wall fetching any wooden beams stored across the camp. He then stood and watched as the enemy artillery prepped.

The first shot hit the wall some ten feet from the gate. The whole rampart shuddered, though the actual damage was minimal. The next two shots, however, were aimed directly at the gate, and, sure enough, could hardly miss the concave towers that deflected shots *inwards* rather than out. Rufinus saw the whole gate shake, and knew that there was going to be trouble there.

Over the following hour, the enemy artillery slowly increased, the pounding of the gate incessant, but as the stones struck and dust and mortar clouded and cascaded, Rufinus's men worked hard, bringing beams into the narrow towers and wedging them horizontally across the interior so that within that hour they had created a lattice that braced that stupid concave wall in both towers and on both floors. It was far from perfect, and far from unbreakable, but it was a damn sight better than it had been, as was evidenced by the notable reduction in shaking and debris.

How long could they hold?

How long did they *have* to hold?

It was around seventy miles to Castra Regina. The message would have reached the governor and the Third Legion by now, unless somehow Ingomer's men had managed to catch and stop the messenger, a possibility that didn't bear thinking about. If the legion moved hard, they could be here by dark the next day, or at a good, sensible pace that would leave them ready for battle, the morning after. That was a long time to hold a place like this with a force this size. There was the *possibility* of relief coming from one of the other local forts, but that was only possible, not likely. They were on their own for a full day yet, then, at least.

He somehow doubted the south gate was going to last that long.

He returned to the dusty ground just inside the gate. This area was being used as a staging post for the defence, stacks of ammunition, equipment, raw materials, food and drink all gathered together in the open space of the main street. The few military slaves held by the fort, along with a couple of healthy soldiers and a number of the walking wounded distributed it to where it was needed. He'd contemplated moving up to the wall walk, where he could get a better look, but had decided against it in the end. After all, what was there to see but what he already knew to be there? Roman siege engines turned on their own people for the betterment of the Alemanni. And there was the danger, of course, too. He'd had every man removed from the gate's towers and upper walkway, for one lucky strike would not only break stone, but kill precious men.

He'd also had three carts brought forward, along with a whole collection of timbers and barrows of earth. Should the gate become an issue, he wanted to be ready to make it troublesome for any invader. Rufinus stood there for the next hour as he listened and watched the fort getting weaker. A soldier brought him some oiled bread and a cup of water, both of which he gratefully consumed before turning all his attention back to the gate.

There was enough artillery working out there now that he could predict every shot.

THUD!

One...
Two...
Three...

THUD!

One...
Two...
Three...

THUD!

It went on. To Rufinus, every thud sounded slightly worse than the previous one, and every shot that hit home – which was most of them – raised more of a cloud of dust and mortar, shaking the whole defences of the fort slightly more.

He was not confident.

'What is your assessment?' a voice asked, and he turned to see that Prefect Veremundus had joined him at ground level once more. He wasn't sure whether it was his imagination, but the man looked more drawn, pale and serious than usual,

'The walls will hold as long as we have ammunition, long spears, and men to hold them. The Alemanni's only hope is to cause a breech and flood through a hole in our defences. I don't know whether Papirius Maximus gave us the south because it is a burning turnip he cannot hold and therefore wants *us* to hold *for* him, or because he truly believes we are good enough to make a go of it, but I tell you this, Prefect: nowhere else in the fort is as dangerous as this. The gate is holding, and thank the gods for good men bringing good timber fast, else I fear both those towers would be rubble by now.'

As if to prove the point there was a dull thud, and the right-hand tower shook slightly, grey dust billowing. Rufinus turned.

'Are you ready, just in case?'

His reserves were far from impressive. Eight infantry and two cavalry with their long spears, as well as three slaves who had been armed for the fight. Military slaves were usually long-term ownerships, bought in markets elsewhere or from passing merchants, never the locals for security reasons. These men, therefore, were no more Germanic than their Hispanic owners, and while there was always the danger with slaves that they might rise up and try to overthrow their masters, here they were in just as much danger from the Alemanni as were the Romans, and could pretty much be trusted to fight, even if only to preserve their own life. That was his reserve: eight footmen, two riders and three slaves. If the south wall suffered a breech, thirteen men would try and plug it.

THUD!

One...
Two...

Three...

The next blow took Rufinus entirely by surprise.

The auxiliary artillerists out there fighting for Ingomer had thus far been aiming for specific points, and had been worryingly accurate. They'd been trying to hit the central part of the widest stretch of wall to each side of the gate, and on the dangerously concave towers at the centre. This shot could only have been a mistake, then. Loosed at one of the flanking towers, the heavy stone had gone off course and had instead struck the very centre of the gate.

Rufinus knew it for a critical blow in an instant. A rock the size of a man's head had struck the arch of the gate, but, worse than that, it had delivered twin blows with the most appalling luck. It had half-hit the stone, and half timber gate itself, where it had torn through the timbers like parchment and ripped them from position, sending the leaf of the gate leaning, slightly off-kilter, revealing through the gaps the dark outside the fort. Potentially worse, the rock had also hit the keystone that supported the arch of the gate, and the blow seemed to have been just so placed that it had actually done true damage.

Rufinus felt his blood chill. This was not good.

The door shook and then fell still, not quite square, but that was not the main issue. The larger problem was the creaks and cracks and stony groans coming from the arch of the gate. Fuck it, but he'd known the towers to be weak spots had had shored them up. Who could have guessed a need to shore up and block the very gate itself. It had been one lucky shot.

One lucky shot.

There was a distant roar. Rufinus told Orthus to stay, then ran to the gate, looking up nervously as he did so. The whole structure seemed about to give way, and he'd just run beneath it. He peered through the gap made by the broken gate. The Alemanni remained on the far side of the ditch system, but a single giant warrior the size of a small trireme had pushed his way to the front and now spat on his hands in a business-like manner.

Rufinus jogged back to the prefect.

'They're coming.'

'The gate is still standing,' Veremundus said.

'For now. Just don't sneeze. We need to get the men down from the walls to help. This is going to be a breech.' He spotted Clemens talking to a soldier on the wall and gesturing wildly outside. He was about to go up there when he realised something else was happening. Soldiers were talking in worried voices, pointing out across the causeway. Rufinus fretted. The best views of what was about to happen would be from the wall top. but there he would be too far away to act, and from the gate arch itself, which was in imminent danger of collapse. Impotently, he watched from where he stood.

The scene seemed not to change for a long time, and then suddenly the great oak door was moving. He watched, heart in his mouth, as that great brute of a warrior suddenly appeared, moving the door, trying to open up the arch for entry. The *lunatic*. Rufinus's eyes went up to the groaning stonework above the man. His own people were clearly equally wary, for none of them had yet followed him, and all stood beyond the ditches, watching. The man moved the door. Dust and mortar cascaded down over him, and there was another crack and a serious groan. The arch was a hair's breadth from giving way now.

Then it did so.

With another crack and another groan, the whole thing settled by several feet, and the arch would have fallen in, but for the quick thinking of the big Germanic lunatic beneath it. The warrior, still gripping the great iron-banded oak gate, pushed it back almost into place, jamming it under the sagging keystone. Rufinus blinked in surprise. The whole gate arch was on its way to collapse, but had been stopped part-way by one warrior, jamming a door in place. The man carefully turned it sideways, risking complete collapse, yet pulling through somehow. The door was open to the Alemanni, the gateway clear. The arch was sagging, yet it held. There was a strange moment of uncertainty, and then the enemy, across the causeway, started to run. All they had to do was duck under the dangerous gate, and they were in the fort. Victory was a moment away.

Rufinus shouted something. He wasn't sure what. It was meant to be encouraging and send his reserves in to hold that gate, yet no one moved. In the most selfish corner of his soul, he could understand that. When a gate had half-collapsed, and only one man with a broken door was holding it up, who felt like volunteering to stand under it?

He was trying to frame an order so that it still sounded encouraging, when he heard pounding feet behind him. He spun, just in time to see Prefect Veremundus pelting towards the gate. Rufinus felt a chill. The man had a shorter space to cross than the warriors outside, but whatever he planned, it had to be quick, or they would be there too.

The big warrior was holding the gate, keeping the sagging arch up. His face was pale with the effort, running with sweat. Behind him, other Alemanni were almost at the bridge over the inner ditch. Veremundus was there too, though. The prefect ran into the gate like a single-man advance on a battlefield. He hit the big warrior hard. Of course, he was nowhere near as strong or as skilled, and the warrior did not falter, turning to face the assault. But the big man was in trouble. The Alemanni fighter had both hands on the gate, holding up the arch so that his compatriots could run past him and flood the fort. The prefect, on the other hand, had his sword out. He hit the man once, twice, thrice, a fourth time. Not one was a great blow, the work of a trained soldier, but even a monkey using a sword could do enough damage given time. The first three blows made the man falter, but the fourth was to his knee, and Rufinus watched in cold but certain horror, knowing what was coming.

The blow was appalling, the warrior unable to stop it without letting go of his door. His leg gave, and consequently, he let go of the gate leaf. The door fell with both the man and the prefect who had injured him, two men and a timber door falling to the dusty ground. There was one horrible sound like a rock being torn in two by a giant, and the south gate collapsed on the pair.

Rufinus leapt back, choking and covering his eyes as a dust cloud billowed out at him from the destruction, and slowly, as it receded, he coughed and blinked into the grey. As the dust settled, the first thing he could make out was the gate itself. The towers still stood – damn but he'd done a good job bracing them – but the arched gate between then had gone. Fortunately, it had resulted in a pile of rubble taller than a man. Of the big warrior, and of Prefect Veremundus, there was no sign. Satisfied than no natives were about to pour over the ruins, Rufinus ran to the nearest steps and joined Clemens on the wall walk. He looked down outside. The falling stones had also demolished the timber bridge over the nearest ditch, making access all the harder. The Alemanni, so close to victory, had realised that their magical way in had sealed, and had pulled back beyond the ditches again.

Rufinus heaved a sigh of relief. 'Looks like we held that one by bloody-mindedness and the favour of the gods. The whole fort could have fallen.'

'That was Veremundus, yes?'

Rufinus turned a frown on his legionary friend. 'Yes.'

'Arsehole.'

Rufinus sagged. 'Good or bad, he did what he could in the end. He gave his own life to block that gate.'

Clemens snorted. '*He* started this whole thing. Without him, there would be no Alemanni, no war, no siege, and he wouldn't *need* to give his life.'

It was a seductive point of view, and for a moment, Rufinus was pulled in by it. Then he shook his head. 'I have scores to settle still, in my life, despite settling more than my share. But I did not have a score to settle with Veremundus. He was stupid, short-sighted, mistaken, but his plans only came from the best of places. He was an idiot, but one driven by hope.'

'He got what he fucking deserved,' Clemens snapped.

'Possibly.' Rufinus could only now remember the Veremundus of last night, sitting on the end of his bed with his head in his hands, shaking. 'I think he got *more* than he deserved, despite everything. Whatever he inadvertently caused, his sacrifice was not inadvertent. It was made willingly, like an old fashioned Roman. Like Horatius at the bridge. He wanted a better world, and who doesn't? When this is over, if any of this is remembered at all, he will be remembered as the man who saved Iciniacum.'

'A thousand ghosts might argue with you,' Clemens said, darkly.

'He's paid the price, and hard. Let his family remember him as a hero. Of everyone in this whole damn disaster, only you, me and Annius know any of the truth. The messages I sent did not name Veremundus as the source of all this. His involvement dies with the three of us.'

Clemens did not look convinced, but Rufinus fancied that he knew the man enough now to know that he would come round to the same point of view eventually. In fact, Clemens reminded Rufinus so much of his younger self at times that it was uncanny.

He shook it off. There was still danger, and a lot of fighting yet to be endured. The gate was largely impassable, and the enemy were out of reach, hovering beyond the ditches, but he felt sure that would change sometime soon. The gate would still not be an easy entrance, but it was a damn sight easier than it had been while intact.

He turned and gestured down to his reserves. 'We have to survive, at least until tomorrow nightfall. Go and find whatever may be of use. Timbers, slates, spears… anything that comes to hand. Make that gate impassable. I don't care how you do it. Just do it.'

He sagged as the men went about their work. Dawn was still maybe two hours away.

And so, therefore, was survival.

CHAPTER TWENTY-TWO

Ingomer was certainly no fool. In the aftermath of the gate's fall, and its recovery, the Alemanni had focused on it as a weak point, but the German over-king was shrewd enough not to deploy his *entire* force there, for that would have allowed the Romans to do the same. Instead, he manoeuvred his warbands so that there were three separate assaults, two of them close enough to capitalise on one another's success when it happened.

A large group of warriors with auxiliary support was still pressing at the south gate, hoping to exploit the weakness of the collapsed arch, while the main artillery barrage continued from the west, now focusing on the southern end of the western wall, close to the corner tower, and the slightly weakened section where the latrines had been destroyed. A large force of warriors accompanied that assault, and, having already ruined the south gate, half the southern artillery was now trying to take down its flanking towers, but the other half were also concentrating on the southwest corner, near that latrine. Meanwhile, the third group, without artillery, assaulted the northeast corner, keeping the Roman forces split around the entire circuit.

As the hours of darkness pressed on towards an inevitable dawn, Rufinus saw only the battle for the south gate, reports of the other parts of the fight coming only through occasional breathless runners. He was down to fifty-six infantry and eight cavalry now, plus his small reserve who spent their time ferrying ammunition and equipment back and forth.

The enemy had come three times so far, roughly once an hour, each time the artillery taking a short break to allow the assault to take place without fear of being hit by their own machines, and also allowing the bringing up of fresh stones for the weapons. Each time, the assault had been a bloodthirsty affair, aimed at opening the breach at the south gate. They were strange attacks, with a mix of Roman and German tactics, for when the auxilia stopped their barrage, a small group of warriors ran to the far side of the ditches and cast javelins up at the wall top, Roman-style, forcing the defenders to drop down behind the battlements and take cover. This bought time for the German-style manoeuvre: a full-scale, head-on swarm of angry warriors hurtling across the defences and trying to cross the rubble mound of the gate.

Those assaults had each been costly in men, but had been repelled with the judicious use of the Romans' long spears, which were excellent for keeping the attacking warriors at a distance and off-balance among the ruins. Rufinus had spent so much of the past two decades fighting in the east, or in Rome itself, that he had forgotten what a Germanic battle was like, for it was entirely different to the sophisticated strategies of the southern and eastern peoples, which was not to say it was any less effective. The Alemanni, when they came, did not come in units, or ranks, attempting formations of wedges, shield walls or the like. They came like a pack of wolves, a group bound with the same goal and the same target, but with each warrior considering the fight his own. That was the German way of war: find a worthy looking enemy, whose death would be the cause of songs in the mead hall, and butcher him, making sure the kill was seen by your peers, then move on and do the same again, always looking for the greatest victory. In assaults on walls, that type of fighting was chaotic and none-too-efficient, but over open ground, or rubble such as the gate, it was surprisingly effective. Thank the gods for irrepressibly optimistic Hispanics and their long lances. Rufinus and Orthus had played their part, too, for this was no time for officers to keep themselves separate and command from the rear, and two narrow stripes of red on his left arm marked his presence in those fights. Orthus, on the other hand, was almost entirely red with other men's blood now: a nightmare shape the enemy were trying to avoid where they could.

The *real* danger was going to come when the gate towers fell. At the moment, the Alemanni were struggling to cross the outer defences, their momentum killed by the ditches, for defenders along the walls could fill them with arrows as they struggled up and down. If a tower fell, though, there was a good chance it would topple out into the ditch and fill it, creating an uneven causeway and allowing an easier crossing. And both towers were starting to look endangered. The pounding of artillery against them was almost constant, and every now and then, Rufinus heard the sound of the bracing timbers inside falling under the pressure. Sooner or later the towers would go, and then the effectiveness of the ditches would be compromised, the assaults would gain momentum, and the fight at the gate would be all the harder. And each time those attacks happened, the defenders became thinner on the ground.

Rufinus was directing the reserves up into position, plugging gaps and committing every man he had, when the runner came with the best news all night.

'What is it?' he said, turning back from Clemens as his friend ran to the wall with updated instructions.

'Begging your pardon sir, but Chief Aemilius reports that Locusta is ready to test.'

Rufinus grinned, and, with Orthus at his heel, ran across the fort for the great siege engine, to find men rolling massive boulders out of one of the storehouses, while the engineer and his men put the finishing touches to the machine.

'She's ready?'

Aemilius gave him a doubtful look. 'She's ready to *test*. There's no guarantee she'll *work*, as I explained earlier.'

'What do you reckon the range is on her again?'

'If she works properly, maybe half a mile.'

Now Rufinus's grin jacked up. 'Can you turn her south?'

'The mechanics of *that* part aren't in question. Direction and distance I can set. It's just whether she holds together on release.'

'The Alemanni siege engines are lined up just out of bow range to the south, I'd say two hundred and fifty paces from the wall and directly south of the gate. There's your test shot.'

'Should I not wait for the prefect, sir? He may want it testing on the west.'

'The west can hold a while. The south gate is close to giving. Test it south.'

The man saluted. 'Yes sir. You might want to be some distance away for this.'

Rufinus nodded, watching for a moment as the men angled the machine according to the artillerist's calculations, and, once it was loaded, he, like most of them, retreated to the safety of nearby buildings, leaving only Aemilius and one man at the engine. As the last adjustments were made, Rufinus jogged back to the south wall, where he climbed the steps and reached the parapet, falling in beside Clemens.

'Pray for luck, my friend,' he breathed.

The two men waited, tense. There was then an ominous wooden noise back across the fort, a nerve-jangling metallic crunch and then a thud, which Rufinus swore he could feel vibrate beneath his feet even half a fort away. He turned to look for the missile, and ducked instinctively, his bowels loosening slightly as a rock the size of an ox-head whirred only just overhead.

It missed the Alemanni war machines by about ten feet, but proved its effectiveness by gouging a furrow through the German ranks, killing a score of men in one shot, the front two men effectively obliterated by it, becoming a shower of gore and bone shards, and even the man at the back of the shot lost a leg to the boulder as it hammered deep into the turf just behind him.

Beside Rufinus, Clemens whistled. 'Shit, I'm glad *they* don't have that thing.'

338

Rufinus grabbed the nearest man. 'Run to Aemilius. Tell him to keep going, but a little to the left.'

The man ran off through the fort, and Rufinus took a deep breath. 'For the first time, I'm starting to think we might hold out.'

Twenty heartbeats later that noise came again, followed by a slight vibration rippling across the fort. Rufinus ducked again, even as the great rock hurtled over his head. Aemilius had angled it perfectly this time. The great boulder flew straight at the five war machines even as they primed for their next shot. It struck the second weapon from the right, and the result was so impressive it took a moment for the carnage to settle sufficiently for Rufinus to make out the damage. The boulder had completely obliterated the catapult, leaving only shattered timbers, twisted metal, and lengths of shredded rope. It was too dark to make it out properly, but he would be willing to bet that half a dozen auxilia lay scattered around in pieces, too.

But that was not all. The machine the boulder had struck had effectively exploded, sending shards of timber and metal flying in every direction, which had ploughed deep into the ranks of the nearby warriors, but had also struck the machines to either side. The result was the semi-destruction of the flanking engines, both of which were instantly out of commission, their crews ruined.

In one shot, Aemilius had removed sixty percent of the enemy artillery on the southern side. Rufinus grinned like a madman, and turned. The runner he'd sent was just returning, panting with exertion. Rufinus whistled at him, then pointed back to the fort's heart. 'Another, the same distance left as last time.'

The soldier stopped, leaning on his knees for a moment, sucking in air, then straightened, saluted, turned, and pelted off across the fort once more. The great machine's third shot was slightly higher than the previous two, perhaps the result of a lighter rock, and for a moment Rufinus thought it might miss. He was relieved to see, though, that the rock went straight through the top spar of a remaining catapult, snapping it in its passage, then nicked the arm of a great twenty-pound ballista. It was only a glancing blow, but such was the tension on these machines that even the slightest damage could cause disaster, and as the arm cracked, the whole thing exploded, the torsion pulling it apart and sending shards of timber and metal out among the crew. The shot had been almost a miss, and yet through immense luck had put the remaining artillery out of commission. The barrage ceased instantly, no more pounding of stones against the gate towers, and Rufinus heaved a great sigh of relief. They would still face hard fights at the south gate, but at least the enemy had no serious advantage now.

He waited for that exhausted runner to reappear, and when the man did, turned and gave him an apologetic smile. 'Tell Aemilius that the south is safe and he can turn west.'

He decided not to pull the soldier up on the fact that he rolled his eyes and sighed before saluting, turning, and running back across the fort once more.

'Rufinus!'

He looked up at the call to see Clemens waving from the wall and then pointing out to the south. Tense, wondering what the man had seen, he jogged over to the steps and bounced up to the wall top, with Orthus close behind. Soldiers recoiled as the blood-soaked dog passed, despite knowing he was on their side. He reached Clemens and turned to look out.

Another assault was in preparation, but this time it looked serious. Each attack thus far had been carried out by a part of the warband, strong enough to stand a chance of opening the breach for the rest, but still small enough to cross the ditch bridges opposite the gate without occupying too much of the land to either side, where they would come under increased missile barrage from the flanking walls. This time, every man out there looked to be brandishing weapons, readying for the attack.

'Shit. This is it. They're committing every man.'

Clemens nodded. 'We can't abandon the walls, but the gate needs reinforcing.'

Rufinus fretted. They simply didn't have the manpower to do it all. He considered sending for support from the other walls, but there was a very good chance that this was only part of Ingomer's plan, and that if he drew men from the other walls, the enemy would use that to break the defences elsewhere. He did not have enough men, but they would have to do. The south wall had to stand. They were on their own.

He looked back and forth. 'Send the infantry down to the gate. The long spears are more useful on the walls than shorter ones or swords. I'll send my cavalry up to replace them. You'll have fewer men, but all of them will have a longer reach.'

Clemens gave him a professional nod, and Rufinus smiled at the fact that his friend's expression betrayed none of the uncertainty he must now be feeling. Reducing his number by even a third made holding the walls a much more difficult proposition. But the ruins of the gate were the real danger point now, and Rufinus would need all the men he could get.

As he ran back down to the open space where the reserves had been until he'd been forced to commit them, he waved his men over.

A headcount after the last assault had been worrying. He now had thirty-one infantry, two slaves, and ten cavalry. Forty-three men, plus himself, Clemens, Annius and Orthus. The ten cavalry were now committed to the walls with their long spears, five on each stretch to either side of the gate, each commanded by one of his legionary friends. Down by the ruins, Rufinus now had thirty-three men. Looking up at the walls, fretting about the numbers, he had four of the infantry retrieve their bows and bolster the wall defences, two to each side. They looked a little better up there, though that now left him with twenty-nine men, thirty including himself.

He gestured to the slaves. 'You've earned your freedom tonight. Either of you stands with me through this fight, I will see you get not only manumission, but an offer of a career in the cohort.' It was a sign of how hard the struggle was fought and how much of a part the slaves had played that there was not a hint of surprise or disagreement among the soldiers. Somehow sharing such dangers as this tended to strip away the layers of social order. All of them were just men fighting to survive.

He looked at the array of soldiers. Several were sporting wounds already, all of them were tired.

'There are at least a couple of hundred out there,' he said, deliberately downplaying the numbers, which he'd estimated from the wall top to be at least twice that. 'That's serious odds. But we have the advantage. They have to come to us. They will be hit by arrows from the walls, and they will have to face the contus lances if they want to get over them. We have the gate to hold. They can't get more than ten or fifteen men into that gap at a time, and we have enough of us to face that and hold. Here's what I want. Every man here who has a bow, grab it and move over there, the rest get your swords and shields ready.'

He watched as his twenty-nine men separated into two almost even groups. 'Good,' he said. 'Sixteen men for a shield wall. We're going to do that the old fashioned way. Get into the breach and form a line, braced. Any man who won't fit, form up behind, ready to fill any gap that forms. No heroics. Stand hard and stab any bastard who comes close enough, but make sure to keep that shield wall up. Preserve your own skin above all, because a dead man is no use, am I right?'

A roar.

'The thirteen archers, I want deploying as you see fit. Each of you find a good place among the ruins or in the towers where you can see past or over our shield wall. There will be no command to loose arrows. You're all professionals and you all know your skills and limitations. Find a good place, wait for the enemy to come, and as soon as you see fit, plant arrow after arrow into them. Don't stop until you run out of ammunition, then grab your sword and shield and come join your friends in the gap. I will take position in the left tower. There is a doorway there that the enemy could exploit, so I'm going to block it with a one man shield wall. Have we all got that?'

Another roar. Rufinus nodded. 'Let's kill some Alemanni.'

Still roaring, his men ran to their positions, readying weapons and shields. The swordsmen clambered up into the rubble of the gate and found the best place with the safest footing, then formed their wall, locking their shields and bracing, eyes on the south, even as the enemy came, running from the dark, closing on the outer ditch. The archers were each finding a place now, and by the time the first German rose from the furthest ditch, an arrow thumped into his chest and sent him tumbling back down into it.

Rufinus ducked into the gate-tower, swallowing his nerves. He could see how badly the tower was damaged. It would need major repairs if they survived, and had been just one or two shots from demolition. He ignored the dust and mortar that continued to drift down from the walls above, and crossed to that doorway. It was the size of one man, and would grant access through the tower and into the fort. He had to hold it, and his job was every bit as critical as that of the others. He looked at the Alemanni swarming towards them, and knew damn well that there were a heck of a lot more of them than he'd said. His men knew it too, though no one had commented. Good lads.

We are Bracari.

He smiled to himself as he hefted his sword and the shield he'd borrowed from stores. He was not used to these lighter auxiliary shields, flat and oval, instead of curved and rectangular like those of the legions and the Guard. Maybe not quite as protective, but a sight more manoeuvrable.

He turned at a noise behind him, alert to danger, and realised that one of the slaves was picking his way across the rubble into the tower. Rufinus frowned for a moment. Was the slave coming for him for some reason? Had the Alemanni somehow got hooks into him? He glanced out to the side, through the door he guarded, and could see a solid shield wall now formed, then looked back at the slave. No. The man had fought hard alongside them throughout the siege. He stood to lose or gain along with them.

'You are supposed to be in reserve if not in the shield wall.'

The slave looked embarrassed in an odd way, and when he spoke it was with an eastern accent – Thracian, Rufinus thought. 'I *am* in reserve, sir. They told me *you* needed a reserve too.'

Rufinus nodded. True. He smiled at the man. Just make sure you stick that sword in Germans, not Romans.'

The slave nodded, and Rufinus returned to watching the enemy. Unlike the other three gates, the prefect had left the bridges intact across the three ditches outside the south gate, though the falling masonry had demolished the nearest one. The bulk of the German force was trying to pile across the bridge, while other men were simply dropping into the outer ditches and struggling up to plunge straight into the next one. Wherever they came, across bridges or across ditches, the Bracari archers went to work, sinking feathered shaft after feathered shaft into the mass of men, almost every arrow finding a target, the Alemanni falling away in droves as they ran. Not that it was making any grand difference to the numbers. Even had they an hour to loose their missiles, the Romans would still be horribly outnumbered.

The nearest Germans finally clambered up the near bank of the inner ditch, and were on the defenders at the gate ruins. The shield wall braced, and the first few Alemanni who reached them were dispatched with professional ease. There were many, many more behind them, though.

Rufinus watched, surprised that none of the enemy as yet seemed to have noticed him. The doorway he occupied had originally been an entrance from the gate itself into the tower, and they could use it to bypass the shield wall in small numbers, and yet no one had apparently picked up on that. They ran, instead, howling for blood, directly at the auxiliary shieldwall.

Then he saw it. For just a moment, he spotted a familiar figure, then lost it, and wondered if it had been real, until suddenly he saw it again. Out on the edge of that force, not committed at the front, but waving his sword and bellowing at the Alemanni, rallying them, pressing them on to fight, was a figure he had last seen at that camp in the forest.

A king. Not Ingomer, but that *other* king.

Rufinus frowned. The Alemanni were a new nation, still formed of tribes who had only been working together for a few months. It struck him then what was happening. That was why there were three different assaults. Not because Ingomer had split them that way, but because the three forces were all separate tribes, each led by their king. And Rufinus knew from those days against the Marcomanni what value a Germanic king held. Just like a Roman general on the battlefield, when a leader died, it sent ripples of despair through the entire army.

His eyes narrowed. They had a chance, all of a sudden. Not a good one, but a chance, nonetheless, if he seized it right now. He turned to the slave behind him. 'What's your name?'

The man looked confused for a moment, and Rufinus realised he was trying to work out whether to give his slave name, foisted on him when he was sold, or his original, true name. 'Bato,' he said, shakily. An Illyrian name, Rufinus thought, smiling still.

'Well, Bato of Illyria, soldier of Rome, I'm about to do something monumentally stupid, and that means you are now the man holding this doorway. Get over here and kill any man who tries to get through it.'

It was odd to watch a sudden flush of pride in the face of a slave, but that was what he saw as he acknowledged not only the man's free status and origin, but effectively labelled him an equal of any man here. A look of steely determination fell upon the slave as he stepped over to join Rufinus, who in turn walked out into the open beyond the tower, onto the rubble being crossed by the Alemanni, Orthus still at his heel.

Warriors began to spot him, and men started to peel off from the main force and hurry his way. His exhaustion was still there, plaguing him, even after his brief sleep, but now a tantalising possibility lay before him, and the excitement it brought overrode the weariness, filling him with adrenaline.

He ran, his dog an ever-present accompaniment.

Across the rubble of the fallen gate, to one side and on the periphery of the attack, they ran. He met the first of the warriors who'd stepped aside to fight him, with a swing of his sword that caught the man's own weapon with such force that he tore it from his hand, breaking fingers in the process. The man howled, but Rufinus ignored him. He was past already, and still running, because no matter what got in the way, his eyes were set upon that one figure, and he was coming ever closer to it. Another warrior snarled Germanic curses and angled for him, only to have a hound's iron jaws clamp on his leg, sending him shrieking to the ground even as Orthus released him and ran on after his master.

Rufinus reached the inner ditch just as a panting, struggling German clambered up it, and simply planted a booted foot in the man's face, sending him tumbling back with a cry, as he leapt on past, still watching the king, making sure he didn't lose him. Then, his plan suddenly came undone. The king turned and spotted the Roman running at him through the pre-dawn, just the faintest purple glow announcing the approach of sunlight. The king pointed a sword at Rufinus and roared. Immediately, half a dozen burly warriors leapt in the way to protect their king, and Rufinus, though he was still running, knew it was over. He'd lost his chance. Even with Orthus's help, he would never get past them all to the king now.

And then the scales of warfare tipped again. With a belligerent roar, the Alemanni sub-king pushed through the protective line of warriors and out into the open. He was not going to be protected when there was an important Roman to kill. Ah yes, that Germanic impulse in battle, to seek out the greatest opponent and kill them, securing your status as a revered warrior. But the man's confidence now just played into Rufinus's hands.

Indeed, as the king, bellowing his fury, started to stomp towards Rufinus, those men who'd been peeling away from the mass to intercept him stopped, instead darting out of his way, not interfering with their master's fight. Only one kept coming, but when a dog's jaws closed on his manhood and the animal hung there, growling, his advance stopped with a keening wail.

The two men met on the end of the wooden bridge at the middle ditch. The king roared and hammered his sword against his shield, then threw his arm out to the side, sword wide, inviting an attack. Rufinus just gave him a single nod. The man was supremely confident. Good. Such men were easier to surprise.

He had to make this good. A powerful victory to shock onlookers. And he already knew how. Just as when he faced men in the ring and could see from early on how they might fall, he could picture *this* fight, blow by blow, and would let it play out the way it must.

He walked close, lifting his sword and his shield. The German king came just close enough and with a roar, swung that sword. It was a powerful strike, for sure, but lacking style or skill, relying simply on strength. Foolish. Still, Rufinus let the blow come, as though powerless to stop it, throwing his own sword in the way to parry and watching it knocked aside. It deflected the blow, only just, the tip of the German ring-pommel sword whipping a palm-breadth past Rufinus's nose, and he felt the achy vibration of the weapons' meeting echo up his arm to the shoulder.

The king gave him no time to recover. The sword came back the other way, back-handed, and this time Rufinus's shield caught it. Even as the sword struck the iron boss, Rufinus let go of the grip, and the shield was thrown away, off to the side, where it fell to the turf. He staggered, only partially playing the part, for the king's blow had again been a powerful one. He lurched, now, left arm hanging as though damaged when the shield fell, right holding a sword that was lowered, open to a killing blow.

Predictably, with a bellowed oath to some war god, the German swung a third time, another wide slash with the power of a blacksmith's hammer. Rufinus let it come, then at the last moment took one pace forward and left, inside the blow, too

347

close for the blade to hit him – too close for *any* sword play at all, but that was fine. Sword play was not his intent. As the king's blade swept round harmlessly behind him, his free left hand came up, bunched into a fist with the middle knuckle extended slightly.

The punch was accurate, and one that no boxer could use legitimately in the ring. The fist slammed into the king's throat, just below the chin, and there was a distinct crunch. The German staggered back, eyes wide, making a desperate wheezing noise, his windpipe crushed, lungs starved of air. As Rufinus took a step after him, the man threw his sword away, both hands coming up to claw desperately at the neck that would not allow the passage of oxygen.

A hush fell over the previously loud Alemanni force as they faltered now, watching their king, uncertain what was happening. Nearby, Orthus let his maimed victim go and stepped over to Rufinus protectively, teeth bared at the others, growling.

Rufinus took a deep breath. This had to be perfect. He looked at the man, took note of his neck, the way he stood, his hair. He stepped to the side slightly and pulled back his sword to the right, gripping it with both hands.

'Jupiter, I give you this man as a sacrifice, for all your columns he toppled,' he bellowed at the top of his voice.

Then he swung. His sword was a spatha, a long sword of the sort the cavalry always used, but was now en vogue with the infantry. It was long, very sharp, and heavy, and Rufinus was stronger than most men, and had put every ounce of his remaining strength into the blow. Moreover, he had been careful with his aim, and as the sword came round, slamming through that long, braided black hair, it struck the back of the neck, roughly halfway between skull and shoulders, the two vertebrae he knew to be the weak spot for such a blow.

The sword cut through the spine with sheer force, and the momentum carried it on through muscle and tendon and crushed windpipe.

The German king's head rolled free.

Rufinus lowered his sword, and treated the nearest Alemanni warrior to the fiercest, most maniacal grin he could muster as he gave the disembodied head a hefty contemptuous kick, sending it off into the ditch and out of sight.. Orthus's snarling probably only added to the effect.

The cry of dismay and panic rose from that man's throat first, even as the head hit the ground and rolled away to a halt, staring up at the sky. But in heartbeats, that cry had caught in the throat of every warrior at the south gate, turning into a chorus. The rout began as a few men turning and running, but took only moments to become a tidal wave of panic as the Alemanni broke off the attack and fled the gate. Some of the treasonous auxilia behind them, knowing that they could hardly rely on Roman clemency, tried to arrest the Germans' flight, but the Alemanni simply fled *through* them, butchering their auxiliary allies as they ran.

Rufinus looked around. His men in the ruins of the gate were cheering, particularly Bato the slave, where he stood blocking that doorway.

They had broken the enemy and saved the south gate. And with the south wall secure, the enemy could now be broken.

The siege had turned their way at last.

CHAPTER TWENTY-THREE

The flight of the Alemanni warband triggered the inevitable. Even as Rufinus watched them disappearing into the pre-dawn light, he could hear raucous shouting from across the fort. By the time he'd settled his men, sending the injured to be treated by the capsarii, while the whole, yet weary, survivors took position along the walls and gate in case anyone returned, a runner arrived announcing that the warband attacking the northeast of the fort had routed and fled. The destruction of a full third of the Alemanni force had broken the confidence and will of another third, leaving only the warriors at the fort's western side pressing the attack.

That, Rufinus decided, was their win. Until now, they had been seriously outnumbered by the Alemanni. Now, the odds had become more or less level, and everyone was equally tired, but the Romans had the twin advantages of the defences and a series of successes under their belt to give them heart.

Leaving the lads at the south wall to it, under the capable charge of an optio, Rufinus departed his command, content that it was safe, and went to find the last great struggle. With him went a small force he'd come to think of as his companions: Orthus trotting alongside, crimson and shaggy, with Clemens and Annius at his back. He was going to regret sending them back to Castra Regina and their legion, when the time came. Of course, they had to make it through dawn here, first.

That did not seem to be an issue. As he reached that corner where the enemy artillery had been pounding the ramparts, he could sense the change even before he ascended to the wall top and saw it. For a start, there was no thud of catapult shot against the stone walls. Locusta had done her job, silencing the enemy

351

siege weapons out there and making any breach of the walls more or less impossible. There were places where it was shaky, but would hold, and with a little work could be repaired to full strength. And the enemy had stopped their periodic surging across the ditches against the western walls, for each time, they had lost a huge number of warriors with little to show for it. As Rufinus jogged wearily towards the west gate with his three companions, he could see in the growing light what was left of the Alemanni force out there on the far side of the ditches, waiting, glowering, uncertain. Occasionally a man would move a little closer, and be pinned by an arrow from the defenders, teaching the rest to retreat out of bowshot.

Rufinus found Prefect Papirius Maximus at the gate with his signallers. He was leaning on the parapet, breathing deeply, and turned as they approached.

'The south held then.'

'Just. *They* broke the gate, but *we* broke *them*. This, I think is all that's left.'

'And your prefect?'

'Veremundus sacrificed himself to hold the gate.' He tried to ignore the grumbling that issued from the men behind him, the only two who knew the truth.

'Sad. But noble, I suppose.' The man's gaze returned to the waiting forces of the Alemanni. 'What are they up to? I've known these people only a couple of years, since my arrival here, but I've yet to find a tribesman who dithers. They get an idea in their heads, and they just push for it until they succeed or die trying. So why are they just waiting out there, across the ditches?'

Rufinus shrugged. 'Maybe they're hoping their friends will return, though they won't. One warband routing might be recoverable, but two is too much. They've gone. They'll be crossing the border again and seeking their villages. The attack's over... unless there's another force coming we don't know about.' He paused and shook his head. 'No. That's not it. They wouldn't have been trying quite so hard if there were others yet to come. And the second warband might have stayed. So…'

His gaze had been playing across that gathering of Alemanni outside the fort as he spoke, and he'd noticed the reason without even realising it. He frowned, and looked back and forth again.

'What is it?' the prefect asked.

'Where are their leaders?'

As the prefect followed his gaze, Rufinus felt his spirits sink. That small knot of horsemen at the rear had gone. Ingomer and his companions had departed and left them to it.

'They're leaderless. The king's gone.'

Papirius Maximus gave a vicious smile then. 'I am very tempted to lead a sally.'

Rufinus frowned at him now, and the prefect laughed quietly. 'Men in that state break easily. We have veteran soldiers here, eager for the kill. An infantry sally from the west gate, and a cavalry one from the north hitting them in the flank, and we can carve them like a side of beef.'

Rufinus nodded. He had other concerns whirling around his head. The fight here was over. That was clear. Even if the prefect didn't break that remaining force, they would eventually just go away, leaderless and impotent, though it sounded as though the man was determined to deliver a killing blow anyway.

With the failure of this siege, and with word racing to the other forts along the border and to the governor and the legion at Castra Regina, Rufinus was content that any mass crossing of the border by the Alemanni could now be halted and contained. The plan formed by Veremundus in his delusions, and twisted by Ingomer to his own end, had failed. The Alemanni that *had* already crossed, and met failure at Iciniacum were largely fleeing back to their homelands outside the empire. They would come again, Rufinus thought. Veremundus had inadvertently created a monster by banding the tribes together under one king and forming the Alemanni, and now that they were one great tribe, they would try again, and again. But not for a while now. They had been broken and would take time to regroup and come once more. Raetia was safe for now.

But none of that was what was nagging at Rufinus.

His mind was filled with a series of images. Of Ingomer the king. Of men's heads rolling in the dust at that woodland camp. Of Publius…

Ingomer had gone.

He could not have got far.

'Lead your charge,' he told the prefect, but turned and stalked off along the wall towards the steps. It took him a few moments to realise that as well as the patter of paws on stone behind him, there was a purposeful tread of hobnailed boots. He glanced over his shoulder to see Clemens and Annius were still with him.

'You should stay with the prefect.'

'And let you get yourself killed?' Clemens snorted. 'I don't think so.'

'I don't even know what I'm going to do.'

'Yes you do,' the legionary said flatly. 'You're already heading straight towards the stables. You know he won't be alone, so neither should you.'

Rufinus shook his head. 'He'll have a strong guard. One man might be able to sneak in and get him. Three will just make a noise.'

'There won't be three,' Clemens murmured. As they neared the stables of the unit's cavalry contingent, situated in the southwest corner of the fort, the legionary looked up past the buildings, towards the southern wall they had so recently and so valiantly defended. 'Baebius?' he yelled, making Rufinus jump slightly, the shout unexpected and close to his ear.

A Bracari cavalryman leaning on his long spear on the wall turned at the shout, spotted the three men and the dog, and waved.

'Bring your mates,' Clemens shouted. 'We've a job to do.'

Rufinus frowned for a moment, then remembered that Clemens had been in charge of the cavalry on that wall for most of the night. They would know him well, and respect him and automatically follow his orders. For a moment Rufinus almost argued. It was unlikely that Papirius Maximus was going to be hugely pleased, when he gathered his cavalry charge, to find part of the unit missing. But then quite apart from Rufinus's personal reasons to see the man fall, the death of Ingomer would be a massive blow for Alemanni unity, and would set back the danger they posed to Rome by years. The prefect would appreciate that in the long run.

As he reached the stables and pulled open the door, he could see nine cavalrymen, the entire mounted contingent from the south wall pounding his way. And in their wake came Bato the Illyrian, a determined look on his face. Rufinus decided not to question or refuse the former slave. Sometimes a man needed to be allowed to take a step forward.

Nodding to the others, he entered, looking along the line of horses until he found a chestnut mare who met his gaze and held it, even in the presence of Orthus, who was making several of the animals skittish. He waited to see if any of the riders claimed this one, but they all found their own horses swiftly, and so Rufinus located the harness and quickly geared his steed up. The others did the same, and in a few moments Rufinus was leading a small force towards the rubble of the south gate. One Praetorian, nine auxilia, two legionaries, a former slave and a blood-soaked hound. A motley bunch, but a fearsome one. Thirteen men and a dog – all tired, some with minor injuries – and yet Rufinus would think twice about facing them even with a small army at his back. He grinned like a madman.

'Let's kill a king.'

With that, he clattered out across the gate ruins. The only real obstacle was the inner ditch, though it was now clogged with sufficient rubble and bodies that it was only half the depth it should be, and in a few moments they were across, climbing the last stretch to the remaining length of timber bridge. Clopping out across it, he and his small cavalry force were free of

Iciniacum. He could see the remaining warriors of the Alemanni off to their right, and men were shouting now and pointing at the escaping riders, but Rufinus put heel to flank and raced off west, leaving them behind with no real chance of pursuit. As he rode away from the fort and the Germanic force outside, he could hear the cohort's horns blowing for the call to arms. The prefect was about to break that last warband.

And Rufinus was about to finish it all.

The men with him were more than just capable. He knew Clemens and Annius for good horsemen, after travelling with them so many days, and the nine auxiliaries were trained cavalry, but the skill with which Bato handled his mount suggested that in earlier days he had been quite at home in the saddle, too.

'Where are we going?'

Rufinus turned to Clemens. 'Ingomer will be heading back to his home and his own people, but he is guaranteed to have left things at the forest camp, and he will have to go back for them. Even if it's just spare weapons and the like for his people. We need to catch up with him either there, or before he gets there.'

Clemens nodded, and they rode, hard. As they angled across and met the road along which the Alemanni had first arrived, even Rufinus, whose tracking skills were no great thing, could see that they were on the close trail of their quarry. There was plenty of churned ground, prints of boots, hooves and wheels, but one small group of hoofprints sat atop it all, going the other way, mute evidence of Ingomer's recent passage.

In what seemed no time at all they were passing the empty walls of Castra Numera, and racing up the slope towards the frontier gate. The trail led straight there, and this time, the border was completely deserted and unmanned, those warriors who'd controlled it the last time Rufinus had passed now gone north with Ingomer.

He raced through the open gate, leaving the Roman empire for the second time in recent days. This time, though, he was not unconscious and bound, lying in the back of a cart. This time he was armed and determined.

Down the far slope, across the open ground, and onto that forest road that he knew led directly to the camp in the woods they rode. They paused, then, at the edge of the forest, and listened. They could hear the rush of the river nearby, but no sound of their prey. Ingomer was too far ahead. They needed to catch up. Once the man left the camp and went back to his own lands, Rufinus would lose the trail and any chance of catching him. Along with the others, he kicked his tired horse into a gallop, racing along the woodland road as fast as he could manage.

He'd underestimated the Alemanni king, though, and he realised this to his peril at that bridge where they'd taken the horses. He burst clear of the trees with his friends at his back, and almost died there in an instant. Light javelins came from both sides, and three of the cavalrymen fell, two injured and one on a wounded horse, before Ingomer's warriors burst free of the woods to engage them.

Rufinus, shocked, desperate, looked this way and that. The king himself was nowhere to be seen. He had left his warriors to trap them. Sure enough, as he peered at the road ahead, he could still see hoof prints racing off in much smaller numbers.

'Go,' one of the riders shouted, waving at him even as the man turned and caught a sword in a parry with his own.

The Alemanni were now engaged with Rufinus's force. He nodded and left them to it, kicking his horse to speed once more. As he crossed the bridge, a warrior tried to chase him down and stop him, but Bato was there suddenly, holding off the man, fighting hard. Rufinus left them struggling, one goal in mind now.

He was some way on when he heard hoofbeats over the receding din of the fight, and turned to see that Clemens was still with him. He nodded. Just one man, but one of the most capable and trustworthy men Rufinus had ever met. The legionary caught up, and the two men galloped side by side for the last stretch.

The fortifications came into view all too quickly, close to where they'd effected their daring escape. The gate lay wide open, which came as no surprise. The place was deserted now, and Ingomer had no reason to expect company so swiftly. Over that last stretch of road, as the light continued to increase, Rufinus had peered at those tracks they were following. Three horses, he had determined. There were three of the Alemanni. Fine. There were three of the hunters, too. A fair fight.

They pounded through the gateway and into the camp, and Rufinus spotted movement instantly. Horses milled about aimlessly over near the headquarters building, in that same open space where Orthus had been caged, and then a human figure appeared among them and shouted, pointing. Rufinus rode straight at the man, Orthus loping along on his left, Clemens clattering forward on his right. The German pulled himself up onto one of the horses, still shouting his warnings in his native tongue.

'The other two are inside,' Clemens shouted, and Rufinus remembered then that his friend spoke their language. The warrior turned his horse, sword out, and rode for them.

'Go. Find the king,' Clemens shouted, and put on one last extra turn of speed to intercept the Alemanni rider. Rufinus nodded, silently thanking his friend, and angled wide to skirt around the warrior, making straight for the headquarters building, whose door stood wide.

He heard Clemens and the warrior meet, their conflict marked with the clang of sword on sword, but now Rufinus simply concentrated on his own task. Reaching the building, he vaulted from the saddle, sword out, and ran for the three wooden steps that led up to the doorway, Orthus keeping pace with him, the animal now a strangely dark red/brown colour, the blood having dried into his white hair and darkened. He truly was a thing of nightmare.

Rufinus burst into the outer room of the building, and found their prey at last.

Whatever Ingomer had been doing, he'd stopped, and he and his warrior had turned at their friend's warning, weapons drawn and ready for their hunters.

The warrior to the king's right snarled something in his own language that was clearly a curse. In response, Rufinus pointed at the man and said, quietly, 'balls.'

A red blur shot past him and hit the warrior like the fury of gods, the two shapes disappearing to the floor in a welter of snarls and screams. Rufinus left them to it, content that Orthus was going to have the better of that one. Instead, he focused on Ingomer. The Alemanni king was going to be no pushover. He'd already known that, for the man had risen to this height largely on his strength and skill and fearsome reputation. That was how a German king was made. As he waited, eyes on Rufinus, the Praetorian could see no obvious tells in the way the man stood. He was good, and confident, and bright enough to wait and give nothing away. Such a man was not going to be easy to get the drop on. As he took a couple of paces forward, his spatha out in his right hand, he pulled from his belt the remnants of a broken blade in his left.

'This,' he said, 'was the sword of my brother, who commanded the cohort at Batavis, until you had your men hunt him down and take his head. And in the sight of Nemesis, daughter of darkness, from whom there is no escape, I will use it to take your head, Ingomer of the Alemanni.'

He knew the king spoke Latin and understood, and the man nodded slowly.

'You will not kill me with your broken Nemesis blade, Roman.'

Rufinus leapt the last short distance between the two of them. He kept the broken sword lowered, ready to parry, while swinging his own longer sword wide, testing the king's skills. Ingomer's blade moved like lightning, blocking the blow, turning it aside, and somehow twisting into an attack of its own. Rufinus, surprised at the man's speed, only just managed to duck back out of the way, the tip of the man's sword scraping across the links of his chain shirt.

The Roman found himself reassessing the man he faced. He'd thought to use the disparity in weapons to his advantage, the king having only one sword, while Rufinus in effect had a parrying weapon, too. But Ingomer was faster than him, and had already proved that his one sword could match Rufinus's two, and still manage to attack.

He had to find another way.

Even as he pondered this, Ingomer was coming for him again. That blade flicked out, caught Rufinus's broken sword and yet somehow, once again, bounced from it straight into an attack that the Roman only just turned aside with his other weapon. He was not going to beat Ingomer in a straight fight. Perhaps if he was fresh and whole, he might be a match for the king, but tired and bruised and achy as he was, he was in trouble.

As he fought, each engagement little more than an attempt to save himself from injury with little opportunity to do any damage to his opponent, Rufinus's mind raced over everything he knew about fighting, everything he'd learned in his days in ring, in the legions, the Guard, and among the Frumentarii.

He smiled.

The frumentarii.

Sometimes success was not about being better, but about making your opponent worse. His time among the frumentarii had taught him that more victories could be achieved through stealth and quick thinking than through strength and skill. If he couldn't *outfight* Ingomer, he would have to *outwit* him.

He smiled, a new plan forming even as he staggered back, avoiding the latest blow. In a heartbeat, he went on the attack at last. The broken blade lanced out in his left hand, coming straight for Ingomer's face. With a contemptuous snarl, the king swept his own sword up, and knocked the half-blade out of the way, the blow hard enough to numb Rufinus's hand and send the weapon flying through the air to clatter against the wall and then fall to the floor.

Sometimes a fight was not about skill, but about misdirection. Just as the frumentarii would turn an opponent's strengths into weaknesses, Rufinus had done as much throughout his days boxing for the cohort, using misdirection time and again. Throw a wide swing that draws the eyes, then jab with the unseen hand.

Even as that all-important blade of Publius's whirred away across the room, the king's victorious grin ignoring it, locked on Rufinus's face, the Praetorian's right hand came up, bearing his long spatha. It was not a strong blow, for it was impossible to get a really good hit in at such close range with such a long sword. But the tip slammed into Ingomer's armpit from below, and drove into the unarmoured and soft, giving flesh until it touched the inside of his shoulder blade.

The king gasped, his gaze dropping to the sword that had pierced him. He staggered back a step, the blade slipping free, blood following in a small fountain. Ingomer tested his injured left arm, but as he swung it, he winced and hissed with pain. He was down to one hand.

But Rufinus was not done with him.

Misdirection.

His sword came up again, sweeping round for Ingomer's right side, and the king lifted his own blade to knock it aside, and bellowed in agony and surprise at Rufinus's simultaneous kick that drove hobnails into his left kneecap.

The king lurched and staggered with the pain, his leg wobbling, threatening to give way.

'This is for every Roman officer you had killed,' Rufinus snarled,

He swung his sword, and was gratified to see that Ingomer's attention was suddenly split with indecision. His gaze, even in half a heartbeat, leapt from the approaching sword to Rufinus's other hand, to his feet, to his eyes, wondering where the next secondary blow would come from.

361

Because sometimes the best misdirection is to be unexpectedly direct.

By the time the king realised that this was no trick, he had insufficient time to block the blow properly. He managed to get his own sword in the way, but only just, and the blade simply deflected Rufinus's powerful blow slightly lower. The sword bit into his hip, hard, jarring against bone, and Ingomer howled. He staggered away again, barely able to remain upright, now. His back hit the hut wall and he stood there a moment, trying not to fall, breathing hard, staring at this Roman who had somehow bested him when such a thing had seemed inconceivable.

Rufinus's next blow was a careful one. His sword struck Ingomer on the right wrist, and hard, but with the flat of the blade. He did not even break skin, but he *did* break bone. The king's wrist snapped audibly and as he cried out, his sword fell away, useless.

The over-king of the Alemanni fell to the hut's wooden floor now, every limb in trouble, left arm out of commission and bleeding from the armpit, right with a broken wrist, left leg reeling from a hobnailed kick to the knee, right from a wounded hip. Ingomer of the Alemanni lay in a shaking heap on the floor, trying desperately to pull some life and strength back into his limbs. Rufinus took a step over to him, and then brought his foot down hard on that broken wrist, putting all his weight into the stamp, heel first. There were more, horrible, audible crunches. Ingomer screamed, but before he could even end that first howl, Rufinus had repeated the blow on his left wrist, now broken and mangled to match. He could do little to stop it now as Rufinus stamped down on first one knee and then the other, breaking each with little difficulty.

The ruined king flailed, unable to make any limb work, every tiny movement a symphony of agony.

Rufinus nodded to himself, then walked slowly across the room, past where Orthus was busy getting a fresh coat of crimson from the writhing corpse he had made. As he stooped to sweep up the broken sword of Publius, Clemens appeared in the doorway, clutching a wounded shoulder.

'Hades, but that's a mess.'

Rufinus wasn't sure whether he meant what was left of Orthus's victim, or the broken king of the Alemanni, or perhaps both. It didn't matter. He walked back across to the German king and crouched by him.

'I lost another brother once, long ago, and for a very long time, I could not look into the eyes of a dying man, for it just dragged me right back to that day, hunting in the forest. But then I learned to overcome it. To face what I saw in a man's dying eyes. Sometimes it still haunts me. Sometimes I feel nothing. Today, I will savour it, because today my other brother, Publius, will rest peacefully in Elysium, known that I did so.'

He pulled his scarf free and wrapped it round and round his left hand, then used it to grip the broken sword near the twisted, shorn end, his other hand on the hilt. With a silent prayer to Nemesis, he placed the blade over the staring, panicked king's throat, and slowly pushed down.

Beheading a man was difficult, even with a powerful swing. Slowly, like this, as though slicing through cheese, it required every ounce of strength Rufinus could muster. The king started trying to plead, though it lasted only a moment, for then the blade was through his voice box and his windpipe, driving through the resisting muscle and tendon of his neck until it reached the spine. The king was dead by then, for it was not a quick job, but as he worked, Rufinus kept his eyes locked on those of the dying Alemanni, every moment a whisper of vengeance for his brother. The neck broke with a sharp crack and the rest was easy, the head rolling free.

Rufinus simply stayed there, crouched, looking into those clouding, unseeing eyes. He was barely aware of the arrival of the others as Bato the Ilyrian crouched and retrieved the head, working it with difficulty onto the tip of a spear he carried. Rufinus almost fought against it as Clemens reached down and tried to help him up, but then he rose, shakily. Emotions whirled through him in a maelstrom, threatening to unman him, to make him throw up, and with the release of tension at long last, days of exhaustion and privation caught up with him in a single moment, threatening unconsciousness in the blink of an eye. He managed to get to unsteady feet, and then Clemens and Annius were at his sides, one at each shoulder, helping him. By the time he reached the door, a small amount of strength had returned, and he could at least walk, shakily.

Outside, Bato had taken Ingomer's head on a spear and planted it in the open ground before the headquarters, on display to anyone who might come here. Rufinus wandered over to a log and collapsed to it, sitting hard. He remained there in silence as men brought heads. The one who'd tried to stop them in this very open ground. The one who Orthus had mangled inside. The others who had ambushed them at the bridge. Rufinus knew he'd lost a few men, but he was too tired to count right now. He just watched as the Alemanni over-king and his chosen warriors were put on display in the camp. In a line.

It was done. Raetia was safe, the Alemanni disarmed, for now at least, the border forces warned, and Publius avenged, along with every other soldier butchered unnecessarily over these recent months. He even almost chuckled as one of the Bracari riders produced a bucket of water and threw it over Orthus in an attempt to clean some of the blood off him, then ran away, yelping, as the dog snapped at his heels angrily.

Things may never be quite the same now, but perhaps they could be nudged back in the right direction.

It was over.

CHAPTER TWENTY-FOUR:

EPILOGUE

Tasgetium, summer AD 198

The man behind the mansio counter was just how Rufinus remembered, neat, Roman and official, and he was surprised when the man nodded at him in recognition after all this time, and gave him a tight smile.

'Did you find your man, sir?'

'After a fashion,' Rufinus replied wearily. The man nodded professionally, perhaps sensing that his customer did not particularly wish to discuss the matter any further. The man scratched his short, curly beard, and then looked at his listings of occupied and empty rooms.

'Are you seeking accommodation for the night, sir? We have no four directly together, but I can do you three chambers on one floor and one on another, or two twos, as it were.' The man looked past Rufinus at his companions, and down at the dog. He seemed unfazed. 'All dog friendly,' he added.

'Yes please,' Rufinus replied. 'Two pairs would be ideal, and for the single night only. In the morning we will be heading back to Rome after we heartily break our fast.'

The man nodded and began to work on his forms, and Rufinus stepped back. He turned to look at his companions with a tired smile.

365

Following the siege at Iciniacum, and then the fights in the forest and at the camp, Rufinus had returned to the victorious home of the Bracari and spent the night in the fort's accommodation, with the gratitude of the prefect for his part in it all. The following morning, after a long and very well-earned sleep, Rufinus and his friends had used the baths at leisure, and then reequipped as best they could from the stores. The prefect had agreed to sign and seal the manumission documents, freeing all the slaves who had helped fight and save the fort, and releasing Bato to Rufinus's party. Then, with a last wish of good fortune from the officers and men of the Third Bracaraugustanorum, they had set off east.

They did not stop at any of the forts on their way to the home of the legion, instead relying on that local place that Clemens knew and where they had stopped before. What they *did* notice, in every trouble spot they passed, was that all evidence of Germanic head-taking practices seemed to have vanished from public view. There were no heads on spears or grisly skull shrines outside any of the forts, now, just subdued villages watched over by Roman walls with armoured figures atop. Whether the occupying garrisons had been punished on the orders of the governor, or had perhaps disposed of any evidence of wrongdoing before that happened, upon receiving word of Ingomer's failure and subsequent demise, Rufinus couldn't say, but the whole area looked awfully normal and under control now.

They reached Castra Regina towards the end of the day, and Rufinus went to report in, only to discover that the governor had taken a cohort of men and returned to his capital at Augusta Vindelicorum a day earlier, while other units had been dispatched both east and west. The legion's senior tribune and camp prefect greeted the visitors warmly in their commander's absence. There had apparently initially been some scepticism over Rufinus's rather hurried and panicked report a few days ago, but just a few hours of scouts prying into the matter around Batavis had confirmed the truth of it for all. Legionary vexillations and

366

trusted non-Germanic auxilia had then immediately been mobilised to reinforce the frontier and to take command of any fort that seemed to have edged towards Alemanni control, manning all the suddenly empty watchtowers. In short, the border region had swiftly been brought under control.

The two officers had been less than enthusiastic about Rufinus's request that night, but they had grudgingly agreed to it, given his status and the fact that he may well have just secured the border and saved rather a lot of lives into the bargain. So, he had left the next morning with not only Bato in his entourage, and a now-clean Orthus trotting alongside, but also with Clemens and Annius in his wake, each clutching their transfer papers. Rufinus was sure he would have little argument getting the prefects to sanction their entry into the Praetorian Guard in Rome, and their promotions to the rank of centurion as well. By the gods, they certainly both deserved it. And there would undoubtedly be openings following the Guard's sojourn in the east, in the land of the bad tempered Parthians.

'I'm looking forward to a proper meal and a proper bed,' Annius murmured.

'I'm just happy not to be bouncing around in a saddle for a change,' Clemens agreed.

Rufinus looked across at Bato, who was grinning. He was just happy at life in general.

'I'm afraid I had to keep these,' the man behind the desk said, suddenly. Rufinus turned, to see him holding a pile of four scroll cases. 'I considered forwarding them to Augusta Raurica, where I gathered you moved next, but I decided best to keep them here, pending your return.'

Rufinus nodded his thanks, and took the scrolls, noting on each his own seal, telling him they'd all come from Senova.

He waited impatiently as all the formalities were taken care of, and then followed the others through to a communal room where wine and beer were being served while the various officials in occupation awaited the evening meal. As the other three chatted,

Rufinus moved to the end of the table and stacked the scroll cases, then took the one with the earliest date on it, sent not long after he'd left Rome.

It was mostly a collection of inanities and platitudes, gentle and pleasant, and it made him smile to think of Senova sitting bored in their triclinium, trying to think of anything to tell him. He put it aside, and then drew out the second. This was a little sharper. The tone suggested that he had not lived up to his part and kept her informed, and that he was supposed to have been back quickly. The letter did soften towards the end, with her hope that he had found Publius and that all was good, and that she missed him and hoped he would be home soon.

He put that scroll aside, looked at the date on the third, and then braced himself. Sure enough, it began by berating him for not sending her letters, which left him slightly irked, given that he'd been in captivity and being beaten at the time. She'd then gone into a short passage where she told him she'd picked up a stray in the city, because she was just too cute to leave to the elements, and that Sheba had taken to the new companion, and she just hoped that Orthus, disobedient mutt that he was, would do so too. Rufinus hoped it wasn't a cat. It sounded like a cat, and he didn't like cats. She ended with a tone of slight worry that he had not been in touch, and vowed to write again every market day until he returned or replied, but that if he had not replied by midsummer, she would hire a small guard unit and make the journey north to find him. He resolved, upon reading that, to pick up the pace a bit and get home before she decided to set out, lest they cross paths unknown somewhere in Northern Italia and miss one another entirely. He did not like the idea of her arriving here and asking after him while he was arriving back in Rome.

He opened the last one, expecting more of the same.

He was wrong.

And surprised.

And worried.

GNAEUS.

COME HOME VERY SOON. THINGS HAVE
GONE FROM BAD TO WORSE HERE, AND
TROUBLE DARKENS OUR DOOR. IF YOU GET
HOME AND I AM NOT HERE, LOOK FOR ME AT
TIBUR IN OUR FAVOURITE SPOT.

HURRY.

Rufinus lowered the letter to find that Clemens, Annius and
Bato were all looking at him.
'You've gone pale,' his friend said. 'What's happened?'
'From the morning onwards, we ride fast,' he said, 'and with
relay horses. There's trouble at home.'

HURRY.

Damn it.

The end.

The Nemesis Blade

HISTORICAL NOTE

In Rufinus's last outing, I portrayed Severus's war in the east against Pescennius Niger. I worked the story such that others would be dealing with the war against Clodius Albinus, as I really did not want to base two consecutive books in consecutive civil wars. For a similar reason, I also did not want to send Rufinus once more out to war in the east. From a personal point of view, I had just written about a campaign in Parthia under that very emperor in my novelised biography of Caracalla, so I had no great wish to rehash it through Rufinus's eyes. Besides, I already had the bones of this plot idea in my head while writing the last Rufinus book, a few years back, and so I needed him in the west, and alone.

Severus was one of those emperors who habitually took the Praetorians with him on campaign. After all, they had been rebuilt only recently out of his trusted Pannonian legions, and would therefore be perfectly suited to war. But clearly the Praetorian fortress in Rome would never be left empty while the Guard was on campaign. Even if logic did not tell us that, it is made clear by Tacitus, who tells us that the Praetorians were set by Vitellius to guard the approach to Rome in AD 69, when a number of cohorts went over to Vespasian, and yet when the Flavians reached Rome, they had a hard fight taking the Praetorian fortress.

Who was left in charge when the bulk of the army was away remained to be seen. The Guard seems to have had their own equivalent of the legions' camp prefect in the fort of a 'Princeps Castrorum' but it seems more than reasonable to have one cohort left behind to guard the emperor's interests in the city. That they would be the troops of least use on campaign makes further sense, and if a cohort remains behind, then it seems natural to have a tribune left in command. Thus we have Rufinus, with his wife and his new dog, still in Rome. I presume the reader has already read Blades of Antioch, and will now know why Acheron is no longer at his master's side, but to have Rufinus adventure without a dog has become oddly inconceivable, and so Orthus (a multi-headed dog in classical mythology, brother of Cerberus) was created.

This book was born of four elements. Firstly I wanted an adventure for Rufinus that was personal and full of travel and mystery, similar, in a way, to my other favourite Praetorian book so far, Eagles of Dacia. The story of Rufinus hunting his brother's killer was what produced this book's title, way back, of course. Secondly, I have always been struck by the difficulties of the German/Raetian border – the Roman limes – in this region, and particularly the Agri Decumates. The Rhine and its tributaries form a natural and powerful border, and so does the Danube. At one point, near the sources of the rivers Danube (Danubius) and Neckar (Nicer) they are not ten miles apart. Yet Rome chose to advance the border into the lands beyond the rivers and create a man-made boundary that did not rely upon natural features. This region, between the two rivers, would cause Rome headaches over the ensuing centuries, and would be the place where Roman borders become wholly consumed by Germanic tribes on the move (indeed, these very Alemanni around AD 260). Following that, in the later empire, Rome would indeed do what is proposed in this book, and fortify the line of the Rhine, back down in Switzerland and southern Germany, as it had been in Neronian times. So that was another reason: I wanted to explore the thinking of this border region. Thirdly, I am from northern Britain, and we have our own Roman frontier. This has been as much explored as the Germanic borders, and I am something of a student of Roman frontier culture as a result. I was interested in exploring this in a German context for a change. And lastly, there is the matter of the Alemanni. This super-tribe, formed from lesser, yet still powerful, German tribes, would become so influential historically that the French name for Germany is still based on their name even now. And the history of the Alemanni's formation remains cloudy. The first reference of them comes in the reign of Caracalla, only 15 years after this book's setting, and by AD 260, they were powerful and fearless enough to swarm across that border. Since they do not seem to have been influential or dangerous enough to be mentioned during the Marcomannic Wars, which extended into this region between AD 165 and 180, it is reasonable to assume they became a power between AD 180 and 213, slap bang in the middle of Rufinus's adventures. Thus I wanted to write their origin story into the text.

To pick up our story in Rome, little, I think, needs to be said of the arrival of the letter and Rufinus's initial journey north, although I have included another little author's conceit in the faint suggestion that the villa in which Rufinus fights the Germans in Liguria is either that of Agricola's mother, or of Ostorius Scapula, both of which appear in the second volume of my Agricola series (which is not out yet, so keep an eye out for that one.)

The western passes of the Alps leading to Genava (clearly modern Geneva) are a known Roman route that it was natural to have Rufinus follow, all the way to Tasgetium, a small Roman settlement with a walled enclosure at the top end of Lake Constance's Unterzee branch. Little is known of its history, though a later Roman wall from the fortress is still visible in the town of Stein am Rhein. The city of Augusta Raurica existed, too, and is now the town of Augst (and its suburb Kaiseraugst) just outside Basel. The remains there are extremely impressive, though they were only a stopover in this book, and I was unable to make the most of them here. The stretch of the Rhine between these two places meanders, and is quite impressive, and the site of the native temple they find is my own addition.

The temple itself, though, is based upon an example found at Roquepertuse in the lands of the Ligures. That it was clearly designed to hold skulls or heads is a given, which tells us that the tribe there had been head-hunters. We know the Germanic peoples of the era to have also been head-hunters, even when serving in the Roman military (as evidenced on plenty of carvings and even in texts.) So copying the French temple and transplanting it to their neighbours seemed fair.

Batavis was an auxiliary fort on the peninsula now occupied by the city of Passau. It was, indeed, the home of the Eighth Bataviorum, and later a second fort occupied the far side of the Inn River, on the Danube's south bank.

I suspect there will be reviews of this book that accuse it of being an outlandish plot. Readers will think that such a corrupt scheme on such a grand scale is unrealistic. To anyone of that opinion, before you reach for your angry keyboard, I would ask you to compare the events postulated in this tale with a number of recorded incidents throughout Roman history…

Arminius's convoluted plot to gather German tribes while tricking a Roman governor into leading three legions into the forests beyond the empire? The Batavian Revolt of AD 69-70? Governors of German states taking power into their own hands in spite of senate and emperor: Vitellius and Gaetulicus leaping to mind. Or governors, generals and clients who actually manage to break away from the empire entirely, such as Postumus, Carausius and Zenobia. Such Earth-shaking plots are surprisingly common in Rome, and this one is actually only mid-range compared with some of the above. And if one might argue against Romans deciding deliberately to go against imperial policy and rearrange the borders, I might point the reader to Tacitus, writing of Agricola's campaigns: "To retreat south of the Bodotria, and to retire rather than to be driven out, was the advice of timid pretenders to prudence," suggesting that when Agricola met heavy resistance in Scotland, his more conservative officers advocated retreating to the line of the future Antonine Wall.

In some respects, the pulling back of the frontier in the region might have given Rome stronger borders and allowed her to redeploy many troops to other areas.

With reference to the fort locations and the troops involved in the book, there follows a brief, perhaps tedious, list of unit locations, dates and justifications for those of you like me, who pedantically need to know about the truth of the forces mentioned. I selected for my units swayed by Veremundus only those of native Raetian or Germanic origin. These included Cohors IX Batavorum, who served at Vindolanda in Britain, then in the Dacian wars, and were then sent to Raetia. An altar at Weissenburg certifies the presence of at least one member of the unit there, but Passau bore the name Batavis, and the unit are certainly attested there by the time of the Notitia Dignitatum. Cohors III Tungrorum (often confused or combined with IV Tungrorum) is only ever attested in Raetia in one diploma. IV had been at Abusina but was moved to Mauretania under Marcus Aurelius. The Abusina (Eining) fort was occupied by Cohors II Britannorum by the Notitia's time, and they are on stamped bricks there, but they were at Kumpfmuhl in the Flavian era, so their occupation of Eining at the turn of the 3rd century is uncertain. I have therefore chosen to place III Tungrorum there. Cohors I Raetorum was likely based early on in Moesia, then served in the Dacian wars before being sent to Raetia, where they are attested on tile stamps at Schirenhof. We can say without doubt that II Raetorum were at Straubing (Sorviodurum) and the Ala I Flavia Singularium was at Pforring (Celeusum.) However, Cohors VI Raetorum are only recorded at Windisch (which was a civilian site post AD 101) and Aarau (undated.) The garrison of Dambach, whose Roman name is unknown, and so I have called Tannum, is also unknown, and so I have placed Cohors VI

Raetorum there. The cohort was known to be in the region, and by the time of the Notitia was at Neuburg an der Donau (Venaxamodorum) but that fort was unoccupied and far behind the border at this time, and so their location in AD 198 is unknown. Finally, although I could have jemmied them into my plot, I left out the cavalry units Ala II Flavia Millaria and Ala Gemelliana as not convincingly German enough. Ok, thus ends the technical justification of units. Back to the lighter stuff.

In the episode at Abusina, I think all that need be mentioned is the prefect's body Rufinus finds in the pool. This is a nod to the legendary 'threefold death' of the Celts/druids. Rufinus then returns to the legionary fortress of Castra Regina (Regensburg), and meets a jaded governor. While there is no literary evidence to support a manpower issue in Raetia, it is reasonable to suggest one. We know that border units were consistently below strength, from a number of sources, including original strength reports found at Vindolanda. Add to this the fact that we are only talking 18 years after the Marcommanic wars, which took place over a period of 15 years and then think on how long it took the modern nations to recover from just six years of warfare after WW2. Then note that Upper and Lower Germany, and the Pannonian and Moesian provinces on the Danube each housed two legions, and each had huge rivers to define their borders, while Noricum and Raetia, the latter of which controlled much of the troubled Agri Decumates frontier, had only the 3rd Italica between them, based on the border at Regensburg. It should be no surprise, then, that it was in that very region that the border was overrun in AD 260. All of this points to the manpower problem I have suggested here.

The forts I have described are based as far as possible on physical evidence, and where that was not directly possible, on similar installations across other imperial borders. My reference to statues in fort headquarters is based upon finds in various forts around the empire, and my suggestion that Commodus was favoured by the German tribes is not beyond belief. As well as having granted them favourable terms, it might be remembered that despite the reputation Commodus still bears down to this day, he was still popular with the army and much of the empire beyond his demise. An altar found at Dura Europos on the Euphrates is dated after the emperor's death, clearly before word of it reached that far, and uses the emperor's honorifics for his unit and the date, showing he was honoured even on the periphery.

During the Marcomannic Wars, the bulk of the conflict was fought across the Danube in Pannonia, but there were also parts fought further east, in Moesia and Dacia, and we know that the Marcomanni were allied with tribes in the Raetia and Germany regions, and so the likelihood of there having been campaigns in the area in which this book is set is strong. Roman temporary camps are found occasionally in Germany outside the official border, testimony to one campaign or another. Thus, having a long-abandoned camp the Germans and their prefect and king can use, ten miles north of the frontier, is far from impossible.

The architecture and technology used in the camp is all based on known examples, from the Roman padlock to the barred windows, all the way to the wooden roof shingles (one fantastic surviving example of which was found at Dambach, coincidentally.)

The terrain around the camp and all the way back to the border I have portrayed as forested. These days that land is wide, largely flat, open farmland. However, it should be remembered that the native tribes of the time would not have farmed on such a massive scale, and it is highly likely that forest pre-dated the later farmland, just as it did across much of Britain.

The area of the border, the Upper Raetian Limes, around the place Rufinus crosses back into the empire is one of the most interesting. The border itself, with its towers, rampart, palisade and ditch, would be replaced with a stone wall not many years after this, but at the close of the second century, it remained a timber edifice. How the frontier crossed rivers remains an unsolved question. Streams, we believe to have been crossed by simply adding leats through the base of the rampart, but this could not be the solution for full rivers. On Hadrian's Wall, rivers were crossed with full bridges that carried the wall, but given that Hadrian's Wall was a slightly different system, with the forts and towers on the wall itself, and the whole thing traversable on foot, that makes sense. With the Germanic limes, the same would not be true. They may have been crossed by simple timber bridges that carried the palisade, or they may have simply been left open as I portrayed here.

Atop the ridge I describe in the book, the tower and its crossing have largely disappeared, partly due to the stone's reuse in a monument to Bismarck. The fort at Gunzenhausen, where I have placed part of III Bracaraugustanorum, is now buried beneath the town, but sufficient work has been done to produce dimensions, allowing us to presume it was the home of a numerus, a detachment of a unit from another fort. Though its Latin name is not known, I have named it simply Castra Numera ("Camp of the Detachment," more or less.)

Theilenhofen, known in this book by its Latin name of Iciniacum, is a partially-excavated, but entirely buried, fort close to the limes. It survives as an earthwork, but its form is known in full from surveys and the various digs it has seen. Its ditches were not crossed at the gates by a causeway as was so often the case, but by wooden bridges, the remnants of the southern bridge found in position during excavation. Its south gate is a strange concave shape, as noted in the book, known as a 'niche gate', and other similar examples have also been found at Carnuntum, Lambaesis, and also at the German forts of In der Harlach and Faimingen. There is no record of destruction at Theilenhofen dated to this period, but the fort would be destroyed, along with so many others, when the Alemanni swarmed across the border in AD 260.

My siege at Theilenhofen is, of course, fictional, though entirely plausible. The Third Bracaraugustanorum have left us evidence at the fort in the form of stamped tiles, and of a beautifully preserved ornate cavalry helmet, now in the museum in Nuremburg. The great siege weapon that I named Locusta, after the infamous Roman poisoner, is my own addition, for no such remains have been found on site, but it is based upon examples such as that of Archimedes, which was five times the height of a man. A replica was constructed in the time of Kaiser Wilhelm, and these weapons may well have been in use at times on the Germanic/Raetian borders.

The siege over, we return to the camp outside the empire, and I can think of nothing else that would gain from explanation or investigation. Rufinus has brought down his enemy and avenged his brother. I was pleased to be able to lay to rest one of those little characteristics of his that has been in evidence since the start: his inability to look into a dying man's eyes. And all now appears to be settled. Of course, when things seem at their most calm is when you need to be most cautious. There may be a situation now awaiting Rufinus back in Rome, but that is another story...

Simon Turney, March 2024

If you liked this book, why not try other novels by Simon Turney:

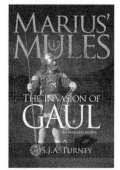

Marius' Mules: The Invasion of Gaul (2009)

It is 58 BC and the mighty Tenth Legion, camped in Northern Italy, prepare for the arrival of the most notorious general in Roman history: Julius Caesar.

Marcus Falerius Fronto, commander of the Tenth is a career soldier and long-time companion of Caesar's. Despite his desire for the simplicity of the military life, he cannot help but be drawn into intrigue and politics as Caesar engineers a motive to invade the lands of Gaul.

Fronto is about to discover that politics can be as dangerous as battle, that old enemies can be trusted more than new friends, and that standing close to such a shining figure as Caesar, even the most ethical of men risk being burned.

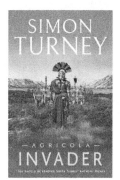

Agricola: Invader (2024)

58 AD, Rome. Agricola, teenage son of an impoverished yet distinguished noble family, has staked all his resources and reputation on a military career. His reward? A posting as tribune in the far-off northern province of Britannia.

Serving under renowned general Suetonius Paulinus, Agricola soon learns the brutality of life on the very edges of the empire, for the Celtic tribes of Britannia are far from vanquished.

To take control of the province, the Romans must defeat the ancient might of the druids - and the fury of the Iceni, warriors in their thousands led by a redoubtable queen named Boudicca...

Other great ancient world reads recommended by Simon include:

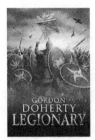

Legionary by Gordon Doherty

The Roman Empire is crumbling, and a shadow looms in the east...

376 AD: The Goths amass at the edges of the Eastern Roman Empire, armed and with madness in their eyes. Emperor Valens frantically mobilises his legions to contain this unexpected tide. Little does he know of the far greater, darker threat that drove the tribes like this: the Huns.

The legions need every new recruit they can find, anyone to hold a spear. Pavo - slave and orphan - is not just anyone. Thrust into the border legions, cast into the front line, he must become a man, or he will die, and the empire will fall with him.

Killer of Men by Christian Cameron

Arimnestos is a farm boy when war breaks out between the citizens of his native Plataea and their overbearing neighbours, Thebes. Standing in the battle line for the first time, alongside his father and brother, he shares in a famous and unlikely victory. But after being knocked unconscious in the melee, he awakes not a hero, but a slave.

Betrayed by his jealous and cowardly cousin, the freedom he fought for has now vanished, and he becomes the property of a rich citizen. So begins an epic journey out of slavery that takes the young Arimnestos through a world poised on the brink of an epic confrontation, as the emerging civilization of the Greeks starts to flex its muscles against the established empire of the Persians.

As he tries to make his fortune and revenge himself on the man who disinherited him, Arimnestos discovers that he has a talent that pays well in this new, violent world - for like his hero, Achilles, he is 'a killer of men'.

Made in United States
North Haven, CT
16 May 2024

52533448R00236